London

Isles of Scilly

Azores

Voyage of the Cynthia Anne

James H. Lovingsworth, Capt.

The
Scourges
of Heaven

The
Scourges
of
Heaven

Especially for Edith Bennett

With all best wishes
for better understanding

A Novel by

DAVID DICK

David Dick

June 12, 2000

THE UNIVERSITY PRESS OF KENTUCKY

Scholarly publisher for the Commonwealth,
serving Bellarmine College, Berea College, Centre
College of Kentucky, Eastern Kentucky University,
The Filson Club Historical Society, Georgetown College,
Kentucky Historical Society, Kentucky State University,
Morehead State University, Murray State University,
Northern Kentucky University, Transylvania University,
University of Kentucky, University of Louisville,
and Western Kentucky University.

Editorial and Sales Offices: The University Press of Kentucky
663 South Limestone Street, Lexington, Kentucky 40508-4008

02 01 00 99 98   5 4 3 2 1

Library of Congress Cataloging-in-Publication Data

Dick, David, 1930-
    The scourges of heaven : a novel / by David Dick.
        p.   cm.
    ISBN 0-8131-2074-8 (cloth : alk. paper)
    1. Cholera—Fiction. I. Title.
PS3554.I287S26   1998
813'.54—dc21   98-29012

This book is printed on acid-free recycled paper meeting
the requirements of the American National Standard
for Permanence of Paper for Printed Library Materials.

Manufactured in the United States of America

For Cynthia

Contents

There is an Eastern fable which tells us that a certain city was infested by poisonous serpents that killed all they fastened upon; and the citizens, thinking them sent from Heaven as a scourge for their sins, kept praying that the visitation might be removed from them, until scarcely a house remained unsmitten. At length, however, concludes the parable, the eyes of the people were opened, for, after all their prayers and fastings, they found that the eggs of the poisonous serpents were hatched in the muck-heaps that surrounded their own dwellings.

—Henry Mayhew,
London Labour and the London Poor

Owl Hollow, Kentucky

October 1998

THE STEEL TEETH of the backhoe made a scraping sound as it struck iron in the ditch, and the yellow machine vibrated with the unforeseen resistance. Luther Duncan felt a curious flutter in his hands and feet. He did not like the interruption, did not like it at all. He was in an all-fired hurry. Luther was digging a new water line from the road to his house, near Owl Hollow, where his life was anchored.

It was October 15, 1998.

The leaves on the pin oaks and black walnuts, the dogwoods and locusts had finished turning to their flaming reds, golden yellows, and sallow, deathly browns. Winds edged with the coming cold of winter worried the leaves, whipping them toward their final cutting loose. It was their annual death dance, the inevitable spiraling down of foliage to provide another layer of humus to the fertile limestone soil.

"Hit sumpin!" yelled Joseph, the hired man, looking intently into the narrow, lengthening trench. He knew a lot more about digging without combustion engine machines than he did with them. As far as he was concerned, the mechanical beasts were much too noisy, too smoky, too destructive, and much too likely to break down. They were forever needing lubrication. He understood better the feel of manual posthole digging, much preferred the mattock to remove stones for mending fences and building water gaps. His right foot felt at home on the spade when he opened hills for potatoes, straight furrows for entwining corn and beans, or double-dug rich, friable mounds for radishes, beets, and carrots.

He preferred to do all practical chores by hand, taking most seriously the responsibility for each kind of digging. Joseph felt bonded when he was personally involved with the earth. It made him feel wanted and needed, less lonely. He was in no hurry. "It takes twice as long to do it wrong" meant doing it right the first time, a nugget of wisdom handed down from his mother. Scooping up soil and letting it slip through cupped fists by the slow, squeezing movements of the fingers was a special pleasure for the O'Malley clan. Joseph came from a long line of Irish stock, clinging to old ideas as stubbornly as moss growing on the smooth rocks of Owl Hollow Creek.

Still, Luther needed a little help with *his* machinery, somebody to watch out for trouble and lend a hand in case anything should go wrong, and Joseph O'Malley was reluctantly willing to do what he could. He hated to make trouble. He had learned that if he waited long enough, trouble would grow tired and move on to bother somebody else. Joseph was almost as stoic as he was Roman Catholic.

"Hit sumpin?" echoed Luther, who had not wanted city water in the first place. He would not be going to all this expense if Old Lady had not been so hardheaded about it. When Old Lady was in a swivet, it was time to pay attention. She went on about wanting *good* water, the kind that didn't make her white things look like they'd been forever dragged through a sulfur swamp. She said if she didn't get water from town like everybody else on Owl Hollow Road, instead of from the old, leaking well to the side of the kitchen, and if she didn't get it "*right* now," she was packing her bags. That's what she said. Said she was "*packing* her bags." She sniffed about how some people she knew had good sense.

At this time in his life, passing sixty, Luther Duncan couldn't afford to lose Old Lady. After forty-two years of marriage he knew she had the upper hand anytime she wanted it. Practically speaking, he frowned on the idea of not having his breakfast cooked or his underwear washed or his porcelain spittoon poured out or the slop jars emptied and washed. Nor did he take pleasure in the thought of Old Lady not being handy and willing when the Devil took hold of his body in the middle of a hot night. When the full moon was soaring and clean and shining, so as to make the pastures sparkle as if they were stark naked in the daylight, and everything seemed light and airy, Luther just might be in a real, honest-to-goodness, rip-snorting conniption fit. When he had such a major need it was better off filled than spurned, not left hanging in the middle of nowhere. He called it being "summer riled."

It could hardly be called "romance." It certainly did not involve kissing. Old Lady understood this and was more than willing to accept it. Luther's constant chew of tobacco was a contradiction to anything else that might be conceivably oral. So far as he was concerned, man was man and woman was woman and breeding was breeding and chewing was chewing and smoking was smoking and kissing didn't have anything to do with it. Nor did the occasion need to be complicated with talk.

The two grown children born of this union were living somewhere in California, rarely forsaking their high-tech lifestyles. They placed their faith in megabytes and the Unitarian Church. They traveled the Information Superhighway and accessed the stock prices of Microsoft and Intel with the click of computer keys. They balanced their checkbooks with Quicken, shopped in fiber-optic malls on the Internet. They acknowledged to their parents on their fortieth wedding anniversary that at Armageddon the children and the grandchildren would doubtless quickly perish, while Luther and Old Lady would likely survive along with the groundhogs and woolly bears. Luther shook his head and said he didn't understand what the hell they were talking about and Old Lady said she wished their children wouldn't say things that weren't nice.

Luther took his foot off the gas pedal, shoved the backhoe's gearshift into neutral, and jumped down to stand by Joseph's side. They stood there together with their hands jammed down in their pockets, like two little boys studying a copperhead snake. Together they stared into the ditch, pulled on their chins, coughed and spat and scuffed the dirt.

They lowered themselves to their knees to get a closer look where the business end of the backhoe had made its purchase on the unseen resistance. Luther took the pack of nonfiltered cigarettes from his left shirt pocket, shook one out and offered it to Joseph, then put the end of another in his mouth, drawing the pack away and back to its accustomed place near his heart. The lighted up and took deep drags, blowing out the smoke in a common gesture, as if that might help solve the unexpected puzzle.

"Hit some *arn*," said Joseph.

"Hit some *arn*?" said Luther, who had a habit of repeating everything anybody said to him and turning it into a question. When Old Lady said, "Luther, I need the ashes took out," he would say, "Need the ashes took out?"

Luther and Joseph began to dig with their shovels. They worked around the sides of a rusty object about four feet long and two feet wide.

"Looks like a coffin," said Joseph.

"Looks like a coffin?" said Luther. "Just be goldern it all, Joseph, what do you mean it looks like a coffin?" craning his neck to see.

Joseph knew when to button up his mouth. His jaws slapped shut like a basement door when a high wind blows out the prop. He spoke very little in the best of times, unless it was in the confessional with Father Devereux whenever he got started on sex. When Joseph was younger he had confessed his sins with dutiful regularity. When Marilyn Monroe was starring in *The Seven Year Itch*, Father Devereux at Mother of Good Counsel Church in Mt. Sterling hammered away on sex and seemed unlikely to stop until every whore in the universe was nailed to the wall, though in recent years the bishop had more than once admonished Father Devereux to stop being an insufferable stick-in-the-mud. Joseph's confessions had of necessity become infrequent. Compassion and sympathy had gradually moderated old invectives in the confessional. Joseph thought Father Devereux had grown soft on sin, but the issue was not discussed.

Peering closer at Joseph's find, Luther let out with "Jeeesus, Joseph, it's got a window in it!" and at once started clearing the loosened soil from around the metal-framed glass. Joseph reached down and rubbed his gloved hand over the small window at the head of the little coffin. The traditions of such coffin making had long ago ceased, but to Joseph the little glass opening window seemed like a fine idea, a peephole to the "other world," giving friends a chance to see each other from both sides.

Joseph was a digger of graves as well as of trenches and gardens and outhouses. The aging Irishman remembered his grandfather telling him how to prepare the earth for the human dead in the old-fashioned way, personal and attentive to detail, using his work-hardened hands to open a grave for the reception of mortal remains. Although Joseph was rarely sought out to perform the necessary work as it was done long ago, he'd heard the tales of premature burials. He feared them, exceedingly.

No one had to tell Joseph O'Malley about the importance of taking a final look inside the coffin before covering it with dirt. His father and his grandfather encouraged him to remember to persuade next of kin to spend a little extra for a small shovel to be included inside the coffin. This was in case the buried recovered and needed a tool for digging out. Others might laugh at Joseph and ridicule him unmercifully, but any-time a family wanted a bell above the grave, attached by a string to the hands of the buried, Joseph could understand that, and time was he could arrange for it to be put in place. There were those who had made a fortune from selling these bell ringers of resurrection, but he, Joseph O'Malley, would never think of profiting at the expense of the dead. That would not be right.

He and Luther bent forward and looked closely, but there was nothing to be seen on the far side of the window. The burial had preceded modern embalming, and judging from the con-dition of the iron casket, there could have been little left inside to remain visible. Where a head might have rested, there was only the trace of life crumbling into earth.

"Mother of God," said Joseph. He crossed himself three times, including miniature crosses on his forehead and his lips and over his heart.

"God don't have no mother, you old geezer," said Luther. "How many times do I have to tell you that?"

Joseph O'Malley, a devout Catholic for all of his seventy years, did not bend or argue. Joseph practiced his religion pri-vately, without debate, which he instinctively knew was the best way and, in fact, the only way he knew how. He prayed each morning and evening in the corner of his one-room shack, where the left hand was missing on his four-foot-tall statue of the Virgin Mary. It didn't matter. Didn't matter one little bit. The blue of her plaster of Paris gown may have faded, but Jo-seph loved the Blessed Mother as much as when he bought her ten years ago "as is" at Court Day in Mt. Sterling. Held every year in October, Court Day used to give dog owners and dog thieves a chance to swap hounds in the streets and lies in the courtroom, but in recent times the powers that be had cut out the dog part of it and stuck mainly to bargains in knives, guns, and other valuable stuff from Taiwan and Mexico. There were local crafts, too: birdhouses, bird feeders, and wooden choo-choo trains and miniature outhouses and dogwood walking sticks and Christmas wreaths and pillows—a mammoth display of artifacts that drew crowds numbered in the tens of thousands.

Joseph lived four miles out from Mt. Sterling on the side of a hill on the farm owned by the Duncans. His hut, the object of ridicule and rock throwing from neighboring children, was a reason for sporadic concern on the part of the public health department.

Joseph didn't have a car or a pickup truck. He didn't have a horse or a wife. He didn't have a dog. He didn't ask for or expect favors. The Catholicism passed down to him from his Irish ancestors sustained him the way spring did in May at the shutting down of winter and provided him with an unspoken structure. When he said the rosary, he always pressed firmly as he counted the beads. He squeezed until he felt pain. He loved the words of the Hail Mary and the Our Father. Silence was Joseph O'Malley's doxology.

Luther and Old Lady were Protestants, although they never used that word. Old Lady, fondly known among her friends as Miss Mary Duncan, attended Sunday services at the Owl Hollow True Believers Evangelical Church, where the service was robust and congregational. Spontaneous "Amens" punctuated the preacher's sermons, and every so often a worshiper uttered a moan and fell into a heap on the floor. About once a year somebody down front would pop up and launch into a solo of "Just a Closer Walk with Thee." Old Lady made a point of seeking a safe corner in one of the rearmost pews, where she sang as sweet and lonely as a mourning dove calling before and after rain.

Miss Mary could always be counted on at potluck suppers (spoon bread and corn pudding were her specialties), and she helped with brides' bouquets, but she had pretty much given up on getting Luther ready for Heaven. As long as Luther Duncan didn't run off with some pretty young thing, and as long as he finished digging the water line before the snow flew, Old Lady knew when to leave well enough alone. She might even forgive him for a pretty young thing, but she wasn't about to let him off the hook about digging that water line.

To Luther Duncan, Sunday mornings were no different from Monday mornings or Saturday mornings. Work on the farm needed doing. There was livestock to be fed in winter and ice to be broken open with an ax so that the cows could get water and keep on making milk. There were calves with their sides sunk in, abandoned in a brush pile, needing some human help in reconnecting with their mamas. Sunday or not, farmers needed to plow their soil on the first fair days of late winter when there was a break in the weather, needed to seed their crops in spring, fertilize and side-dress their plants in summer, and take the harvest to the barn in autumn. A farmer cooperated with weather more than with church or, for that matter, any other tinkering with what was real.

As for running off with any pretty young things, a man would have to be crazy. Shoot. Luther had thought seriously on a young neighbor woman once or twice when he was about forty-five years old, but the whole business looked to be headed for a lot more trouble than it was worth. He considered himself lucky that Old Lady never got a whiff of it. If she had, she might have reached for the snub-nosed pistol he knew she kept hidden on her at all times, and she would have plugged him between the eyes. Or the young neighbor woman's town-working husband might've peppered his rear end real good with a Remington .410 shotgun.

Luther was grateful that nobody could read his mind. When the Lord created the noggin on your shoulders and that other piece of equipment down there, he did a mighty good thing. In fact, the Lord did a fine job on just about everything.

Copperheads might be considered exceptions to the general rule, but Luther had an answer for all poisonous snakes. He once told his California environmentalist son what would happen if the last rattlesnake on the face of the earth crawled up onto *his* doorstep. "I'd shoot the son of a bitch," Luther had said.

Luther and Joseph finished their cigarettes. They had always ignored the warnings about tobacco being hurtful. It was just some more government meddling in their private affairs. Luther had a small government burley tobacco allotment, and he grew it the way his daddy and his daddy's daddy had grown their varieties. Old Lady called cigarettes "coffin nails," but she cashed the tobacco checks, spent the money on necessities and school taxes, and Luther enjoyed his smokes and his chews as much as the public seemed to enjoy newer school buses and better lighted classrooms and bigger and better places to play basketball.

When Luther and Joseph were boys, they'd grown little patches of hemp for their 4-H projects, but it never once had occurred to them to sit in the shade or hide under the porch and smoke that. It was much more elegant and self-important to light up nicely seasoned catalpa pods, which they proudly and sagely referred to as "injun seegars," or to experiment with dried corn silks and torn strips of old newspapers sealed carefully with spit. Sometimes they would sit in the corncrib and make it all the way through a smoke or two. It was there that they had their first hands-on experiments with sex. Luther never felt guilty about it; he considered it a thoroughly pleasant undertaking, messy but pleasant. Joseph, on the other hand, considered each of these occasions of sin a mortal offense and felt a miserable guilt that could be relieved only by confession and penance. He had also heard that playing with himself would cause hair to grow in the palm of his hand, and he daily checked for any sign of it.

In the latter days of his life Luther usually lit up after lying with Old Lady. It prolonged the free and easy feeling. More than once she'd taken the cigarette out of his hand where it dangled over the edge of the bed, to keep him from burning down the house. "Derned old fool," she'd say at times like that. "Derned old fool," and she'd smile, seeing him there, sleeping like a baby. She could hardly stop smiling even if she wanted to, which she didn't.

Luther rubbed his hand back and forth over the letters on the coffin, barely legible below the small window, and read aloud the crudely cut inscription:

Little John
1839-1844

"Want to help wrestle it out?" Luther said, excitedly clearing his throat.

"What out?" blurted Joseph.

"The goldern coffin, Joseph. What do you think I mean?"

"No sir."

"No sir, what?"

"I ain't gonna help you wrestle it out—it's wrong."

"Tell me one thing that's wrong about it," said Luther.

"The dead are with God."

"And?"

"God will decide who comes and who goes. It's not for you and me to know. God might strike us dead."

"Joseph, you're just scared." Luther stared at the coffin, then looked back at Joseph and reprovingly said, "But because of you we're going to let this young feller stay right here in his final resting place."

"We are?" Joseph glanced at Luther and quickly looked away. Direct eye contact with anybody in and around Owl Hollow was like talking too much, a form of trespass.

"And we're not going to open it up to see if there's any gold in there with him," said Luther, remorsefully. Most of his life he'd had visions about buried gold. He only dreamed about digging up scattered, unidentified family graves on the farm. They'd always fascinated him, especially the aboveground slabs serving as sepulchers. He'd put his ear to the top in case there might be something to hear, and he'd peek along the side crevasses to see if there might be buried treasures. Anything from wedding bands to gold tooth fillings would do just fine, though naturally there'd always be the off chance of finding a whole pot of gold. This recurring dream was something else he did not discuss with Old Lady. No telling what she might have done if she'd caught him with a shovel in the middle of the night, making the dirt fly in the honey locust thicket up on top of the hill where unidentified folks had been sleeping in their unmarked graves for a hundred years and more. She might've called the law on her own husband. But shoot. What good did it do to bury things of value with a body that had no way whatsoever to make use of them? Made about as much sense as planting a dog with his collar on, a waste of good leather.

Luther and Joseph gently filled in the earth at opposite ends of the iron coffin and carefully covered the small window. Luther used the backhoe to replace the rest of the dirt, and Joseph used his shovel to even the corners of the hole. He turned the shovel over and patted down the soil.

"All right," said Luther, "we're going to run this water line around the grave, but if we happen to run into any bones I ain't stopping."

"Ain't stopping?" asked Joseph.

"Ain't stopping," said Luther, smelling the coolness of the October air. "If I don't get this line dug and the job finished before the snow flies, there's going to be some hell to pay."

London, England

April 1833

When I heard of men dying upon the street; when I was informed of persons closing their shops in the evening, and having their grave-stones laid upon them in the morning; when I called this day, perhaps in the way of business, at the house of a customer, and returned next morning for the payment of my account, and was told that he was dead and buried, I could not but feel that I was living among the tombs, and that no one could tell how speedily I also might drop into my opened grave.

—*Christian Journal,* 1833

"HEAR YE THE LORD! Worthless sinners! God's Wrath! A-men! His way of punishing mankind for ALL wrongdoing! Scourge sent from Heaven! The Lord has no other way, no choice but to bring down another scourge. This cholera pestilence. A-men!"

The Reverend Daniel C. Goodman's words mercifully died on darkened Borough Road like the prestorm splatterings of oversized raindrops quickly absorbed by a thick layer of dirt, garbage, and excrement. Homeless human beings, cats and dogs, pigeons, and scavenging hogs wandered through the narrow passageways of the city, where Reverend Goodman's words hung in the cool, damp air. The extremes of human experience confounded the zealous preacher: the godforsaken slums of Southwark and the new Buckingham Palace where Queen Victoria would become the first sovereign to dwell in royal splendor; the crudeness of the Isle of Dogs docks and the intellectual sophistication of the Royal Society. Alone, unrecognized and unappreciated, the Reverend Goodman felt himself snared in religious, political, and social ferment. Yet, increasingly, he felt helpless to effect change.

Leaving his adopted street corner, the Reverend Daniel C. Goodman heard the steady clumping of a horse, looked around, and saw a gaunt gray steed straining to pull a cart piled high with bodies of the London dead. Some of the forms were barely shrouded, some entirely naked, arms and legs dangling, eyes staring from sunken sockets, mouths slackened by the final drain of fluids, and a smell so strong as to cause the Reverend Goodman and others to cover their noses and mouths with the palms of both hands. The driver's broad-brimmed hat was pulled down across his forehead. In his mouth he clenched a pipe, channeling the smoke to his nostrils to intercede with the sickening stench of death. Whether he did his job for the pittance it paid or for humanitarian reasons, he was part of a brotherhood of suffering.

At the end of a narrow street the Reverend Goodman saw another wagon backed up among the dead and dying. A man with his face covered was lifting a naked body by the armpits. Another man, also wearing a mask, held the ankles. In Protestant suspicion, Goodman stared at a priest with an upheld cross standing near the place of loading. Bodies lay in a row, some wrapped in filthy, tick-ridden cloth or canvas. In the flickering light of a small bonfire in the street, the faces of the living were despairing and helpless. A woman pulled a scarf in front of her chin. She moved away from the bodies, perhaps her kin or neighbors. A man extended his arms upward in desperation and frustration. A hooded man hoisted a body over his shoulder as a stevedore might carry a sack of coal or potatoes. A man, perhaps the husband of the lifeless form, assisted in positioning the body inside a shroud. Her breasts were bare. Two more bodies were akimbo in the cart. From the upper end of the street, several people were carrying a coffin, something few could afford. Most bodies were heaped into dead-wagons to be carried away for mass burial in a pit.

The Reverend Goodman saw no beauty anywhere. The gloom bore him down. He was aware only of the wagon, the solitary priest with the uplifted cross, and his own guilt-ridden mind. Since his arrival in London only a few weeks before, he had seen many dead-wagons traversing the streets of the city. Day and night he had witnessed the loading and the departures for the open pits in the vacant lots of the metropolis. He had stood on the edge of it all, and he had watched the dumping of the bodies. He imagined he was seeing the end of the world.

Goodman was horrified by what he saw through an open door. In one small room two beds stood end to end; in one, a man sat upright, his back almost touching the wall, his head thrust upward in agony, a blanket covering his body from the hips down. A young man dressed in black, apparently a medical person, knelt on the floor beside a small tub with handles. He had his hands in a smaller pan and appeared to be washing or preparing some application. In the other bed, sat a woman, her flattened breasts exposed, her right arm thrust from the bed in a position of stiff helplessness. Another man, in a black frock coat, approached the bed with a bowl as if to spoon-feed the victim. A nurse, wearing a nun's habit, stood at the end of the bed holding a bottle of medicine in her right hand.

The scene called to mind the words Goodman had read in *Pictures of Pauperism,* descriptions of conditions in Scotland in 1832: "I have entered into hovels where I found frail, aged human beings lying on a miserable pallet of straw, with scarcely a rag to cover them, or any food whereof to partake." The Reverend Goodman realized that he was witnessing much the same conditions in England: paupers living like animals in dark, crowded, dungeonlike basements; men, women, and children wedged into rooms so small there was scarcely a place for a bed.

The Reverend Goodman wandered aimlessly, his conviction wavering as to whether he was actually responsible for clothing the naked and visiting the sick. He brushed by two small beggar boys, their hands extended like blackened cups of pottery. A prostitute wearily smiled, but the man of God walked sternly on. The street urchins followed closely on his heels, looking for a mark, making no pretense of innocence. The idea of suffering little children to come unto him and forbidding them not was vexing Goodman's spirit. He whirled and, pointing an accusing finger, shouted: "Go away!"

Following a man carrying a medical bag, the Reverend Goodman entered into one of the hovels. The room was crowded with forms resembling humans. He heard moaning, and the smell was overpowering. It increased Goodman's anger. He spoke to an old woman: "And so you've come to this?"

She stared back at him.

"Why don't you get up and get out of here?" said Goodman.

"Where would I go?" she asked fiercely.

"Where is your husband?"

"I don't know. He's left me, I think."

"No other family members?"

"I'm too old. They've turned their backs on me."

"Have you minded your prayers?"

"I have prayed for food."

"And?"

"See for yourself." The woman's cheekbones seemed ready to push through skin as dry as parchment. Her eyes were sunken and her body trembled.

The Reverend Daniel Goodman removed a shilling from his pocket and held it out to the old woman. She snatched it away as a starving dog would seize a bone, not chancing that the offer might just as quickly be rescinded. She closed her fist around the coin and with vacant eyes looked at Goodman as if wondering whether there might be more for the asking.

"I have two adopted children, and they are hungry. Would you have a farthing for them?"

Goodman hesitated, because he suspected she might be lying. Nevertheless he produced two farthings and handed them to the woman. "Your church should be helping you," he said.

"Yes," she strained to make herself heard. "The Parochial Board does. The amount is almost nothing. Out of the pittance I receive each month, I must pay rent. There's little left for food. The children you see around you beg on the street. They also steal. Sir, when you're as hungry as we are you'll do whatever you must to survive."

"Why are you here in this corner of the room? Where is your bed?"

"Last winter we burned it for fuel. Now I sleep here on this straw. This is my bed."

The Reverend Goodman drew himself upright. He did not like what he smelled. He felt a sudden revulsion for the old, sickly woman, and he wished to be away from her before she could play any more upon his sympathies. He did not like the condition of her skin, wrinkled and pale, hair as kinked as a soured mop. There was a bald spot on top of her head. Goodman had seen better living conditions for stray cats and dogs. Those Parochial Board members should be ashamed, he thought. Did they not come and see these things? Dribs and drabs of charity, like crumbs for starving people, are nothing less than torture. Still, what could anybody do? Had not the situation gone so far as to be irreversible?

The Reverend Daniel Christian Goodman, founder of the

newly formed Tabernacle of the Living Word, on the eve of his departure for America, arched his thick brows and attributed these conditions also to the sin of drunkenness and other depravities. You could see it on every hand. Men stumbled in and out of pubs like the Billy Goat Strut, and they spent their last farthings on a Devil's brew. Goodman was wearied by the weight of preaching against such odds. How much could one man of God be expected to do? It didn't seem to matter how committed he might be to the call of Puritanism. He believed he had the strength for it. But why were the obstacles so difficult? Why were the people so stubborn? Was God testing him? At fifty-one years he was not sure all the doubts would be resolved before his own arrival in Heaven.

He had created the Tabernacle of the Living Word in his mind when he was a youth, tried to establish it in Oxfordshire, and brought the idea with him to London, but he questioned whether it would ever gain a substantial, tithing congregation of believers. People seemed to be running in another direction. Founding a church was not as quick and easy as he had once thought. Indeed, after a year of attempting to organize even the smallest of followings, he was coming to believe that churches had long since forfeited any claim to legitimacy. Written accounts and oral tales of royal, theologically sanctioned burnings at the stake, beheadings, banishments, and bloody trails leading from subterranean torture chambers had created in Daniel C. Goodman an abiding distrust that had grown to intense hatred for any Mother Churches.

As he climbed slowly up the narrow stairs to his tiny attic room near the River Thames, the Reverend Goodman heard the usual scurrying racket on the third landing, a sound smaller, more rapid than the clumping of the dead-wagon, yet exceedingly more insistent. As his own heavy footsteps made each board groan, the scurrying noises moved farther away. The rats always acted as if they thought it was *their* home, wherever they chanced to be. For what conceivable purpose had they been created? Why didn't *they* get sick? *Did* God create rats? Of course He did. Surely, He did. God created everything in seven days! "And God said, Let the waters bring forth abundantly the moving creature that hath life, and fowl that may fly above the earth in the open firmament of heaven. And God created great whales, and every living creature that moveth, which the waters brought forth abundantly, after their kind, and every winged fowl after his kind: and God saw that it was good."

For Daniel Goodman, the persistent question would always be a nagging, pathetic, and urgent *why?* If God had created man in His image, had He also created the rat, and the flea? This was an absurdity. Were they, then, the creations of the *Devil?* Did the Devil have the power to *create?* Surely, he did not. But if the rat and the flea *were* weapons of the Devil, was it not possible that they would replace mankind? One absurdity led to another.

The Reverend Goodman had heard a lifetime of admonitions to read, study, and accept the Bible as the ultimate word of the Lord. Yet questions persisted. Could the Devil defeat God? That would be blasphemy, according to the earnest teachers of the Reverend Goodman. Then cholera was one of God's means of holy vengeance, along with war and floods and other diseases, a worthy absolute, which fundamentalists would trace to the book of 1 Samuel: "Woe unto us! Who shall deliver us out of the hand of these mighty Gods? These are the Gods that smote the Egyptians with all the plagues in the wilderness."

Sin was definitely the problem, according to the Puritans and many other God-fearing people. But according to the agnostics and the atheists and those who lived in joyful ambiguity, Puritanism and other forms of worship were themselves the problem. Christopher Marlowe had concluded that religion was "but a childish toy . . . there is no sin but ignorance."

With dog-tired steps the Reverend Goodman reached the top of the stairs and rested his head against the door. In the

Book of Job, God was likened to the leviathan. "Canst thou put an hook into his nose? Or bore his jaw through with a thorn? Will he make a covenant with thee?" Goodman was becoming increasingly apprehensive about his departure the next day upon God's vast ocean. The decision to purchase a companion ticket added to his discomfiture. He had gone to the extra expense on the off chance that a deserving person might need passage. He had found no one who seemed to him worthy.

Inside his cubicle, he stood for a moment at the window facing north. The outline of the city created a painful remembrance, reminding him of the hedgerows of Eynsham, Oxfordshire, the home of Aelfric and the Lives of the Saints. The hedgerows and the saints too made odd shapes against the sky. The formations visible in London depended upon the dampness of the night, the heavy fog rolling along the Thames like a cloud from nether regions. It compounded the gloom and muddled his best intentions. The Reverend Goodman did not believe, as many did, that muggy air had anything to do with the scourge of cholera. Many times, he'd heard the foolish arguments for mass bonfires as a way to cleanse the air of disease-causing elements. Unrelated to the cause of cholera, it was as stupid as it was sinful, an excuse for licentious reveling, public drinking, sexual depravities—all sure signs of Sodom and Gomorrah, upon which the Lord rained "brimstone and fire; . . . and He overthrew those cities, and all the plain, and all the inhabitants of the cities, and that which grew upon the ground."

Thoughts of Sodom and Gomorrah were sickening to the Reverend Goodman. The evil practices of perverse fornication played upon his mind in pictures so vivid that he felt himself in mortal combat with the Devil. The rats multiplying exponentially in the building where he spent his nights were the same wicked creatures as the ones running about wildly at Sodom and Gomorrah. Goodman had heard lectures on the scientific explanation for the fire and brimstone on the plain at

Sodom and Gomorrah, that it was simply an earthquake in an area of underground oil beds. He dismissed this theory as more of the Devil's clever strategy for leading people away from God by denying the reality of sin.

Dropping to his knees beside the filthy, salvaged mattress on the uneven floor, fists tightened against his forehead, the Reverend Daniel S. Goodman prayed that his wife and daughters would understand the worthiness of his mission. He had agonized about it and prayed about it daily. He had decided to carry his work to America and send for his family after he had established himself there. It was a brave, daunting thought, but one he was lately beginning to doubt most seriously. Everything, all good things, indeed, would take time. Was that not true? Yes, but perhaps too much time. He understood that, and indecision was a luxury he could not afford. The Lord had spoken to him in Oxfordshire, had told him to pick up his cot and walk, to do it quietly in the middle of the night while Thelma, his wife, and their daughters, Gretchen and Elaine, were asleep. Their threatening dreams reflected their hunger pains. They did not know they were destined for deeper poverty. Goodman hungered for his wife, missing her warmth in their bed, regretting the loss of pleasure that caused him to feel each time as if he were beginning a new life. He believed that carnal love between a husband and his wife was one of God's grandest gifts. "Thou shalt not commit adultery" was one of God's sternest commandments.

Goodman pictured the short, scribbled note he had left behind:

> *Have gone to London, then America. Will send for you soon as possible. Where I go, you cannot go, not at the present time. I love you.*
>
> *God loves you. He will bring us all to Heaven. We will be united there—after the scourges have passed.*
>
> DCG

The Reverend Goodman had, in fact, deserted his wife and daughters in Oxfordshire. But he didn't think of it as willful abandonment, nothing as sinful as that, because such a conscious, deliberate act would surely offend the Great God Almighty. Goodman was a devoted and pious Puritan. His Holy Crusade was to save souls, as many as possible; and more important, he believed his ministry would flower in America, where so many might still be saved. He shunned the Church of England and the Church of Rome with nearly equal disdain. They were both Catholic, both commanded by monstrous impostors, and he, Daniel Christian Goodman, the self-governed, the self-directed, saw this insanity quite clearly.

Not only was Goodman lonely for his wife and daughters. His waking consciousness was awash with doubts about his inner self, his turbulent, libidinous being. Putting the preciousness and vulnerability of that self in direct combat with Evil was the way, he believed, to find a surer pathway to the throne of the One True God. This theory had become his obsession, a spiritual rationale. He must not compromise truth as he conceived of it, as he felt it, as his fingers and toes tingled with it in divine enterprise. Daniel, the individual, the Cromwellian handmaiden of the Almighty, would not, could not accept the insipid intervention of bishops, archbishops, certainly nothing as devilish as creatures masquerading in Rome as Vicars of Christ. They were the true anti-Christs.

"Vicars, indeed. *Vicious,* indeed," breathed Daniel Christian Goodman as he stretched out upon his vermin-infested mattress. He drew up his knees, pulled a dirty sheet over his left shoulder, doubled his right fist for a pillow, then turned toward the wall of his tiny cubicle. He drifted in and out of consciousness until he plummeted into a deep sleep. One of his recurring dreams involved his wife; it was disconcerting because it quickly turned to conjugal gratification. Thelma was as eager as he. She responded to his touch with vigorous enthusiasm. It was the moment of bliss when Thelma's face became angelic and Goodman imagined himself at Heaven's entrance.

There was an insistent rap on the door.

"Mister?" called a woman's voice.

"Thelma? Thelma, is that you?" Why was she suddenly outside?

"Mister, I need your help."

"I don't understand," said Goodman, struggling to rise from the mattress. His head hurt and his right hand was numb from loss of circulation. His fingers were curved into a petrified claw. It did not seem as if he was at home in Oxfordshire, but neither did the room look like his garret on the Thames. Thelma was gone. Where was she? It was not like her to leave their bed in the middle of the night unless it would be to use the chamber pot. Even then he would know she was there. He heard no familiar sound. Shaking his head to clear his thoughts, he stumbled to the door, opened it, and looked into the face of a woman as dreamy-eyed as Thelma. Instinctively, he reached out to h before recognizing one of the prostitutes who regularly conducted business on Borough Road. She was one of those he had often reproved, receiving only smiles in return. He could not distinguish any one of the women by face, certainly none by name. The prostitutes, who had become the special concern of some liberals, especially Gladstone, seemed to be thriving as well as, perhaps better than, many of God's righteous creatures. But this was a superficial judgment; disease did not distinguish between prostitutes and royalty.

"What do you want?" the Reverend Goodman asked fearfully as he looked past the woman for any sign of beguiling serpents or conspirators waiting to creep upon their prey.

"What do *you* want?" asked the young woman, as she brushed back the silky reddish gold hair from her forehead. Her eyebrows were as perfectly etched as new moons on clear nights. The shadows blurred the woman's face, highlighting her friendly,

neutral right eye, intensifying the gleam in the left eye, an unmistakable message that playfully teased with delight. Goodman
had not seen a whore's mouth so close to his. He'd not thought
of such a woman as this having lips so inviting, even refined.
The thought of touching her shining hair crossed his mind, but
instead he caught his hand in midair and nervously smoothed
back his own hair. She appeared to be in her early twenties.
Perhaps beauty had been sharpened, some would say heightened, by her encounters, which caused her smile to be more
tightly drawn. She seemed to him like a she wolf hungry for
prey. She understood the profit in controlled, parted lips and
slightly upturned corners of the mouth. Goodman felt a tin-
gling sensation spreading upward from the tips of his toes. His
heart was pounding, but words did not come easily.

"I want to sleep," said Goodman, lamely. "I'm having
trouble seeing anything clearly. Do you understand? I have
preached until there's nothing left in me. I feel pulled apart on
a rack. I want to sleep."

"I want to sleep *with* you," said the prostitute.

"You what? You what?" stammered Goodman. "Young
woman, I—I don't sleep with prostitutes. Don't you understand?
You are evil. You have no right to affront me, a man of God, in
this obscene manner. I will not—abide it. I am a married man.
And I am old enough to be your father."

"What difference does that make? You are a man. I am a
woman. I will be your Eve."

God had done a curious thing, Goodman puzzled as he
looked at the young woman, in creating Eve from Adam's rib.
Why had he done that? A favorite supposition was that God
had decided that Eve should be the one to gather the firewood,
wash the clothes, cook the food, birth the children, and satisfy
Adam's insatiable desire to procreate. God also said: "But of the
tree of the knowledge of good and evil, thou shalt not eat of it:
for in the day that thou eatest thereof thou shalt surely die."

"You're right. It makes no difference." Goodman was tired to the point of collapse. Has anyone, he wondered, any idea what it means to go out on the street every day and preach until you feel as if you have not one word left, not one ounce of energy remaining? Does anyone know how this makes a man of God *feel?*

"So, you want me to come in? I can make you feel better."

The Reverend Daniel Christian Goodman, lifelong Puritan, had secretly read, with a troubled and anxious mind, Cleland's *Fanny Hill; or, the Memoirs of a Woman of Pleasure.* Temptation had aroused his desire and rocked his self-restraint. Goodman was morally driven to condemn prostitution, wherever it raised its ugly head or—on this moody night in London— its pretty head. This was the first time he had been personally confronted by a good-looking woman at a time when he was worn out and vulnerable. His eyes automatically moved from her radiant face to the cleavage of her splendid breasts. The temptation was as automatic as it was irresistible. The woman turned as if auditioning, revealing nicely contoured hips and legs.

For an instant, Goodman was speechless, a strategic error. The young woman seized the moment and slipped into the room.

"I have no money," Goodman lied.

"I don't want your money," said the woman, unbuttoning her blouse.

"Then what *do* you want?" he stammered.

She said nothing. She opened her blouse and exposed her breasts. "You have no right to tempt me in this way! You must stop!" Instinctively he turned away, looking toward the window.

"I heard you're one of the lucky ones heading for America. I want to go with you. Let me sleep with you tonight. Do you understand? Let me give you pleasure. It won't cost you a tuppence. Let me give you more joy in one night than you've had your entire life."

"Wait just a minute," stammered the Reverend Goodman. "Wait—"

"Nobody'll ever know the difference, except you, of course. Who else needs to know?"

"It's not right," said Goodman, but his resolve was shaken.

"Then take me aboard the ship. Tomorrow, isn't it? You'll never be bothered with the likes of me again—unless, of course, you want me."

"How do I know I can trust you?"

"How do I know I can trust *you*?"

"I'm a minister of the Lord."

"I'm a whore. What's the difference?" she asked, slipping smoothly out of her skirt. She wore nothing under it.

Goodman's knees buckled under him and he sank to the bed. "This is no way to talk to a man pure in his heart. No way to talk to God's missionary. The Lord *hates* sin. You *are* sin. You *are* the flesh," said Goodman, looking at her nakedness. Quickly he looked away again.

"That's true," said the woman.

"You *are* one of the reasons for this *sickness*. I am Daniel Christian Goodman, and I warn you that you are forsaking your soul."

"Do you really think so?" asked the prostitute, advancing like Eve toward her Adam.

"You are leading others to Hell. You are in danger of losing eternal peace."

"You're in danger of losing one of the best pieces you've ever had the offer of," said the woman serenely as she sat down next to Goodman. She turned his face toward her and smiled.

The Reverend Goodman looked toward the darkening window, then back to the prostitute. She sat quietly on the corner of the mattress. The musky odor emanating from her body opened a hidden chamber of the Reverend Goodman's spirituality. Smiling, she reached out, took his hand in hers, and placed it on her breasts. She kissed him on his cheek, and she smoothed back his rumpled hair. "Take me with you," she sighed.

"I want—I want to say this—you are more different than I ever imagined. I have always renounced Satan. I continue to do so. You have drawn me into this—I renounce—"

He felt her left hand on the inside of his thigh as she whispered into his ear: "My name is *Sylva*. I am all yours."

"No—oh, no," moaned Goodman.

"Oh, yes," breathed Sylva into his ear.

Daniel Christian Goodman's face flushed hotly as the last shreds of his Puritan prohibitions were swept away. His breath caught and he found himself spiraling into a strange, dark domain, sensual and inviting, where satyr queens reigned with their reddish golden hair, their long, smooth bodies, their delectably pointed tongues.

At 62 Borough Road, Southwark, outside the closed door of the room where the Reverend Goodman slept deeply and dreamed of exquisite sin, the King of Rats was in control of the third landing of the stairway. He demanded obedience from all his consorts. They approached him and submitted to him. He bred them quickly in their regular seasons, dispatching any males who dared to challenge the totalitarian authority of the kingdom. Let them find their own harems. Let them establish their own courts, their own sovereignties, their own reasons for being.

And they did. With enormous satisfaction, they did. Able to begin breeding at three months of age and to produce seven litters a year, as many as twenty-two pups in each litter, one pair of rats easily became thousands, all multiplying in blinding, exponential progression. And on every level of every building in Southwark there were many kings, many consorts, untold numbers of future kings and consorts, living to breed, breeding to live, their reproductive appetites as rapacious as locusts in ripening fields of golden grain. But there was another spectacle, stranger and more miraculous. The glistening satin back of each of these creatures of God carried other, minuscule members of the natural order. Fleas, wingless but able to jump distances two hundred times greater than their own length, contrived their separate, interdependent survivals. They siphoned blood in the furry fields of the backs of rats, both species of God's creatures in deliciously desperate search for food. Carrier for the bubonic plague and the Black Death of the fourteenth century, the flea alone had killed more people than all the wars of history, including the Holy Crusades. Miniature ministers without ordination or portfolio, they prowled the world for lovely blood, wherever they could find it.

The Reverend Daniel S. Goodman slept the sleep of a fitful angel in diaphanous, dimly lit dreams, rattled by the sounds of God's creatures incessantly struggling to stay alive. The young woman who lay naked by his side, as naked and shameless as Eve in the Garden of Eden, had given the Reverend unimaginable gratification. She too slept deeply and peacefully now. She had put as far away as possible any thoughts of the outside world, where human tragedies continued to unfold.

London, Dockside

April 1833

Let no one dream of an angry Deity, pouring out vials of wrath on his creatures. Shame on any who will make or tolerate such representations. There is no such thing in reality, and there should be none in thought or deed. God is love, and whoever does not so regard Him, alike in adversity and prosperity, has the elements of religion yet to learn.

—Samuel Barrett
August 9, 1832

ST. KATHERINE DOCK was packed with family members hurrying to take their places aboard the *Cynthia Anne*. There was a carnival atmosphere and a sense of desperate urgency. Whole families, uprooted from a decaying agrarian economy, victims of the industrial revolution, clung together in tribal despair. Departure on the graceful sailing ship, it was generally believed, meant escape from miserable conditions. It represented hope for a new and better life. But some would not reach America, and they were seeing their loved ones for the last time.

"Charlsie, me girl, and what am I to do without you?" moaned the elderly Charles Woodall.

"Oh, Grandfather," said twelve-year-old Charlsie Ferguson, "I don't want to go without you."

"Your mama and your papa will take good care of you. If they don't I will come to America and thrash them soundly, I will," said Charles, wiping his nose with the sleeve of his tattered jacket. He used the back of his hand to brush away some of the tears in his eyes.

Sally and Elton Ferguson, Charlsie's young parents, had dreaded this moment when they'd be forced to say goodbye to the old gentleman with the heart of gold and the lively mind of a scholar. It had been his idea to stay behind, a sacrifice to ensure the likelihood of a successful passage for the younger family.

"Father," said Sally, patiently, "it's truly a sad day, and yet as you yourself many times have said, it is the day when your child and your child's child go to find their fortune in another world, isn't that right?"

"True. 'Tis true as Donne's *Valediction:*

Our two souls therefore, which are one,
Though I must go, endure not yet
A breach, but an expansion,
Like gold to airy thinness beat.

"Oh, father, I love you," said Sally.

"And I love you, my beautiful child," he said as he felt the warm goodness of Sally's arms around his neck, her flushed face against his.

"Now, see here Elton, me boy," said Charles across Sally's shoulder to her husband. "'Tis you who have the responsibility of seeing that these girls will be all right."

"Yessir," said Elton, who, Charles could easily sense, had not overcome his uncomfortable feeling in the presence of one who was better educated. But there was no hostility, for that was neither Charles's nor Elton's inclination.

"It is time for us to be aboard the ship," said Elton.

"Right you are," said Charles, kneeling in front of Charlsie. "There is something I wish for you to have." With his hand he fumbled and then removed from an inside pocket a small gold cross and chain. "This was your grandmother's and hers before her. I've saved it for you."

Trembling, Grandfather Charles attached the chain around Charlsie's neck, smoothed back her reddish brown hair, then held her face in his hands. "Yes, you are a beautiful child, and I shall miss you terribly. Now go with your mother and father. It is the way it was meant to be."

"Grandfather," said Charlsie, "I'm going to miss you."

"And I you, child."

"What's to become of me without our chats, I'd like to know?" said Charlsie, tears welling in her mournful brown eyes.

"Remember, child, the illustrious voyager, Donne:

In what torn ship soever I embark
That ship shall be my emblem of Thy ark.

"And what does that mean?" asked Charlsie, with both her hands rubbing away tears.

"It means there'll always be storms, and with God's grace there'll always be calms. It means we have no choice but to live our lives as best we're able. It means it's time for you to be on the grandest journey of your life."

Elton led Sally and Charlsie across the gangplank to the *Cynthia Anne*. They found a spot to stand where they could wave goodbye to the old man with the sloping shoulders, hands thrust into his pockets. He wiped his nose and his eyes again, and, from the dockside, he kept waving as long as he could see the faces of the only family he had.

With the highest of expectations, the *Cynthia Anne* left port on the fairest of days on the Thames in the shadow of the Tower of London. Around the tip of the Isle of Dogs, the last pride and joy of Captain James Henry Lovingsworth sailed like a grande dame billowed with presence born of imperial breeding. The passengers, savoring the brilliance of the sunlit day, crowded the rails to wave bittersweet farewells to relatives and friends. Children ran and played games of "catch me if you can." Exhausted older men and women sat to catch their breaths on trunks filled with as many possessions as they could cram within. The captain knew that some had pieces of gold sewn inside their clothes, but he did not question it as long as fares were paid in advance. Young single women turned demurely with sly and furtive glances, signaling appreciation for liberation and perhaps, if the timing proved just right, lustful adventures, maybe sinful. But, they asked, what of it? Prostitutes watching the passing parade on deck, looking for opportunities, assessing them for their probabilities, bided their time.

Some young men climbed the rigging and scrambled for better vantage points. "You, there!" shouted a member of the crew. "Where you think you're *going?* Get your damned ass *down* from there, before you kill your bloody self."

It was little use to attempt any regimentation at the outset, but once out of the mouth of the Thames, past the Strait of Dover and well into the English Channel, Captain James Henry Lovingsworth and his crew would let the bloody emigrants know who was in charge. The captain would try to get as many passengers as possible to New Orleans, but there were no guarantees. Never would be. Never could be. In fact, with the stench of London's cholera still in his nostrils, he knew that many would probably die and certainly be dispatched overboard as quickly as possible. Lovingsworth was not responsible for cholera. This disease was somebody else's concern. Nor did he have any responsibility for the Church of England's implication in the disenfranchisement of the rural population of England.

James Henry Lovingsworth was the captain of his own ship. He was providing a way out, an opportunity to go to America. That was it. There was nothing more to it. The constant gnawing of daily adversity during years of worldwide economic depression had eaten around the edges and was moving toward the heart of the captain's once substantial wealth. He had his own ledger accounts to balance. End of discussion.

Charlsie Ferguson, finding a tiny space with her mother and father in steerage, did not think of herself as Captain Lovingsworth's or anybody else's commodity. Curiously, in fact, she felt unshackled from the demands of childhood. She was proud to have been born in Oxfordshire, granddaughter of a yeoman farmer who had moved to London after losing his three acres of ancestral land to the local curate in an Enclosure Act proceeding. By now, she imagined, her beloved grandfather was heading toward the one place where he would find solace.

Charles Woodall, voracious reader of newspapers, magazines, and books, was a regular visitor at a pub that freelance reporters also frequented. On the day Woodall saw his girls for the last time, waved goodbye to them and his son-in-law as they disappeared from view, he cried as much as he ever remembered doing. Grimly, his heart pounding as heavily as his plodding feet, the old man with the normally mischievous spirit and love of stout retreated to the Billy Goat Strut.

Charles had left Oxfordshire, the burial place of his wife, Winifred, and he had brought Sally, Charlsie, and Elton to Southwark. One of Charles's hobbies had been sharpening knives. It was a living. It wasn't much, but it helped to support his reading habit and pay for his cherished stout at the Billy Goat Strut.

"Diggery, me lad, I've just seen me only child go off with her husband and child to America. You'll be pleased to bring me the bloody usual."

The owner of the pub brought a brimming mug and set it before the old man.

"This one's on me," said Diggery Blanchard with a rueful smile.

"Cheers," said Charles.

"Cheers," said Diggery.

"Here's to all us frigging farmers and all us stupid knife sharpeners and all our godforsaken children out there on the Great Water," said Charles, wiping his mouth with a trembling hand.

"A poet we are so fortunate to have in our midst, alas another time," moaned Diggery. "And here's to all us bloody bartenders in godforsaken England who have to listen to tales of woe," he added grandly.

Several journalists came through the opened front door bringing with them the sounds of the street—tinsmiths hawking their wares, ragmen calling to second-floor windows, bells ringing at the church of St. George the Martyr, and the smell, the godawful smell of soot and filth. They took a corner table and waited for Diggery to bring their usuals.

"Diggery, me lad," said Charles when the barman returned, "have you had occasion to read of the trials and tribulations of some of the bloody preacher bastards in America as well as the ones on our own lovely shores in the dearly departed eighteenth century?" asked Charles. Diggery knew his customer could be counted on daily for miscellaneous scraps of useless learning.

"I've a feeling I'm about to hear about them."

"True, true, and amazing it is to me that the bloody Americans have had so much trouble converting the bloody savages. I mean, didn't the Calvinist Johnny Edwards have enough on his hands with the bloody likes of the Housatonnuck Indians without burdening us all with his *Original Sin?* And there's our own William Law and his *Serious Call to a Devout and Holy Life,* as if he knew which side of the bed to get up on in the morning. And there's Joseph Priestley and his *Letters to a Philosophical*

Unbeliever. For a fact, now, that's what I've become, Diggery, a bloody philosophical unbeliever."

"Hear, hear," chorused the journalists.

"Aye, and a bloody good one," announced Diggery.

"I'm empty, Diggery. I'll need another stout in order to continue, lad."

Diggery Blanchard filled another mug and brought it to Charles.

"Imagine, imagine, if you can, can you imagine, me good Diggery? There's preachers what want us to believe that the cholera is God's way of *punishing* us!"

"*Do* they now?"

"Indeed! Our God is an angry God, oh yes he is. The pulpits are full of it. The reverend blarsted fathers from Liverpool to Land's End are cracking the poor people's heads open, pouring in the fire and brimstone, slapping 'em closed, and putting their boot on 'em. Yes, darlin' Diggery, they are the hottest of the hot, all around they are exactly that, my dimpled Diggery. And they call themselves *holy.* Holy me arse, for a fact now. Do you know what I think, Diggery dear?"

"What do you think? As if it would stop you, if I said I knew."

"True, true, absolutely true. So, here's what I think. I think it's not the poor people to blame. Don't matter who they are or where they live in our fair land, it's a fact now that the blame is *conditions.*"

"Conditions?" the journalists inquired.

"Aye, conditions. You heard me right, my scribes. Therefore, Diggery, darlin', should we not be on our bloody knees and offering our *Prayer for All Conditions of Men?* The conditions of living in Southwark, for example, are not fit for human beings. 'Oh wearisome condition of humanity!'"

"And whose lovely words were *they?*"

"Sir Fulke Greville, dear Diggery. First Baron Brooke, the

lad who had the bad fortune to be murdered by his old servant. Terrible way to go, sweet Diggery. Terrible."

"And whose fault are *conditions?*" sighed Diggery.

"I'm coming to it. Don't you hear me coming to it? The fault is failing to figure out a way for people to live in cities, if that's what it's come to. Me, I'm living in this bloody city because I couldn't make it on me own in Oxfordshire. Simple. Tried to find a decent tutoring position after I lost me land. The headmarsters said I was a bad influence. Said I drank too much. Imagine that!"

"Bloody awful!" chimed the journalists.

"Did they actually *say* that?" asked Diggery with feigned disbelief.

"Can you imagine that, now? Me, Charles Woodall, couldn't make it there because of new theologies burglarizing me mind, then machines robbing me of the work of me hands. See, it's mostly all a question of economics. Has absolutely nothing to do with bloody theology. I've read me Adam Smith. How's about you, lovely Diggery?"

"How's about me, *what?*"

"You've not been reading. I thought as much," said Charles, wearily shaking his head.

"So tell me, Squire Charles."

"Adam Smith wrote *An Inquiry into the Nature and Causes of the Wealth of Nations,* did he not?" asked Charles, patiently.

Diggery, nonplussed, wiped clean a row of mugs.

"A good Scottish mon he was, although I must take him to task on his notion that land is, of necessity, such a poor bedfellow."

At the corner table, the journalists listened expectantly to Squire Woodall, for he seemed at the top of his form. They were keenly professional in their recognition of inexpensive entertainment—a joy after another long day of barely making deadlines.

"I quite understand the inordinate pretensions and deplorable working-class conditions which have reduced the poor to pawns of economic circumstance," Charles continued.

"Hear, hear," chorused the journalists.

"I am saddened that women are victims of one of Christianity's most cherished beliefs, Adam's superiority over Eve. I also dare to entertain the radical belief that royal personages are likewise victims of the traditional assumption that English 'civilization' is loftier than all others on the face of the earth."

"Nay, nay," shouted the journalists.

"Of course it is not superior," enjoined Charles, "and you gentlemen of the fourth estate above all should be insulted by the Divine Right of Kings."

"'Twill be a long time relinquishing its hold on the royal subconsciousness," said one of the young reporters.

"Aye, with complex battle lines drawn, and the cholera pandemic that has now reached us pardons no one," Squire Charles persisted grandly. "Neither the commoners nor pompous leaders, their heads adorned with periwigs and perukes, seem able to fathom the relationship between open sewers and disease."

One of the reporters rose to go. As he passed, he patted the squire on the shoulder as an endorsement for truth-seeking and -telling.

"And what might your name be?" asked Charles.

"Dickens," called back the reporter, as he headed toward the street.

"Yes, Mr. Dickens, I've been reading your accounts. Keep writing. Remember to seek the essence of the truth."

"Squire," said Diggery, clearing his throat, "what's to become of your granddaughter, do you suppose?"

"Were she here right now, I'd take her into me arms, and we'd have a bloody good time conversing with Macha—"

"Macha?" inquired Diggery, feigning surprise as he made his way to the journalists' table again, both hands gripping tankards overflowing with stout.

"The goddess of war, lad—Macha, the exalted earth mother —Macha, the Badb, the Dana, the Celtic tradition of the Danaides, the daughters of the King of Argos, slaughterers of frigging males, even their own bridegrooms on their wedding nights." The journalists in the reporters' gallery laughed boisterously upon the hearing of the familiar "Macha" tale.

"Have mercy upon us all," said Diggery, winking at the reporters and returning to the long mahogany bar. "Are we ready for another stout, Sir Charles?"

"Indeed. There's nothing so necessary as fortification for the work at hand. Nothing so encouraging as the fair sex, the lively ones, I mean, standing toe-to-toe with the frigging scribes." The journalists raised their stouts in unison toward Charles, clanged them together, drank to the bottoms, and slammed the empties to the tabletop.

"Then here it is, Squire. What should we toast back at 'em?" Diggery inquired.

Charles Woodall paused, looked once at the journalists, then reached deeper into his treasure house. "Diggery, my good and faithful man, shall we toast the *female principle* living in the sorcery of Morgan le Fay, or shall we remain loyal to her brother, King Arthur? That seems to me to be the crux of the matter."

"Hear, hear!" chorused the reporters.

"Squire, for God's sake, don't put me on such a spot. You want *me* to take sides?" Diggery implored.

"Coward! I have nothing but the utmost disrespect for all those lacking in courage, journalists or no. We have no choice but to offer the toast to *she* who suckled the gods."

"Oh, no!"

"Then it's to King Arthur?" demanded Charles.

"Bloody right!" chorused Diggery and the journalists.

"If so, then I must rise to this occasion. This is no time for cowardice. Therefore, I propose a toast to every last one of us. I'll have it no other way, lads."

Charles stood at attention before the table of scribes:

I pray you all give your audience,
And hear this matter with reference,
By figure a moral play—

"Hear, hear!" enjoined the journalists.

Charles raised high his tankard and continued, his voice unwavering:

The Summoning of Everyman called it is,
That of our lives and ending shows
How transitory we be all day.

Charles and Diggery clinked their tankards, drank, and bowed until their heads almost touched. Charles returned to his table and Diggery went to the bar for another round for the reporters, who were laughing and slapping each other on the back.

"Another, Diggery!" commanded Charles, who in his reeling fantasia would confer the title of sovereign princess upon his only granddaughter, forever "Charlsie" to the squire.

"Should be your last for today, Squire Charles, me sweet boy."

"Quite so. Permit me to say what I'm saying another way. Permit me to summarize for the intrepid reporters gathered in yon gallery. Too many bloody people—"

"Too many people breeding, that have no business breeding?"

"Quite right, Diggery. At last, you are definitely onto the main issue even if they are not. Indeed. The breeding will continue. So, now the time has come for many to leave the land. Where should they go? To the Celtic Sea? They ain't fish. Up in the sky? They ain't birds. They are, my good Diggery, *people!*

Therefore, if they cannot stay on the land, cannot swim in the ocean, cannot fly in the sky, then it stands to reason that they must come to the cities. And there's simply got to be a way to pull through *conditions!* There must be a way to muddle through all the nonsense! I cannot say it a better way, Diggery. We have a defecating problem. We have a defecating storm. If there is such a thing as, for lack of a better phrase, a *scourge* of Heaven, then there it is. Too many people relieving themselves. Too many rats running free. And *they* are relieving themselves. Too many pigeons. And *they* are relieving themselves. Too many journalists, too many politicians, and too many preachers running off at their mouths."

"Relieving themselves?" asked Diggery.

"Aye! Bloody right. Too much confusion about what is real and what is imagined. It is, to take it by the throat, my dear Diggery and members of the fourth estate here assembled, a sewer of the mind that contaminates the beauty of the heart."

With the cheers of the reporters ringing in his ears, Charles Woodall left the Billy Goat Strut and wearily walked home, recalling with what joy he had welcomed 1833, the year of the abolition of slavery in the British Empire. He was certain there would continue to be other forms of servitude, including the displacement of another generation of agrarian families from their homelands, from London to Edinburgh, from Cork to Belfast. He'd read the reporter Dickens's descriptions of the horrid living conditions in Southwark, where his father was imprisoned for his debts.

"The problem is numbers, the problem is frigging numbers," murmured Charles as he lurched in the direction of his hovel. "Malthus was absolutely correct—human beings by their unthinking nature will multiply faster than the food supply."

Charles returned to the ramshackle building on the Thames where he would try to find sleep, if only he could disremember Sally and Charlsie. "Damn it to hell!" said Charles to the noise of the rats between the walls and on the landing. "Listen to the bloody bastards!" stormed the old man.

"The ultimate restraint is not morality—more likely it'll be disease and famine and war," he muttered as he lay and tossed on his cot, reliving the moment when he had placed the small gold cross around the neck of his departing granddaughter. Then he cried himself to sleep.

Bishop Rock

April 1833

I know your sorrow well, Everyman:
Because with Knowledge ye come to me,
I will you comfort as well as I can . . .
Here shall you receive that scourge of me,
Which is penance strong that ye must endure,
To remember thy Saviour was scourged for thee
With sharp scourges, and suffered it patiently.
So must thou ere thou 'scape that painful pilgrimage.
Knowledge, keep him in this voyage. . . .
—*Everyman*

MOUNTAINS OF WATER heaved beyond the Isles of Scilly and
Bishop Rock, a logical location for a granite-based lighthouse to
send out final warnings to captains and first mates, navigators
and helmsmen, to beware the many rocks that could tear a ship
apart. The vastness of the North Atlantic became a new religious dominion for pilgrims embarking upon its uncompromising waters, which gave no quarter, expected none. The wind
blew with its own sense of timing. The waves rolled in methodically, never asking what they might be breaking or what new
formations of rock they might be creating. The ocean had com-

mitted no sins, forgave none. No dogma was taught; therefore nothing required confession or penance. There were no cathedrals built with peasant labor. No floors swept by aging women. There were no Holy Orders, no elections of bishops or archbishops.

In the savage days when the Celts were overrunning Britain, countless ships had gone aground on the rocky, fog-shrouded shores of the Isles of Scilly, 140 tiny, foggy protrusions breaking the water's surface thirteen leagues west of Land's End. These islets, warmed by the Gulf Stream, were believed by some to be submerged mountaintops of the lost kingdom of Lyonnesse. For more than twenty centuries the shorelines circling them had been graveyards for sleek Viking longships, the *drakkars* with their moose-jawed female figureheads, Scandinavian *knorr* merchant vessels, and warships of Denmark and the North Sea Frisian Islands. The bones of captains and oarsmen lay scattered in brittle chalk deposits, and their cargo treasures shone like the veritable gold-laden streets of Heaven.

Legends rode the winds above the bones and the gold and silver caches. Folktales enveloped the lives of Celtic bishops who, according to tradition, were said to have used the uninhabited islands as havens to live apart from the Roman world. Bishop Rock, the westernmost of the tiny, craggy islets, would become the nautical zero-milepost for reckoning distances. The rock, which formed the base of the old lighthouse, would come to symbolize both a starting point and an ending point for many emigrants to the Americas who would know no turning back. There'd be pride born of stubbornness, mistakes born of ignorance. Ships filled with peasants would founder in the heavy fog, and there'd be bones for pirates to pick, souls for Holy Men to salvage. There'd be patronizing solaces for the priestly ones to confer and deals to be sanctioned by lords.

The image of a ship bearing black sails would one day live in the memories of storytellers from Cornwall to Kentucky.

Long after King Arthur and the tales of Camelot, the sufferings of the Welsh, the Irish, the Cornish, and the Scots, it would live in myths of the voyage of Captain James Henry Lovingsworth's *Cynthia Anne,* one of the last of the noble sailing ships.

Captained by its owner, a Kentuckian down on his luck and far from home, the three-masted, square-rigged *Cynthia Anne* slanted on a southwesterly course past Eddystone Rocks, Lizard's Point, Land's End, Wolf Rock, across Latitude 49.5 North, Longitude 6.5 West. The graceful bow rose and fell in the waters surging south of the southernmost edge of the Celtic Sea, where winds unendingly howled like Gaelic banshees, as if foretelling death. The *Cynthia Anne* leaned toward the western fires flattening in sullen purple as another night rolled down the long lanes of the North Atlantic.

At supper in the fo'c'sle sailors ate salt pork with brick-hard scones and drank sparingly from tightly kegged water. Like kenneled mastiffs, they eyed with suspicion any shipmate's movement suggesting an overstepping of bounds. These sea dogs were hidebound, plundering adventurers, a polite word for pirates. Many were vicious criminals imprisoned for a brief time within the confines of the ship, held captive by a captain serving as their warden. Some were innocent bystanders seized by thugs in the darkened streets of London and impressed to serve aboard ship. Prompt hanging from the nearest gibbet was the certain punishment for desertion. The trick was to stay alive.

In steerage, a microcosm of Malthusian economics, the survival of human beings was put to another test. In times of impending storm, immigrant passengers—men, women (some about to give birth), and children—were crowded, stacked, then, when the big blow came, scattered like cordwood. Soon they'd be retching and defecating and urinating beneath hatches battened down against the weather, the smell growing as heavy as steaming manure wagons departing Bankside Street in London.

The human cargo on this voyage of the *Cynthia Anne* included English, Scottish, and Irish emigrants to the United States. The Reverend Daniel Christian Goodman was among them. He had begun the voyage by cajoling sinners to repent but was quickly overcome by his own seasickness. At first, green as a frog squatting and then gigged from its lily pad, he was now spending many of his waking moments bent over in blanch-faced despair. The Reverend Goodman could not understand why God was treating him so. What had he done to incur such wrath? Were his sermons not honest? Were they not true? Were they not unselfish? Had he not surrendered the comforts of home in Oxfordshire to preach on London street corners? Was he not willing to risk all by sailing to America to continue his ministry?

All around him were scenes so vile and pathetic as to tempt him to curse God. How could such wretchedness be? Was this not Hell itself? Are little children not innocent? No, they are not, for they have inherited Original Sin. *What befell Adam and Eve on account of their sin? Adam and Eve, on account of their sin, lost innocence and holiness, and were doomed to sickness and death.*

For the first time, the Reverend Goodman doubted himself almost as much as he doubted organized religion. The night spent with the prostitute had enormously increased his guilt and compounded his confusion, and Goodman was trying mightily to put that out of his mind, a most difficult challenge. He had brought Sylva aboard as part of his companion ticket, and no one had questioned her identity. But after that, whenever he was near her, he refused to make eye contact, and she made no further attempt to speak with him. Goodman had been true to his word, and he was grateful that she was being true to hers.

Amidships, Charlsie, Sally, and Elton Ferguson were surrounded by other families with equally sobering countenances. Only the smaller children laughed. Women tightened their bonnet strings as if to gain a feeling of security, while menfolk stood erect in their waistcoats, apprehensive and guarded on unfamiliar territory. There were many stony-faced misgivings. Some mothers nursed their infants, while labor pains began for others. The drama of birthing fascinated Charlsie, who sensed a need to help but did not know how. She watched as a family huddled, one woman taking charge because there was only one doctor aboard ship. The confidence and trust involved in one woman helping another, although unrelated to her family, seemed strangely praiseworthy. Charlsie questioned her own ability to have, one day, a child, and she brooded over the possibility of there being no one to help. She prayed such a fate would befall no woman.

Beyond Bishop Rock, ocean valleys were as drenched as rain forests, ridgelines boiling in saline froth like bubbled beads in pans of fire. Lightning flashed in the blackened west, streaking the horizontal plain, followed by the rumbling of distant thunder. The heavy seas punished the starboard beams of the *Cynthia Anne,* laying her over to port. Her spars, swelled by the mounting wind, bore sails gathered full as maidens' aprons. The ship's timbers ached and groaned with the crashing swells of water.

On deck briefly for his nightly pipe, Doctor Laurence M. Hanover moved forward on the fo'c'sle and watched the silver-pointed breasts of the *Cynthia Anne's* figurehead bearing into the coming storm, her eyes staring, her hair streaming with ocean spray, her drenched, ankle-length gown resembling a shroud.

The helmsman, Paul Westlander, steering southwesterly toward the Azores Plateau, was joined at the wheel by the ship's young doctor.

"Evening, Mr. Westlander."

"Evening, Doctor Hanover."

"I can smell it coming," said Hanover.

"Smell what, sir?" asked Westlander.

"Trouble."

"The storm out there?" calmly asked the helmsman, a veteran of many years of North Atlantic crossings. "Don't worry. Now that we've cleared the Channel and brought ourselves past the bloody tips of Lyonnesse, we're out in the open, sir, where we can maneuver."

"Have you seen what's happening in steerage, Mr. Westlander?"

"Hell, no. Don't plan to. They ain't exactly human down there, are they, sir?"

"They're a community of humanity." Hanover caught himself, realizing that Westlander had his limitations. "Oh well, I probably can't explain it, and maybe you've got better things to do—like seeing that we don't all drown. Right?"

"Right!"

"Nonetheless, Mr. Westlander, people are people and they deserve much better than they're getting."

"Aye, aye, sir," said the helmsman. "What you say is true, no doubt."

"By the way, Mr. Westlander, what do you make of the captain?"

"Just between us?"

"Just between us."

"I think he's the craziest son of a bitch God ever strung a gut through, sir. But, by God's love, he's the captain and it don't matter a damn bit what any of the rest of us think about it."

"He's sick," said Doctor Hanover, "but I don't think it's the kind of sickness any doctor is going to be able to cure. I know I can't. I'm going to my cabin, Mr. Westlander. Bring us home if you can. Good night to you."

"Aye, aye, sir," said Westlander, his grip firm on the *Cynthia Anne's* wheel. "I'll do the best I can. As for the captain, the best thing is to hope he leaves us alone so we can do our jobs."

As Doctor Hanover emptied the bowl of his pipe and turned toward his cabin, he was persuaded that Malthus's warning was not only true but generally misunderstood and unheeded: "Diseases have been generally considered as the inevitable inflictions of Providence, but, perhaps, a great part of them may more justly be considered as indications that we have offended against some of the laws of nature. . . . The human constitution cannot support such a state of filth and torpor. . . . In the history of every epidemic it has almost invariably been observed that the lower classes of people, whose food was poor and insufficient, and who lived crowded together in small and dirty houses, were the principal victims."

In the captain's cabin, just aft of the quarterdeck, James Henry Lovingsworth reached for the quill his wife, Abigail, had given him the previous Christmas. Squinting in the dim light from the lamp on his desk, he dipped the quill into the ornate, glass-lined brass inkwell on his desk and made his journal entry for April 15, 1833:

> Land's End abaft. Cleared Isles of Scilly. Bishop Rock astern. No turning back. Usual course. Sailing for Azores and Sargasso Sea. Storm ahead. Black as a son of a bitch. Hatches battened down. No choice. God knows, 200 emigrants on deck would soon be 200 emigrants overboard. Then, where would business be? Should be arriving in New Orleans in about a month. Any longer could mean bankruptcy.

He paused, morbidly preoccupied with the thought of dwindling profits. Until the bottom fell out in 1819, Lovingsworth believed he had accumulated enough gold to maintain Abigail and himself in considerable style for the rest of their lives. All that was changing with the arrival of steam-powered iron ships. Upon his arrival in New Orleans this time he'd advertise the trade or sale of the *Cynthia Anne*. Surely somebody would be stupid enough to swap prime land for a magnificent sailing ship despite the advent of steam. Then he'd buy property in his native Kentucky. He'd smoke fine cigars, sip mint juleps, and watch the sun go down over rolling bluegrass pastures. He'd breed imported Aberdeen Angus cattle, merino sheep, and maybe thoroughbred horses. He'd build the best distillery and keep the French Quarter well stocked with the best sour mash bourbon! That's what he'd do, he thought, smiling to himself. He'd raise acres of golden-leafed tobacco and give the ladies something devilish to hold in their hands as they privately discussed their charity bazaars. Whenever possible he would barter for goods, holding back his final cache of golden eagles and pieces of eight down to the very last shining picayune. Abigail would never know where all their money had gone. She had never known the many secrets hidden in his moneybags.

The captain set his pen down to contemplate the starfish tattoo on the skin between his thumb and forefinger. He had acquired the prideful symbol in a shop near St. Anne's Limehouse on the East India Dock Road shortly after his first arrival in London. The Sea Star was a mark to commemorate his Aquarius birth date. And now this was his last voyage on the *Cynthia Anne*. A part of him did not believe retiring was such a splendid idea, even when there seemed to be no alternative. He'd been on or near waters most of his life—the Bay of Bengal, the Arabian Sea, the Indian Ocean, the North and South Atlantic, the Caribbean and the Gulf of Mexico, the sea lanes connecting Calcutta, Bombay, London, and New Orleans.

Softheaded landlubbers believed storms at sea were instruments of the Almighty. Captain James Henry Lovingsworth knew that when heavy seas turned maniacal and Davy Jones was after you, you'd better hold tight to the seat of your pants and trust the man with his hands on the helm. If your time had come, it had come. If you were destined to drown, you would. With a heavy leather belt, James Henry would tie himself to the captain's cabin center beam, grit his teeth, and ride like a hunter after the hounds of Hell.

When it hit, the force of the storm picked up Sally and Elton and pitched them like ragamuffins against the opposite bulkhead. Charlsie was momentarily separated from them. Thrown against a center stanchion, she instinctively wrapped her arms and her legs around it and held on fiercely. Passengers screamed, the tumult almost deafening. It was Bedlam, the violent wrenching of the *Cynthia Anne* continuing for what seemed an eternity. Actually, the worst was over within a quarter of an hour. There were bruised ribs and bloody noses, but it would have been more devastating if Captain Lovingsworth's helmsman had not succeeded in steering around the storm's periphery. At daybreak, families did what they could to restore a semblance of order to their lives. It was as if a tornado had struck and scattered a gypsy encampment.

By nightfall a more hideous dread had replaced violent weather, a catastrophe that helmsman Westlander could neither control nor circumvent. More feared than cyclonic winds, almost as disastrous as fire at sea, a scourge of Heaven suddenly visited the *Cynthia Anne.* It arrived in silence, without warning, and like a godly thief it struck—the worst fear of 1833: Asiatic cholera.

The first victim was Sally Ferguson. Her face blanched, her stomach in convulsions, she was barely able to speak. She writhed in excruciating pain.

"Mother, what is it?" asked Charlsie.

"I don't know," she breathed.

"For God's sake, Sal," said Elton, "What can we do?"

"Pray for me—please—"

Charlsie bit her lip and stared into her mother's face, the

bewildered expression becoming vacant. The once-beautiful eyes were now deep depressions. Flesh once vibrant was drawn tightly around her cheekbones. She vomited profusely and her bowels went out of control. Charlsie and her father stood by, helpless.

"Ship's doctor!" yelled Elton. "Ship's doctor!"

"It won't do no good," said Harmony Fischer, a woman who had taken a spot near the Fergusons.

"What do you mean?" asked Charlsie.

"It's cholera. When it strikes there's no hope. Your mother, rest her soul, could be gone in less than an hour. If she lasts any longer it'll just mean more pain and terrible suffering."

On the starboard side where he had completed the bandaging of what he believed were a man's broken ribs, Doctor Hanover heard Elton's call and quickly responded. He knelt beside Sally, searched for a pulse but detected hardly any. He bent closer and listened for a heartbeat but heard only a faint flutter.

"I'm afraid," he said, "she'll soon be gone."

"How can she soon be gone?" cried Charlsie.

"Oh, my God," moaned Elton.

Listening close by, Sylva, the prostitute, heard the doctor's words. She quietly advanced to Charlsie. "Come here, child. Let me hold you."

A loud knocking at the door interrupted Captain Lovingsworth's journal entry recording the storm now moving astern. "Storm passed. Westlander brought us 'round. Might have some sunshine. Might open the hatches—"

"Captain!"

"Who is it?"

"First mate, sir."

"Come in," roared Captain Lovingsworth. He stood up quickly, for he intended never to be seated in the presence of persons beneath his rank. First Mate Thomas S. Moreland, six-foot-two, twenty seven years of age, ducked his blond head and lowered his broad shoulders as he entered the small cabin. A strikingly handsome, proud Kentuckian, he understood and accepted the reality that he was caught between the unchanging demands of the captain and the certain inconsistencies of the crew. Captain Lovingsworth, this ship's authority on the open seas, could not waver on matters of purpose. Stated simply, the mission of the month-long voyage was to connect the ports of embarkation and debarkation—London and New Orleans. How that was to be accomplished was a capricious balance, accommodating fallible human ingenuity and unforgiving natural order.

Storms, fires, icebergs were realities without feeling or compassion. Once they were encountered, it was solely the captain's responsibility and the first mate's orders to implement the precisely timed furling and unfurling of the mainsail, the trimming and manipulating of the topsails, the forecasting, the evading, the outwitting of all natural forces. It was the first mate's obligation to ensure that every sailor's job was performed satisfactorily, especially the helmsman's.

"By the grace of God, sir," said Moreland, "we've come through a bad storm."

"God don't have a goddamned thing to do with it. Trying to convince you muttonheads of such a simple thing is beyond me."

"Captain, my God is my God and you won't convince me to the contrary."

"Sit down here, Moreland, and allow me to give you another slant on God—He created the natural forces and turned them *loose*." As ordered, the first mate sat and the captain continued: "He created man and woman and turned them *loose*. It was up to human beings to figure out the rest. Survival was in their hands. Some would live; many would die."

"How did you know?"

"How did I know what?"

"That they are dying now in steerage?"

"That's their problem. It's the ship's doctor's problem," said Lovingsworth, standing with his arms crossed over his chest. "I hate complainers wherever they crop up. Emigrants who paid to sail on the *Cynthia Anne* should have understood this. This ain't no son of a bitching afternoon tea at Buckingham Palace, Mister."

First mate Moreland looked down to his salt-hardened hands. He folded them together and squeezed as if to release tension and to appease a desire to throttle the captain. Then he looked squarely into Lovingsworth's eyes, which did not blink.

"Well, what is it, Moreland?" snapped Captain Lovingsworth.

"There's a corpse in steerage, sir. It's a woman."

"Cause?"

"Not sure."

"Hell you mean, 'not sure'? What does surgeon say?"

"Says he's not sure. May be cholera."

"'*May be*'s not good enough, Moreland."

"What about the corpse?" asked the first mate.

"Dump the son of a bitch. Quicker you get it overboard the better."

"Aye, aye, sir."

Although he made a conscious practice of not personally admitting it to Moreland, the captain valued his first mate highly. The crew, on the other hand, was the usual combination of greed, mean-spiritedness, and stupidity. Practically speaking, as most successful captains knew, this was not all bad. Greed, mean-spiritedness, and stupidity make for excellent mastiff guard dogs. Frills and unctuous bravado were no match for icebergs and lifeboats. Life aboard the *Cynthia Anne* was a constant brute struggle with the elements.

"Moreland, my boy, life is unforgiving."

"I believe you are a good captain, sir. But for some reason I do not understand, maybe God is not pleased with us."

"Waste of time."

"What do you mean?"

"I mean that no prayer can make the wind abate or become more favorable. The wind does not negotiate terms. The hurricane season does not wait for invitations."

First Mate Thomas S. Moreland, standing at the center of a triangle of captain, crew, and God Almighty, drew his strength from a middle ground of broad experience, natural executive ability, and faith in a command higher than the captain's. Now he was dumbfounded and speechless.

"Moreland!"

"Yes, sir?"

"Send the goddamned surgeon to me."

"Aye, aye, sir."

Moreland obediently returned to steerage, where the emigrants were wedged like caged, frightened rabbits. The expressions on their faces had become wounded and confused.

"First mate!" said Harmony Fischer, "I wish to speak with you about—"

"Yes, what is it? I don't have time to waste."

"—the burial of this child's mother, that is all."

"I will assist you after I speak with the doctor."

Moreland found the boyish surgeon bending over an elderly man. Dr. Laurence M. Hanover wore gloves and a cloth tied over his nose to mask the stench of steerage. He had already confirmed the absence of any pulse. Now he smoothed back the straggles of the dead man's graying hair and covered his face. Hanover stood and turned to see the first mate.

"Captain wants to see you, Doctor."

"Doctor wants to see the captain. We've got ourselves a mess, First Mate."

"I know," said Moreland. "And the captain is in one of his royal 'sons of bitches' moods."

"None of us appreciate being called 'sons of bitches,'" said Sylva, holding Charlsie.

"Just because the eastbound cargo from New Orleans to London was cypress boards is no excuse for treating paying passengers as if they were planks," said the Reverend Goodman. "Surely the captain is not aware of these conditions."

"He is," said Moreland.

"Well, then, just as surely he should be reported to the authorities."

"Right. You do that. See how far it gets any of us. I'll have the bosun assist you in the burial."

"Damn," said Hanover. "Two, at least two deaths. Probably from cholera. There'll be more. There'll be many more."

"Doctor," said the first mate as they made their way through steerage to the main hatch, "what causes it?"

"Causes what?"

"Cholera. Do you have any idea?"

"Don't know. Don't know for certain. Many explanations. No solutions. Probably something that'll be discovered in time. Maybe *we* won't see it in our lifetimes. See here, Moreland," said the surgeon as they crossed the quarterdeck, "my advice to you. Don't expose yourself any more than you absolutely have to. Whatever you do, don't put your dirty hands into your mouth. Be careful what you eat and drink, especially what you drink."

As Hanover approached the captain's cabin, he shook his head as he thought of the emigrants caught and bedeviled in an overcrowded, evil-smelling warren. Laurence Hanover was not an atheist. He believed in the Great Creator, but he had no tolerance for oversimplifications, whether religious, medical, or intellectual. When Defoe compared the plague with certain men of God, Hanover savored what he believed to be the wisdom in it: ". . . of all plagues with which mankind are curst, Ecclesiastic tyranny's the worst."

When the doctor raised his hand to knock at the captain's cabin, the oak-paneled portal suddenly burst open. Captain Lovingsworth filled the space, putting the young surgeon off balance—precisely the captain's intent. He secretly admired Hanover as a graduate of Transylvania University's medical department, but he sensed the distinct advantage of putting a more intelligent man at any disadvantage, no matter how contrived or petty. The new doctor had signed on board the *Cynthia Anne* to be able to continue his studies of cholera and other infectious diseases. Now his extraordinary academic record was meeting its match in the unschooled dictatorship of James Henry Lovingsworth.

"Cholera?" demanded the captain.

"Probably. Most likely. May I come in?"

"Doctor Hanover, you are new at this game, I can see that very clearly. Yes, you may enter," said the captain with a tired sigh weighted with exasperation.

"Game?"

"Call it anything you like."

"I call it madness. I call it inhumane. I call it a damn poor way to run a ship. I call it the authoritarian oversimplifications of second-rate minds."

"Is that a fact?"

"Yes, it is. It is also a fact that the Great Plague of 1664-65 killed more than 100,000 in London—"

"Ancient history."

"—all paling in comparison with the Black Death of 1349, when 25 million people died in Europe, including one-third of the population of England, more than 35,000 in London alone."

"And what son of a bitch was to blame for that?" asked Lovingsworth.

"It doesn't matter. What matters is *now!*" Hanover exclaimed.

As a student in the internationally acclaimed medical department at Transylvania University in Lexington, Kentucky, Laurence Hanover had become well aware of some well-intended but nonetheless outlandish teachings.

"Have you ever heard of Professor Benjamin Rush?"

"Not lately," said the captain.

"At the University of Pennsylvania he taught his 'noxious miasma' theory relating to the treatment of infectious diseases."

"Wrong?" asked the captain.

"Wrong," said the doctor. "As wrong as his belief that tobacco caused insanity, or his notion that black people were black because of leprosy, and especially his reliance on bloodletting as a remedy for many disorders—"

"Wrong?" asked the captain.

"Wrong. Sadly wrong," said the doctor. "Did you know that a disciple of Rush, Dr. Cooke, came to Lexington in 1827 to accept the Chair of Theory and Practice of Medicine at Transylvania?"

"Nope. But, of course, he too was wrong."

"I have read his *Treatise of Pathology and Therapeutics*—"

"I haven't—"

"And I reject his reliance on calomel as a purgative."

"I hear it works wonders," said the captain, laughing.

"The last thing a cholera victim needs is more purging—or laughing."

"The last thing a cholera victim needs is a young doctor running around trying to convince the world that he has all the answers."

"Captain—"

"Now, now, my young, overwrought man, my fresh-out-of-college surgeon, you are only now *beginning* to see the central problem. Do you think that I do not appreciate the wisdom of the ages? Let us not become overheated in our sophomoric judgments."

Captain Lovingsworth put a condescending hand on Doctor Hanover's shoulder and guided him as a father would a prodigal son, from the cabin to the starboard rail of the *Cynthia Anne,* where the ocean swells had for the moment lessened. Still, from time to time, it was necessary to shout above the wind-blasts and the slapping of the seas against the ship's hull.

"Now, tell me about this madness, this 'inhumanity,' did you call it? No way to run a ship? Authoritarian oversimplifications of second-rate minds?"

"Captain Lovingsworth, we both started out in the same town."

"Aye, we did, my boy," said the captain, his voice unctuously solemn. "Dear old Lexington."

"Captain, I am not your 'boy.' I am your surgeon. While others spent most of their time at Postlethwait's, drinking their bourbon and branch, laying plans for the Kentucky Jockey Club, I was in my father's library, reading."

"And while you were reading, I was out working my ass off."

"Fair enough. I was reading, you were working, and neither of us was obeying God's commandments."

"Should we have?"

"I assume you've not read Defoe:

Wherever God erects a house of prayer,
The Devil always builds a chapel there;
And 'twill be found, upon examination,
The latter has the largest congregation.

"Aye. And thank you, my good doctor, for *all* your enlightenment. Since school is over and church is out, and since I've paid you good wages to be my ship's surgeon, I think it only fair that you tell me as quickly and as exactly as you can what in the name of the Devil is going on down there in steerage!"

"For once, why don't you just come and look at it?" said Hanover. "Why don't you come with me and smell it?"

"When I do and if I do, it'll be for the captain to decide, not *you!*"

The captain's insistent, ingratiating manner had vanished, replaced by his normal, full-chiseled, deep-bore bravado. His voice was a match for any wind born of the Celtic Sea, even though his heart often frightened him with its worrisome palpitations.

"Captain, you cannot cram two hundred people into a filthy, rat-infested hellhole and expect anything but disaster. You cannot—"

"Don't tell me what I can and cannot do, young man. I can put *four hundred* human beings anywhere they are willing to pay to be. I can squat them down on Bishop's Rock and let them piss in each other's faces. How's about *eight hundred?*" sputtered Captain Lovingsworth as the palpitations became chaotic.

"Even if it were only *one,* it would be wrong."

"For God's sake, don't you understand that many of these sons of bitches would have died in the hellholes of Southwark if I had not given them at least a *chance* to survive?"

"So you have given *some* a chance to survive. Are they to die at sea instead of London? Or in New Orleans? Is that an improvement? And then there will be those innocent people throughout the United States who have never been to sea, never been to New Orleans, certainly never been to London or Bombay or Calcutta, yet they will die without ever stepping from their homes because you have brought the damned cholera *to* them. Is that what you call a chance to *survive,* Captain?"

"Now, you pay attention to me, boy. You don't want to be crossing me. I *am* the captain of this ship," Lovingsworth roared. "You are the surgeon on this ship. *Your* job is to take care of the sick. You graduated from Transylvania University. You're a doctor. I never went to college. So you figure it out, Mister Educated Smart-ass. In fact, tell you what: You go to work on what's to blame for cholera. But first, you go back to London and you forbid anybody to board a ship to America. That's what you do, *Doctor.* You go to Calcutta where you tell me this damn plague started, and tell millions of people to stop praising their gods and shitting in the Ganges River. You go back and tell them that Captain Lovingsworth has sailed his last voyage. You tell all those universal sons of bitches that there's this crazy-assed captain who is selling his ship to the highest bidder or maybe even scuttling it as soon as he arrives in New Orleans, and he's taking his wife home to Kentucky, where he's going to build a blasted high fence around his land to keep out all the immigrant sons of bitches. Tell them that he wasted a lifetime trying to help people get from here to there."

Captain Lovingsworth clutched his chest, whirled, and returned to his cabin. He sat in his chair and waited for his heart to resume its normal rhythm. At such times, he feared death and wanted no part of it.

Doctor Hanover slowly walked aft to witness the burial of Sally Ferguson, the first corpse to be buried at sea on the final voyage of the *Cynthia Anne.* Her husband, Elton, was unable to attend, for he lay prostrate in steerage. Harmony Fischer and Sylva stood at the rail alongside Charlsie. Reverend Goodman was noticeably absent. Hanover joined the brief service.

"She had dreamed of a new life in America, a fresh start for themselves and their daughter, Charlsie, released at last from the slums of Southwark," said Sylva.

"She was beautiful," said Charlsie.

Bosun Whittaker had carefully wrapped the shrunken little form in a winding-sheet and sewn it securely. It was now ready to be leveraged overboard on a greased plank fulcrumed like a seesaw on the fantail rail of the *Cynthia Anne.*

Sylva and Harmony stood with their arms around Charlsie as her mother was committed to the deep.

Precisely at midnight, before Captain Lovingsworth had climbed into his rack for his usual four hours of sleep, he placed a small bowl of gruel on the deck in the middle of the cabin, a practice he'd begun when he was first mate for the East India Company. Lying stretched on his left side, facing inward from the after bulkhead, Lovingsworth cocked his right eye in anticipation of his nightly visitors. They rarely failed him. Shortly after midnight, signaling a new day of survivorship, a pink nose would appear in the opening where the forward bulkhead met the oaken deck beneath the captain's table. It was a small entrance left open by the captain, a gateway for the restless, satin-backed rats staking their claim to sovereignty. The pink nose would be followed by the stiff whiskers, the coal-black eyes, and the tiny pink ears, erect, quivering.

Always on guard, always ready to detect food, these indomitable mariners were the descendants of the unconquerable *Rattus rattus,* which traced its roots to the fourteenth century before Christ. When Tutankhamen was reinstating the deities destroyed by Amenhotep IV, when Nebuchadnezzar I was king of Babylon, and when Moses received the Ten Commandments on Mount Sinai, the rats were there, multiplying faster and more efficiently than Malthus would ever dream possible.

"Aye," said Captain Lovingsworth, holding back a yawn, "the First Mate is here with his lovelies. Come in. Come in. You are welcome to sup. You will find the usual." The first rat proceeded to the bowl of gruel, and the rest of the family, six in number, quickly scampered after. They took their places on either side of their leader. They watched the captain as they devoured the meal.

"How are things in steerage, my well-paid First Mate? Are the lovely, emigrant sons of bitches being honorable? Ungrate-

ful, I'll wager. Insensitive to the legitimate needs of their com-
rades with the good eyes and the long tails. Are conditions to
your liking? Tell me something. When we arrive in New Orleans, will you be debarking at once? Plans? I should tell you
that you are losing a very fine captain! It is doubtful that the
next captain will be so hospitable and so honorable. The next
one, lacking in experience, will probably cover the hole, and
you will have to create another one, which I'm certain you will.
But there will be no bowls set out for you. You will miss me,
then? Aye, that is most likely, because I am heading for Kentucky to live out my days, and there will be no place for you
there in the land of hemp and tobacco. No, you see, you would
have to learn to smoke, and I judge that you are too smart for
such foolishness. You would have to learn to groom magnificent horses. And you, of course, would be good drinkers. You
would sit in your rocking chairs, twirl your tails, and have most
obedient slaves serve you your bourbon and branch. Naturally,
if there be a nice quadroon among your slaves, you will spend
nights of ecstasy with her. Even the blackest of your slaves are
possibilities for rapture. You are the multipliers. That is your
longevity. That is your answer. I? I have no children of my
own.

"I hear that a woman in steerage wants me to adopt a little
girl. You believe I should? What do you know of adoption? You
are the breeders and the feeders. By Jesse, you are survivors. I am
in awe of this, your nature. I do not understand why God set
upon this earth so many rats and gave them this ability to popu-
late the land. But yes, I have it. He put rats on the land, fish in
the sea, and birds in the sky. Then, for punishment for these
two-legged creatures who can't seem to do anything but fight
one another, he set them down in this Hell on earth and sat
back and watched them wiggle. Did he smile? Of course he did.
Still does. Perhaps Almighty God established you as the final
punishment. See, fish have gills. Birds have wings. You, my pre-

cious First Mate, have feet, nose, eyes, and ears, and over time you will destroy the human race, and you will inherit the earth."

Captain Lovingsworth burst into laughter, startling his visitors, who finished their meal and retreated through the hole as quickly as they had entered. The captain blinked, then his right eye closed, and he was asleep. The usual dream appeared. It involved a kingdom of rats.

The kingdom, located in the luxuriant Lyonnesse Mountains in the northeast corner of the Gulf Stream, to the west of Land's End, had a stupendous fleet of sailing ships. One was called the *Cynthia Anne*. The ships all bore black sails, signifying death to any creatures acting in defiance of Viking superiority or even showing disrespect. The captain of this *Cynthia Anne* was a large rat, standing six feet tall. There was the usual knock on the door. It would be the First Mate, standing seven feet tall, and the entire crew of rats would be in line behind him. They swished their tails like whips on the backs of galley slaves. The First Mate would announce that he had come to remove the Captain because he had become too old to function in the best interest of the King and Queen of the Kingdom of Lyonnesse. The Captain would stand his ground. He would reach for his blunderbuss. His finger would be on the trigger. He would squeeze it. Again and again, he would squeeze it, but the weapon would not fire. The First Mate would take the blunderbuss, and the crew would seize the Captain and lead him away to the scupper. The bosun, a dark and burly rat, would blindfold the Captain and tie his hands behind his back, and he would be forced to walk the short plank extending over the starboard side. And just as the Captain was falling toward the water, James Henry would suddenly awaken. Cold sweat would be pouring from his face.

By the time the *Cynthia Anne* had passed through the first storm and crossed the Mid-Atlantic Ridge at the Azores Plateau, approximately fifty bodies had been committed to the sea, Elton Ferguson among them. Morning, noon, and night, death and burial had become so regular that the passengers began to resemble ants on a restless migration from hill to hill: They would hesitate a moment when they encountered a lifeless form, but the main desire of the living was to survive. Disposal of the corpses had lost almost all semblance of ceremony. It had become a simple act of quick removal, like the discarding of worn-out clothes.

Among those interred in the sea were the mortal remains of the Reverend Daniel Christian Goodman. Shortly before his death he had shared a small communion cup of grape juice with a Southwark family, and within hours the husband, wife, and two small girls had also died. When Doctor Hanover returned to his cabin from the starboard rail, he looked closely and with curiosity at the dirty, silver-plated goblet from which the latest victims had drunk. It bore the inscription: *"The Tabernacle of the Living Word, Merry Christmas, Your Girls, Oxfordshire, 1830."*

Doctor Hanover wrote in his journal: "A good man died today. A family of four died almost at the same time, within hours of each other. What did they have in common? They had a belief in common. They had a religious service in common. They sipped from a common cup. Their lips shared the same spot on the goblet's edge. The juice, representing their belief in divine Resurrection, contained *something* that produced a shutting down of life, more crucifixion than resurrection. There must be a connection. There must have been an agent in the substance of the communion. What else *could* it have been?

"The juice was not alcoholic. The agent was living in the juice. What was its origin? How was it sustained? It entered the bodies of the victims. They died. Simple. Let me not forget this day. Let me not forget these deaths. We must discover and identify the killer agent. Even if God designed cholera as punishment of sinners, no man should surrender to it without using his God-given brain to try to understand it and then to resist it. It is paradoxical. God, the Creator, gives humans their brains, then sets up barriers. Now, is it not essential, even wondrously beautiful, when people *use* their brains to scale the barriers?"

Doctor Hanover's brain told him that theological arguments were plainly silly in the face of the realities of disease. He believed this so passionately that he would risk his own immortality in order to understand and alleviate suffering. Of course people could not live forever, but he believed both instinctively and as a result of his medical studies and his lifetime of reading in his family's library that they had a right to live as long as possible. It was wisdom derived from the Greeks: Hippocrates, the Father of Medicine, born 460 years before Christ; Alemaeon of Croton, who 500 years before Christ had learned the different natures and functions of veins and arteries—he had ascertained the connections between the brain and sensory phenomena. And Anaximander had taught that humans evolved from amphibians, that in fact, the universe had arisen from a single primordial substance. From the time of the Greek civilization in Rome to the advent of the "Athens of the West" in Lexington, however, there had been perpetual, insidious rivalry between the proponents of the physical and the advocates of the metaphysical explanation. For every ten Platos there had been only one Aristotle, or so it seemed to Dr. Hanover.

Aboard the *Cynthia Anne,* equality in steerage meant that all were fair game for a disease for which neither cause nor cure was known. Survivors clung to individual sets of beliefs, and those who willed to live reached deeply within themselves to find sustaining shreds of inner strength. They hunkered down, seeking their own warmth and nourishment. Those who lived ate and drank as little as possible. With Dr. Hanover's encouragement, they boiled and carefully preserved their water supplies. They washed their food. They washed their hands before eating. They conserved their energy and curtailed their appetites. They wore dour faces and made no excuses or explanations for unfriendliness, laboring stoically like dwarfs in labyrinths of deep mines where oxygen was at a constant premium. Social intercourse was undertaken only by the foolish. Such brazen acts as sexual intercourse could scarcely be concealed, yet those with better sense hardly took note. Conditions in steerage, especially during storms and epidemics, resembled a madhouse in which the inmates cowered in corners.

Charlsie Ferguson sat huddled in one corner, beholding the insanity and longing for a quiet afternoon with Grandfather Charles, who might take from the shelf of his mind's eye a story of green pastures and lazy afternoons along the brooks of Oxfordshire. They'd lie on their backs and look up at a sky of white clouds with only a hint of rain, birds would sing and flowers would understand that they were not forgotten. Charlsie dreamed of the day when her mind and body would be incorporated into the new world beyond the western horizon, but the deaths of her mother and father had been devastating. She felt terribly alone and, she feared, beyond any possibility of help.

The Sargasso Sea

May 1833

O my Brother, my Brother, why cannot I shelter thee
in my bosom, and wipe away all tears from thy eyes!
Truly, the din of many-voiced Life, which, in this soli-
tude, with the mind's organ, I could hear, was no
longer a maddening discord, but a melting one, like
inarticulate cries, and sobbings of a dumb creature,
which in the ear of Heaven are prayers.
                                        —Thomas Carlyle

MRS. HARMONY FISCHER had cared for her elderly husband
as long as he could draw a painful breath. When he died, she
closed his eyes, fixed his hands in the traditional way, wrapped
him in bedsheets, hoisted him to her shoulder, and carried him
herself to the starboard scuppers of the *Cynthia Anne*. She almost stumbled going up the ladder to the top deck, but if anybody had offered help, she would have told them to stand out
of the way. She had carried sacks of coal. She had carried firewood. She had carried buckets of water. If there was anything
to be carried that could be carried, she did it without complaint.
It all came naturally to Mrs. Harmony Fischer.

When she reached the railing, without hesitation she

dropped her husband overboard and watched the water close around his shrouded body like the giant mouth of a leviathan opening to gather food. Mrs. Fischer suspected that she would soon follow her husband, but until that time she would take certain matters into her own hands. It was not her nature to capitulate without having her say, without conducting certain housekeeping chores for the landlord, so to speak.

Harmony Fischer had helped to look after young Charlsie when she was left behind by the deaths of her parents. The girl's eyes shuddered with a dull sadness that brought out the fullness of Mrs. Fischer's mothering instincts. She and her husband had had no children of their own, a lifelong grief and an unforgettable frustration. It caused doubt and recriminations to spread through the family like the ripples of a bad coin thrown into stagnant water. Jasper Fischer had to explain to his friends at the Billy Goat Strut why he had no sons, not even any daughters. It was nothing of which to be proud. Childlessness brought forth in Harmony Fischer a motherly zeal for homeless youth, especially girls.

Mrs. Fischer returned to steerage and went directly to Charlsie. "You have such a fine name, my child."

"What does it matter?" asked Charlsie.

"Why, of course it matters. Our good name is our priceless possession. We all have our names, and we all have a right to be proud of them. Permit no one to make you shameful of your name."

The child bit her lower lip. Her chin began to tremble. She looked down at her soiled and threadbare dress, trying to smooth the sticky cloth with the palms of her hands. She looked around for Sylva, upon whom she'd come to depend.

"Now, we don't want to make you unhappy. We want to help you. We're your new family."

"Don't need no more help," said Charlsie as she worried at the stains of her garment.

"I'm afraid you do, my child. You're all alone. I know your parents are in Heaven. I believe I'll be seeing them there very soon. But until then I have an idea that will help you and maybe many more of us on this bloody stinking ship."

"There's nothing you can do about it," said the child.

"I've already had a talk with the first mate," said Harmony Fischer, looking up in the direction of the captain's cabin, "and we're just not going to be taking *his* bloody 'No' for an answer."

She clutched the child's hand and, holding it tightly in her own, climbed out of steerage and strode deliberately through the swarm of passengers and crew on deck toward Captain James Henry Lovingsworth, who at the moment stood at the starboard rail, studying with fascination the formations of green weeds floating in the Sargasso Sea. The shapes on the surface of the water mingled with the captain's own imaginings to produce monsters of evil description, providing James Henry with a morbid measure of satisfaction. It was one of the few things in the world that could put a smile on his hardened face. A Lovingsworth smile was as warm as a line chiseled by a hollow gouge.

"Captain," began Harmony Fischer, her left hand on her hip, the right hand holding tightly to the child. "I told First Mate Moreland that I wish to speak with you."

"You wish to do *what?*"

"I said, I wish to *speak* to you," said Harmony with her customary, blunt assertiveness. She punctuated "speak" with a punch into her side and a stomp of her foot.

"What's the matter with you? I have already told the first mate, you have no business talking to me!"

"My name is Harmony Fischer. I am one of those who has paid you well to take me to America. My husband also paid you well. Now that he's at the bottom of the ocean, he does not expect any passage money returned, nor will I when I am with him down there. Until that time, I have plenty of business talking to you."

"Madam, as I've explained many times—perhaps you were

not listening—if you have medical problems, you speak with Doctor Hanover. Anything else, you speak with First Mate Moreland. You don't want—"

"Yes, I do *want* to speak to you, Captain Lovingsworth, about adoption of this child, who has barely been surviving down there in that stinking hellhole you politely call steerage."

"No! A thousand times, no. Not now, not ever. You are crazy. I do not like crazy women." You let crazy women get their foot in a door, he thought, you can kiss everything else goodbye. There are too many crazy women in the world, as it is.

"Adoption of *this* child, Captain."

Captain Lovingsworth focused on the girl for the first time, the flickering, dark eyes, the stringy hair matted and blown by the salt spray, the worn garment barely covering her shoulders. The child's small nose was running with mucus, her thin lips looked as if they'd been stamped on her face. The chin was prominent, with only a hint of the beginning of a dimple. She looked like a miniature monster, a pale, green troll netted from the Sargasso Sea.

"What is it about *this* child, madam, and what is it about *you* that brings you to talk so insanely? Is this a plot of some nature? Am I being set up by the Devil's agents?"

"Captain, I'm here to remind you that this child has lost her mother and father to cholera, and they have been fed to the damned sharks, or maybe they're down there with the Devil himself, Captain, I don't know, but they are *gone*. Don't you understand calamity when you see it before your very eyes?" Mrs. Fischer began to cry. Her shoulders shook.

"All right. All right—"

"No, it's not *all* right, Captain. It's not *all* right at all. You as captain have a responsibility for the care of this little girl. She has no one, no one at all in the world. She may have relatives back in England, but they cannot help her now. I surmise she has no one expecting her in America. If you do nothing else good in your life, Captain, you will take this little girl and see her safe for the rest of the voyage. That is *not* asking very much. That is *not* asking very much at all."

"Not my job, ma'am. Damn sure not my job," said the captain, turning back to the rail. He watched as the seaweed spiraled, forming a face with a single, piercing eye. It opened and closed and opened again. "The son of a bitch winked at me," snorted the captain.

"*Make* it your job, for the love of God! This is nothing to laugh about. Do it for all that's decent. Is it too much to ask that you adopt—"

"Adopt? Listen to me, crazy woman," said the captain, whirling back in the direction of Harmony Fischer and the child.

"No, *I'm* not crazy, Captain, you know I am not. *You* are the one who is losing his mind. *You,* Captain. Anybody can look at you and tell it. You need your sanity brought back to you. Adopt this child as your own. Give her decent food to eat. Let her sleep in your cabin. She can do chores for you. She can wash your clothes. She will more than pay her way."

Captain Lovingsworth looked sternly at the child. Her eyes returned the stare. They did not blink. For a moment the memory returned of a ten-year-old boy arriving in New Orleans, homeless too, with nothing to eat. There had been only the clothes on his back, and those nothing to speak of. The youth had pounded on doors, and they had all been slammed in his face until a riverboat captain on Barracks Street in the French Quarter invited him in and gave him a place to sleep for the night. Captain Schilling allowed the boy to stay for a week, enough time for the youth to explore the waterfront and find the first opportunity to stow away on a ship bound for England. Then there had been employment with the East India Company, including years as a seaman on the trade routes to Bombay and Calcutta. Lovingsworth had survived that time, and he had risen to become first mate. He had the watch the night of the return to England when the ship went aground in the Isles of Scilly. Among the handful of survivors on the shore of St. Agnes, James Henry had vowed that he would not only become the captain of his next vessel; he would own it.

A decade of plunder, of scavenging in the Isles of Scilly, of hoarding treasure and making barters finally resulted in his own ship, which he named the *Cynthia Anne*. Captain Lovingsworth had bought it at auction and commissioned an artisan in Greenwich to create the figurehead in memory of his mother. "She was strong-willed," the captain had told Reginald Matthews, the carver of figureheads for vessels operating from the Isle of Dogs to the markets of the world.

"And she was beautiful?" asked Reginald, as he whetted his wood-carving knives.

"Indeed. Oh, yes, indeed. I always thought so. And she was filled with courage. Her name was Cynthia Anne. She died quite young."

"A scourge?"

"Oh, no. She died in Kentucky."

"And where might that be?"

"In America, where there are no scourges."

"Do tell."

"My mother, Cynthia Anne, grew up in the Bluegrass."

"I see," said the wood-carver, tucking in his chin, doubtfully.

"She was taken from one paradise to another—"

"Oh?"

"She wore out. But a scourge certainly didn't have anything to do with it. God likes Kentucky too much to send scourges there, I suppose," said the captain with a laugh. "Besides, my mother never sinned. That is the memory I wish to perpetuate."

"Indeed, indeed. I'll have your mother immortalized within, let's say, four weeks. Then you can come and see whether it meets with your approval. I shall take special pains to re-create her. You will be proud to have her there on the prow of your ship. She will live again. She will bring you good luck! She will protect you and your crew from plague."

Reginald Matthews's skill in creating figureheads had been passed down from his father and his father before him. They would be true to their craft in every respect, in each exacting detail.

"I should like to have the figurehead for the *Cynthia Anne* finished as you have promised, in one month. There'll be a bonus of a bit of gold if it's ready then."

"It shall be done," said Reginald Matthew.

The flight of memory into which Captain Lovingsworth was transported had become typical of late. Sometimes in the middle of a conversation he would stare off into the distance. There seemed to be no help for it, even if he was the captain. At times of aggravation, he felt faint and short of breath. Another moment passed, and he looked blankly into the face of Mrs. Fischer.

"The child must return to her place in steerage," said Captain Lovingsworth, his voice low and even, his heart palpitating.

"Good God, Captain," said Mrs. Fischer, "you have less of a soul than I thought." She turned in disgust and anger and led the girl back to her bondage below decks.

One by one, sometimes two by two, and sometimes by fours, the victims of cholera were heaved overboard. From Bishop Rock to the Bermuda Rise to the Gulf of Mexico, the *Cynthia Anne* left its wake of human bait. Sharks feasted and fattened. There was no cure, a fact and a frustration well known by Doctor Hanover. There was hardly prevention once the disease had begun to spread. The only hope was that the *Cynthia Anne* would make good speed to landfall, where there was at least a chance for an intelligently managed quarantine. A count of the dead had been given up—no one would know the number for sure until there'd been an official roll call of survivors upon arrival in New Orleans.

The young doctor, worn down by lack of sleep, methodically picked his way through the dead and dying. He offered whatever comfort he could and words of condolence. He noticed two women and a child sitting together. Mrs. Harmony Fischer had covered her face with her hands. She was weeping convulsively. The other woman Hanover recognized as one of several prostitutes among the passengers. They were fairly easy to spot. They wore their clothes in a suggestive manner, and there was an unusual openness about their behavior. She had her arms around Mrs. Fischer and Charlsie, who was not crying but seemed distant, confused, and bewildered. The young doctor sat down next to them.

"What seems to be the matter?" he asked.

"He won't do it," said Mrs. Fischer, lowering her hands. "He won't do it."

"Who is 'he' and what won't he do?"

"The captain won't adopt this little girl. He won't accept responsibility for her. She has no one. I am sick. My husband is dead. I begged the captain to take this child. He won't do it."

Doctor Hanover did not speak for a moment.

"I believe I might be able to persuade him," said Sylva. "Since he won't listen to reason, perhaps there is another way."

"Why have you not asked *me* to adopt the child? Why ask the captain, of *all* people?" asked Hanover.

"Doctor," said Mrs. Fischer, "you are a young man with a bright and promising future. You will have many patients. Some will be children. Some will be old, as my husband was old, as I am old. Remember this: you cannot *adopt* your patients. It is one of those realities, is it not? If you were to adopt this girl, then every orphaned child would deserve the same right. Isn't that true?"

"Perhaps," said the doctor.

"The important thing, yes, the essential thing is for you to help the sick. What happens after that is somebody else's responsibility," said Mrs. Fischer, wiping her eyes.

"Doctor," said Sylva, "I do not know what you think of me—"

"I think you are quite beautiful, to speak the truth."

"Thank you. I think you are beautiful, too. Maybe that rings false, but I mean it. All I would like to say is that I am a woman who has a mind as well as a body. I hope I have a spirit. I'm trying to understand my self, my true self. I'm trying very hard to do that. I reject the idea that I am nothing more than a prostitute."

"I understand," said Doctor Hanover. "At least, I think I do."

"Thank you. I cannot tell you how much it means to me to hear a man say those words."

Sylva and the doctor looked at each other, silent communication surpassing sexuality. There were thoughts of seduction, but intellect rose above it.

"I have an idea," said Sylva, throwing back her long hair with the sudden toss of her head and movement of her hand that usually helped to cool a heated moment. "Here it is. This child needs help if she is to stand a chance to arrive safely in New Orleans. Mrs. Fischer is not well, and she cannot give that help. As she has said, doctors cannot adopt the world; their job is to try to cure the world. Isn't that right, Doctor?"

"Yes."

"A prostitute has no business adopting a child. What do prostitutes know about being good mothers?" asked Sylva with a rueful laugh. "That leaves somebody stupid like the captain. He can keep her out of steerage, and he'll be smart enough to be the first off the ship after we arrive. I think he's perfect for the job, and I think I'm the one to talk him into it."

"Please," said Charlsie, speaking up at last, "don't I have anything to say about this?"

"Of course you do," said Sylva.

"I would like to be adopted by you."

"Come here. Sit in my lap. Let me put my arms around you and hold you," said Sylva to Charlsie. "That's good. Isn't that good? Now, listen to me. The doctor will tell you I'm right. Mrs. Fischer will tell you I'm right. When the captain agrees to take you in, *accept* it, for God's sake. You and I can remain good friends. Mrs. Fischer will remain your good friend. The doctor will remain your good friend. The captain will be your guardian as well as your challenge. It will be what we call an *arrangement.* Nothing is perfect. But this stands the best chance of working."

"I'll listen. I'll think about it. That's what Grandfather Charlie would do," said the child.

"Fair enough. Listen and think. First, then, you're getting a new name," said Sylva, gently rocking Charlsie.

"What is it?" asked Charlsie, looking into Sylva's face.

"Cynthia Anne," said Sylva.

"Cynthia Anne? Why Cynthia Anne?" asked the child.

"Genius," murmured Doctor Hanover. "Beyond any shadow of a doubt, pure genius."

"Good God!" said Mrs. Fischer.

"Look," said Sylva, "until now you've been called 'Baby' and 'Child' and 'Daughter' and maybe 'Little Darling.'"

"My real name is Charlsie. I was named for my grandfather. I don't know if he would like Cynthia Anne."

"It doesn't matter now what he would like, but given all the circumstances, he might think well of my idea. Stay here, my little family, and leave the rest to me."

When the Outer Banks were sighted off the Carolina coast, Captain Lovingsworth felt a sense of new warmth in his aching bones. True, his head still hurt and his heart still thumped and he was as tired as he ever remembered being, but his step was light as an eagle's feather. Old men, he reminded himself, should be careful about sporting and soaring with young women. Old age was as inevitably treacherous as North Atlantic storms, as deadly as hurricanes roaring out of the West Indies. Youth, with its sparkling, irresistible seductiveness, would in time become as broken and shredded as tin roofs after hurricane winds had blown through. Tidal waves followed to cut away shorelines. The grave was the final and irrevocable scourge of Heaven.

Chief Helmsman Westlander took professional pride in threading the close passage between the outer Carolina islands and the western edge of the Gulf Stream. With favorable winds the *Cynthia Anne* glided toward the Florida territory with ease and grace, the ship's majestic appearance belying the disaster in steerage. Soon the eye of the needle would narrow even more and the pristine water would become deceptively inviting, coral reefs as dangerous as the rocks of the Isles of Scilly. One mistake and all could be lost. Captain Lovingsworth stood alone on the starboard side, studying the cumulus clouds. A waterspout appeared as if to bar the way, then turned and slowly moved in the direction of the Great Bahama Bank. Death on this voyage had been dark and devilish, and James Henry was confounded in the aftermath of Sylva's magic.

Captain Lovingsworth returned to his cabin and made an entry in his journal, notable for its deceptiveness by omission. His practice, formed out of habit over the years, was to address his journal entries to his wife, especially when there was something to hide.

> My dearest Abigail—
> Cholera. Poor business. About half the immigrants in steerage have died of this scourge. It shows no mercy. For every one thrown overboard, another corpse is ready to be carried to scuppers. Lost two seamen. First mate beginning to look sick. Could become a ghost ship.

If God is still in His Heaven and still punishing the human race for its sins, wouldn't you think there'd been *enough* retribution?

I have been asked to adopt one of the children aboard ship. And I have agreed that it is something we ought to do. It may lead to complications for us, but it seems only right.

I have made the decision. Maybe it is crazy. Why would we want to do such a thing? Maybe I'm becoming warmhearted, but I doubt it. I think that others are trying to make me feel guilty. *They're* the ones who are crazy. *My* mind's as good as it ever was. It's not my fault that so many have died on this voyage. How could it be my fault?

When I heard that the child's name is Cynthia—not only Cynthia, but Cynthia Anne—I could not resist. Maybe God is telling me something. I saw a waterspout a few minutes ago. It could have ripped us to shreds. Could it have been a warning? He knows this is my last voyage, so He makes me this little gift. A child. One who has lost her real mother and father. Maybe I'm superstitious. Maybe God is testing my faith. What faith? Maybe Cynthia Anne is my one last good luck charm.

Three small raps on the door interrupted the journal entry. Cynthia stepped inside the cabin and turned in a pirouette.

"Captain," cooed Cynthia, "how do you like my hair?"

"You've combed it. Somebody's combed it. That's good."

"Yes, and see this piece of ribbon in the back?" she said, as she made another full turn.

"Would you rather be Cynthia or Cynthia Anne?" asked the captain, matter-of-factly.

"Cynthia Anne sounds very nice, I think. Do you like the ribbon?"

"Cynthia Anne was my mother's name. She died when she was a young girl. I named this ship in her memory."

"Is that *true?* I have her name *and* the ship's?"

"Yes," said Captain Lovingsworth. "Yes, both."

"Then I shall be pleased to be called Cynthia Anne. Do you like my ribbon? I did it for you. What is my last name?"

"You are a Ferguson, or so I've been told."

"Not a Lovingsworth?"

"No."

"Why not?"

"Because Ferguson is *your* family name. You should remember your Irish and English roots."

"Where does Lovingsworth come from?"

"Comes from nowhere. You don't want to be a Lovingsworth. Ferguson is much better," the captain frowned.

"I will be Cynthia Anne Ferguson, but I like the sound of Lovingsworth. I may even use it: Cynthia Anne Ferguson Lovingsworth!"

"All right. Fine with me."

"Captain, why have so many died on this ship?" said Cynthia as she secured the ends of the small hammock made especially for her by Bosun Whittaker.

"Because cholera is sweeping the world."

"Where does it come from?"

"There's a lot of it most of the time in India. It has spread from there. Nobody seems to know how."

"Does it have anything to do with God?" said Cynthia, eyeing the captain.

"Everything has something to do with God, it seems," said the captain, smoothing his shirt inside the back of his trousers, remembering the sight of the powerful waterspout. "He made the world and everything in it. Cholera is in the world, so God must have made cholera. How does that sound?"

"But cholera is bad. God is good. Why would God want to make something that is bad?"

"You ask too many questions. We'll soon be heading on down the coast to the Florida Keys. It's a son of a bitch staying off the reefs and out of the hands of the thieving wreckers, but with good luck we'll make it past the Dry Tortugas to the Gulf of Mexico. After that it should be a short passage to New Orleans."

"Captain?"

"Yes?"

"Am I here because—and are you adopting me, *really*—because of Sylva?"

"Cynthia Anne?"

"Yes?"

"I do not wish to discuss this, not now or at any time in the future."

"Why?"

"Because, there is an *agreement*." The moment the words were out, the captain profoundly wished he had not spoken them.

"What *kind* of an agreement?"

"Let's drop it. Let's drop it right now. I have given you a place, a hammock in which to sleep. I have taken you from steerage. I am feeding you. I am asking nothing from you in return. It is obvious that I am crazy. Behind my back it is *said* that I am crazy. That's what all crews do when they have nothing better to talk about, they sit around and slander the captain. It doesn't mean anything. Let them think me mad. I'll pocket the insult and walk away."

The captain, leaning forward from his chair, was nose to nose with Cynthia. "What do *you* think? Do you think I am crazy?" he demanded.

Cynthia Anne turned her head to one side. Then she

reached out and touched the captain's hand. "No, I do not think that. You have been very good to me."

Rain squalls moved in and out of the mangrove entanglements in the prehurricane season. The heat rose and fell along the Florida shoreline stretching for three hundred miles. Some days Cynthia Anne gazed up at huge clouds, towering spirals of whiteness as high as mountains that suggested to her new possibilities. The *Cynthia Anne* made safe passage between the Dry Tortugas and Rebecca Shoal, and winds came pleasantly out of the east-northeast. Twin porpoises arced ahead of her prow, their own figureheads real, uncarved, unpainted. In the years before cholera, this last leg of the homeward-bound voyage had been a time for celebration. But in the late spring of '33 the nightmare remained with the ship.

It was one thing to lose human cargo. It was intolerable to watch First Mate Tom Moreland succumb to the disease. For a captain, to lose his first mate is to lose a central bearing in the helmsman's wheel. To lose a first mate is to lose the primary link between captain and crew. When the first mate is taken away during a voyage, mass confusion, even mutiny, is a strong possibility. The death penalty is a deterrent to mutiny, and every sailor is aware of the gibbet and the uncompromising tradition attached to it. Mutiny on the high seas is worse than murder in the dark corners of the Isle of Dogs. But confusion on a ship at sea is a derangement leading to despair.

When Tom Moreland's tall, once handsome body was wrapped and sewn inside a piece of old sail, six crewmen bore it to the starboard side of the quarterdeck. Doctor Hanover, standing next to Captain Lovingsworth, was predictably uncomfortable. Hanover saw no difference in the ranks among the dead, but he could recognize the degree of this loss to his fellow Kentuckian. The young doctor also felt the anger of a captain who doubtless believed there had been professional failure:

doctors were expected to *do* something, not just *think* something. Anything was better than nothing.

"Should've bled him, goddamnit, should've bled him," exclaimed Captain Lovingsworth.

Hanover knew it was as senseless to argue with the captain as it was useless to practice the damnable bloodletting theories bequeathed by Professor Benjamin Rush. To revere him as the Hippocrates of American Medicine, as many of his followers did, was a mockery. It was not only the cultivation, harvesting, and application of green, four-inch-long Gnathobdellidae leeches as a cure for everything from headaches to whooping cough; it was also Rush's missionary zeal for puking and purging that offended the intelligence of Laurence Hanover. Captain Lovingsworth was as woefully shortsighted as Benjamin Rush was wrongheaded. Together, they represented a continuing age of superstition and oversimplification, as powerless to prevent the spread of cholera as the ancient Celtic rites of purification.

The canvas-shrouded corpse of First Mate Moreland was placed on the plank over the starboard scupper. "I should like to offer a prayer," said Doctor Hanover. Captain Lovingsworth nodded his assent and removed his hat but crossed his arms firmly across his chest. Cynthia Anne stood by his side.

"God in Heaven," began Doctor Hanover, "give us the will and the courage to discover the cause of this disease. May Thomas Moreland not have died in vain. May all those who have died in steerage and who now have been committed to the deep, may they not have died in vain. Protect us from the deceptions of those who preach the theology of Almighty punishment. Amen."

"Push it overboard," said the captain.

The two-hundred-pound dead weight of First Mate Moreland fell straight to the water. A one-hundred-pound anvil was included for extra weight. Captain Lovingsworth had ordered it. Doctor Hanover stood by the rail and watched the form sink out of sight.

"All right, you sons of bitches," said Captain Lovingsworth to the assembled crew, "you're taking orders *directly* from me. With any kind of luck, and God knows we're overdue for that, we'll soon reach New Orleans. I'll tolerate no trouble. The bosun will fill in temporarily for the first mate and may occupy his cabin, but not until I have personally gone through it to see what has been left behind. Doctor Hanover, you will accompany me. I do not wish to be accused of looting."

"Captain," said Doctor Hanover.

"What is it?"

"May I have a word with you in your cabin?"

"We can talk in the first mate's cabin. Kill two birds with one stone. Cynthia Anne, you will go to my cabin and wait for me there."

Lovingsworth and Hanover entered Moreland's small quarters, sparse and stringent, as became a sailor's necessity. The hammock was stowed, the sea chest squared away on the opposite side. On top lay a relief etching of a house with a stream flowing past. Farm animals grazed in front, and children played along a path leading from the two-story house. Giant water maples framed the front yard. A weeping willow shaded a springhouse on one side, a barn built for storing hay and wintering sheep stood on the other.

"Be careful what you touch," said Doctor Hanover.

The captain looked at him disdainfully.

"We don't want to lose our captain," Hanover said truthfully, although it didn't at all sound sincere.

"And we don't want to lose our doctor, Doctor," said Captain Lovingsworth without semblance of sincerity.

The captain held up the etching for closer inspection. "Looks like a place in Kentucky. It could be," he said, setting it on the deck. He produced a key taken from the first mate's pocket, opened the sea chest, and rummaged through the neatly stacked clothes. There was a swath of blue, finely textured cretonne, which the captain unfurled. It covered him from his shoulders to his feet.

"I think your first mate was a romantic at heart," said Doctor Hanover. "He was probably taking that home to his sweetheart, or his sister or mother."

"What did you want to talk to me about?" asked Captain Lovingsworth, who knew nothing about romanticism.

"Here, let me fold it up," said Doctor Hanover, taking the fabric from the captain. "I want to talk to you about the quarantine in New Orleans."

"What about it?"

"I'm only recommending to you—"

"Recommend away."

"—that we be sure to do it correctly."

"And what would that be? What *is* correct, Doctor?"

"First thing, let's clean up the ship the best we can. Have the bosun put the fear of God into the crew and the passengers: nobody throws *anything* over the side. Stuff that's contaminated will wash ashore and ragpickers will descend on it and cholera will spread. I will try to explain to the passengers, but I'll need the support of the captain and the bosun to be sure that nobody throws bedclothes overboard. Let's pile all such stuff in one place topside and allow the authorities to decide how to dispose of it. Let's not try to hide anything. An epidemic is an epidemic, and the only way to stop it or even slow it is to get control over what people *do* and not what people *think* or what they pray about."

"You don't believe in prayer?" said the captain, sarcastically. "My, my—"

"God takes care of those who take care of themselves. That's prayer enough."

"Try to tell a bunch of religious fanatics not to pray," sneered the captain.

"I'm not going to try to tell *anybody* not to pray, and I'm not going to tell *anybody* not to believe in God. But I am going to tell them that cholera spreads in *filth*. That is rule number one."

"And what might rule number two be, *Captain?*" asked Lovingsworth.

"Please don't be so insulting. It does no good. I don't know what rules two, three, and four are. I just know that *your* ship is a cholera ship, and it has the potential to continue the spread of a monstrous pandemic from India to England, from England to New Orleans, and now with you, God forbid, to Kentucky. We cannot outrun the disease. We have to start someplace, and that someplace is the quarantine station. We can only hope that well-intentioned officials will be manning it. If not, if they can be bribed, if they can be bought and paid for, then cholera spreads no matter what we do *or* think."

"So, we'll be delayed in debarking?"

"Of course we will. Absolutely. Each passenger and crewman will have to be checked. The sick will be transferred to hospitals. And, just as important, the ship must not go *anywhere* until it's clean as a hound's tooth. Especially, this means the extermination of the rats."

"Rats? A ship wouldn't be a ship without rats. I like to make sure they're well-fed. Until Cynthia Anne came along I used to make a practice of setting a special bowl for them each night. Some of my best conversations were with rats. Now I spend all of my son-of-a-bitching time listening to the kid pound me with questions."

"I'd only read of the ancient practice of feeding rats and making them feel at home. Now I've met somebody who admits doing it, and I *still* think it's crazy."

"So, now *you* believe I'm crazy? The Fischer woman told me I'm crazy."

"You are if you feed rats. You are if you talk to rats. You are if you accord them equal status with people. They go where there are squalid conditions, not to mention crazy people who'll feed them."

"Tell it to the people of Bombay and Calcutta."

"I will, whenever I have the opportunity."

"How many sons of bitches have died on this voyage?" asked the captain.

"They're people, and they're not all sons of bitches. Counting First Mate Moreland, I'd estimate about a hundred have been buried at sea. As for the rats, I'd say if there were five hundred when we left England, there are now a thousand. It's a game of numbers, Captain. We humans are about to be overwhelmed by numbers. Maybe you don't think we can become extinct, but we can. And rats *can* inherit the earth. And wouldn't that be a damned shame? And wouldn't it be glorious if a rat fed *you* each night! Talked to you and tucked you into bed and said a prayer or two for you?"

"All right! Enough. I've heard enough. I'm the captain of this ship and I'm going to remain the captain as long as I have breath in my body. You may have no respect for me. Frankly I don't give a good goddamn. Go talk to the *people* in steerage. You might remind anybody contemplating swimming when we get close to shore that the Gulf waters are full of hungry sharks. Big, fat, hungry sharks. You tell the *people* in steerage to be my guest and swim into Choctawhatchee Bay. Old Chief Osceola needs new recruits for his next war with the United States. Or let 'em try Mobile Bay and swim up the bloody Tombigbee to Demopolis for all I care. I bet we've got some real fine swimmers down there among the *people* in steerage. And I'll tell you what I'll do, *Doctor* Hanover. I'll tell the bosun to break open the brains of anybody who tries to throw *anything* overboard. How's that?"

"That's fine."

"You know what else I'm going to do?"

"No, sir."

"I'm going to my cabin for a cup of brandy. Maybe two. Maybe three. Join me there after you've made your speech to the *human* beings in steerage."

The *Cynthia Anne* was tacking on the final leg, northwest to Cape St. George, west-northwest to Santa Rosa Island, then due west to the passage between Cat Island and Isle au Pitre. So far as could be determined, nobody tried to swim ashore, and the bosun caught only one man throwing bedclothes overboard. Bosun Whittaker did not take kindly to a blatant breech of orders. He thrashed the guilty man and plunged his head into a bucket of swab water until the man thought his lungs would burst.

Passing Grand Isle, entering Lake Borgne, angling through the tight passageway of the Rigolets, the *Cynthia Anne* entered an ill-omened world rich in the tradition of pirate Jean Lafitte. Captain Lovingsworth was like a dog guarding his own territory, a sunbaked jungle of bald cypress with awl-shaped leaves and aerial roots. Submitting to quarantine authorities sent out from forbidding and protective Fort Pike was as onerous to him as standing by and watching strange mongrels show up to dig and gnaw on hidden bones. But at least the *Cynthia Anne* could not be blamed entirely for bringing cholera to New Orleans. It was already there.

"Captain," said one of the boarding authorities, "you've no idea how bad it is. Ours is not the only city. New York has been devastated. Halifax, in Nova Scotia, is a mass graveyard. Here in New Orleans people are dying by the thousands. Many haven't been buried; they're rotting where they fall. We must do all we can, anything to stop its spread. If we don't, we may not have a city left. Now, here's how it works. Everybody receives a medical examination."

"Including me?"

"Including you."

"Then what?"

"Since you are the captain, as soon as you've been examined and have received a clean bill of health, you will be permitted to leave the ship. You'll be free to come and go as you please, but your first mate or someone you place in authority must be present on board at all times."

"The first mate is dead."

"Then who will be responsible?"

"I'll designate the ship's doctor. He can be trusted."

"Who is this little girl with you?"

"I'm her guardian. Her mother and father died of cholera, and they were buried a short distance from Land's End. I would like for her to be examined at the same time I am, so we can debark together."

"All right. Do you have a bosun who is reliable?"

"Yes."

"We would like you to anchor here at the entrance to Pontchartrain, not too close to shore. We don't want anybody trying to swim in. We'll have a boat for you, Captain. A reliable local coxswain will take you down to Fort Macomb, where you'll likely find a driver who'll take you on into New Orleans."

"Sir," said Cynthia, "may I come and go too?"

"It would be better for you and all concerned if you did not. It would be better for you to stay ashore."

"She'll stay with my wife at our place in the Quarter— assuming we still have one," said Captain Lovingsworth.

After the doctors had cleared them, the captain and Cynthia climbed down to a flat-bottomed Spanish pirogue with small twin masts that had pulled up beside the *Cynthia Anne*. It was piloted by a Cajun, looking earnest and sadly wild-eyed. He resembled a creature briefly arising from the steamy surface of a nearby swamp. Hair matted like Spanish moss hung down to his jaws, his fingers blunt and crusted like fishnet mending pegs. He smelled worse than a Southwark fish market.

"What's your name?" asked Cynthia.

"Boo-*dro,* mon cher," he said in a husky voice, deep as a bullfrog in Grand Coin Bayou.

"Well, Mister Boo-*dro,* my name is Cynthia Anne Ferguson

Lovingsworth, and I'm glad to meet you." It was Cynthia Anne's first encounter with an American in this mysterious new world, more primitive than she'd imagined possible, a land of steaming heat, rough and natural, a fishmonger's paradise.

"Boo-*dro*," said Captain Lovingsworth, "I've seen some pirogues in my time, but I've never seen one with *sails*."

"Been wucking fo' *me*. What wuck *fo' me* ees wha' mad*der*, no *how*." Through a hole in his Spanish moss beard, Boudreaux winked at Cynthia, and she winked back. "Bes way ees to hug dee sho'line down to Chef Pass en Bayou Sauvage to Fo't Macomb," said Boudreaux, maneuvering in and around the flotillas of other small craft, shrimpers and oyster bed hunters, brothers and sisters of the catch, innocent, honest, and loving as any of the extended families of Pierre and Jean Lafitte on Bayou Barataria and the voodoo queen, Marie Leveau, in the Vieux Carré.

Captain Lovingsworth loved the sight and the fetid smell of Pontchartrain, and he was especially proud of its size even though it was shallow and more tidal lagoon than it appeared. "This one lake is forty miles long," bragged the captain to Cynthia. "You could take the whole city of London and set it down here on this water and still have room to spare."

Cynthia wondered what Grandpa Charlie would have to say about that. He'd probably say it didn't make a damn bit of difference. He'd say you could take all of America and drop it into the ocean. But Lord, surely the squire would have been curious about this new world of water, narrow channels with shacks built on poles, people fishing as if there were nothing else left to do, possibly nothing better to do. Her first impression of America was that it was hardly a civilization, neither street nor park, just entwined vegetation and twisting waterways. She liked it because here there was space whereas in London all had been so crowded. The heaviness of the air in the bayous made Cynthia conscious of her own breathing, reminding her of the preciousness of cool, refreshing air.

James Henry and Cynthia stepped ashore on Shell Road, brittle with sunbleached crustacean husks, and the captain handed Boudreaux a piece of shining gold. The Cajun bit down hard on it and smiled one more time. *"Laissez le bon temps roulet,"* he grinned.

"What does that mean?" asked Cynthia.

"It mean, let de good times roll," said Boudreaux, untying the line and wading out to push clear of the dock. "It mean all us coon awses got to stick together *all* de time!"

"What's a coon awse? Can I be one, Mr. Boudreaux?" asked Cynthia.

"I official bestow upon you, mon cher, de title of Coon Awse wit all de rights pertainin' der to. So tomorrow you sees a coon awse, you say 'Hey, Coon Awse, how you *be* dis mawnin?' And de answer come back, 'I be fine, how you *be*, Coon Awse?'"

"Come on, Cynthia Anne," said the captain, "let's see if we can find ourselves a nigger and a buggy." There was congestion at Fort Macomb, people of every description hurrying as if chased by wild beasts from the swamps.

"What's a nigger?" asked Cynthia. "Is it different from a coon awse?"

"A nigger is a—Lord God, Cynthia Anne, you ask enough questions to float a boat. A nigger is different from you and me, that's all."

"Well, is it a person?"

"In a way. But a different kind of a person."

"How is it different?"

"Niggers are black, for starters. We are white. We tell them what to do, and they do it."

"Do you mean they're slaves?"

"Sometimes. Sometimes not. Depends."

"Depends on what?"

"Depends on how a white man feels about it. Depends on his necessity. Now, see here. God made us what we are. Some of us He made *white,* which is good. Some of *them* He made *black,* which is not good at all. Some He made brown, which is better than black but not as good as white. Some He made red, which is somewhere in between brown and black."

"I see," said Cynthia, soberly. "What about a coon awse?"

"A coon awse—good God, I don't know. He lives in the swamps with all the other creatures."

"Mastah, you be needing a ride somewha?" asked an aging black man who reined in his old horse alongside the captain and Cynthia.

"Yes, we do," said the captain. He helped Cynthia into the buggy and then pulled himself up.

"Where to, Boss Man?" asked the black man. He wore a top hat and a piece of bright red cloth around his neck, like the remnant of a tie, that fell only halfway down his white shirt-front. His eyes, recessed above the large nose and mouth, had a loving sadness. His long, tapered hands, black on top and white as a pearl in the palms, gently raised the reins and let them fall easily to the old horse's swayed and crusty back. The old man whistled softly. The horse took one step and then another and finally locomotion occurred, accompanied by a methodical clumping sound, pleasant to hear.

"Vieux Carré. Rue Dauphine and St. Peter," said the captain.

"Yassah, Boss. Vieux Carré! All right. That's where we be going soon's this old hoss get a move on herself. Get up, hoss!"

"What's your name?" Cynthia asked the black man.

"My name? My name is Chawles."

"That's funny."

"Miz Lady, what's so funny about my name being Chawles?"

"My grandfather back in England. His name is Charles."

"That's nice. Real nice. You come all the way from 'cross the water? And this be your daddy here?"

"Can I come up there and sit with you?" asked Cynthia.

"Can I go up there and sit with Mister Charles?" she asked the captain.

"If he says it's all right."

"Sho, you can," said Charles.

"Go ahead," said the captain.

"He's not my real daddy," said Cynthia as she rustled into her seat beside Charles.

"He not?"

"No. My real father and mother died of cholera on the way over here from England."

"Lord, have mercy. Seem like ever'body dying of cholera. Right here in N'Orlans, ever' day, more is dying ever' day. It a mess."

On the precarious way along Bayou Sauvage, where the large eyes of alligators blinked against the sunlight slanting through the cypresses, Charles allowed his mare to rest from time to time. He sat patiently and said to Captain Lovingsworth, "Boss Man, this place is crazy—plain, lowdown, voodoo crazy. If you don't mind me asking, what you white folks going to do when they ain't no more running from the cholera?"

Cynthia Anne looked around on both sides of Shell Road. It reminded her of nothing she'd ever seen before. Where were the farms of Oxfordshire? The rock walls surrounding flocks of fat sheep? The tenements of Southwark, row on row? In America there was this huge wilderness, strange and filled with uncertainty. And there was the coon awse creature, Boudreaux, and there was Charles, the black man with white palms, who talked softly and treated her as an equal. And there were those eyes as large as saucers tilted on the stagnant water. "What are *those,* Mr. Charles?"

"Alligators," replied Charles. "They git ahold of you, one dead little girl."

"Who's running?" asked the captain, annoyed by what he judged to be insolence on the part of an inferior species.

"Never seen such comings and goings. More goings than comings. The French, they move in. The Spanish, they take over. The Irish, they show up. Then the Kaintucks, they blow down the river. Now they looks like lots of folks they be going in the other direction. Ever'body going. It a mess." Charles spoke evenly to his horse. "Up there, darlin'." He whistled, then clucked, and the horse plodded on again along the winding path strewn with chalky, white shells that crunched softly under the weight of horse and carriage.

"Better watch out for the 'Kaintucks!'" said the captain.

"Yassuh!" said Charles.

"The Kaintucks would as soon run a long rifle up your backside as blow your brains out," said the captain, drawing himself up.

Charles turned and looked at the captain. Then his eyes met Cynthia's.

"Hmm hmm," said Charles, recognizing that it was time to rein in his words. "Hmm hmm," he repeated.

"Let me tell you something, Charles."

"Yassah."

"Takes all kinds to make a world. And that's what makes New Orleans what it is. It's a world full of just about every kind of son of a bitch."

"Hmm hmm," said Charles, looking at Cynthia.

"He don't mean anything, Mister Charles. He calls just about everybody a son of a bitch."

"Hmm," said Charles.

"Mister Charles, are you a nigger?" asked Cynthia.

"Well, now, chile, that depends."

"Depends on what?"

"Depends on what you mean when you use that word, 'niggah.'"

"I don't know what I mean. The captain said we needed to get ourselves a nigger and a buggy."

Captain Lovingsworth shifted one leg over the other and gazed out over the Elysian Fields, where Pierre Philippe de Marigny had carved out his maison Marigny, the kind of wealth Lovingsworth had aspired to but had missed.

"Well?" asked Cynthia.

"Yassum?" replied Charles.

"Are you a nigger?"

"Let me put it this way. If you means, is I a *free* niggah or a *slave* niggah, then I'se a *free* niggah. If you asking whether I'se a *good* niggah or a *bad* niggah, I'se a *good* niggah. If you asking whether I'se a *live* niggah or a *dead* niggah, I'se a *live* niggah. Well, missy, the same's true of you and all the white folks. Now then, you wants to know the difference 'tween *white* folks and *niggahs,* don't you? Well, they ain't much difference a-tall. Some us *free,* some us *slaves* to this, that, and the other. Some us *good,* some us *bad.* Some us *living,* some us *dead.* The great God Almighty made some us *white,* some us *black.* Look here. You see my *right* hand? You see my *left* hand? *Both* my hands *black* on top, *white* underneath. Now you tell me, missy, wha's the *niggah?*"

The sounds of the desolate bayous, the splash of the pelicans, the growling of the alligators were gradually replaced by the hammering of carpenters repairing old docks, constructing new houses on pilings. New Orleans did not arise dramatically—it was a logical extension of the primitive naturalness stretching from Fort Pike to the Vieux Carré.

As they drove through city streets, Cynthia saw bodies lying on the banquettes. Some had been burned where they had fallen, arms, legs, and torsos resembling thorn trees cut and set afire. She covered her face with her handkerchief. New Orleans looked like Southwark. It looked like steerage. She cried and stamped her foot.

Charles reined in his exhausted horse at the corner of Rue Dauphine and St. Peter. Captain Lovingsworth stepped down, and before Cynthia climbed out she gave Charles a wet kiss on his right cheek.

"Thank you," she said.

"Anytime you wants to ride in my buggy, you send word for Chawles. Now, they several Chawleses in the Quarter, so you ask for Chawles T. Adams, the free niggah from Kaintuck."

Captain Lovingsworth handed Charles T. Adams a small piece of gold. "I'll call for you, Charles, and if ever I go back to Kentucky, I'll take you with me!"

"Yassah, Boss, you call me whenever you need me. But Boss, there be one thing for real certain. I ain't goin' back to no Kaintuck with you or nobody else." Charles laughed until his sides hurt. "No suh, I ain't gonna go back to no Kaintuck. I may've got myself out of a slave mess into a free mess, but anytime I got the chance, I take the *free* mess. Ain't *no* way you gonna get me back to no Kaintuck. Get up there, darlin'. Take this here free niggah where he can find some more bidness with some more white captains with gold to give away. Hmmm, hmmp!"

New Orleans

May 1833

In almost every house might be seen the sick, the dying and the dead. All the stores, banks and places of business were closed. There were no means, no instruments for carrying on the ordinary affairs of business, for all the drays, carts, carriages, hand and common wheel barrows, as well as hearses, were employed in the transportation of corpses instead of cotton, sugar and passengers. . . . One day I did not leave the cemetery till nine o'clock at night, the last interments were made by candlelight. Reaching my house faint, I found my family all sobbing and weeping. They had concluded from my long absence, that I was certainly dead.

—Dr. Theodore Clapp

WHEN LOU BELLE, the black maid, opened the door to the captain's house on Dauphine near its crossing with St. Peter, she cried out, "Oh, Lord, it's the Captain. Lord, Lord, Lord, Miz Abigail, come see, come see! The Captain, he's home, he's home!"

Lou Belle opened the iron gate with the large letter "L" in

the center and swung it wide. "Come in this house, Captain, and who's this chile you got with you?"

"My name is—"

"Lord, Lord, Lord," Lou Belle squalled at the top of her lungs and all the way up to Abigail Lovingsworth who, in her light, billowy daytime dress, was lurching down the long, straight cypress staircase. That is to say, she was hurrying as fast as her worn-out legs would carry her, for she was not the Abigail of a year before, or even six months before. "Heavens, no," Abigail thought as she descended the stairs. "Each new day is a burden. I wish it were not so, but it is. My voice is weaker. Nerves on edge. The heat in the Quarter is simply too much. The pounds I've put on are not any help. Oh, James Henry, hold me—hold me—"

When she reached the bottom of the stairs, the captain was already there, and he held her kindly in his arms. Briefly, it felt comforting to Abigail, but her patient, long-suffering nature had nearly run its course. Her ability to think had become as knotted and brittle as dried shrimp nets. Once she had felt beautiful and wanted. Now she feared that she, like her mother before her, was sinking into senile dementia, a condition her grandmother had reprovingly called "softening of the brain."

"James Henry, I was sure I'd never see you again," she sobbed. "I was sure I never would." She kissed him, and her small hands beat on his back, the rhythm of it sending puffs of shell dust into the shafts of light streaming through the stained glass window above the landing.

"I'm home," said the captain. "And would you just look here what I brought you!"

"My name is Cynthia Anne Ferguson Lovingsworth," blurted the child.

"You are *who*?" said Abigail, stepping back, hearing the string of names clearly yet confused about the inclusion of "Lovingsworth," which she *thought* belonged to the captain, a name he had given her in everlasting marriage. *Why* had these names and faces become so puzzling?

"Let's sit down and I'll explain," said the captain as the three crossed into the high-ceilinged, heavily brocaded parlor. Abigail's portrait, the work of Kentucky artist Matthew Harris Jouett, hung over the mantelpiece, the painted eyes notable for their ability to follow James Henry or anybody else who entered. Cynthia became riveted to the intense, pleading stare. A John James Audubon original of two quarreling female Iceland Falcons and a large pencil sketch of the *Cynthia Anne,* commissioned by Captain Lovingsworth, hung on opposite walls. Over the years, the name of the Isle of Dogs artist had been lost and forgotten.

"Lou Belle," said the captain over his shoulder to the eagerly solicitous, faithful-to-a-fault black maid, "bring me a little bourbon and branch. A little wine for Miss Abigail. Fix a little pink lemonade for Miss Cynthia Anne."

Lou Belle hurried away, murmuring, "These white folks headed for trouble, they are, they headed for some kind of big trouble. Miz Abigail need something better than wine. She need help. She need her laudanum, what she need."

"Now then, James Henry, what's this about a 'Cynthia Anne?' And what's the, the—the—where is the—the—*Cynthia Anne?* James Henry, I *am* so mixed up."

"It's a long story. This child's name is actually Cynthia Anne. She's a Ferguson, a Catholic girl from England. Mother and father," said the captain, looking toward the hallway, impatient that Lou Belle did not instantly produce his bourbon so that the words might come more easily, "they died of cholera on the way over."

"Who did?" asked Abigail with a nervous cough and a sudden turn of her head.

"This child's mother and father," said Lovingsworth, puzzled.

"Heavens, child," said Abigail as she sat down heavily on the nearest chair to prevent her trembling knees from buckling. She'd been in wretched health for most of the year. She tried to put on a special smile for James Henry, but there was no hiding her worsening condition. She was often flustered of late because she was having trouble remembering the simplest of things. It was as if doors and peepholes were closing in parts of her brain, and she was helpless to keep it from happening. A tincture of opium with her daily libation gave temporary relief, but the smallest aggravation would vex her spirit. She was distraught by the fear of becoming permanently infirm, perhaps being committed to a lunatic asylum. In better times, James Henry's return from a long voyage would signal a round of parties, and there'd be laughter long into the night. But this time he seemed strange, and Abigail sensed a gap widening between herself and her husband. She was beginning to believe that God was punishing her for some wickedness. She was as helpless as one of Jonathan Edwards's spiders suspended over the pit of hell, her softening of the brain another scourge of Heaven.

"A difficult voyage?" she asked, tremulously.

"Ain't the half of it. We lost about half the passengers, the sons of—excuse me—the sons and daughters of a whole generation of people trying to get to America," said the captain, leaning forward with his stiffened hands upon his knees, "Hey out there, where the hell's my bourbon?"

Lou Belle returned with a silver tray upon which sat a goblet of 100-proof Kentucky bourbon and a glass of homemade wine as gross as it was potent. There was a tall glass of pink lemonade. "I hurry fast as I can, Captain. Sometimes I know I don't move as fast as you want me to, but I do the best I can with what I got. Now that's just all there is to it."

"*Half?*" asked Abigail.

"Half what?" asked the captain, removing the bourbon from the tray and taking the first swallow.

"You said you lost *half* of the passengers?" asked Abigail, sipping the wine and dabbing her mouth with her handkerchief.

"And the first mate to boot."

"Terrible," said Abigail, shaking her head as she did when vexed by bad news, looking at Cynthia and motioning for her to come closer. Abigail patted the settee near her chair, and Cynthia obediently and politely sat there, sniffing and sipping the pink lemonade.

"What's this about *you* being a Lovingsworth?" asked Abigail, cheerful now with the effect of the wine and its touch of laudanum, as if one of the peepholes in her mind had snapped open in expectation that the mood of the homecoming might improve.

"Well-l-l-l," Cynthia hesitated, rocking back and forth, returning the look of Abigail's portrait, then regarding the toes of her scuffed shoes. "There was this nice lady aboard ship."

Two Abigails stared.

"Some said she was *not* real nice, but I thought she was *very* nice. It was because of her that the captain agreed to adopt me," said Cynthia, cutting looks first at Abigail and then at the captain, lastly at the portrait.

Captain Lovingsworth was suddenly having a problem swallowing his bourbon and branch. He pressed his doubled fist against his mouth and coughed, hoping his heart would not begin to pound. He wished he were somewhere else, anywhere distant. He fleetingly thought of Sylva and just as quickly swept her from his mind.

"Adopt?" exclaimed Abigail, as if confronted with a foreign word.

"Well, he told the nice lady that he would look after me. I don't have anybody else in the world, except Grandpa Charlie, who's back in England, and I may never see him again."

"I do declare," began Abigail.

"I promise not to be any trouble, and I promise to

work for you to help pay my way, which is what the nice lady said."

"What else did the *nice* lady say?" Abigail mocked as her glare bore through the gloom of the parlor to the captain's face, white above the rim of his glass.

"She said, you should always work for your pay," said Cynthia.

"James Henry," said Abigail, "what about the *nice lady* who made all these arrangements?"

James Henry felt the sharp edge of the bourbon against his lips. Lou Belle had added hardly a dash of water, less than the amount of laudanum she had dropped into Abigail's wine.

"Stop your drinking long enough to explain. *Who made all these arrangements for us?*"

"Long story, Abigail. And a short story too. Nothing much to it, actually. It was pure hell on that ship, Abigail. In quarantine. The ship's in quarantine, Abigail. It's over in the Rigolets. Near Fort Pike. Don't know when it'll be cleared to bring through to Pontchartrain. When it is, I'm selling out. Last voyage, Abigail, last voyage—and—"

"Oh, yes, James Henry Lovingsworth?"

The icy flatness and the querulous upturned tone at the very end of Abigail's question puzzled him. Suddenly she seemed a stranger.

"Like you're just drawing your last breath and taking your last bourbon and branch. Taking your last fling at the quadroons and the octoroons of the Vieux Carré."

"Now, Abigail—"

"James Henry, I'm worried to death about the cholera epidemic. Never mind what women you've been with. No matter the color of their skin. I'm scared to death about the *cholera,* James Henry!"

"I *know.*"

"Thousands of people are dropping like flies here in

N'Orleans. Now you come home to tell me our ship's in quarantine. Tell me you've lost half the passengers *and* the first mate, and now I'm informed that some nice *lady* talked you into taking a child off her hands."

"Abigail—"

"How old are you, child?"

"Twelve years, and—"

"Now, at our age, we've got a twelve-year-old child going on twenty-one, for goodness sake, James Henry! My health is slipping away. Don't you know that? Cholera everywhere, and on top of everything else, I'm losing my mind. Just like Mama. She finally got to the place where she couldn't *speak* at all. But maybe that would be better than this. James Henry, what *are* we going to *do*?" Abigail sobbed.

"Well, here's what I was thinking." The captain paused and called, "Lou Belle, another bourbon and branch." Then turning back to Abigail, he said, "Why don't we take a trip back to Kentucky, Abigail, so we can just kind of get away and rest a spell? Take a nice and easy steamboat ride on the *Thomas Jefferson* if it hasn't already blown sky high, and, who knows, why don't we see about maybe even buying a piece of land up there in the Bluegrass? We could sell the *Cynthia Anne,* lock, stock, and barrel." James Henry was warming to the idea.

"I don't understand," said Abigail, softly under her breath. "Buy it with *what?* I don't think we have enough money. I don't think we're as well off as once we might have been."

"Don't you worry. We're going to be just fine. Why, we could invest what we do have in a piece of land in one of the most beautiful places in the world. See, we could have two homes; spend some time in Kentucky, spend some time here in New Orleans. We could do that for the rest of our lives. Back and forth, back and forth," said the captain, as he drained the last of the bourbon from his glass. "Sound good? Lou Belle, bring that bottle in here and leave it."

"You are serious about selling the *Cynthia Anne?*" said Abigail.

"I can be your Cynthia Anne," said the child.

"Hush, child."

"Yes, ma'am."

"Lord, have mercy upon my—upon *all* our souls. It's true, if ever there were a time to be getting out of N'Orleans for a little while, only just a little while, this would be it."

"That's right," said James Henry.

"If we don't, we may all die of the cholera. James Henry Lovingsworth, *are* you serious?"

"Mo' sherious then ah've evah been in mah whole life," said James Henry, artfully lapsing into a Deep South dialect induced by bourbon-laced insincerity and the hope of distracting Abigail's attention from matters better left unspoken.

"You're lying. But I love your lying. We probably don't have a pot to spit in. Lord knows, I've put up with it long enough," sniffled Abigail, cooling her face with her jade-handled fan, a gift from the captain after his return from an earlier voyage. "I *do* want to take a trip back to Kentucky. I *do* want to go right away, because I *am* scared out of my wits, James Henry."

"It'll be all right," said the captain, taking the bottle from Lou Belle, who looked at him with a stern frown.

"When cholera comes knocking on this door," said Abigail, shaking her head from side to side, "I don't want anybody to be here, except maybe Lou Belle. She'll know what to do. *I* certainly don't know what to do anymore, James Henry. More and more, every day, I do *not* know what to do."

The fanning became more rapid as her eyes filled with tears. "I really don't know what's the matter with me. Sell the *Cynthia Anne.* Adopt the Cynthia Anne. Try not to think too much about all the little *lagniappes* from the 'nice ladies,' who'll always be out there, somewhere, just waiting to be nice."

Abigail began sobbing, bitterly.

Captain Lovingsworth went to her and put his arm around her and motioned for Lou Belle to take Cynthia Anne from the room. "Show her where she'll be schleeping," he said. "Scrub her good and find some different clothes for her to wear. She don't smell too good."

"Just where am I supposed to find clothes for a little girl?"

"I don't have the slightest idea. Borrow some from somebody. Abigail, don't you have shome old clothes the child could wear?" the captain inquired.

"Clothes? What clothes, James Henry? Do you mean some of my younger days' clothes? Is that what you mean? What *do* you mean?"

"Come with me, chile. I'll find some better rags for you to wear. I'll fix you something special to eat. Bet you never had crawfish étouffée. I'll fix you a hot bath and scrub your bottom 'til it blisters. How about that? You hungry? The Captain and Miss Abigail sure enough got some catching up talk to do."

In bed, on his first night home after the last voyage of the *Cynthia Anne,* James Henry and Abigail tossed and turned and occasionally bumped into each other's arms, with only vague remembrances of passion, while in the guest room their "adopted" child was wide awake, gazing out at the courtyard on Rue Dauphine. Her mind was awash with the waking nightmare of the *Cynthia Anne,* her parents' deaths, the unceasing burials at sea, the frightful sights and sounds of all that went on long into the night, the moaning and the gasping for air in steerage—and, then, there they were again at each daybreak. Always the same thing. Over and over again it was the same scene. The faces changed yet all looked so much the same. And now the bodies on the streets of New Orleans, and the captain's drunken behavior, and Miss Abigail's fear and confusion.

Perhaps it was the beginning of the end of the world, Cynthia thought.

Asiatic cholera, endemic in India in 1817, might be sweeping across the entire world, yet nothing had changed in the rising of the sun over Lake Pontchartrain. The first morning after the end of their voyage from London to New Orleans, Captain Lovingsworth, with Cynthia Anne in tow, walked across Bourbon and Royal Streets to Pirate's Alley, where they entered St. Louis Cathedral. It had been a traditional practice of the captain to go there upon his return to the city from each voyage, to light a votive candle and kneel in silence. He did not know why he did it. He was drawn to it, but maybe it was just superstition. Officially, he had never considered himself a Catholic or any other sort of churched person. The whole notion of sacramental worship vexed his spirit. He did not receive Holy Communion, and confession and penance seemed to him ridiculous. The lighting of the candle and the moments of peace were as warm and satisfying as swimming in Gulf Stream waters, but intellectually or spiritually the captain had no desire to go beyond that.

Cynthia also lit a small candle and knelt before the Virgin Mary, the stillness broken only by the softened footsteps of people coming and going, protective cloth across their faces. A priest passed in front of the altar, devoutly and mechanically nodded to the crucifix, and entered the room on the right side of the sanctuary.

Their devotions completed, the two walked together toward the massive front doors of the cathedral, Cynthia feeling small, swallowed up by the enormity of the vaulted structure. It felt better outside in the bright sunlight of the Place d'Armes, traditional parade ground for military forces, especially in 1815 when General Jackson successfully defended the city against the British assault.

"Well," said the captain, "like Old Hickory, we've come here and we've paid our respects."

"Thank you," said Cynthia. "I've offered prayers for my

mother and father and grandfather Charlie. I've prayed for Miss Abigail. And I've also prayed for you, Captain."

"Don't waste any on me. Let's go for beignets and café au lait if there is any such thing left in this sockdolloger. And then let's find ourselves passage for three on the *Thomas Jefferson* or some other such boat that looks like it might get farther than Natchez. With all that fire in those boilers it's no wonder the sons of bitches don't blow up more than they do."

"What's a sockdolloger?" asked Cynthia.

"Fist in the face."

"I don't understand."

"Cholera has just about shut down this city. Look around you."

"Will we ever see the nice lady again?" asked Cynthia, as she and the captain walked on from the cathedral. She turned once to look at the spires reaching high above the Vieux Carré.

"Cynthia Anne, there's something you have to understand about Syl . . . I mean, the 'nice lady.'"

"And what is that?" asked Cynthia.

"Remember, we agreed we would stop talking about the 'nice lady.'"

"Why?"

"Because an agreement is an agreement, and because I said so."

"Are you ashamed of her?"

"Stop it! Just damn well stop it."

"Captain, I only asked if we would ever see her again. Please don't be angry with me."

"We're going to sit down here on this park bench, and we're going to have a lesson in how to watch our mouths."

"I'm listening."

"You're impudent as hell, and you know it. I'm going to level with you, and I expect you to use your head for something besides a place to grow hair."

"All right."

"Good. Now, this is how it is, and you might as well know about it. Men need women for different reasons. There is a time in a man's life when he needs respectability."

"So he gets married?" ventured Cynthia.

"Yes, he does. After a while, usually one year, the children start to be born."

"But you and Miss Abigail don't have any children. Except me."

"Except you. That's right. Sometimes, there are no natural children. But, whether there are or not, the man and his wife begin to change."

"How? Do they stop loving each other? I don't think my mother and father had stopped, do you?"

"Not necessarily. How in hell would I know? I never knew them, so I would like you to be quiet and listen. Just close your mouth and open your ears. What I'm going to tell you could be very important for you to understand in a few years."

"I'm listening."

"A man is made different from a woman. A man has a strong desire, which God gave him, and a woman, usually, has not so strong a desire."

"For each other?"

"Yes, for each other. I mean, no. I mean a good woman understands this and handles it accordingly. It is not unusual for a married man here in New Orleans to have relationships with other women. Happens all the time. Happens all over the world, in fact. Everybody knows it. Most of us don't go running around talking about it."

"Please," said Cynthia. "I want to speak."

"So, speak," said Captain Lovingsworth, looking toward the landing where the steamboats were jockeying for position, unloading cotton from Mississippi, Arkansas, and Tennessee, tobacco and bourbon whiskey from Kentucky, and human beings in bondage—men, women, and children—heading for the slave markets. "Speak," said the captain.

"I may be only twelve years old, but I understand more than you think. Grandpa Charlie used to tell me to watch out for anybody 'running wild as a March hare.'"

"What are you trying to say?"

"What I'm trying to say is, I think you're wrong, Captain. Maybe not entirely wrong, but wrong all the same."

"Thank you very much."

"I'm not going to mention the 'nice lady' again, but if I see her on the street, I'm not going to act as if I don't know her. She's the person I owe my life to. If it had not been for her, you would not have adopted me."

"Now wait a minute—"

"You wouldn't listen to Mrs. Fischer, but you sure did listen to Sylva."

"Cynthia Anne, damn it all—"

"But, if Miss Abigail is with you, I will keep your secret. I owe my life to you, too."

"Can I trust you?" asked the captain, peering into Cynthia's wide eyes.

"Can I trust *you?*" said Cynthia, smiling cheerfully.

"You should know by now."

"And so should you."

"Deal?" pleaded the captain.

"Deal," said Cynthia.

"Let's shake on it."

"What does that mean, shake on it?"

"It means, give me your goddamned hand and hold it in mine and squeeze and know that nobody goes back on their word."

"All right!"

"By the way, I've been thinking."

"Yes?"

"It comes to all of us that we must die. So if ever there's the time when I come to my end, and you are there, I want you to take whatever of value there is on my person. Take it before any of the sons of bitches get their hands on it. All I have is what I carry with me. Banks don't trust me anymore, and I don't trust them. The hydra-headed monster, that's what Old Hickory calls 'em. When he finishes with 'em they'll sing a different tune."

"Old Hickory?"

"Andrew Jackson. President of these United States of America. Stands for what makes us different from England."

She never again mentioned the words "nice lady" to the captain, but Cynthia couldn't help wondering where the woman was and how she was and hoping that someday she might be able to repay her kindness. Thoughts of a spirit so free and honest made a warm place in the girl's memory.

Hand in hand, the captain and Cynthia approached the long line of steamboats. She kicked some pebbles along the way, and once she picked an oleander and held it to her nose. The fragrance was pleasantly aromatic, unlike the wharf where an air of gloom hung heavy. The prevalence of cholera and its twin scourge, yellow fever, had tried and almost succeeded in sucking the wind out of the normally boisterous and irreligious throng of heathen dockhands.

Captain Lovingsworth found an agent who was more than happy to book their passage on the *Thomas Jefferson*. Professional courtesies were exchanged, and then a piece of gold made a capital difference, one of the nicest kinds of *lagniappe*. "Do you know of anybody who might want to buy a sailing ship?" James Henry asked, indifferently.

"A *what?*" replied the agent.

"You heard me—a sailing ship."

"I see," said the agent, thoughtfully rubbing the gold. "I take it that you possibly own a commercial sailing vessel." The agent leaned forward and peered into Lovingsworth's face. "Perhaps you are—"

"The captain, the goddamned captain," Lovingsworth exploded.

"Yes, you are the captain," said the agent, carefully taking two steps back as one would when confronted by a snarling dog. "And the owner?"

"The owner and the captain of the *Cynthia Anne,* as fine a ship as ever bore three masts upon the ocean!"

"Yes indeed. And now that steamboats have replaced sailing ships, you think there might be a market for your—what did you call it?—your *Suzie Q?*

"Listen to me, you insulting little—"

"Now, Captain. Don't be offended. I mean no harm. Surely you are aware that the times are rapidly changing. Look around you. Look at the stacks. They are talking to all good men just like yourself."

Captain Lovingsworth was well aware of what would soon overtake the age of sail, but there was something about steam-powered ships that repulsed him. Move on water without sails? Without good and generous wind gathered? The idea of relinquishing control of the mainmast and the jib to a smoke-belching contraption was an obscenity, truly a royal son of a bitch.

"Captain, to tell you the truth, if I had a sailing ship right now, I'd get rid of the crew any way I could, and I'd give the damn thing away."

"Captain," said Cynthia, "I'm hungry. Could we just go home?"

Feeling helpless, the captain glowered at the agent. For an instant, James Henry thought of fighting. He would smash the face that grinned at him. Speaking evenly in a tone that was low but unmistakably clear, James Henry said to the agent: "Mister, I don't know your name. I don't want to know your goddamned name. You may have given me an idea."

"Let's go, please," said Cynthia, fearful that Captain Lovingsworth was going to plant a sockdolloger in the agent's mouth.

"We're going home. We're going to do something that's needed doing for a long time."

The agent, increasingly apprehensive, retreated two more steps.

"It's all right," said James Henry. "Consider yourself lucky that I'm not going to run a Kentucky rifle up your butt and squeeze the trigger. I'm not going to hang a mainmast on the end of your nose. I'm going to thank you for giving me the best advice I've heard since we landed back in this son of a bitching town. Now let's go, Cynthia Anne."

"Captain!" called the agent to James Henry as he abruptly turned, took Cynthia's hand, and stomped away.

Over his shoulder, the captain yelled, "Go to Hell!"

On Royal Street the captain in his agitated frame of mind wondered about some little gift for Abigail, something that might divert her enough for him to clear some decks quickly. She had always loved brooches. There were many hanging from a chain around the neck of an old woman slumped against the wall of a building at the corner of Royal and Iberville. A rag picker long ago fallen from society's grace, she trafficked in the odds and ends of a devastated city. The captain thought a bauble might brighten Abigail's spirits. On the other hand, he doubted that anything would help.

"How much for that brooch, that one right there?" asked the captain.

"For you, sir, I make you special price. Let's say ten reales."

"Let's say five."

"Let's say you got yourself one fine brooch. Now then," said the old woman as she removed the chain from around her neck, "I have a small gold cross, which would be nice for this child you have with you, sir."

"How much?"

"One eagle."

"One half eagle."

"Captain, if this gold cross ain't worth ten dollars it ain't worth nothing."

"One half eagle, take it or leave it."

"It's yours. And with it goes a blessing upon this child."

The captain took a half eagle from his leather pouch, like pinching crust from a loaf of bread, and handed it to the woman. She placed the cross around Cynthia's neck and kissed her on both sides of the face.

"Bless you, child," said the old woman. Now Cynthia had two gold crosses, one from the captain and the other from Grandfather Charlie. She felt doubly blessed as she walked with the captain through the Quarter.

"Do you think I might have a new dress? Or maybe a blouse?" asked Cynthia.

"I thought Lou Belle found something for you to wear," the captain grumbled. "You look all right."

"Well, yes, she did, but it doesn't fit all that well. She tightened the waist a little, but it still pouches out like I'm going to have a baby. She turned up the hem and tacked it but I still have to be careful that I don't step on it and fall, and I just thought—"

"Women are all the same. Give them something nice and they always want more. Give the son of a bitching crew a little more grog and they want a barrel."

"I need some better shoes, don't I?"

"What you need and what you get may be two different things, especially now when the shops are closed. The banks are closed, and soon I'll be closed. Cholera has changed everything. Ask Lou Belle for some shoes. We don't have time to waste."

They walked on toward Dauphine and St. Peter. From time to time, a young woman would be looking down, sometimes wistfully, other times arrogantly, from an open second-floor window. Now and then, three or four would be laughing on flower-bedecked balconies, where ferns were luxuriant, moist, and cooling. Occasionally a voice would call down, "Who you got there, Captain? Out for a little stroll? How's the café au lait this morning? Did you find any? You keeping ahead of the cholera? You coming back here sometime?"

"Who are they?" asked Cynthia. "There are so many of them," she said, looking up at the balcony.

"Whores," said the captain.

Once when they had sat cross-legged in steerage, the ship rising and falling like a playground seesaw, Sylva had told Cynthia, softly, after the deaths of her mother and father, "Let me advise you, luv, you got to look out for yourself. You just remember that. You got to figure out what you can do and what needs to be done and then, well, you just go and do it!"

"But what if what you do is *bad*?" Cynthia had asked.

"Let me tell you, sweetheart," said Sylva, combing her long, reddish gold hair, "*you* decide what is bad. *You* have to do that. If you don't, somebody else will decide it for you. There are many who profess to be *good* when in fact they are very bad and don't have the foggiest notion of the difference. And there are people, like me, who are outcast because it is said that we are bad, yet we are not nearly as bad as many of our accusers."

"Am I an outcast?" asked Cynthia.

"Look at me," said Sylva. "Some call me whore, and some call me worse, but I am what I am. I'm a woman who works in order to live."

"What is a whore?"

"Someday, you will remember me as the nice lady who persuaded the hard-hearted captain to provide you with a home."

"How did you talk him into it?"

"I did not do it by mopping his floor. I did not do it by

waiting for him to think that I *might* be beautiful. I did not do it by hiding until he accidentally stumbled upon me. Let's say I presented him with a gift. It was a gift of *myself.*"

"Your*self?*"

"Yes. It was all I had at the time. Maybe I could have waited until I was invited to a very fine party in New Orleans. And we might have played games with our eyes. See, think about it. I could have waited until he invited me to dance a waltz with him. We might have secretly squeezed each other's hands. Our knees might have touched. He would have courted me. There would have been flowers, and there would have been promises. And if I was good at playing this game, I would have encouraged other men to dance with me too. Some would have sent flowers and tried to steal kisses. Others would have pinched. Then there would have been jealousies. There are many good girls who employ such strategies. To be fought over, who knows, maybe in a glorious duel, now wouldn't *that* be *good?*"

"So, you chose to be bad?"

"What I did caused no harm to anybody and did some good. If God disapproves, then he disapproves, and I will stand responsible for that judgment. What more can be asked of anybody, anywhere?"

Cynthia considered these words. She felt a stirring in her body that she could not identify, a restlessness that would not retreat. She knew that Sylva was taking time to talk to her as no woman had before. It was good to feel a part of an adult matter so intimate, whatever that might involve, however it might unfold.

"Well?" asked Sylva.

"Do you think I should become a whore?"

Sylva took a deep breath. She reached to touch Cynthia's hands, raised them up together and kissed them. "No, you should not. But you should always remember to be true to yourself. You should always consider what seems the *right* thing to do at the right time. 'Right' is a tricky word."

"And *truth*?"

"An even trickier word. *Truth* has a million faces. My truth is not necessarily your truth or any other person's truth. Let me see if I can explain it a little better. Truth is like a bee. When a bee stings you, then you understand the meaning of that kind of truth. You have been stung, and that is a truth. Now, who created the bee and gave it a stinger?"

"God."

"All right. It was God. But why did God give bees stingers, when he could just as easily have left that part off?"

"He gave it to them so that they could defend themselves."

"Possibly so. Probably so. But we are still not sure of the original intent. We just know that if you get too close to a bumblebee, it probably will sting you and that will get your attention. It might even kill you. But the truth of the relationship between the pain and you is a mystery."

"And what else?"

"You should honor the memory of your mother and your father. That is also a piece of the puzzle. Growing into womanhood, your own womanhood, is not an easy thing."

"Why?"

"Because of having to live with the reality of *men.* Do you want to know another truth?"

"Yes."

"Some men are the worst of whores. Men go to women like me, bargain for them, lie and cheat for them, call *them* whores, then return to their respectable lives and never think any more about it until the next time. So, I ask you, who is the higher-ranking whore?"

Cynthia remained silent for the remainder of the walk, absorbing pungent New Orleans atmosphere, occasionally the aroma of fresh bread baking, the piquancy of spices, the reek of raw fish and oysters and boudin blanc and boudin noir mixed with the smell of the unmistakable and strangely sweet stench of bodies unremoved.

"Abigail, have Lou Belle pack lightly for our trip," said Captain Lovingsworth, when he and Cynthia reached home. "We leave early the day after tomorrow on a boat heading north."

"We *do?*" said Abigail, startled by the announcement.

"We'll head for Memphis and on to the Ohio. With any kind of luck, we'll book passage there to Maysville."

"The captain says we're going to *Lexington,*" said Cynthia with a newfound sense of measurement.

"For Heaven's sake, child, stop interrupting. Go play. *Do* something."

"You mean, I'm not going with you all? You're serious?" whimpered Lou Belle as she led Cynthia from the room. "I see it coming. I'm going to stay here and keep the cholera fed. Hmm, hmmm. Expected as much. Hmmp! C'mon, Cynthia, we gonna do some packing of bags. I'll find you another pair of shoes. You all going to Kantucky and leave this here old workhorse right here, right here in N'Orlans, ain't you? Well, all right, you all do that, you hear? You all just do that." She tossed the last of the bitter words over her shoulder toward the captain and Abigail.

The next morning the only stirring of air in the depressingly hot parlor came in tiny wisps from Abigail's small, collapsible fan. She stared at her husband through silence as heavy as her brocades, their raised gold and silver threads dulled by long, solitary afternoons in the Quarter.

"James Henry, you come home after being gone for months." Abigail spoke in measured phrases because she feared the loss of composure. "You waltz in with a prissy little girl that some 'nice lady' has presented to you. And right away you tell me we're going to Kentucky? *Is* that it?"

"You said you were afraid to stay here. People are dying by

the thousands and those that can are getting the hell out of the city. Well, that's us, too."

"It *is*?" Abigail felt more waves of confusion. Having to think clearly caused her to fumble with her forehead, which reminded her of a large ball of twisted yarn. She was having trouble remembering where she'd last hidden the Bracken family banknotes, her inheritance after the death of her mother. She'd kept it secret from James Henry, which was easy enough because he was gone most of the time. She imagined that it was not a huge fortune but that it was a substantial amount, perhaps $100,000. The only thing certain about it was Abigail's determination that James Henry should not lay his hands on a penny of it.

"We're making our own exit as fast as we can," said the captain. "We're going to outrun the cholera. We're going to get ahead of it and stay ahead of it. I need time first to go back out to the *Cynthia Anne* and take care of a little piece of business. Then we leave."

"Are we moving for *good,* James Henry?"

"We'll have to wait and see."

"There are so many things left undone."

"What you need to do now is to pull yourself together. Make ready your necessaries. Do you understand? Pack *lightly.*

"Pack *lightly*?" asked Abigail, remembering now that the banknotes were last stored in the bottom drawer of the linen chest, hidden beneath two copies of the school of Ingres originals. She would remove the notes and place them among her unmentionables in her traveling bag.

"We'll have a good time. From Maysville we'll travel by stagecoach on down to Lexington. We'll stay there until we know it's all right to return to N'Orleans," said James Henry.

"It may never be all right. I want everything to be like it was when you first courted me, James Henry."

"What?"

"I know everything can't be the way it was then."

"It's going to be all right, everything is going to be all right when we get to Lexington. It's a progressive place. Beautiful place. Remember me telling you about King Solomon?"

"I don't *want* to lose my mind. Do you hear me, James Henry? For the very first time in your life, do you *hear* me?" she shouted.

"Yes, Abigail, I hear you."

"What about '*King* Solomon'? Who's *he?*"

"Friend. Used to know him a long time ago in Lexington."

"Is there a Queen of Sheba, too?" asked Abigail with flinty, rekindled fire in her eyes.

"What are you talking about?"

"I mean, after all, what's *lagniappe* for N'Orleans is probably *lagniappe* for Lexington."

"Abigail, what—"

"Wherever we go, we *have* to have our 'nice ladies,' don't we, James Henry?"

"I don't know anything about any Queen of Sheba. 'King' is just a nickname for Bill Solomon, a town character in Lexington."

"*Lagniappe* for Lexington—"

"We were boys together. My ship's doctor knew him later and told me about how big he turned out to be. Giant. Fine specimen. Shouldn't be wasting his time digging basements and graves and holes in the ground for outhouses."

"James Henry, you *are* crude."

"Probably so. But who knows, maybe he could be my next first mate."

"I thought so. You're no more going to sell the *Cynthia Anne* than I'm going to grow hooves and pull carts in Gehenna."

James Henry seized his captain's cap and stomped outside. From her room Cynthia heard the commotion and followed in a flurry. "Wait for me! I'm coming with you."

"No, you're not. You're staying here."

"Please, let me go with you," pleaded Cynthia.

The captain yelled at the first cart rounding the corner of Dauphine and St. Peter, and he and Cynthia took their seats.

"Yassah, Boss, where we going this time?" said Charles. "I been thinking you all about ready to go for a ride. How you been sweet chile?" he said to Cynthia.

"Back to the place where you picked us up at Fort Macomb," said the captain.

"Why?" asked Cynthia. "I been fine, Mister Charles."

"Me to know and you to find out," muttered the captain.

"Oh, Mister Charles, what are we going to do about us?" asked Cynthia, feeling comforted by the closeness of the old, black driver.

"Lawse me, chile, don't know nothing about nothing when it come to other people's business, especially when they's *white* folks, most *especially* when they's white folks."

The ride back through Elysian Fields was little different from the first. There were more bodies unburied, and vultures were doing their work. Cynthia held a handkerchief over her mouth, and the captain stared straight ahead. At the edge of Chef Pass several pirogues were tied up, and Boudreaux was grinning from one of them.

"Can you take us back out to our ship, the *Cynthia Anne,* in the Rigolets?" asked Captain Lovingsworth.

"Be most proud to take you out der," beamed Boudreaux.

"Charles," said the captain, "I need you here late this afternoon, but before it starts to be dark. If we're running late, wait for us. We don't want to be stuck out here in this godforsaken swamp."

"Yassah, Boss."

"Cynthia Anne, you are going to stay with Boudreaux while I'm finishing my business aboard ship. You are not permitted back on it. Do you understand?"

"Aye, aye, Captain."

"You're a guttersnipe, is what you are."

"And the old rag woman who sold you the gold cross, she is a guttersnipe too? But you are the *Captain*," Cynthia smiled in pert resignation. "I know that."

Boudreaux helped the captain and Cynthia into the pirogue, and quickly they were on their way in a good breeze that carried them up Pontchartrain to the Rigolets. They coasted past Fort Pike, with its parapeted cannon guarding the primary passageway connecting Lake Pontchartrain and the northwestern lip of Lake Borgne. There rode the *Cynthia Anne* at anchor.

Boudreaux maneuvered in tight to the port side, and the captain climbed up the rope ladder. Staying with Boudreaux made the waiting easier and more inviting for Cynthia. She learned some Cajun words. They talked about what it meant to be a Catholic and a coon awse all at the same time. It was Boudreaux's opinion that a Catholic was what you were when you were in the confessional and at the kneeling rail and taking Holy Communion and being baptized and confirmed and in the end having a funeral mass said for you. "I'm goot Catlic, *som*'time," smiled Boudreaux. He told Cynthia a coon awse was what you were if you were fortunate enough to live in bayous like the Atchafalaya, where you feasted on gumbo, shrimp, softshell crabs, and fresh-shucked oysters. In your spare time you hunted alligators and ate squirrel brains. A coon awse was a good friend to other coon awses, showing respect and not dabbling with another man's wife, *som*'time. A coon awse's dog was usually a catahoula, one eye blue, the other green.

"Captain," said Bosun Whittaker, who'd had a hard time believing he was really in charge after the death of Tom Moreland. "I'm be damned glad you're back. Is it possible for us to talk in your cabin?"

"As long as we make it fast."

Lovingsworth and the temporary first mate sat down in

the captain's cabin. "All right," said the captain, "Where do we stand?"

"Captain, if we're not standing in gumbo mud and up to our sweet asses in alligators, I don't know what is. What I would like to do is to set this bloody ship adrift and let everybody but me and the crew fall off the end of the earth."

There was a knock on the cabin door. "Yes?" said Captain Lovingsworth with uncharacteristic mildness, lacking the will to contest the interruption.

"It's Doctor Hanover. May I join you?"

"Come in."

The young doctor came in and took a seat. He looked ashen, as if he had not slept in days. "Captain," he said, "the quarantine will last a few more days. May I ask if you are back to stay?"

"Yes, you may ask. And no, I'm not. I'm booked this week for Kentucky with my wife and our adopted child."

"Just like that?"

"Just like that."

"Abandoning ship?"

"Call it whatever you damn well please."

"Captain," said the bosun, "we need you here."

"No, you don't. Not as much as you think. Not as much as a hole in the head. Tell you what. I spoke with a plug-ugly Jonathan today who made a lot of sense. For once, I'm going to follow a yankee's cheap advice. There comes a time to take in chips, cash 'em in, and head for home."

"These surviving passengers aren't *chips*, Captain," said Doctor Hanover.

"Doctor, I cannot tell you what to do. You can stay with cholera as long as you like. Get real close. Stare it in the face. Twist its nose. It's out of my hands. The quarantine officials are in charge. In fact, you, Doctor, are more in charge than I am. I've decided what I'm going to do. Two things. Number one:

I'm making Bosun Whittaker, First Mate Whittaker, *permanent*. Number two: I'm turning over the *Cynthia Anne* to you, Doctor Hanover. She's all yours. In fact, I'll pay you to *take* the bitch. Piece of gold for you, piece for the first mate, pieces for whatever crew has not jumped ship and swum to shore," sputtered Captain Lovingsworth, the loaf of bread growing smaller.

"Captain—" began Doctor Hanover.

"No, you've got it wrong. *You* are the captain. *And* the owner. *And* the doctor. You can sell her or you can scuttle her. Work with the quarantine bastards to process the dead, the dying, and the ones who look like they might survive. I really do *not* care."

"Captain," said Doctor Hanover, "I don't know what to say. I really—"

"Then, don't."

"Captain, Doctor," said First Mate Whittaker to Hanover, "make it legal, pay me and the crew, and most of us will stay."

"Incredible," said Hanover, shaking his head.

"What's incredible?" asked Lovingsworth.

"The whole blessed thing," said Hanover. "Before you change your mind, put it in writing, and I will notify the quarantine officers. I just want to say one thing, Captain Lovingsworth—the *Cynthia Anne* has sailed her last voyage. You can count on that. The bosun and I will bring her in after she's cleared quarantine. The crew will be paid and sent packing. This ship is heading for a museum. If there isn't one, I will see that one is built, and the *Cynthia Anne* will be the showcase. It will become a monument to the stupidity of the cholera pandemic of 1833. I know this may hurt your feelings, Captain Lovingsworth, but every rat on this ship will be hunted down and exterminated. No more will people be kept in steerage, at least not on this ship, and this will be the beginning of a more extensive effort to discover the cause of this disease."

"No gold for the son of a bitching rats?" bellowed the captain.

"God's wrath," said Bosun Whittaker. "God's wrath," he said again, shaking his head, wisely. "God Almighty has kicked our asses."

"Believe that if you want to, I will not argue with you about your beliefs *or* your superstitions," said Doctor Hanover. "As for me, I prefer to call it 'God's challenge.' In fact, gentlemen, let's play a little game. Since that is what you seem to think all of this has been. Take the word 'wrath.' Remove the first and the last letters. What do you have?"

Bosun Whittaker and Captain Lovingsworth gaped at Doctor Hanover. They knew nothing about spelling words. He dropped the matter.

As Boudreaux prepared to push away from the ship, Cynthia and the captain looked toward the quarterdeck for the last time. There she was. Sylva, standing at the scupper and gazing down to them. "Take me with you," seemed written on her face, yet she did not call out. She had too much pride for that. She was resigned to her situation. The wind hugging the swamps of the Rigolets corridor stirred her hair, and she smiled as if across the ages.

"Stop!" screamed Cynthia.

Boudreaux was startled. He hove to.

"Get going," yelled Lovingsworth.

"If you don't stop, I will jump into this water and climb up there to her," Cynthia shouted back, removing her hat and reaching for her shoes.

"Captain," said Boudreaux, "we ain't going to see this little one in that water, nohow."

"Good God," said Lovingsworth, recognizing defeat when it confronted him, face to face. "Doctor Hanover," Lovingsworth called to the quarterdeck, "is that woman by any chance cleared to go ashore?"

"She was cleared two hours ago. Is there room for her with you at this time?"

"We make room," said Boudreaux. "For such a good-looking woman as she is, naturally, we better make room, ain't dat right, Cap'n?"

"I am no longer the captain," answered Lovingsworth. "If she wants to go with us, send her down," he called up to Doctor Hanover.

Sylva came down the rope ladder with an ecstatic smile on her face. Cynthia reached for her hand and helped her take her seat in the delicately balanced pirogue. Boudreaux pushed back from the ship and rounded the bow, where the figurehead of the *Cynthia Anne* peered directly and solemnly ahead. Cynthia Anne and Sylva fell into each other's arms. Captain Lovingsworth looked toward the parapet of Fort Pike and under his breath he muttered, "Son of a bitch."

"Dis nicest lookin' woman, Cap'n, she be your friend som'time?"

"I never saw her before in my life," said Captain Lovingsworth.

Sylva and Cynthia held on to each other, laughing and crying at the same time.

Charles Adams was waiting when Boudreaux landed the pirogue in very nearly the same place as he had the first time, at the end of Shell Road between the mouth of Bayou Sauvage and Fort Macomb. A pinch of gold was exchanged, and Boudreaux was as happy as he ever remembered being. He solicitously helped Cynthia and Sylva onto land, and he grinned and slapped the captain on the back. "She som good lookin' woman, Cap'n, you one lucky coon awse."

Charles climbed down and assisted the women into the cart. Captain Lovingsworth felt as if he had met a storm and it had beaten the hell out of him.

Charles whistled and clucked to his old dray horse. The black man felt as if he were driving royalty back to the palace, although he could tell something was definitely godawfully odd.

Charles was no fool; he understood humanity as well as anybody. He could see the pained look on the captain's face, the girlish pleasure on the faces of Cynthia and the mysterious woman who had joined them. As for her, Charles had seen hundreds like her in the Vieux Carré. They were as natural to it as the azaleas in front of St. Louis Cathedral, as the Spanish moss hanging from the live oaks. Oh, yassir, there be those who say the whores they be evil and they be going to hell in handbaskets, but the truth is that the whores almost always pays their bills.

"Now, Boss, what do we want to *do?*"

"Sylva, where do you want to go?" asked the captain, warily.

"She wants to come home with *us,*" said Cynthia.

"No, she does not want to come home with *us,*" said Sylva. "Please take me to a convent."

There was a stunned moment of silence in the cart. The only sounds were the vultures flapping their wings in the live oak trees.

"And for what purpose, may I ask?" said Lovingsworth, clearing his throat.

"You may ask."

"Well?"

"Well, nothing. Captain, never once have I asked about *your* purpose. Never once. I assume the purpose of this driver is to take us where we wish to go. He does it for money. I assume your purpose in abandoning the *Cynthia Anne* was to tar and waterproof your conscience. I assume the purpose of the child you have adopted is to live a good life and at the same time try to make some sense out of what grown men and women do. But I do not ask these questions. Therefore, do not ask what is *my* purpose."

"I'll ask anything I damn well please."

"Well, maybe you think a prostitute is a weed that pops out of nowhere. I had a mother and father, and we were a family until my father started drinking heavily and my mother went to work on the streets. They were educated, and I was educated in good Catholic schools. As a child I attended Mass daily. I have read St. Francis of Assisi and Geoffrey Chaucer. I have seen the best and the worst. We could not help what happened to us."

"Nobody to blame?" gibed the captain.

"Nobody to blame. Not even myself. We all pretty much do what we have to do."

"What will you do in the convent, Sylva?" asked Cynthia.

"Perhaps I will become a nun, but first I'll have to be accepted as a novice. I will scrub floors, wash dishes, prove my intentions. Perhaps I will spend one night, two nights, three nights with the sisters and then go back into the streets. I do not have answers. I sold all I had to ensure passage on your ship. I sold *myself* to ensure that you, Cynthia Anne, have a chance to live a halfway decent life. But no matter what you may think, I have never sold my soul. So, Charles—"

"Yassum."

"Do you know where there is a convent?"

"Sho do. There's the new convent out on Dauphine."

"Take me there," said Sylva.

"Yassum."

The Mississippi and the Ohio

May 1833

We mortals are all on board a fast-sailing, never-sinking world-frigate, of which God was the ship-wright; and she is but one craft in a Milky-Way fleet, of which God is the Lord High Admiral. . . . Thus sailing with sealed orders, we ourselves are the repositories of the secret packet, whose mysterious contents we long to learn. There are no mysteries out of ourselves. But let us not give ear to the superstitious, gun-deck gossip about whither we may be gliding, for, as yet, not a soul on board of us knows—not even the Commodore himself; assuredly not the Chaplain; even our Professor's scientific sur-misings are vain. On that point, the smallest cabin-boy is as wise as the Captain.

—Herman Melville
White-Jacket

THE ACCOMMODATIONS ABOARD the *Thomas Jefferson* were sumptuous, far and away superior to the best of any cabin space aboard the *Cynthia Anne*. Captain Lovingsworth, who had his own definition of obscenity, was not used to being pampered. Waited on hand and foot, indulged to the utmost, he missed not having an excuse for breathing fire on an underling who wasn't moving fast enough to catch a good wind. As a prominent passenger aboard one of the grandest of steamboats operating on the lower Mississippi, Lovingsworth felt discomfited, disoriented, and fidgety. He had booked the honeymoon cabin as a comfort, a restful place, for Abigail. As for himself, he was like a desert cactus pulled up by its roots and set down in greenery too lush. He longed for the hardship of the seas.

Leaning against the rail on the starboard side of the *Thomas Jefferson,* watching the wilderness of Mississippi sliding by, James Henry's mind once more was wandering, turning back to his boyhood. Even at ten years of age, he had known exactly what he wanted, and he had gone after it, full bore. He had accompanied his father on a flatboat from Maysville, Kentucky, down the Ohio and Mississippi rivers to New Orleans, and he had learned to cope with storms and human treacheries. He'd run away from his father when they'd reached the Bonnet Carre Bend, downstream from Baton Rouge, and he had walked the last thirty-five river miles to New Orleans. Little Jimmy Lovingsworth had taken his last whipping from his father, drunk *or* sober. Little Jimmy Lovingsworth was going to grow up to be *somebody.* He was going to make something of himself, damned to hell if he wasn't.

The boy had slept by day and moved by night, past the grand plantations where the songs of slaves could be heard as clear and clean and sweet as the baying of hounds in the back country of Kentucky's bluegrass. Where the full moon descended as bright as the sun rose, only lovelier. Occasionally, there'd be a rustle by the side of a bayou.

"Be you, Ned?" a needing, silky voice would whisper.

"Be me. That you, Sugah?"

"Be me, oh, Ned, be me."

Little Jimmy would wait until the lovers were well connected and lost in themselves, oblivious to all else in the universe, and then he'd head on down the Big River toward the Crescent City. He had close encounters, too, with runaway slaves. They might make a slight, unavoidable noise in the forests between the cotton plantations and the Big River's edge, but they'd dare not speak. Staying downwind from the bloodhounds was the first order of business for any slave running to save the hide on his back. Jimmy Lovingsworth did not know what to make of slavery. It seemed necessary on the one hand. On the other, to a young boy, it seemed as strangely wrong as tying cans filled with pebbles to the tails of cats, or dipping them in tar and setting them afire. Slaves were human beings, weren't they? Jimmy Lovingsworth wasn't sure. From time to time, he was uncomfortably puzzled by the question.

His father had hated most whites and certainly all blacks and Indians with equal, uncompromising ferocity. The son inherited a definite measure of racial loathing. He'd sailed once as deckhand on an illegal slave ship and was only slightly troubled by it. He would remember the sight of naked living bodies flung overboard at the sight of a British warship. He thought it was a practical diversion, because the penalty for operating a slave ship was the gallows.

In New Orleans, he found a sailing ship bound for England, and he stowed away. The year was 1793, a year after Kentucky's statehood, the year the United States passed a law requiring all escaped slaves to turn themselves in to their owners.

Jimmy Lovingsworth had been born in 1783 in Fort Lexington, Kentucky, the only child of Cynthia Anne, still in her teens. She'd gotten into trouble with an unwashed pioneer trapper, George Lovingsworth, who spent most of his time hunting and welcoming opportunities to deflower young girls, white or black, brown or red. It had been said of old George that he'd take a flying fling at a nanny goat in heat. He rejoiced in the rewards for the capture and return of runaway slaves. He was surgically proficient in the removal of Indians' scalps; he said they all looked better after a haircut. George Lovingsworth did just about everything for the sheer, maniacal fun of it. As trade began to open up from Lexington north to Maysville, then south to New Orleans, George "Tom Cat" Lovingsworth went along and made the most of it.

After Cynthia Anne's early death, Jimmy became the exclusive property of his father. On their first trip south, the boy picked the night when his father was drunkest as they came booming around the Bonnet Carre. He slipped into the water and, being careful to avoid the snags, swam ashore. It was the last the boy saw of his father. No one in Kentucky or Louisiana would ever know or care that, as he was returning home to Kentucky on the Natchez Trace, robbers murdered the "Tom Cat," hacked his body to pieces, and kicked it into the Chiwapa River. Much later it would be common knowledge that the orphan boy had become the captain of a sailing ship and would marry above himself to Abigail Bracken, descended from a distant branch of pioneer Virginia stock. They too had the appearance of wealth.

Abigail was not used to boats of any kind, regardless of the accommodations, and she felt more threatened than she had ever imagined possible. She dreaded the blast of the steam whistle and stuffed her ears with cotton to try to block it from her throbbing head. She didn't like being fussed over by strangers. Where was Lou Belle when she needed her so? I told her to pack my laudanum. Now, damn it all to whoremongering hell anyway, where *is* it? What am I going to *do* if I don't find it? Why are these awful slave traders allowed to sit at meals with civilized people? They suck air through their teeth, pick their teeth with knives, and actually spit whenever and wherever it suits them, even at the dining table. Their language is gross and generously obscene. On top of everything else, it's scorching hot by day and insufferably humid at night. The mosquito net makes it worse, but without it there'd be no surviving the whizzing creatures, designed for what earthly or heavenly purpose? They're as useless and menacing as Vieux Carré cockroaches. Why did God *do* all this thoughtless creation? Why does He make my head hurt? My God, I've found it! Lou Belle, bless her sweet soul, hid my laudanum compact inside my sachet! I'm going to help myself until it's all gone and done with!

Cynthia raced barefooted from one end of the sternwheeler to the other, experiencing more joy than she had ever dreamed of in her wildest fantasies. The rhythmic sound of the paddlewheel churning the water held her spellbound. She wished she could share it with Grandfather Charlie. The sunrises and sunsets were as magnificent as any she had witnessed on the horizons of the North Atlantic or in the Gulf of Mexico, perhaps because the light shining through the live oaks and the hanging Spanish moss cast filigree shadows like spiders' webs.

The plantation homes, gleaming in the sunlight, were splendid from Good Hope to Belle Pointe to Golden Grove. Before 1790, in St. Charles Parish, Pierre Trepagnier had built Ormond, with its ten-foot galleries facing the Mississippi River, another object of Lovingsworth's coveting. The property was later purchased by another family, many of whom were swept away by another scourge—Bronze John, the yellow fever.

Ignoring all scourges, the mighty Mississippi rolled past Bayou Lafourche, Bayou Plaquemine, and the city of Baton Rouge. Just a few years before, it had created and then abandoned False River. It curled around Tunica Bend like a sleepy cat, contemplating New Cut Off in order to shorten and leave behind Old River. It received the waters of the Red River and ignored Impassable Swamp and Dismal Swamp. Oozing past the southwesternmost corner of Mississippi, it gave Fort Adams in Wilkinson County a reason for being. It received the floods of the Homochitto and permitted the existence of a Lake Mary. It gave the city of Natchez its place in the Mississippi sun. The big river shaped and reshaped the lives of a people and their polyglot civilization.

The symphony of wildlife sounds echoed along the main channel and out on the bayous, deep in the Achafalaya. The great blue heron, the Louisiana heron, and the great egret thrilled Cynthia, for she had never seen such splendid creatures. By night the bullfrogs croaked their throaty bass notes, "Too-Deep, Too-Deep," the insects hummed, and the rattlesnakes shook their horny rings. Whenever the riverboat stopped at a levee after sundown, the evening études merged the mysterious "hoo-hoo-h-h-h" of the great horned owl and the saddened "coo-coo-o-o-o" of the mourning doves with the fluttering epilogue of the passenger pigeons, and the child who had left Southwark far behind knew she would never return there. She was becoming a young woman and discovering a wonderful and tragic new country.

The songs of the slaves, heard against the backdrop of the puffing of steamboats heading in both directions on the Father of Waters, lent a deep, mysterious, melancholy quality to the river's music. Cynthia silently watched the trafficking in slaves on the lower decks or on the landings the boat came alongside. She could not sort out slavery. It was a deep puzzlement within the young girl's budding sense of morality. No matter how those who practiced slavery might try to rationalize it, Cynthia was as bewildered as any creature looking through the last door of the abattoir. Surely slavery was not tolerated in Kentucky, surely not in Lexington, which the captain so often called the Beautiful City. Everything would be different once they arrived in paradise. There'd be neither black nor white—there'd be *people*. Cynthia had been neither schooled nor conditioned for prejudice.

Abigail stayed on board when the *Thomas Jefferson* docked

at Natchez. She'd heard enough stories about the dangers Under the Hill—the drinking, thievery, whoring, and hellraising on the landing beneath the cliff where Natchez perched—and she had neither the will, the desire, nor the strength to walk up to the picturesque city, even though civilization there was closer to the life she knew and loved. While Abigail slept deeply, the captain and Cynthia went for a stroll, the one acting as a shield for the other. As long as it was daylight, and as long as they avoided arguments with any Kentucky riffraff, they stood a reasonable chance of surviving the mayhem. To the child, the frontier city was raw and primitive and devoid of graces. Even the captain felt intimidated by the angry, murderous behavior. The Isle of Dogs was paradise compared to Natchez's Under the Hill.

The *Thomas Jefferson* completed the 632-mile journey from New Orleans to Memphis at an upstream average speed of nine miles an hour. It took four days and part of a fifth, allowing for stops, and by this time the arduous nature of the pilgrimage had made itself plainly felt.

Abigail might have insisted that they disembark, find a southbound boat, and return as soon as possible to New Orleans had it not been for the thought of cholera knocking on their front door in the Vieux Carré. Even though she'd used her last laudanum, she knew there was no turning back. The only choice was to stay ahead of the epidemic. She was as frightened as she'd ever been in her life. Either way, the journey was madness. It was crushing the life out of her sagging body. She continued to revert to childish thoughts, haunted by the memory of her mother's final days as softening of the brain changed her speech from lively patter to disobliging mumble and finally to nothing at all.

At night, lying in his bunk, a cup of brandy never far from his lips, Captain Lovingsworth wished he were back aboard the *Cynthia Anne,* taking on a better kind of passenger, a wealthier kind without the scourge walking around as if it were wearing pirate's boots and a cocked hat, indeed, swaggering around as if it owned every moment and all the world too. He missed his midnight chats with the first mate of the rats. The rats: precious little trouble, asking for so little. Why couldn't people be as unselfish? Why couldn't human beings be as intelligent as rats? There was no excuse for it. People should figure things out. They should solve problems. They should survive. The human race should not die.

James Henry refilled his cup from the nearby decanter. He mused that the mortal remains of the marvelous Lord Nelson had been returned home in a barrel of brandy in order to preserve them for burial in St. Paul's. They'd pickled the son of a bitch.

Moreland. Thomas Moreland. Where are you tonight? Why aren't you here to knock on my door and bring me news from steerage? Why were *you* not more careful? You should not have died. You should not have been prayed over and sent to the bottom of the ocean. You have no business being down there. You should be with me. I cannot be a good captain without a good first mate. Don't you know that? Come back! Do you hear me? Come back and instruct the helmsman to turn around. No. We should not be turning back. That would be stupid. Oh, Tom, Tom, sweet Tom, you should never have let the cholera overcome you.

Sylva, most wonderful Sylva! What are you doing in a convent? That is no life for you. It is *wrong!* One so beautiful and talented has no business being locked up with a bunch of stupid nuns who don't understand the first thing about making a man happy. When I return to New Orleans, I'm coming to take you away from that terrible place. And I'll tell you what I'm going to do, Sylva. I'm going to make you an honest woman. Yes, I am. You will see. You will be *only* for me. All is finished with Abigail and me. I can see that. It is not her fault. It is not my fault. It is nobody's *fault*. Goddamn it, why are we always ladling the blame? You yourself said, there's no one to blame for this and to blame for that. There is nothing left between Abigail and me. We are finished. But for you and for me, Sylva, there is eternity, and I will give you everything I have, I promise. Please do not smile as if you don't believe me. I am telling you the *truth!*

Suddenly, the captain was awakened by the shouts of the crew making the *Thomas Jefferson* secure at Memphis. It was a reality he did not appreciate, for he was feeling the magic of Sylva so intimately that he was nearing the supreme moment of his dream. "Son of a bitch," said Captain Lovingsworth as he blinked his eyes and realized that he was alone on his side of the canopied honeymoon bed and Abigail was nearby, alone on hers, the two of them, each irreversibly alone.

Cynthia Anne had drifted in and out of sleep. From her bunk, during the predawn hour she heard crew members shouting orders and hurrying fore and aft. When the fearsome whistle blew three times she leaped up and ran to the pilothouse. "Where are we?" she yelled.

"Memphis town, little darling. Big old cotton picking, cotton baling, cotton shipping Memphis town," said the pilot.

Cynthia whirled and ran back to the honeymoon cabin. "Captain, Captain," she shouted, without thinking to knock, "they say we've arrived at Memphis. Could we go ashore for a little while? Please? Didn't you say we could see all the exciting places? Yes, you did. You said that. So you better be getting up, and Miss Abigail, you'd better be getting up too. We're at Memphis! Just think! Another big city where I've never been before."

"I never thought we'd make it this far," said Abigail, struggling to arise. "I mean, I never thought *I'd* make it this far. James Henry, help me. If you expect me to get off this danged old boat, you've got to help me up. You've got to steady me. Please don't let me fall, James Henry. Will you promise me that you will not let me fall? That's a good boy. Now take hold of me,

James Henry, so I can get to the slop jar. It's the least you can do."

They didn't go ashore in Memphis. The *Thomas Jefferson's* captain, Edward Tolliver, and pilot, Sam Dorsey, were eager to take on passengers and cargo and head quickly up the last 234 miles to the mouth of the Ohio. "What you're going to see farther on will make up for not going ashore, little darling," said Sam to a pouting Cynthia Anne. "We're going to steam around the big loop called the Kentucky Bend, and I'll show you where a little more than twenty years ago there were all these bodacious earthquakes. I mean, jugful big'uns. Why, they lasted for a year and whole towns were swallowed up, and the course of this big old river was changed. Why, my daddy, he had to learn to find his way all over again. And you know what, little darling?" said Sam. "One of these times God's going to get mighty upset about all the carryings on down here, something or other, and he's going to send another bunch of earthquakes and plenty of folks are going to be swallowed up. Swallowed up whole by the biggest whale of water you ever did see. And what do you think about *that?*"

"I think," said Cynthia, "I'd like to see it. Do you suppose, Mister Sam, you could point out the places where some of those towns used to be?"

"Why, you're a mighty spunky young lady, and I don't mind showing you at all. I'll even let you take the wheel when we pass around Kentucky Point. That's right across from New Madrid."

Cynthia Anne spent most of her time in the pilothouse, learning the names of the Kentucky tributaries to the Mississippi—Obion Creek and Bayou du Chien—and she marveled that there could be so many people moving up and down the waterways. Why were they so restless? Were they forever running away from one scourge or another?

"Mister Sam, there goes another one," said Cynthia to the pilot.

"Another boat? Sure is, if I ever did see one."

"Another boatload of slaves," said Cynthia.

"Heading south, little darling, heading south."

"Why?"

"No market for the rascals up north. Leastwise, not yet."

"Rascals? Why are they rascals?"

"Born that way. Fit for nothing much. Have to take care of 'em."

"Why not take care of each *other,* Mister Sam?"

"One of these days, maybe. Might have to fight a war over it, though. Say now, who's side you on?"

Cynthia watched the *Homer Jones* slip by the *Thomas Jefferson.* She gazed for an instant, although it seemed like an awfully long time, deep into the silent faces of the children lining its rails. She thought of calling to them, even thought of swimming to them, but it was only a heated and perplexing thought. She bit her lower lip and kept her eyes fixed straight ahead.

At the confluence of the two mighty rivers, the Mississippi and the Ohio, Sam Dorsey directed the *Thomas Jefferson* up the Ohio fork to Cairo, port of entry to the magnificent valley curving almost a thousand miles to Pittsburgh. Destined to become a major depot for Union forces during the Civil War, Cairo, in 1833, was an inevitable frontier settlement with a commanding vantage point overlooking the sloughs of western Kentucky. The *Thomas Jefferson* navigated only on the New Orleans to Cairo run, though on special occasions it might go as far as St. Louis.

After the landing at Cairo, Sam Dorsey grabbed his traveling bag, shook hands with Captain Edward Tolliver and, looking for the last time at Cynthia, said: "Going to miss you, little darling." With that he was down the ladder to the main deck, across the gangplank, and through the crowd on the dockside, hurrying to meet his woman, to take his usual of venison and his lodging for the night at the Riverboat Hotel. Cynthia waved goodbye until he was out of sight.

There had been little time for pleasantries between Memphis and Cairo on the part of Captain Tolliver, even for someone as noteworthy as Captain James Henry Lovingsworth, his wife Abigail of Kentucky and Louisiana, and their charming young lady, Miss Cynthia Anne Ferguson Lovingsworth of London, England. The exchange of a gold piece from one captain to the other, however, made the awkwardness a bit more manageable.

"So long, old top," said Captain Tolliver after the *Thomas Jefferson*'s lines were secured and the watch was set for the day. "I wouldn't mind taking you all on up the Ohio, but we don't handle the falls at Louisville too well," he laughed, "especially in drier times. You'll find yourselves a good packet here, and before you know it, you'll be cutting up past Paducah, Henderson, Owensboro, Louisville, Cincinnati—homeward bound to Maysville for certain!"

"Thanks, Captain," said James Henry. "You've got yourself a fine piece of machinery here. 'Course, it could use some sails. Let me know if you ever come to your senses, and I'll be there to show you how it's really done. In fact, I know where there's a damn good sailing ship that might be had for the asking."

"Right, Captain. Tell you what. Next time I'm in the mood to go over to London to check out the wine and the women, I'll look you up. I'll sign on as your first mate," laughed Tolliver. "You can show me everything I need to know."

"Got yourself a deal. Only right now I don't have a ship. Do I?" asked James Henry as he fumbled absently inside his pockets, a blank look spreading over his face. The *Cynthia Anne*, full sails straining with North Atlantic winds, boomed across the captain's memory like black clouds heavy with water.

"Are you all right, Captain Lovingsworth?" asked Tolliver.

"I gave my ship away, *didn't* I? Or did I let the sons of bitches *steal* it from me?"

"Why, I don't know. Let's hope not. Let me help you ashore," said Tolliver, gently taking James Henry by the elbow.

"That's what I did. I let the bloody sons of bitches take it away from me." Pitched high like a woman's voice with a tone as disconcerting as it was surprising, Captain Lovingsworth's laugh was almost hysterical.

"First Mate," said Tolliver to the officer standing on the quarterdeck, "let's help this fine family if we can."

"It wasn't my fault that all those people got cholera and died, *was* it?" James Henry asked the first mate.

"Whataya mean 'all those people got cholera and died'?" exclaimed the first mate, backing away.

"I didn't have any business agreeing to let the *Cynthia Anne* be hauled into a museum. Why did I *do* that, Captain?"

"It's going to be all right, Captain. I'll help your wife. Easy, ma'am, there's a step up right here. Don't catch your toe."

"It was that son-of-a-bitching doctor from Lexington that did it. I knew I never could trust him. And then my first mate deserted. He went and died of the cholera."

"Cholera? Wait a minute. That's the second time you've said *cholera!* Were you captain of a cholera ship?" recoiled Captain Tolliver, drawing back his hand from Lovingsworth.

"It was desertion, that's what it was. It was mutiny, and if I ever get him back, I'm going to make Tom Moreland fly from the gibbet, the good-for-nothing son of a—"

"Captain—" said Cynthia with a firm grip on his shirt-sleeve. She squeezed down hard. "It's going to be all right. We have to go now. Please help me with Miss Abigail so we can get ashore." Cynthia purposely looked at the retreating Captain Tolliver. Every day she felt a little more as if she was the one in charge.

Their departure from Cairo the same day on the packet *Kentucky Lady* canceled the possibility of spending the night ashore. That would have been most difficult for Abigail, who could hardly stand unassisted. James Henry, in no mood for unnecessary delay, had rushed arrangements. On the 377-mile journey to Louisville, the packet's captain, Daniel Wiggins, was able to maintain a steady and slightly faster speed than the *Thomas Jefferson.*

"Ten to eleven miles an hour," responded Wiggins to Lovingsworth's question about the packet's capability.

"Thought it would be faster," said James Henry.

"Did?"

"Well, you don't have as strong a son-of-a-bitching current as on the Mississippi."

"True," said Wiggins, scratching the seat of his pants and looking off to Cumberland Island sliding by on the starboard side. "The old Mississippi, back yonder, gets about two-thirds of its outflow from the Ohio. Plus, you've got the currents of the Tennessee and the Cumberland rivers and what you've got is one tricky piece of goddamned navigating business, Captain."

"Just thought I'd ask," said James Henry, doubtfully, "don't mean to be nosy."

"That's all right. Don't blame a horse that's heading for the barn."

Warming to Wiggins's obliging Kentucky manner and his earthy speech, James Henry said, "Lot easier to get down the son-of-a-bitching Ohio than it is to go up it, I'll wager."

"Yessir, that's a goddamned huckleberry over a persimmon," said Captain Wiggins, again scratching his backside. He had a rash there that wouldn't heal, and scratching it was one of his major pleasures. He bit off a hunk of chewing tobacco and continued, "Now this here Ohio River may have struck them fancy French explorers, them *coureurs de bois* as they liked to call themselves, might have struck *them* as La Belle Rivière." Captain Wiggins took his time before using his brass spittoon. "As far as I'm concerned, it's a goddamned muddy stretch of snags."

Lovingsworth laughed. "Damn sure wouldn't want to drink from it."

"You do, you might come up with a serious case of shits," said Wiggins. "Might develop a case of the Kentucky crud."

"What's the Kentucky crud?" asked James Henry.

"Sudden rush of shit to the heart," said Daniel Wiggins, concluding with a volley to the spittoon.

"See here, how long's this trip going to take?" Lovingsworth persisted, returning to his first line of inquiry.

"From Cairo to Louisville—let's see—two to three days. Good thing we got the new locks around the Falls, though."

"How's that?"

"Takes most of the gamble outta getting past. Used to be, you got low water, you ain't going to *get* through. The *Kentucky Lady* fits into the new locks—barely. Three years ago we'd be hung up 'til the river rose. Locks too small to take big boats. Had this here *Lady* built to fit." Wiggins spit.

"How long from Louisville to Maysville?"

"Oh, from Louisville, say, it's 113 miles to the mouth of the Great Miami, this side of Cincinnati. Then to the mouth of the Licking River on the Kentucky side. Another forty-some-odd miles to Augusta—now you take Augusta, that's as fine a little place for trading as you'll want to find between here and the Gulf of Mexico—we'll stop there for mail and passengers. Then it's less than twenty miles on to Maysville—add it all up, I'd say, oh, better part of five days total *if* we're lucky and don't have no breakdowns or run into no bastards who don't know their ass from a hole in the ground."

"Son of a bitch!" said Lovingsworth, stomping his foot.

"Hold on!" said Wiggins, "What's the matter? Main thing is we're going to get you there. Don't mean to be personal, but how's your missus?"

"She's tired of being on paddleboats and so am I. We've also got a girl with us that has to be looked after."

"Why don't we all have a ration of calf's head and a jugful of white lightning to wash it down after the sun drops? It'll be on me," said Wiggins.

Lovingsworth nodded assent, clapped Captain Wiggins on the shoulder, and said, "I'll ask." Retreating to the small cabin reserved for very important passengers, James Henry felt cornered and helpless in the face of mounting odds. When he entered the tiny living space, he found Cynthia sitting cross-legged at the foot of the bunk, combing Abigail's hair.

"What do you think, Captain? Doesn't Miss Abigail's hair look nice?"

Abigail was blissfully silent until James Henry spoke: "Captain Wiggins has invited us to have supper with him. He mentioned calf's head and white lightning. I told him I'd ask."

Abigail looked at her husband and serenely replied, "No, James Henry. No, I'll stay right here. I'm enjoying this too much."

"I'll stay too," said Cynthia.

"You have yourself some man-to-man talk," said Abigail. "Cynthia and I will be just fine."

"Just send us a little something civilized for Miss Abigail and me to eat. She doesn't need much, and I don't either," said Cynthia, cheerfully smiling.

"Don't go and get drunk and lose your temper, James Henry," cautioned Abigail.

Lovingsworth suspiciously eyed Cynthia and said, "You watch what you say while I'm gone."

She blew him a kiss.

After the captain left the stateroom, Abigail decided the time had come to act. "Cynthia Anne, you and I will have our own little secret."

"About the nice lady?"

"Oh, heavens, who cares about that? I wish only the finest for her. It is you, my dear, that concerns me most. I want to provide for you. And I will. Please find me something to write with."

Cynthia spotted a quill on a pull-down desktop and brought it and a small bottle of ink to Abigail, who had removed the banknotes from her unmentionables. "I'm signing these precious pieces of paper over to you, child, and you must never mention them to the captain."

"What are they?" asked Cynthia.

"My inheritance, is all. Banknotes purchased by my father when I was a child. They could be worth lots of money. I have no use for them. They are yours. Hide them. Don't spend them." Abigail's hand trembled as she signed her name twelve times.

"There have been no known cases of cholera on the *Kentucky Lady*. None on the *Tom Jeff*, I'm hoping," said Captain Wiggins, spooning up a generous amount of calf's head and directing it into his mouth. After chewing and swallowing he used the back of his hand to wipe his mouth, crooked his little finger and, from between his teeth, dug out a strand of something resembling meat. He placed it inside his mouth and swallowed.

"Too much talk about cholera, it seems to me," said Captain Lovingsworth as he looped the jug over his shoulder and let the burning glory of the white lightning descend his gullet, the effect of it reaching his fingertips and the soles of his feet. Wiggins's black servant took the jug and set it before his master.

"Can't say as I agree," said Wiggins. "We've been getting reports of people dying from New Orleans to Pittsburgh." He drank from the jug, belched, then continued. "The dying and the stories of suffering are enough to make you wonder if we might be heading for the end of creation. What do you think about that, Captain?"

"I think people like to talk," replied James Henry, studying his trembling hands.

"You ain't eating much, my friend. Tobias here, he knows how to boil up a mess of calf's head, and he knows exactly how I like the brains fixed. But that ain't all. Tobias," said Wiggins to the black man, "fetch my friend a piece of the bread you made special for me."

"Yassah, Mr. Wiggins," said Tobias, slicing a generous chunk of bread and setting it before Captain Lovingsworth. The slave stood back and watched both men for the slightest sign of needing something.

"Now, way I hear it, the biggest concentration of the goddamned epidemic is in the major ports—New Orleans, New York—and that's where we have all these goddamned immigrants coming in."

"That's true."

"Why the hell don't they stay where they come from? We got enough problems without them making it worse, especially if all they're going to bring with 'em is the goddamned cholera."

"Couldn't agree more," said Lovingsworth.

"Why, last year alone, I'm told, there's been a right smart slew of dying from cholera and yellow fever in New Orleans, no telling how many boodles in New York City. Around the world?" Wiggins dipped his bread in calf's head gravy and slid it into his gaping mouth. "Who knows? More than likely we never will know. But I'll tell you this much—it's plenty bad and getting worse."

James Henry dabbled with the food on his plate. "Do you suppose," he said, "you might have somebody take a little something to eat to my wife and child in our cabin?"

"Well, Lord God, why didn't you say so? I'm a damned fool for not thinking of it first. Tobias, round up a couple of plates and take it to the captain's family."

"Yassah, Mister Wiggins."

"Before you go, make sure we ain't about to run out of shine. If we're low, we'll need to find some more first thing."

"Yassah, Mister Wiggins."

"You've probably been just about everywhere, Captain. Is it true that conditions in Russia are as bad as they say?"

"Never been to Russia."

"Tobias, before you go, hand me that letter from over there on my desk. That's the one, right there. Pick it up and hand the goddamned thing to me."

"Yassah, Mister Wiggins."

Captain Wiggins snatched away the letter and handed it to Captain Lovingsworth. It was a copy of a letter written in London. "Just look ahere what this preacher feller told his congregation. See, it's a copy of a letter, which has been circulating over here up and down the river. This Phelps feller said it was written from Russia. Go ahead, take a look at it and tell me it ain't bad all over the goddamned world."

Captain Lovingsworth unfolded the letter and read:

Business of every kind is at a standstill, the bank has suspended its operations, the shops are shut, in the market not a whisper is to be heard, the streets are nearly abandoned, and the gloom is only heightened by the few solitary individuals who are seen walking about with slow melancholy steps, and holding handkerchiefs to their faces to prevent infection, as the air is full of impure odours. The number of funerals is from 480 to 500 a day, and at one time about a thousand were buried in a large sandpit, for want of graves, which could not be dug so fast as required.

With similar scenes occurring in England, the cleric warned: "Every mind should dwell with most serious and deep-searching inquiry upon its own state of soul and body, and with true and heartfelt humility search out all those secret sins, and lament over all those public transgressions which have so justly incensed and provoked our offended God to visit us with His wrathful displeasures."

"Well, what say you, Captain?" asked Wiggins, shoveling a final spoonful of calf's head into his mouth.

"I say it's time to be at home in Kentucky."

"Yessir, but I'll tell you now, there's cholera just about everywhere, and once the Almighty sets His mind to it He's apt to track down ever' last one of us that has gone out and played the fool. Now that's just how I see it, Captain. I could be wrong but I doubt I'm very far off the goddamned mark. You ain't *sinned*, have you, Captain?" Wiggins laughed and took two more swallows of white lightning.

Lovingsworth felt uncomfortable. He thought about his sins, and they troubled him. "Captain Wiggins, if you don't mind I'd like to turn in for the night. Thank you for your hospitality."

"And thank you for your company. Hell, I don't know what we're headed for. I've got a few more years here on this goddamned river and when I'm finished I'll be satisfied just to be planted somewhere along the way."

On the rest of the journey Lovingsworth stayed out of the pilothouse, and he refrained from joining the gamblers at the card tables. He spent hours at the railing of the *Kentucky Lady*, alternating sides, watching the debris float by on the muddy water. He slept fitfully, dreams of Sylva recurring with stirring effect. After each of her dances of love he was left with a feeling of weak abandonment. Sylva seemed to provide a release from everything that bound him to earth, the peeling away of his layered mortal distress. It was mental transport, bodily rapture, a lifting up from the muck of disease and corruption.

Cynthia was all over Captain Wiggins's smoke-belching steamboat, from stern to bow, including the pilothouse, of course, where she was again allowed to take the wheel with both hands and pretend she was actually steering through the narrow channels. In the evenings she sat, quietly mesmerized by the low moaning of the slaves in their below-deck heapage. "Go Down, Moses" was a song that troubled Cynthia's soul. She did not know why. She combed Abigail's hair, brought her warm water for washing, and offered her food, which went mostly uneaten.

The days continued to be suffocatingly humid, and the nights were almost as oppressive in the tightness of the Ohio Valley. Abigail languished and relapsed into deeper wishes that she'd remained in New Orleans and taken her chances there. The captain abandoned all hope of reviving her, and each time he went to her bedside he expected to find her expired. When he looked at her, he could not help but remember those youthful nights in the Vieux Carré when Abigail Bracken was the belle of the ball, one of the most sought-after damsels in a culture that delighted in the bacchanalian.

At 11:30 on the morning of June 1, 1833, the deckhands of the *Kentucky Lady* threw out the mooring lines and tied up at Maysville, one of the busiest ports on the Ohio, a collecting point for southbound shipments of tobacco, iron, bourbon, and slaves. The trip from New Orleans to Maysville had taken nine days—a hot and unforgiving eternity, especially to Abigail who had no more laudanum and no hope of finding any. The rainbow that suddenly arched upon their approach to the Maysville landing appeared to Cynthia as a sign of promise. She did not see it later flatten into leaden clouds that blackened and moved up the river as the frontal system of a new storm.

Washington, Kentucky

June 1833

Lost Angel of a ruin'd Paradise!
She knew not 'twas her own; as with no stain
She faded, like a cloud which had outwept its rain.
                    —Percy Bysshe Shelley

BY THE TIME OF THEIR ARRIVAL at Maysville, Abigail was virtually on her deathbed. She had remained in her cabin through most of the grueling ten-day journey. She was able to walk only slowly and haltingly across the gangplank with the careful assistance of the captain and Cynthia. Abigail's shoulders were slumped forward, and with a twisted linen handkerchief she caught some of the water flowing from her eyes. When she wasn't fast enough, she dabbed the corners of her mouth. It was mortifying to a gentlewoman who had lost all dignity in her latter years.

"James Henry, why am I being punished? What have I done to deserve this?"

"Now, Abigail—"

"Have I sinned? Name me one sin I've committed. All those times you were gone from me, James Henry, was there one time when I sinned?"

"No—"

"I could've. I thought about it. But I never *did* it. Octoroons, indeed. *Lagniappe,* of course. Oh, yes. Oh, yes."

"Miss Abigail," said Cynthia.

"What is it?"

"You are as beautiful as you ever were."

"You lie so well. Out of the mouths of babes come little bitty lies."

"No. I am not lying."

"Like cheap beads thrown to the crowds along Canal Street. Oh, how I dreamed when I was your age, dreamed of being queen of the ball. Oh, to wear a mask again and to let myself *go!* Listen to me, child. When I'm dead and buried in these awful clothes, I want you to take what's left, the rest, the trinkets, the comb and the sachet, the perfume and the folding fan, and I want you to *use* them, for goodness sake."

"Miss Abigail—"

"No, let me finish." Abigail whispered to Cynthia when the captain turned to look for a coach. "Those twelve state banknotes are in my overnight bag. Last night, when I endorsed over to you, I said to myself, someday this child is going to return to N'Orleans, but I know I never will. These notes may in time be worthless; on the other hand their value may have considerably increased."

"When I say you are as beautiful as you ever were, I mean *all* of you. I mean the best part of you," said Cynthia.

"Look at him," said Abigail as James Henry returned. "Look at our captain, our Jean Lafitte."

As he approached, Cynthia saw an expression of deep doubt, perhaps guilt, on the captain's face.

"He could be king of anybody's dress-up dance," said Abigail, bitterly. "Big and strong. *Joie de vivre!* Full of himself. Look at him!"

James Henry, miserably trapped, felt a deadening sensation across his chest. Cynthia patted him on the arm as Abigail gathered what remained of her strength.

"He's ready to go out and whip a whole jungle of tigers. Look at me. A baby tiger could eat me alive." She began to cry again.

"Now, Abigail. We've had a long, hard trip, but there's only a little farther to go. Just a day's ride in a stagecoach down to Lexington. Just a—"

James Henry and Cynthia caught Abigail before she hit the ground. They revived her with smelling salts, rested for a while, and then moved on to seek temporary shelter, at least for the night.

To their dismay, the normally bustling town was experiencing the panic of many other cities on the Ohio and Mississippi Rivers: "Cholera's coming! Cholera's coming!" shouted the people as they scurried for safety. The mayor of Maysville had already succumbed to the disease. With bewilderment, the Lovingsworths stared at the scattering crowds. It was not the reception they had expected upon finally setting foot on Bluegrass soil. Where was the loveliness? Where was the peace and quiet? How could such a thing as this disease have come so far? Were they not running fast enough? James Henry called out to the driver of a stage wagon, because there were no coaches in sight for the short ride to the county seat.

"We need a ride up to Washington," said James Henry.

"People in Hell want ice water," said the driver, a boy in his teens.

"Will you take us there?" demanded the captain.

"Cost you."

"Young man, I know it will *cost* us. But it'll cost you more if I climb up there and whip your ass."

The driver looked at James Henry and decided it would probably be worth more to provide the transportation than to get into a fight with such a gnarled-looking old beast.

"Climb up," said the youngster, sullenly. "I'll take you for a dollar a head."

James Henry helped Abigail gain her footing on the rear plank of the wagon. Cynthia climbed up and gave the teenager a scolding look, and the captain threw up the three bags and climbed aboard himself. The wagon had no springs to help smooth out the bumps, and there were no backrests, so Abigail fell over into James Henry's lap. The three-mile ride up the hill to Washington jostled and punished her to the depths of her being.

She was dying.

Upon their arrival at the courthouse, built in 1794 by a Baptist preacher who was also a master stonemason, Captain Lovingsworth paid the driver three dollars and helped Abigail and Cynthia climb down to the dusty road. A woman standing in the door of an inn across the way, watching the awkwardness of the three travelers as they looked about for anything that might offer a friendly face, a place to rest, and some nourishing home-cooked food, hastened to the visitors and threw out her hand in greeting: "Welcome to Washington, Kentucky. My name's Sarah, and I run this little establishment here. You can spend one night or as many as you wish. Wouldn't want you to stay for the rest of your natural lives, now would I? On the other hand, might be willing to consider it. You all just come on in this house and I'll draw your bath water and fluff up the pillows and add some more meat to the stew pot. I can tell, what you need more than anything else is a good night's sleep, and I, Sarah Bartholemew, will see that you get it."

"Lord, God," said Abigail, "I never thought I'd see another honest-to-goodness human being again as long as I lived."

"What be your names?" asked Sarah.

"I am James Henry Lovingsworth, formerly of Lexington, and this is my wife, Abigail, also formerly of Kentucky, and this is Cynthia Anne Ferguson Lovingsworth, formerly of England.

I was captain of a sailing ship recently arrived in New Orleans. We consider that city to be our permanent home, although we're on this excursion here to see about buying some land in Kentucky and maybe a nice house on it."

"My, my," said Sarah Bartholemew, "we haven't had celebrities in town since General Lafayette came through in '25. Might say, we haven't recovered from it. Our most recent visitors," sighed Sarah, reaching for the guest register just inside the front door, "were some young do-gooders from Cincinnati. See here—Mary Dutton and Harriet Beecher. They were in a considerable muddle about our slaves. I told them until they came up with a better idea for dealing with these wretched people, we'd go on handling them the best way we knew how. Don't you agree? You aren't abolitionists are you?" Sarah laughed.

"Hell, no," said Captain Lovingsworth. "Do we look like it?"

"Well, no, meant no offense, but you can't be too careful these days. Now then, Captain Lovingsworth and Abigail and little Cynthia, did you say? Just put your names down here for the record. You can mark after it 'Not Abolitionists' if you've a mind to. Separate you from those do-gooders. Say you're all the way from New Orleans and England, and who knows where else? Now, you all just relax and make yourselves to home and I'll take care of all the rest. By the way, hate to ask," said Sarah looking at Abigail, "you all haven't encountered any cholera along the way, have you? Personal, I mean?"

"You should've seen how bad it was aboard ship," began Cynthia.

"Oh?" interjected Sarah Bartholemew.

"What she means is, we did have some trouble on the sea voyage to New Orleans, but we cleared quarantine, and as soon as we saw how dangerous it was in the city, we headed in this direction."

"Well, you look just fine to me," said Sarah, but looking

again at Abigail, added, "My dear, I can tell you've had a really awful time of it."

"I'll be all right," Abigail whispered.

"You need rest. You truly do. I'll see that you're in a nice bed afore you can say, 'Sarah Bartholemew.'"

It seemed odd to James Henry that Bartholemew's Inn did not lurch and wallow in the churning waters of a system of rivers. But that evening, after a supper of browned and simmered pork tenderloin, green beans cooked with squares of fatback, collard greens, corn pudding, and thick wedges of cornbread well drenched with sweet country butter, all washed down with cool apple cider, he had an especially fine Sylva dream. But it still troubled him to think of her in a convent of virgins. Surely the tradition of the founder of the Order, whoever in Hell she was, would discover Sylva's true nature and cast her out to the devils of the Vieux Carré. She would not be able to conceal the truth. How could she? "Jezebel" was written all over her pretty face.

Cynthia felt as if she had arrived in the Promised Land. The air was so much cleaner in Kentucky than in New Orleans. There was a peacefulness that could hardly be described—perhaps because the village of Washington, unlike the wharves of Maysville, Cairo, Memphis, and New Orleans, was so uncluttered and uncrowded. Cynthia wondered how many residents of Washington and Maysville had fled to the countryside, putting as much distance as possible between themselves and the advance of cholera. Whenever the word "cholera" was whispered, much less shouted, panic ensued and reason vanished.

Early on the morning of June 2, 1833, Abigail "faded, like a cloud which had outwept its rain." Death came mercifully shortly before sunrise. She'd been dreaming of home in New Orleans and home in Kentucky, of home somewhere on the face of the earth, of clear water flowing brightly. She was no longer fearful. The passing over was effortless; for the first time in months there was a peaceful expression on her face. There was no time for remorse, no reason for tying together any loose ends. Her last thought had been the words from her youthful Vieux Carré nights: "If ever I cease to love—"

When Abigail's body was discovered, Sarah Bartholemew reacted quickly and with authority. "Captain," she said, looking at Abigail's covered form, "I don't know why she died. I have no earthly idea why she did. I'm assuming it was not cholera, but we don't know for sure, do we?"

"No, we don't."

"Do you have any idea what might have been the cause?"

"She had not been well for some time—the last year or more, actually, or so I'm told. She was just worn-out."

"I see."

"The trip up from New Orleans took every ounce of strength she had left."

"There was cholera on your ship, I believe you said?"

"Yes."

"I see. Well, the important thing's to get her buried as soon as possible."

"Yes. You are right."

"I suggest that we get the grave dug, *immediately.*"

"Do you have a shovel?"

"I do. And I have a man who'll do it for you. No man should have to dig his own wife's grave. Cynthia, go outside and don't come into this room again until I tell you it's all right."

As soon as the grave was dug in the open field behind Sarah Bartholemew's backyard, Abigail's body, covered in a winding-sheet, was placed in it and John, the black slave, shoveled in the dirt. Then he propped the end of the shovel beneath his chin and waited.

"Gracious Heavenly Father," Sarah prayed, "send your richest blessings upon this your daughter. Take her soul into your mansion on the hill. Watch over this her husband and this her adopted daughter. Be with them in the days ahead. Protect us all with your loving grace. And we will do well to remember to give you all the honor and the glory. Amen."

Sarah turned to James Henry and took his hand. "Do you have anything you'd like to say?" she asked. He shook his head and drew his forearm across his eyes. Sarah dropped to one knee and spoke softly to Cynthia. "Dear, would you like to make a little prayer?"

Cynthia pursed her lips and tucked her head to one side as if tilting one ear, the better to catch a thought. Then she looked to the sky. "Please, God, while you're watching over us, could you try to be a little nicer?"

Sarah Bartholemew frowned as if stung by a bee. She looked with bewilderment at Cynthia.

"Miss Abigail loved you." Cynthia went on. "I think she loved you a whole lot. She hardly ever asked for anything."

Sarah took a half-step back and stared, wondering what else would come from the mouth of this peculiar child.

"I bet you love the captain. Maybe you know what's good for the captain," Cynthia blurted with the force of Grandpa Charlie at the Billy Goat Strut.

James Henry shifted his weight from his left foot to his right and looked at Cynthia, her face wizened in the early morning light.

"You could make it better for us, if you wanted to, isn't that true? Now that you've tortured Miss Abigail into her grave, why don't you—"

James Henry seized Cynthia's arm and tried to drag her with him toward the house. She stumbled and in that instant from a hedgerow came the piercing sound of a rabbit's scream, signaling ultimate distress.

"You're hurting me!" cried Cynthia as she wrenched herself away from the captain. She ran back to Abigail's grave and dropped to her knees. She made the sign of the cross. James

Henry heard the child pray: "What sense does it make for people to be born only to die? Why, many times, do good people die while bad people live? I'm only asking. Please don't punish me for asking. Soon I'll be thirteen years old. I want to understand. I want to know. Why are there so many scourges?"

That night in Bartholemew's Inn, James Henry Lovingsworth sat at the window of his bedroom. It troubled him that he and Cynthia Anne, sleeping in another room, were so alone and distant. He reckoned that the odds of ever seeing Sylva again were next to none. He knew the time was at hand when he would have to leave Cynthia Anne. He wondered what would become of a young girl so gifted. For the first time, thoughts of gold and silver seemed strangely petty. Horse farms and tobacco fields and distilleries seemed far away and unanswerable to many questions: What *really* mattered? Where was *true* wealth? What was the real meaning of being in bed with a woman? Captain, first mate, ship's doctor, the lowliest person in steerage—where were the differences that counted when all was said and done? The final resting place—did it matter how it was marked? Shouldn't all ship captains go to the bottom of the sea? Or whatever water they spent their lives on?

There was a knock on the door. "Captain, are you all right?" asked Cynthia Anne, contritely.

"Yes. I'm fine," said James Henry.

"Then, I'll see you in the morning," she said, "I'm going back to my room at the end of the hall. Miss Abigail told me I could have her personal things, but I thought you might like to have the little fan you gave her."

"You can have it. Take it all. I don't want anything that was hers."

"Yessir," said Cynthia. She returned to her room.

Lovingsworth reached for a piece of stationery left by Sarah Bartholemew for the convenience of her guests. He dipped a quill into ink and wrote a final note. It could have been to

Cynthia Anne. If not she, perhaps Sylva. If not Sylva, then the message would be for anyone who found it. It was his final statement. Writing it only once, changing not a word, he signed his name and placed it inside an envelope. On the flap he appended eight words.

Paris and Lexington, Kentucky

June 1833

. . . the epidemic made its appearance among us, and up to this time there have been nearly eighty deaths out of a population of about 1200. We must too take into the account, that as soon as it broke out, our citizens began to fly, and nearly every family who had it in their power left the place. Under the circumstances of the case, we believe we can surely say that in no place in the United States has the Cholera been more fatal than in Paris.

—W.C. Lyle

THE RIDE IN THE CHARTERED Concord stagecoach on the old Buffalo Trace from Washington through Paris to Lexington was a jarring, lurching trip lasting, with one change of horses, from sunrise to sundown. The driver's surly behavior and the frequent blasts of his bugle must have been annoying in the best of times, and these were certainly anything but that. Cynthia's shoes, which Lou Belle had provided from one of Abigail's closets, pinched her toes, and Captain Lovingsworth was deep in a thicket of confusion mixed with both grief and undeniable re-lief that Abigail was gone so quickly. He stomped his foot re-peatedly on the stagecoach floor. He could barely tolerate the notion that the driver of the coach considered himself the cap-tain of the passage, while he, the real captain of his ship, was now as lowly as if he were in steerage.

He glared through the window. How could this terrible thing be? Abigail had been aging, that was a fact, so rapidly that her once beautiful body had become increasingly fragile. Her firm breasts of days gone by had long since lost their vigor, but her voice had kept its silky, southern tone, and her eyes had still flashed at a moment's notice. She'd once been as warm as Sylva, and certainly more than the captain's better half. She had been his only claim to civilized grace and delicacy. Without Abigail, he was probably a direct throwback to his father, the Tom Cat. Memories of the father's meanness produced ambivalent im-pressions, accounting for stubbornness, insensitivity, and occa-sional spiritual longings.

There'd not been enough time for his mother to have much influence on him. James Henry Lovingsworth had been shaped by the winds blowing from New Orleans to Land's End, Lon-don to Calcutta. His first school, after the flatboats on the Ohio and Mississippi Rivers, had been the Isle of Dogs on the River Thames. From there he'd moved on from the Limehouse dis-trict to the East India Company. The lessons had been hard, but he had soaked them in as naturally as breathing air. He had grown to become a more moderate edition of his raw and treach-erous father. But James Henry was capable of compassion, and from time to time it got the best of him.

"Where we going?" asked Cynthia.

"We're going to Lexington."

"What is there?"

"Probably more dead people," said the captain, ruefully.

"Why are we hurrying in that direction?"

"For old times' sake," he answered.

"Will we be warning those still in the city?"

"They know. If they don't have sense to leave, they deserve what they get."

"Then why are we going there?"

"Good question. I don't have an answer," he said, trying to hide himself in the collar of his coat.

Cynthia struggled to remove her high-buttoned shoes. It was a relief to rub her feet together and look out the window on her side of the bouncing coach. The green, rolling country-side of the Outer Bluegrass began to remind her of Oxfordshire. There were fewer hedgerows, but there were many sturdy trees, and the winding waterways feeding the north fork and the main channel of the Licking River were delightful to view from atop the hills. The clouds were solid puffs of whiteness connected by strands of blue; Cynthia began counting the times the tall trees poked through, like an artist's hand pointing at a canvas. She quickly lost count. She thought of adding one more tree, pos-sibly two planted at the gate to *her* place, her home of homes. After they passed through the Knobs to the Inner Bluegrass, she began to see some small flocks of sheep, though not nearly as many as in England. The roofs of the houses were not thatched, but there were occasional stone walls built strikingly like those in England. Cynthia wondered if some of her ancestors had pre-ceded her here. She wondered if she'd have the strength to grapple with stone to build enclosures for sheep and cattle. Cynthia watched farm roads leading away from the national highway to unknown ghostly villages where the small popula-tions, like Elizaville's, were either scattered or unsuspecting vic-tims of the scourge of Heaven.

"Captain," said Cynthia, "do you still plan to buy a place here?"

"What's that?"

"Do you still plan to buy a farm in Kentucky?"

"No."

"Why not?"

"I don't have to have a reason."

"It is very pretty. Said you were tired of being aboard ship, even as captain. Said you were tired of it. Said you—"

"Did I say all that?"

"Yes, you did."

"Well, I've changed my mind. I'm going to Lexington one more time. We're going to find a place for you to live, and then I'm going back to New Orleans. I have no business being here. It was all Abigail's idea," James Henry lied. "She had friends here. I have nothing. No youth, no ship, no money—"

"I thought you were wealthy."

"A few pieces of gold stand between me and the poorhouse. I damn sure can't afford to keep you."

"You mean, I'm not adopted anymore?"

"You never were adopted in the first place. Didn't you understand that? I've done all I can do for you."

"What do you mean?"

"You can't go back to England. You can't tramp around the world with me. New Orleans is no place for you."

"That means I have no place."

"We'll find a children's home for you. Maybe we'll find somebody to take you in. That would do."

Cynthia jammed the shoes back on her feet and resumed her stare through the coach window. Tears welled up, and she wiped her nose with the back of her hand. The jolting of the large wheels made her cough. The infernal bugle blasted again as the coach, with two fresh pairs of horses, lunged southwest from Blue Licks. For a while, Cynthia could not stop either coughing or crying. A sharp pain in her chest reminded her how the sufferers of cholera had usually reacted in the first stages of the disease. They had vomited violently, but at this moment, overcome with grief, Cynthia felt more threatened by abandon-

ment than by cholera. She remembered something her grandfather Charlie had told her once when a hornet had stung her:
"It'll hurt for a little while, but it won't hurt forever. Grit your
teeth. Keep on going. God has given you more sense in your
little finger than he's given a hornet in his entire being, stinger
and all. You'll never have more pain than you can endure."

"Do you know *anybody* in Lexington," Cynthia fretted.

"Played with a boy named Solomon," the captain replied.
His eyes widening, he watched the village of Millersburg come
and go. Where were the people? The strange feeling that he
would not be traveling this road again left him dizzy with the
sensation of spiraling down into a whirlpool of memory. It was
accompanied by the damnable rapid beating of his heart.

"That was ancient history, and I don't know why, of all the
people I've ever known, Bill Solomon would come back to
haunt me," the captain said under his breath. "Yes, haunt me,
the son of a bitch. That is all he could possibly be good for. Why
is that, anyway? Why is there this haunting business? This
double-dealing guilt business? Why doesn't God just go on and
deal a straight hand? Why does He employ these jokers, these
Solomons with their long, sad faces?"

"Did you say something?" asked Cynthia.

"No. Nothing at all. Talking to myself about Bill Solomon."

"Was he *wise?*" taunted Cynthia, taking small pleasure in
another fleeting remembrance of her grandfather, who sometimes hummed a merry tune with words he resurrected from
the Old Testament. He called it, "Solomon, me Lad, and his
many strange women": "And he had seven hundred wives, princesses, and three hundred concubines: and his wives turned away
his heart," sang Grandfather Charlie, devilishly, as the court
jester of the Billy Goat Strut.

"Bill Solomon? *Wise?* He was so dumb we used to play
plenty of tricks on him. You could tell him almost anything,
he'd believe it."

"Did he have seven hundred wives, princesses, and three hundred concubines?" sang Cynthia.

"What are you talking about?"

"Oh, just remembering Grandfather reading some of his favorite parts from the Old Testament. He liked to *sing* the Bible."

"Well, don't sing it to me."

"Were you cruel to your friend?"

"Who?"

"Your friend Solomon."

"I didn't say he was my friend."

"I thought you did. It doesn't matter," said Cynthia, resuming her stare through the stagecoach window. She remembered how children in Southwark had made fun of her because her hair was short like a boy's and she could recite long poems. Grandfather Charlie's constant recitations found a new life in Cynthia's mind. She wondered if it might not be possible to remember every line and intonation of all the authors alive in the mind of one Squire Charles. When she did well in her studies, the other children teased. She wondered why children were so cruel. She wondered why grown-ups were so cruel. She reasoned it was because children grew up to become adults. They continued the practice of cruelty. And some of the lads grew up to have seven hundred wives and three hundred concubines.

"Captain, did you ever have a *concubine?*"

"Good God! Where do you come up with these things?"

"Well, what *is* a concubine? Can they be nice ladies too?"

"How the hell would I know? A concubine is kind of— another kind of—wife, maybe. Hell, I don't know."

"An extra wife?"

"Maybe."

"One isn't enough?"

"Young lady, you are a prissy piece of plunder. And it's going to get you in plenty of trouble."

"Captain, why are you being so nasty to me?"

"The thanks I get for taking you out of steerage! I save your life, and you call it being nasty."

"Isn't it nasty and cruel to adopt a child and then, when things don't go exactly right, turn the child away?"

"I'm not going to argue with you. We're going to Lexington because I want to look at it one more time. I have no intention of ever returning. We're this close. Abigail would want me to look at the place; I want to look at the place. That's all there is to it."

"And, your friend, Mr. Solomon, will you see him?"

"Not likely. Probably dead and buried."

"If he's alive, he might let you borrow one of his concubines," said Cynthia, gibing.

"Keep it up, Cynthia Anne. Just keep it up!"

"Do you plan to pay a call on Doctor Hanover's family? That would be a nice thing to do."

"They've probably all left the city. They have money. They can afford it."

"Why did you not like Doctor Hanover?"

"Too smart for his own good. Like somebody else I know."

"How can that *be*? I don't understand."

"You don't understand what?"

"How anybody can be too smart for their own good?"

"Cynthia Anne, you ask too many damn questions, and you're smart-alecky to boot, and one of these times somebody's going to straighten you out."

"Captain, I am now twelve years old," Cynthia asserted, becoming increasingly agitated and annoyed with the curtness of the captain and the driver.

"And?" scorned the captain.

"The catechism we learned in school said, before the age of seven we are not held responsible."

"Is that a fact?"

"But, after that time, we begin to grow spiritually."

"Not interested in Christian claptrap," said the captain.

"Grandfather Charlie had his own version of the church's rule. He said we're always in a state of grace and we ought to be on guard against anybody who would mess with our innocence," said Cynthia, looking straight ahead.

"Is the sermon about over?"

"I'm five years past the age of knowing right from wrong, Captain."

"So, that gives you a license to sass your elders," the captain said, matter-of-factly.

"No."

"Sounds like it."

"Captain, tell the driver to stop. I want to get out."

"What do you mean, you want *out?*"

"I have to piss."

"For God's sake," said Lovingsworth, leaning around from his side to make himself heard to the driver. "Stop the coach so that this girl can step outside and relieve herself."

"Jesus," blurted the driver. "I'll just be Jesused. Whoa, horses. Hold up here so's a little darling can go squat. How in the name of God we're expected to be anywhere on time with a lot of people running around shaking the dew off their lilies is more than I can figure out, no way, no how. Whoa, horses! Damn it, I said, Whoa. While we're at it, why don't y'all cut loose too? Let's just all sit here and piss until we float away *together.*"

Cynthia climbed out of the coach and found a small clearing a short distance from the road where there were no blackberry briars. Lowering herself to the ground, she watched a small bird with two black bands across its breast making a high-pitched cry, furiously flapping its wings, as if injured. Just to her right, she spied the nest of four baby birds. When Cynthia finished, she rose silently, returned to the coach, and unperturbedly said to the driver, "Thank you, *kind* sir." She was in no mood for any toffee-nosed talk from drivers *or* captains. If Grandfather Charlie were still alive and kicking at the Billy Goat Strut, he'd be banging his tankard for Diggery to bring him another stout. She wodden 'er grandfodder's nipper fer nuttin'!

"Anytime, anytime," said the driver to the woods flanking both sides of the road. "Get up, hosses! We're good 'til her bladder fills up again. Anybody else needs to go, just ring my bell. I'm right here. At your service. I said, get up, hosses! We gonna get *in*to Lexington, we gonna get *outta* Lexington. Can't tell about nothing no more."

Cynthia did not hear the driver talking to his horses; she was focusing her attention on Captain Lovingsworth, who was wearing a look of exasperation and mustering his usual high-handed attitude. He was about to find out that a well-announced piss could represent quite a turning point.

"Captain, I *was* a child. Then I lost my parents in steerage. You said you were adopting me. Now you say you're *not* adopting me."

"That's right."

"So now what am I? Shepherd's pie?"

James Henry glowered.

"A young girl, maybe? Or am I a young *woman,* a twelve-year-old young *woman*? Does that sound about right?"

"Cynthia Anne—" the captain snorted, trying to interrupt.

"I have left my country. I have no way of returning, even if I wanted to. I have no choice but to go forward," she said, biting off the words and again looking straight ahead.

"Cynthia Anne, you—"

"*You* are going back. That is *your* choice."

"Damn it, *you* listen to *me*—"

"You see, Captain, we're all in this thing together, aren't we?" said Cynthia, stiffening her legs and studying her upturned shoes. "But whenever something breaks apart, like a family, for example, then it's up to each person to be strong. Go it alone and be strong."

"I've had enough of this."

"No you haven't." She whirled. "Let me finish. This may be one of the last times we can talk. Since you are throwing me out, I've a right to speak my mind."

But before she could continue, the driver's bugle sounded for Paris. The stagecoach rumbled over James McLaughlin's Cotton Town Bridge spanning Stoner Creek, and the bugle reverberated again, causing pigs, chickens, and a few stray dogs to scurry to either side. Up the hill, around the courthouse, to the front steps of Burr House, the driver reined in his horses. They were lathering heavily and chewing on their foam-covered bits. The hot spume rolled from their lolloping tongues, and their flanks quivered.

The situation in the seat of Bourbon County reminded some local ministers and their scattered congregations of the coming of the apocalypse. Businesses shut down. Carpenters could not keep up with the demand for coffins. Bodies must have been placed in shallow graves, because a putrid odor permeated the village. Doubtless the living had fled to the countryside.

"Going to be here exactly ten minutes. Better relieve yourselves and be back aboard when the time is up. Going to wait for exactly nobody," said the driver as he looked around and felt threatened by the empty street in the hot, desperate summer of 1833.

"Listen, whippersnapper," said Captain Lovingsworth, "you ain't got call to be ordering nobody around."

"Sir, I weren't born in no woods to be scared by no owl. Now, you chartered for Lexington. And, as I see the unraveling of the thread, my job is to get you and your little hellion there, if the cholera don't get us first or if she don't drown us in little girl piss. You wanna fool around here in this sorry town, fine with me. This coach's leaving Paris in ten minutes. You not on board, you one gone coon. You done wasted two minutes being huffy."

As soon as the captain and Cynthia had used the privies, they immediately returned to the stagecoach and took their seats, the captain still fumbling with the buttons on his pants. He held a copy of *The Western Citizen* under his arm. The newspaper contained lists of the names of the victims, but nothing about cholera was front-page news.

The driver gave a bugle blast at precisely the moment he had promised he would, waved the reins over the lathered backs of the two pairs of horses, and guided them up the last eighteen miles to Lexington. Cynthia would remember it as the last time she talked in any meaningful way to Captain James Henry Lovingsworth.

"Captain, will you please listen to me?"

"I'm listening. But it won't do any good."

"I just want you to listen."

"I'm listening."

"Thank you for bringing me this far."

"Thank *me* for saving you from steerage," said the captain, mordantly.

"You're going back, you say. Fine. The way I see it right now, I'm going to stay, no matter what."

"Cynthia Anne—"

"I have nothing to go back to. My mother and father are gone. Grandpa Charlie is probably gone. I have nobody but myself. It looks like that's going to have to be enough."

"Listen to me—"

"I may find a home, or I may not find a home. All I know is, I have *myself*. Maybe I'll be able to adopt somebody or something."

"Wait a minute—"

"For the first time in my life, I'm going to ask myself, 'Cynthia, what do *you* think? What do *you* want to do?'"

"What do you mean?"

"You were the captain of the *Cynthia Anne,* but you're not

the captain of *me*. The driver is the captain of this coach, but he is *not* the captain of you *or* me."

"Hold on, now."

"We're our own paddlewheels. Did you hear what I just said?" Cynthia yelled up to the driver of the stagecoach.

"Have to piss again?"

"I said, we're our own paddlewheels," yelled Cynthia.

"Jesus," said the driver, "deliver *me.*"

James Henry Lovingsworth looked at Cynthia, then pulled her to his side. She huddled close to him and remained there until the driver sounded the bugle at the edge of Lexington, but the end of the journey produced no cheer. The sound of the coach's creaking wheels and the whip's cries to the horses were like the heralds of Hell. What the captain and Cynthia began to see was anything but paradise. Most of the living had disappeared from the north side of the city. There was no reason to believe that it was different in any other direction. By far, more coaches were heading out of town than coming in, and deserted city streets in broad daylight were foreboding. The grounds of Transylvania University were empty. From there to Main Street the town looked as lifeless as Pompeii. Grass was beginning to grow wherever it was not trampled by the pounding of hooves and the weight of commercial traffic. In a few minutes the wheels of the stagecoach rolled to a dusty, disconsolate stop in front of the Phoenix Hotel on the corner of Main and Limestone. As soon as he saw the captain and Cynthia step down from the stagecoach, the driver pushed their baggage to the ground and lifted the reins. A family pleaded for passage away from the city, but the driver refused.

"No sir, and no ma'am, this coach's whip ain't accepting no more passengers for no amount of money. These hosses are tired. They're headed for a rest. I don't know where, but *out* of here."

"But, don't you see, we have no other way? We are all well.

We are not sick. But we fear for our lives. Please take us to the country. Anywhere, but just away from this place," begged the man.

"Keep looking," said the driver. "I don't know you, and I don't know whether the plague is *on* you or *in* you or all around you. All I know is, I ain't got the scourge, and I don't aim to get it. So, good luck and goodbye."

"Hold on!" yelled the captain, grabbing the bridle of the lead horse.

"Stand back!" snapped the startled driver.

"Gold!" boomed the captain, waving his small leather pouch above the horse's head. "Gold!"

"What? Whoa, there!" ordered the driver.

"Hear me out! Take this family back north on the trace. Leave them in the country. Take some of these gold coins for your trouble. It's a safe bet." The captain produced from the pouch several half eagles and offered them to the driver.

"How many do I get?" asked the driver, leaning down.

"Ten half eagles ought to keep you warm this winter."

"Make it twenty."

"Ten's what it is. If it's not worth fifty dollars to take these good people out of this godforsaken place, it ain't worth a damn thing. Take it or leave it."

The driver took the money and barked an order to the family of four. "All right, you heard what the captain said, climb on board, and let's get the hell *out* of here."

The mother kissed the captain, and the father shook his hand. The two small children, who had never ridden on a stagecoach before, scampered inside as soon as the door was opened. The captain helped the man place their two suitcases in the baggage rack. When the doors were slammed shut, the driver blew the bugle out of nothing more than habit and whipped the horses for the start as he was accustomed to doing. It was his main claim to importance.

"God bless you," called the woman, as the coach made a tight turn left, then right, and rumbled out of sight up normally congested but now deserted Limestone Street. The vainglorious blasts of the bugle and the unnecessary snapping of the whip faded in the distance.

The captain turned, took Cynthia by the hand, and entered Postlethwait's Tavern in the newly constructed Phoenix Hotel. The inn was empty. Chairs were pushed back from tables. Empty glasses lined the bar.

"Anybody here?" boomed the captain.

There was deathly silence. A slight echo petered away.

"I said, anybody *here?*" shouted the captain, who'd always disliked silence when he made an inquiry.

A black boy peered around the corner of the oak bar. He looked like a rabbit, frightened and alert. He wanted to run, but experience told him to stand still and not move.

"I'se here," said the wide-eyed youth, quivering.

"Come here. We won't hurt you," said Lovingsworth. "But, listen, Hoss, where is everybody?"

"They's all gone. The sickness done come. I wants to go, but I gots no way. I don't wants to be sick."

"What's your name?" asked Cynthia.

"Jem," said the boy.

"Jim?" asked Cynthia.

"Yassum. Jem's what they calls me."

"Are you sick?" asked the captain.

"Nawsir, I ain't sick. I's fine, 'cepting I don't wants to be here by myself. They come and they takes away Marster Posselways. He dead when they come for him. King Solman, he comes and carries off several in a wheelbar. The King been right busy, he has."

"Bill Solomon?" said the captain, a smile appearing on his face.

"We calls him the King, that's all we niggah folks calls him.

He one big white man. He been living with Aunt Shawlette round the corner here."

"Do you know where he is at the present time?"

"Spec I do."

"Well, then, Jem, why don't you come with us and take us to King Solomon?"

"S'pose I could. Onliest trouble with that is, he spends most his time at the burying place, and I don't think too much of the burying place."

"You'll be as safe there as you will here," said Cynthia. "C'mon. I need a friend. Don't be afraid of the captain, don't be afraid of me, don't be afraid of anybody, you hear?"

"Trouble is, I'se a free niggah. Me and Aunt Shawlette is free niggahs s'porting one another. That mean trouble, most usual."

"Well, how's about it if I adopt you?" asked Cynthia.

Jem halted in his tracks. He look incredulously at Cynthia. He cocked his head and said, "I'se black. What you talking about, 'dopting me? I ain't never see no white person 'dopt no black person. I seen 'em *buy* lots. I never seen 'em 'dopt any."

"Well, we'll break the rules," said Cynthia, snapping her fingers, "just like that."

"You's white, I'm telling you. You can snap your fingers any time you wants to, but I has to be careful how I snaps mine. You can't 'dopt me."

"All right. We'll pretend you're my slave."

"Don't want to be nobody's slave."

"I said, we'll *pretend.* Nobody'll know the difference. Come on, Jem, as far as I'm concerned, you'll be my brother."

"Now I *knows* you crazy."

"Anybody asks, I'll say you belong to my family. How's about that?" asked Cynthia.

"Jem," said the captain, "just come with us, and we'll take good care of you. You won't be a slave but you damn sure won't be a brother either. You'll just be *with* us, and nobody will know the difference."

"Yassir."

"Take us to the burying place. I want to speak with King Solomon."

"This way," said Jem. The captain stowed his and Cynthia's bags behind the bar, and the three went outside to Main Street. The only signs of life were scurrying rats, chattering like their distant cousins on Borough Road in Southwark.

"The lovelies of Lexington," sardonically muttered the captain under his breath.

Jem led the way up Limestone to Third Street. Stores were closed and abandoned. Lavish parties planned for the popular Mill Street establishment of Monsieur Mathurin Giron had been hurriedly postponed. The racing of Thoroughbreds had been rudely disrupted. One of the busiest parts of town, which included the tracks of the new Lexington and Ohio Railroad, was deserted.

The captain and the two children turned right toward the Old Burying Ground. When they arrived, it was growing dark with shadows. A macabre mound of bodies lay at the entrance, only a small measure of all those dying throughout Lexington. Cynthia took Jem by the hand and held it tightly. He closed his eyes.

"Follow me," said the captain. They walked into the burying place. The stench was stomach turning. The captain covered his face with a handkerchief. Cynthia and Jem went to the old stone fence, where they threw up. When they were finished, they stumbled after the captain, who was standing by a pine tree. Dirt was flying from a shovel flashing from an open grave. Lovingsworth walked to the other side and watched a Goliath of a man digging furiously, as if driven by demons.

"Bill?" said the captain.

There was no response.

"Bill Solomon?" asked the captain.

There was no response.

"King Solomon?" yelled the captain.

The huge man rested on the handle of the long shovel. "Don't you see I'm busy?" he said.

"Yes, I know you're busy. But do you remember me?" asked the captain, squatting down next to the open pit.

Solomon looked up toward the face of Lovingsworth and squinted against the light.

"No. Am I supposed to?"

"No reason why you should. I'm James Henry Lovingsworth. We were boys together a long time ago. Now do you remember?"

King Solomon wiped his face with his bare right arm. He peered at the captain for several moments and then looked back into the grave he was digging. He did not appreciate being interrupted when he was engaged in his profession. All his adult life, William Solomon had been a digger. He specialized in basement and cistern excavations, but he did not sidestep requests for outhouse holes. Gravedigging, on the other hand, was a higher calling, and Bill Solomon accepted the challenge with a reverence that brooked no nonsense. When it was time to dig a grave, that became his obsession—a reliable, steady habit.

Without replying to Captain Lovingsworth, Solomon shoveled out more spadefuls of dirt speckled with shards of limestone. He spotted what seemed to be an arrowhead, and he dropped to one knee to pick up the relic. Amused, he held it close to his right eye, his better one.

"You see here," said Solomon, "this here's something. This here's a piece of a man's work. He chipped it just so. Then he used it for a purpose. Might have killed a squirrel with it. Most people today don't give a tinker's damn about such things. But I do."

Captain Lovingsworth, Cynthia, and Jem fastened their

attention on the King as he climbed out of the completed grave. He sat beneath the tall evergreen, and while he rested he rubbed his large thumb around the edges of the arrowhead. He held it between his thumb and forefinger and stretched it out toward the setting sun. "A piece of a man." He drew it back and rubbed it on his pant leg, then held it again to the sun's rays. The stone glinted faintly.

"Jem, who are these people?" asked King Solomon, removing a small bottle of Ole Wildcat from inside his raggedy shirt.

"Lord, Mastah King, I don't know. They comes into Posselways and they wants me to take 'em to you and that's exactly what I does."

"They want a grave dug, I reckon? Or two? Or three?" asked Solomon as he twisted the cork from the bottle, eyed the contents, and took a swallow. The liquor must have burned, then soothed his gullet wonderfully well.

"Bill," said Lovingsworth, "Bill, I'm your old buddy, Jimmy Henry. We don't want any graves dug. You remember, we used to play together when we were boys along Town Branch?"

"Did we?" asked the King, taking another enormous swallow.

"Remember the time we turned the outhouse over? With old Miss Ashbrook still in it?"

Solomon tipped the bottle again. A slight smile of recognition stole across his huge face. He drank once more, and this time a complete picture might have returned. "I remember the time you and a bunch of your raggedy-assed friends had me climb up a tree to bring down a coon, and you all started chopping down the tree."

"Now, we was just having fun with you, Bill, that's all. Ain't that right? Just having some good clean fun. See here now, this town's in a helluva mess."

"Is that a fact?" Solomon belched.

"I want you to lay down that shovel and get out of here before you catch the cholera. I'm heading back to New Orleans, and I want you to go with me, man."

"What do I need to be going to New Orleans for? You want a drink?" asked Solomon, holding the small bottle out to Lovingsworth.

"I've got this ship. I had this ship. No, I've got this ship, because it's all mine. I'm the captain of it. I've lost my wife. I've lost my first mate. You're the man for the job. I'll make you rich. And you won't ever again have to dig a grave or an outhouse. The job is yours. I'll take a drink."

"What job?"

"Being first mate, damn it all, Bill Solomon," said the captain, choking for a few moments on the fiery liquid. It burned into his throat and a sensation of indigestion flashed across his chest.

"My job is here. I ain't going to no New Orleans. You may not be going either, come to think of it. Take another drink and give me my bottle back."

"What do you mean?"

"I mean, you done returned to Lexington. And guess what?"

"What?"

"You're the one up the tree to get the coon. Watch out I don't start chopping down the tree."

"Is that a fact?"

"Never mind. You just might not be a-leaving Lexington. You just might catch the cholera, same as ever'body else. Ain't that right, Jem?"

"S'pose it is."

"I may be digging the captain's grave. Then whose coon'll be up the tree? What I want to know is, who's going to dig King Solomon's grave?"

Captain Lovingsworth looked at the bottle and took a

short snort before handing it back to Solomon. Cynthia and Jem giggled. She took a small stick and stuck it between Jem's toes. He pulled back in astonishment.

"What you doing there?" Jem exclaimed.

"I'm checking the condition of your feet. I want to know if you're fit for running. Can't have no slave with bad feet. Might have to run from ghosts. Never can tell!" Cynthia burst out in peals of laughter.

"Stop that! You playing with me! You shouldn't be doing that."

"Oh, go on. Can't you pretend anything? You're no fun at all!" Cynthia pouted.

The children's banter and King Solomon's warnings made Lovingsworth feel like a helpless hammerhead in a steel-meshed whaler's net. The time he'd spent a season on a whaleboat had convinced James Henry that definitely it was a lot more agony than it was worth. The opening of the trap had been Maysville. Drawn in by the sudden death of Abigail, the all-day stagecoach ride to Lexington, the confrontation with Cynthia, and now the Old Burying Ground with bodies piling up faster than even King Solomon could lay them to rest—Captain Lovingsworth felt his life's circle tightening. Soon, a harpoon would puncture his brain, and his blood would fill the net, and he would suffocate and drown.

"Jem, who's this little girl?" asked Solomon.

"She say she owns me."

"Owns you? Now, just a goldarn minute. You're free, Jem. Like Aunt Charlotte's free. Like I'm free. And I reckon this young lady girl is free too, ain't she? And the captain, he's free. We're all free. What do you mean, she *owns* you, Jem?"

Jem looked puzzled. He studied his feet. "Said she do."

"Sir, my name is Cynthia Anne Ferguson. I don't *own anybody*."

"Wouldn't think so," said Solomon.

"I was joking. I could never say I own somebody and be serious about it."

"Wouldn't think so," repeated Solomon.

"I came over from England with my parents on the captain's ship. My mother and father, they died of cholera. A nice lady persuaded the captain to take care of me. He and his wife left New Orleans for Lexington to see about buying land up here. She died on the way. She was a very tired, good lady who just lay down and died."

"I'm sorry," said King Solomon.

"Now the captain is talking about going back to the sea. Look at him. He's out of his mind. He wants to find a place here for me to live. I've already told him, he wants to leave me, then leave me. I'll find my own way. I can do it." Cynthia began to breathe rapidly. "The first person we met was Jem. He just looked like *he* needed a home too. So I said he could be my brother. But he says he doesn't want to be my brother. The captain says he *can't* be my brother. So I said he could be my slave. He said he didn't want to be a slave." Cynthia was beginning to choke with emotion.

"That's right," said Jem.

"I don't blame him. I wouldn't either. He just looked scared, and I was only trying to help him. That's all. I would never *own* anybody. The captain knows—"

"Enough!" blurted the captain. "Enough, damn it!" The harpoon was slanted downward at a relentless, unmerciful angle, as unerring as a pistol at close range. James Henry's heart surged. There was a heavy pain, but it passed.

"Hold on, Captain," said King Solomon, "remember, you're in my tree now."

The captain felt a momentary stay of execution. "What?"

"There's important work here. Make you a deal. Help me get more bodies from the front gate, help me lay them out in their graves, and I'll talk to you about going to New Orleans.

We'll drink plenty of Ole Wildcat while we work. See, the trouble here is, Captain, that we're at the bottom of the grave ourselves. You might call it Hell, Captain."

"The preachers say it's the wrath of God, punishment for all our sins," said Cynthia.

"They can call it whatever they want to call it," said King Solomon. "They don't know what the hell they're talking about, but whatever the trouble is, we're in it and there may be no way out of it. Now, we can be cowards and cut and run to New Orleans, or we can stay here and do what we can for these innocent folks who have died."

"Tell you what—" said James Henry.

"Tell *you* what, Captain. Take hold of that wheelbarrow there and follow me."

Captain Lovingsworth moved mechanically. He knew that he'd lost control. He felt as if at any moment the spear would break open his brain and a gaff would bring him aboard for the knives to cut him up into small pieces. He was thrashing in water in the worst nightmare of his life. Ole Wildcat seemed to be helping him some, though, working in his veins, giving him courage. The wooden handles of the wheelbarrow were sticky and stained with human stench. Following King Solomon to the entrance of the Old Burying Ground, Captain Lovingsworth felt drawn down a long, slippery path.

"See if you can help me load up three bodies at a time," said Solomon calmly, as if asking a carpenter's helper for pieces of wood. "Use that child's body there for some balance in the middle. Be careful you don't spill 'em out. Take your time bringing them over there where I'll be digging. When you get tired, set the barrow down, easy. Try to make one trip do it without spilling anybody out. It's worse each time you have to handle them. You there, Jem, you and the gal who says she owns you but says she don't own you, says she's your sister but she ain't your sister, whoever in the hell she is—you all try to stay out of the way."

"We want to help," said Cynthia.

"Do what?" asked Jem, tucking his chin down closer to his chest, his eyes rising to the tops of their ebony lids.

"I'm going to help. And if all you're going to do is to act scared, then you ought to get on back to the place where we found you."

Jem gawked at his bare feet, but he hurt all over from his eyes to his toes.

"Look here, Jem, we can cover up faces, that's the least we can do. We can straighten out clothes a little bit. If there are any eyes that are open, we can close them."

"Ain't closing no eyes for nobody."

"Oh, you're just a little sissy, Jem, that's what you are. Just a little sissy. These people are dead. They can't possibly hurt you. They need us to do right by them. The important thing is to keep your fingers away from your mouth. That's what the good doctor and the nice lady said aboard the ship after my mother and father died. She put her arm around me and held me tight, and she said, you do what the doctors says, you keep your fingers away from your mouth. That's exactly what she said."

As Captain Lovingsworth plodded along, pushing the wheelbarrow weighted down with the bodies of two adults and a child, he remembered Sylva's knock on his cabin door. It had been after midnight. The *Cynthia Anne* was booming along to the south of Bermuda. The winds were fair and the moon was full. The face in the moon was distinct. The captain had fed the rats and watched them scamper appreciatively back through the small hole in the bulkhead. He had spoken at length with the first mate of the rats and had wished him continued good sailing—protocol set firmly in tradition. Being the captain of one's own ship was as lonely as it was difficult, and loneliness was what Captain Lovingsworth was feeling when the soft knock sounded on his cabin door on that moonlit night—the night that haunted him now, each memory adding an undeniable ache.

"Who is it?" demanded the captain.

"Sylva," the voice replied, as serenely as a female gull gathering ocean breeze so as to climb a little higher toward Heaven.

"What do you want?"

"I wish to speak to you about pleasure."

"You what?"

"Do you understand? Pleasure is what I wish to *give* you."

Captain Lovingsworth slid from his rack, pulled on his breeches, and opened the door.

"Hello," said the prostitute, in the softest tones of a voice honed in recent years to achieve its best effect. "I'm here," she purred, as confidently as a goddess.

"Oh, to hell with it and come in," said Captain Lovingsworth.

He had known many prostitutes. He considered most of them to be dedicated to their profession, the way a first mate handled his crew, the way a seaman handled the lines when coming into port. Of course, there were bad prostitutes, truly bad ones. There were inept ones. There were stupid ones. There were clumsy ones, dirty ones, diseased ones. They were fairly easy to spot. The bad ones were also dishonest. They giggled and told stupid lies, laughed and robbed you of your last halfpenny. Some of the bad ones were dangerous criminals. Some had connections to the underworld, straight to the heart of Hades. The bad ones were a central part of a community of crime, could get you killed in a heartbeat. At the same time, they could be killed as quickly. Their lives were fragile and brutal, but Captain Lovingsworth did not care about that. They got what they deserved. He did not consider the possibility that a prostitute might be intelligent, educated, a member of a once respected family.

"You stowed away, I presume," said Captain Lovingsworth.

"Not at all," said the prostitute. "I came aboard as personal secretary to the Reverend Daniel Christian Goodman, may his soul rest in peace."

"He is one of the cholera victims?"

"Yes. And a good man he was, Captain, though I realize he was a burden to you."

"I never gave him a second thought."

"In reality, he was a burden to himself. That is the way it is so often, Captain. Men are a real challenge. They need pleasure, the kind a woman can give. The Reverend Goodman was a tormented soul. I tried to help him."

"You did?"

"I really did. I was able to give him a little happiness, which I am sure he had never known before. It is very simple, Captain, is it not?"

"What is very simple?"

"Giving and accepting pleasure."

The words penetrated Captain Lovingsworth's psyche like a sturdy, well-sprung arrow. "Depends. Don't trifle with me. I've had prostitutes in my cabin, and I've had them in their little rooms administered by their big, fat madams and assisted by their smelly little pimps long before you were born. So, tell me, what are you offering that's any different and what's the price?"

"All right. I can tell you are not an ordinary man. So be it. I respect you for your strength and your character. What am I offering?"

"That's what I asked."

"I am here to worship at your throne. I am here to dance for you. I am here to give you an ultimate experience. I have special oils to anoint you. When we are finished, you will be so good as to tell me if you have not had an unbelievable deliverance. The terms? Simple, or as complicated as you wish, depending upon your definition. I want no money. I want no gold or silver. I want no clothes or precious perfumes. I want no future commitment to me. I am yours for pleasure this one time, or for as many times as you want me or need me during the rest of the voyage."

"I have a wife."

"Doubtless. She is probably beautiful. She is probably loyal and very intelligent. She probably has a maid to do her bidding. She probably does charity work. When she has had nothing else to do, she has probably waited on you, hand and foot. If you wish to remain true to her, of course, that is your choice. I can return to steerage and leave you here to think of your beautiful, dutiful wife. I have nothing but respect for her."

"So what is the deal?"

"All right. The deal—the arrangement—is that you become the guardian of one child in steerage—"

"Son of a bitch—"

"—the one the old woman brought to you, but you turned them away. You sent them back to steerage without even inquiring as to the child's *name*."

"I'm not going to adopt that child for all the whores in or out of Heaven."

"Even if her name is Cynthia Anne?" asked Sylva with a sudden cant of her magnificent head.

"That child's name is *Cynthia Anne?*" asked the captain in bewildered disbelief.

"You don't have to adopt her. All I'm asking is that you give her safe haven."

"Her name is *Cynthia Anne?*"

"That's right. Can you imagine such a thing? Such a coincidence? Such a beautiful happenstance?" asked Sylva, flouncing her hair.

"My wife and I are going to Kentucky."

"Wherever you're going, it will cost you very little to watch over one child, one child out of all the children suffering down there in that hellhole. Especially if her name is Cynthia Anne. Take her with you. Find a home for her. She'll become your good luck charm. She'll be a damn sight more helpful to you than the figurehead on this ship."

"And you?"

"Let me off in New Orleans. Let me live my life the best way I know how. I will always be able to find work. There's no telling what I might accomplish if I really put my mind to it. You see, Captain, I am proud of what I do, for I do it superbly, if you don't mind my saying so myself. I think—in fact I am sure—by sunrise tomorrow you will agree with me. All delicious things will be yours in exchange for the saving of one child, one *Cynthia Anne!*"

"And for that you will 'worship at my throne'?"

"Yes."

The captain bit his lower lip and moved his tongue across the top of his mouth. He looked at the woman and knew he'd be stupid to send her away. He did not think about his wife's possible forgiveness. He did not think about Abigail at all. In fact, he stopped thinking altogether. He was like a stag in the woods during breeding season; the scent of musk was overpowering. He began to throb with desire. Yet wisdom told the captain not to be in a hurry. Experience told him to relax and enjoy what was coming.

"Stay the rest of the night," said the captain.

"And the child?" asked the prostitute.

"Bring Cynthia Anne to me tomorrow," replied the captain, taking his seat of sovereign authority in the celestial chair reserved for him by virtue of his hierarchical rank.

"How do I know I can trust you?" asked Sylva.

"How do I know I can trust *you?*" asked the captain.

"I am a whore."

"I am the captain."

"We are even," said Sylva, as she began to undress.

The captain looked at Cynthia, who was talking earnestly to

Jem. The boy had begun to accept her attentions. They stopped when the captain staggered with the wheelbarrow. Even a single body was an awkward cargo; three bodies at a time were more than the captain could manage. When he raised up the handles and moved forward once more, Cynthia and Jem kept in step. From time to time, when the arm of a corpse fell over the side and dragged the ground, Cynthia would place it back in the wheelbarrow.

"You see, Jem," said Cynthia, uncertainly, "there's really not a lot to dying. And there certainly is nothing to be afraid of. When you're dead, you're dead. Did you know that, Jem? When you're dead, you're dead as the tallest tree cut down."

"Yassum," said Jim, doubtfully.

When they arrived at the grave King Solomon was digging, the captain set the wheelbarrow down.

"Won't be long," said Solomon. "I just need to get a little more dirt out of here, and we'll be ready. I'm running out of time to dig a personal grave for everybody. Unless, you want to give her a try? You could do that, and I could go look for another bottle of Ole Wildcat."

"You're the boss."

"Jem," said Solomon, "go down to Postlethwait's and fetch us a bottle of something. It don't matter what it is. If it looks like firewater, bring it here. If anybody asks you about it, you tell them it's for King Solomon and that I sent you for it. They'll know to leave you alone. If they've got any sense they will."

"Yassir," said Jem, turning and running in the direction of Postlethwait's.

"Wait for me," said Cynthia, "I'm coming with you. You might get into trouble."

The two children disappeared, hand in hand, along Third Street.

"Now then, Captain," said King Solomon, "let's fill up this grave and cover it over. Anything you want to say?"

"Yes. I want to say that this is madness. This is the end of the world, and I believe the two of us are crazy, and I think we ought to be gone from here."

"Amen," said King Solomon, and he began to shovel in the dirt.

"Bill Solomon," said the captain, "you did not even hear what I said."

"Oh, I heard all right. I heard just fine."

"I think I am not going to get out of this place alive. I've got a pain in my chest that won't go away."

"I'm going to tell you what I think, Captain. I think you're probably selfish. More than likely you're greedy, too. You're probably no different from a lot of people I know. They think as long as they can steer their boat all over creation and not be responsible for anything except what suits them, they don't have a quarrel. They use the world as if it were their personal toy. They lie. They cheat. They steal. They run over anybody and anything that gets in their way. They don't care how many die in America, as long as they make a profit. But when they've come down to the last day of their lives, when they're down to their last pieces of gold that they've saved up to buy just about all the acres their hearts desire here in Glory Land, what they discover is Old King Solomon working his ass off, burying people."

"Now, just wait a son of a bitching minute—"

"Let's say, Captain, that everybody dies *except* you. Who's going to be left to plow your fields for you? Who's going to be left to grow your tobacco and distill your bourbon for you? Who's going to be left to bed you down? Where's the fair young thing that's going to ease all your aches and pains? Who's going to pray for you in church? And then, Captain, my friend Jimmy Henry, who's going to be left to bury *you?*"

As Jem and Cynthia turned the corner at Limestone Street, she pulled him up short and held him tight by his shoulders. "I want to ask you something."

"What's that?"

"Who takes care of you?"

"Takes care myself."

"Where do you live?"

"Lives with ole Aunt Shawlette and ole King Solomon. You hurting my shoulders, Miz Cindy. Turn me loose."

Cynthia released him, and they continued down the street. The stores were locked shut. No merchants were anywhere in sight. A family of rats hurried from one corner to another.

"What I want to know is this: who is old Aunt Shawlette and what do you mean, you live with her and old King Solomon?"

"I means exactly what I say. Ole Aunt Shawlette is a free niggah, just like I is. She the flower lady of Water Street. She own ole King Solomon. Bet I can run faster than you can," and Jem began running the last two blocks to Main Street.

"Hey, you, wait for me!" shouted Cynthia as she sprinted after him.

"Gals can't run fast as boys," said Jem, turning and grinning at Cynthia as she finally caught up. Panting, they came to a clomping stop at Postlethwait's. Inside, the dark, smelly place was as quiet as a tree full of owls blinking their large eyes in the middle of a hot afternoon. Jem disliked owls, even the very thought of them, as much as he did snakes. He hated snakes. Cynthia and Jem stood there listening, trying to catch the sound or sight of something. All they heard was the scratching of rats under the bar and in the back wall. Jem did not seem frightened, not yet anyway, maybe because he was on familiar territory, but Cynthia had the feeling that some large animal was about to jump out and grab her by the throat. Goosebumps sprang up on the nape of her neck, and the prickly feeling descended down her arms and legs and settled in her feet. She felt as if she were naked and nailed to the floor. There was a large painting of a racehorse above the bar. Its head was turned in her direction, and it was very clearly a stallion that looked to be as strong as it was beautiful. The thought occurred to Cynthia that she might need to go to the privy. Jem had vanished.

"Boo!" he exclaimed as he reappeared from behind the bar.

"Don't you ever do that again," snapped Cynthia, closing her right hand against her chest, trying to catch her breath. She had wet herself. "Don't you *ever* do that again!" she gasped.

"Do what?" said Jem, grinning grandly.

"Scare me like that. You just scared the daylights out of me. Please don't do that again."

"Aw, I didn't mean nothing. Old Jem playing with you, didn't mean nothing a-tall."

"Did you find what you were looking for?"

"Yassum."

"Well, let's get out of this spooky place."

"How come this place spooky but that dern old graveyard *ain't* spooky?"

"Because, out there I can *see* what I'm looking at. I *see* big eyes and they are *staring* at Jem and me. And sometimes I think they might not be *dead*. They might *jump* up and grab little Jem by the throat and choke and choke and *choke!*" Jem was out the front door as fast as his legs would carry him, and Cynthia could not catch him until he stopped at the entrance to the Third Street burying ground. He was waiting for her there.

"Don't scare Old Jem again like you just did," he said, sternly.

"I promise," said Cynthia, joyfully gasping for breath.

"Here's your bottle of stuff," said Jem to King Solomon.

"Took it right off the shelf," said Cynthia, "and nobody said anything, because there *wasn't* anybody to say anything!"

King Solomon took the Ole Wildcat from Jem and rubbed him gladly on the top of his head. "You're a damn good little free black boy," said Solomon. "You may not go far, but you're all right in my book."

Solomon jerked the cork from the neck of the bottle and walked over to where Captain Lovingsworth was still sitting beneath the black walnut. "Here," said Solomon, "you take the first swig. You're going to need all the help you can get. And so am I."

The captain raised the bottle to his lips and felt the fire descending his throat. "Let's get back to work," he said, rising unsteadily to his feet.

"Go get me some more bodies. I'll be digging," said the King, tipping up the Ole Wildcat to his mouth. The King and the captain were hail-fellows-well-met and well-employed.

As night fell, Cynthia and Jem curled together beneath a giant double-forked American elm with its deep-fissured bark and its double-toothed leaves. Cynthia pulled her feet up tightly and placed her left arm around Jem's shoulder, bringing him in closer to her, giving and getting a small feeling of security. It was a long, dull, humid Kentucky night.

After several more wheelbarrow loads of corpses had been moved, an equal number of graves dug and covered over, and more bottles of Ole Wildcat stolen from Postlethwait's, there was one body left at the entrance to the Old Burying Ground.

"Captain!" boomed King Solomon. "Any more bodies for tonight?"

Nothing.

"Captain!" shouted King Solomon. "Where are you?"

The silence in the Old Burying Ground was broken only by the raucous answering caw of a carrion crow. King Solomon walked to the front entrance and found that last form on the ground, face down.

It was the body of Captain James Henry Lovingsworth.

He appeared to have died instantly where he fell. Later, people might say that the captain had died in the massive cholera epidemic of 1833, that he was one of those buried by ole King Solomon, and they would, of course, be partly correct.

But *Vibrio cholerae* was probably not *directly* responsible for the demise of the Tom Cat's son. More likely it was too much physical effort and too much Ole Wildcat in too short a time for an aging, damaged heart.

"Damn," muttered Solomon under his breath. "Damn, damn, damn. Told him so. Didn't I tell him? Yessir, I did, for a fact, I did. Told him his time might be coming, that nobody gets to live forever, that when that time does come, that's it."

The King gathered up the captain in his arms and carried him into the graveyard. "Damn, damn, damn," the King moaned low under his breath so as not to awaken the spirits.

"Caw," rebuked the carrion crow. "Caw!"

"What's the matter?" asked Cynthia, awaking from a fretful sleep filled with demons.

"The captain is dead," said King Solomon.

Cynthia jumped to her feet. Then she slumped back down again next to Jem, turning to him for solace. She had little breath, little strength of her own. Jem stirred but did not awaken.

"I'm sorry," said Solomon, "there's nothing we can do but bury him. We'll give him his own place. We can do that much."

King Solomon laid the body of Captain Lovingsworth down upon the ground and, without speaking again, began to dig. Cynthia covered Jem entirely with Miss Abigail's favorite shawl that she'd given to Cynthia the last night aboard the *Kentucky Lady*. She stood silently beside the captain, looking at the peaceful expression on his face. Her memory went back to the first time she'd met him beside the rail of the *Cynthia Anne*. He had seemed then entirely intimidating; but now he appeared as blissfully harmless as a sleeping child. Cynthia remembered what the captain had told her after Abigail's death at Washington, that if anything happened to him and she was present, to be sure to take his leather money pouch and clean out his pockets.

She knelt down to do what she had been told. With a guarded glance over her shoulder at King Solomon, Cynthia removed a small, loaded caplock pistol from an inside holster near the captain's heart. She placed the pearl-handled weapon inside her skirt pocket. From his wrist, she untied the thongs of the captain's pride, his soft leather money pouch. She opened it and peered into what seemed to be a hidey-hole for gold coins. In another pocket there was a small envelope with the words, "Do Not Open Until The Need Is Great." She studied the words on the flap, folded it twice, and placed it inside the pouch. She retightened the drawstrings and looped them around her wrist. She sat down on the ground next to Jem, encircled her legs with her arms and began rocking, back and forth.

Cynthia could hardly comprehend the death of one as seemingly indestructible as the captain. Jem, sleeping, was no help, although it was a comfort to have him nearby. King Solomon was as mountainous and scary as he was dull and uncompromising. Her mother and father were dead, and the nice lady aboard the *Cynthia Anne* had disappeared into the convent or the shadows of the Vieux Carré in New Orleans. Abigail was gone to her reward, and now the captain, who had once seemed as permanent as any Bishop Rock, had been brought down fast and hard. By what? He had shown no sign of cholera, and he had been drunk before. It was not time for him to die no matter what the preposterous King might have to say about it. No time would be a good time for the captain to die. Perhaps it was the work of the gods that Grandfather Charlie used to talk about. Grandfather Charlie knew all about the stupidities of the gods.

Cynthia looked up and saw the carrion crow watching intently from its eventide perch near the top of the elm tree, while down below Jem slept the rapturous sleep of an angel, and the captain slept the sleep of the destroyed. She decided to open the envelope. There could be no time when there'd be greater need.

She carefully removed a folded piece of paper upon which these words were scrawled:

> Beware of gold. Beware of silver. Believe in yourself.
> Don't let the sons of bitches get you down.
> Captain James Henry Lovingsworth

Lexington

June 1833

We are distinctly told in Scripture that the sword, the pestilence, and famine are God's sore judgments; we may not therefore shrink from the assertion, that a pestilence, whatever be the nature of it, whether what is known as the plague or the cholera, is a visitation of God.

—Jacobson Augustus Atkinson
August 12, 1866

"WHERE ARE WE GOING?" Cynthia asked King Solomon after he'd buried the captain.

"We're going to Aunt Charlotte's."

"Who is she?"

"Old black woman."

"Remember, I told you, she a free niggah, like me," said Jem.

"Why are we going to see an old black woman?" asked Cynthia, ignoring Jem for the moment.

"She free like me," said Jem again, softly, toward his feet.

"She's all we got, is about the size of it," said King Solomon.

"I don't understand what you mean," said Cynthia.

"Like Jem is trying to tell you, Aunt Charlotte's a freed slave."

"I don't understand what that really means, or what it has to do with anything else."

Solomon, Cynthia, and Jem walked to the edge of Town Branch, which flowed from the confluence of two smaller rivulets on the eastern edge of the town. The flatness of Main and Water Streets stretched westward like the palm of an open hand, gently tapering downward from Henry Clay's plenteous and enviable plantation, Ashland.

King Solomon was bemused by Lexington's becoming the Athens of the West, center for the arts, gracious living built upon timeless agrarian values. Since 1799, Transylvania University had become a flourishing institution in the liberal arts, law, and medicine. Henry Clay was one of the prominent members of the faculty. King Solomon admired Clay as a determined individual but considered it somewhat stupid that there was so little recognition of everyone's need for sanitary conditions.

On the putrid waters of Town Branch, Cynthia watched gas burst from floating bubbles and covered her nose with her hand. Feces were carried along as easily as fleas on the backs of ravenous dogs. Rats squeaked and scurried in advance of King Solomon's ponderous steps. The polluted water made a mockery of the work of the pioneers who had built the town near McConnell's Spring, a pure and sparkling beginning for a refreshing place filled with promise.

"Where you been, Bill Sol'mon? Lawse, mercy, where you been?" jovially fretted Aunt Charlotte, as the giant and the children entered from the second-floor landing of the dingy rooming house on the edge of Town Branch. The building teetered near the center of the outstretched hand of prosperity, everything Abigail and James Henry had hoped for. Surrounding the city, for those with the means to obtain them, were green fields where sleek five-gaited horses frisked with their tails tall and forelegs teased and trained to rise and fall gracefully. King Solomon could usually count on the butts of expensive cigars tossed aside on the street outside Postlethwait's. Aunt Charlotte had helped cook for grand dinners in candlelit mansions where there were champagne and chateaubriand with richly delicate sauces. She'd helped to prepare for cotillions throughout the year, and she'd scurried down hallways past rooms where fine ladies and gentlemen drifted into whispering after their rendezvous in high, canopied beds.

"Jem, who in God's name you got with you?"

"Whoever she be, she say she own me," said Jem, shaking his head. "And I reckon she do if she say she do."

"Tell her who you are," grumbled Solomon, slumping down on the edge of an old, creaky bed in the corner of the dismal room. He found a swallow of bourbon hugging the bottom of a spare bottle of Ole Wildcat, and he felt the goodness of it, the golden beauty of it, easing down his gullet. It was like new honey for an old bear, tired of wandering in the woods. He removed his heavy shoes and scratched the soles of his aching feet.

"You wash your hands, Bill Sol'mon, afore you do another thing," said Aunt Charlotte. He reluctantly complied.

"My name's Cynthia Anne," said the child looking directly into Aunt Charlotte's smooth chocolate face.

"Well, well, well. Now where in tarnation do my Jem and my Bill Sol'mon come up with you, chile?"

"He buried the captain."

"Buried the captain? Deed he do? My, my, my and double my. I expect my Bill done buried admirals and some colonels thrown in for good measure. What do this captain got to do with you, Miz Cindy?" said Aunt Charlotte, turning to stir the green beans in the iron pot on the wood-burning stove.

"Aunt Charlotte," said Cynthia. "Jem and I are hungry."

"You chirrens help yourselves to some of this here hot water and lye soap before you eat a blessed thing, you hear me?"

"Captain James Henry Lovingsworth and his wife took me in after my mother and father died on the trip over from England on the captain's ship," said Cynthia, feeling the roughness of the cake of gritty soap, earnestly trying to lather with it and then handing it to Jem. "It was the *Cynthia Anne,* and I was told by a nice lady that I had to have the same name as it—the ship, I mean," said Cynthia as she washed between her fingers and then rinsed and dried her hands. Jem washed last.

"Do tell. You named for a *ship*? Lawse me. Never knowed nobody named for no ship."

"Yes, ma'am. We landed in New Orleans, which is where Mrs. Lovingsworth was waiting for the captain. They always wanted to return to Kentucky. They always talked about buying land here. Trouble is, I don't know whether they had enough money," said Cynthia, working the captain's leather pouch up higher so that her hand would fit around the top of it.

"Is that so?" asked Aunt Charlotte. "You look to me to be about starved. You and Jem ain't had nothing to eat. Hmmm, hmmph. I'll fix you right up. Got some cornpone and got some fresh beans with plenty of fatback. Fix you right up, yes siree."

As she and Jem ate, Cynthia continued explaining. "Said they wanted to build up an old home place, but they never told me where it was. The cholera in New Orleans helped them to make up their minds."

"The chol'ra? My, my."

"We came upriver in a hurry on a boat with a big paddle in the back. I loved watching that big, red paddle, yes I did. The captain and Miss Abigail—she was the captain's wife—they didn't like watching the paddle turn at all," said Cynthia with a mouthful of cornpone.

"Didn't?"

"Right after we landed in Kentucky, Miss Abigail got very sick."

"Did?"

"Yes ma'am. She died."

"The chol'ra?" asked Aunt Charlotte.

"Yes, ma'am, I think so. Maybe. I'm not sure."

"And the captain. He die of the chol'ra, do he?"

"Yes, ma'am. I mean, no, ma'am. I mean, we're not exactly sure. He didn't have any sign of cholera. Maybe it was his heart just quit."

"Lawse me, chile. Chol'ra kill your real mama and papa?"

"Yes, ma'am."

"Lord, Lord, Lord. Folks die, then more folks die. You the most orphan chile ever I do see."

King Solomon's snoring filled the corner of the little room. In the streets outside, deserted by the town's fleeing population, the stillness was broken only by the chattering of rat families and the howling of hungry dogs. Cats whined, and the carrion crows cawed, and the silent buzzards soared on the steamy air above Town Branch, humid and heavy with stinking gases.

"Yes, chile. Why you standing so close to me? You want some more fixings on your plate? Want another piece of corn-pone?"

"Yes ma'am, and I want to ask you an important question."

"What is it?"

"I don't want you to think I'm being a fraidy cat."

"What is it, chile?"

"Have we come to the end of time?" asked Cynthia, pinching off a piece of pone.

"Lord, how you talk."

"Have we? I'm afraid. Jem is too. Why shouldn't we be afraid?"

"Come here. Set that plate down. Sit in this lap. You can eat more whenever you feel like it. I'll keep it warm for you. Let Auntie Shawlette put her arms all round her two chirren."

The old black woman extended her arms, and Cynthia was

drawn into the warmest embrace she'd felt since Sylva had rocked her to sleep in steerage on the *Cynthia Anne*. The child's own mother had not done as much at home in Southwark or Oxfordshire, maybe because there wasn't time. For Jem it was an everyday pleasure to be snuggled up close to Aunt Charlotte—the only person who had wanted to take him in after he'd become an orphan.

"I'm going to tell y'all a story, little Miz Cindy and little Mastah Jem. Spec' y'all soon be sound asleep, so listen long's you can. In the first place, Miz Cindy, you probably wondering how ole King Sol'mon and ole Aunt Shawlette come to be together. Ever'body say he a bum, poorest kind of white trash. Now, I ain't much better, 'cause I'm just a free niggah, like little Jem here. Hard to say which us the lowest down the ladder, the po' white folks or us free niggah folks. The white folks that done take wing and fly out of Lexington ahead of the chol'ra, they got the money to do as they pleases. The white folks that *ain't* got the money, they run out of the town, but a whole big bunch of 'em don't run fast enough, and the chol'ra it cotches 'em and *throws* 'em to the ground. Then my Bill Sol'mon, the one they all wants to call the bum of Water Street, he be the one to bury 'em best he can. Did you know, Miz Cindy, that I *buy* Bill Sol'mon at *auction*? Sho did. Me, an old niggah flower woman, she buy herself a *white* man on the coathouse steps, and she gets him for thirteen dollar. It was the highest bid. Lawse. Nobody else want him. Some smarty-pants med'cal students from Transylvania wants to buy him so's they can sit around till the ole King die so they can chop him up to see what's inside such a big man. But they don't get him, 'cause they rather spend their money on beer. After the sheriff hammered down my high bid, the crowd moved away, and there stood Bill Sol'mon standing so tall over me, and you know what he say to me? He say, 'Now you bought me, what do you want me to do?' And you know what I say to him? I say, 'I don't want you to do nothing. You're *free.'* Well, that make him feel mighty good, I guess, 'cause after that he been staying right here with ole Aunt Shawlette, just like he belong here. He's a member of the family!" King Solomon's snoring continued unabated, deep, husky, and rhythmic as a chorus of bullfrogs under a full moon.

"They say he mine for one year of 'dentured servitude, whatever that is, cause they tired him being drunk all the time. They declare him a public nuisance, say they tired him awalking around picking up cigar butts and stuffing 'em in his mouth. But now, sho nuff, they ain't so tired him burying the dead of the chol'ra epizoodic. I begged him. I begged him over and over again. Begged my Bill to leave town with me. But no-o-o-o, he wouldn't do it. I told him he free to do anything he want to do, and he choose to stay, and I choose to stay with him, cause he need somebody to look after him. Jem, he stay too. The Lord knows we all free. We all free to do as we pleases, Miz Cindy."

Cynthia was sleeping. Jem played drowsily with the outline of Aunt Charlotte's heavy breast. The flavors of food cooked in an iron kettle on a wood-burning stove made her smell mighty good all over.

The Reverend Josiah Carter Abernathy of the United Lollard Church had held his wife in his arms in the bedroom of their Third Street house in Lexington. During the final hour of her long agony he'd heard but had not accepted her last words, just as he had never paid her much mind except as an act of condescension. A bright woman who understood more than she ever publicly acknowledged, she had lived in the shadow of her husband, remaining there in loyal servitude until she approached the final threshold of a world wherein she had been so little appreciated.

"Listen to me, Josiah. For once in your life, listen to me. This is not the wrath of God. Do you hear me?"

"Yes, dear."

"This is *not* the wrath of God. Has nothing whatsoever to do with it. Please, Josiah, please don't preach any more of your 'punishment for sins' nonsense. Please, promise me that you won't do that. God is love, Josiah. Don't you understand? God *is* love. Please, God, help us to help ourselves."

"Now, dear—"

"We are given life. Death is necessary, but we should not be dying of cholera. There is a *cause* of cholera. There's got to be a *cure* for cholera. But it is not going to be found in preaching that causes people to believe that a horribly wrathful God sends disease as punishment for sins. Do you hear me, Josiah? Do you hear me?"

"Yes, dear. You are delirious. You must rest now. We must pray for forgiveness and deliverance for *all* our sins. All of us, each one of us, has sinned. We sin every day of our lives, and finally we're going to have to face the judgment for it." Abernathy's faith was as firm as Sir John Oldcastle's, "hanged and burnt hanging" for Protestant heresy four centuries before.

Margaret Walton Abernathy abruptly pushed back from her husband. She called upon the last shreds of strength in her wasted body. The fire that had once burned warmly to consummate her husband's physical passion now fused in her eyes, flaring a beam of words, frightful in their soul-searching intensity, unmistakable in the nature of their conviction.

"No more!" she screamed. "I'll hear no more!" she shrieked again. "Silence!" she moaned a third and final time—and fell back to her pillow, fiery eyes fixed.

The Reverend Abernathy slumped to his knees. He clasped his hands against his forehead and prayed in a loud, slow sob: "Deliver her, oh God, into thy keeping. Cleanse her of all her sins. Cleanse this city of its sins, so that thy WRATH be appeased, so that this terrible scourge of Heaven will be withdrawn, never to return as long as the people of God depart their sins. May our children and our children's children come to the fullest knowledge of how much thou hatest sin. Receive this woman now at the judgment table."

He placed the sheet over his wife's face, then backed out of the room and wandered out to the deserted street. The loathsome smell of death, sickening in its soured sweetness, permeated the summer morning like rancid contents spilled from old perfume bottles.

The deacons and elders of many of the Protestant churches in Lexington had joined with a small band of Roman Catholic clergy, each trying in accordance with his fundamental belief system to appease the Angel of Death. In Lexington, a microcosm of Christian tradition, conventional wisdom typically assumed the wrathfulness of a deity; to ignore the belief was to invite the punishment of eternal damnation. But questions remained unanswered.

Why had Aunt Charlotte and Bill Solomon lived, while the preacher's sweet, angelic wife had died? If Margaret Abernathy had sinned, surely they had too. Since the arrival of cholera, some churchgoers had pondered: What was God's point? Philosophy professors had speculated: Was determinism alive and well? Young theologians wondered: Was free will so debased as to be inconsequential? Cynics had sniffed: Perhaps it had never mattered; life was nothing more than a shell game or a roll of the dice, redemption so unpredictable as to be nothing more than sixes and sevens.

Preacher Abernathy had seen King Solomon bury many of the dead, moving methodically, yet almost like a man possessed. There was no denying the endurance and dedication of this giant who could have left the city but chose to remain. But was the choice actually his? Or had God predetermined what the "King" would do?

If he was not at the burying ground, Abernathy knew that Solomon would be resting from his labors—drinking Ole Wildcat or sleeping. It was common knowledge that he had gone to live with Aunt Charlotte after her successful bid at the auction, a farce concocted by the sheriff for entertainment. On the eve of the arrival of the cholera menace, the loafers at the court-house needed a circus. What they got could hardly have been scripted finer. Town drunk with aristocratic Virginia lineage sold into a year of indentured servitude to a black woman for thir-teen dollars. The two of them go off to live together under the same roof in the same room. God Almighty, what a comedy. Ordinarily such relationships were considered scandalous, per-haps even justification for a lynching or tar and feathers and a ride out of town on a rail. But these two unlikely creatures lived together as naturally as a black cat and a white dog.

The Reverend Abernathy crossed deserted Main Street and walked directly to the rickety building inhabited by Aunt Char-lotte, King Solomon, and Jem. The preacher saw no choice. He lacked the strength to dig his wife's grave himself. He feared he'd die of exhaustion. Better men had.

When she heard the loud knock on the door, Aunt Char-lotte eased out of bed so as not to disturb Cindy and Jem from the place where last night she'd tucked them beneath an old sheet, then huskily called to the knocking. "What you want down there?"

"Aunt Charlotte?"

"Said, what you want?"

"This here is Preacher Abernathy."

As she troubled herself to descend the stairs, a common courtesy, she wearily acknowledged, "This here's Aunt Shawlette a-coming." When she reached the bottom, through the shut-tered door she said with the little breath she had left, "Well? Asked you, what you want?"

"I've come for King Solomon."

"What you want with *my* Bill Sol'mon? Shoot," she added, low enough for no one to hear, "I expect I knows what he want with my Bill. Expect I do, 'deed I do."

"I want him to bury my wife."

"Lord God, have mercy. You one of the top dogs in one of the big white man's churches in Kentucky and the chol'ra done got your wife, and now you want my good-for-nothin' Bill to put her in the ground. That right?"

"Aunt Charlotte, there's not time to talk. My wife is dead. She must be buried. I've come asking for King Solomon's help."

Ponderously she mounted the steps, shaking her head and whistling air to conserve it. "I see if I can get him up. Maybe I can. Whew! Don't knows if I can or not. Expect so. I go see if I can. Lord have mercy upon our souls. One thing, it's another. Never seen nothing like it."

Aunt Charlotte shuffled to the side of Solomon's bed. She shook him awake.

"Bill, Preacher Abernathy say he *need* you. His wife gone and died and needs be buried. Bill, you hear me?"

"I hear you. Goldern it, I'm coming. That woman should not have died."

Cynthia and Jem stirred on Aunt Charlotte's bed. Cynthia was dreaming of being left in steerage on the *Cynthia Anne*. Jem was dreaming of being left alone in a graveyard. They sprang up, bewilderment on their faces. They both looked as if a party of ghosts had visited them. By the time Solomon had reached the door, Cynthia was on her feet, determined that she would not be abandoned again, not if she had an ounce of strength left in her spindly body.

"Get back in that bed," scolded Aunt Charlotte.

Jem clung to Aunt Charlotte's skirt. When she told him not to do something, he didn't do it. At least, not while she was in sight. Jem was as bound to Aunt Charlotte as glue is to the bottom of a pot.

"No, ma'am, I'm going where the King goes," said Cynthia, and she followed him down the stairs to the front door. The Reverend Abernathy stood there, his face ashen, his pink and pointed chin trembling, the way it did when he got to the hellfire part of one of his two-hour—sometimes three-hour—soul-stirring, evangelical sermons. Especially at revival time, there were few ministers in Kentucky who were longer-winded or more stubborn than Preacher Abernathy. There were many who dedicated their lives to their ministries and did so with practiced dignity and natural goodness. Abernathy was accustomed to dealing with extremes. He lived by them, and he was prepared to die by them. He believed that black people ought to do what white people told them to do, and white people, he believed, lowered themselves by living with black people. The Reverend Abernathy was a creature of his culture, and he was not inspired to rise above it.

"Bill Solomon," said Josiah Abernathy, "I need you to bury my wife."

"What makes you think I'd want to do that?"

"I've seen you burying many the past two days. Besides, she considered you a friend."

"Preacher, how do you say it? 'I'm not worthy to gather up the crumbs under thy table'?"

"Listen, Bill Solomon. My wife is dead. She needs to be buried right away. I will pay you to do it. Will you?"

"How much?"

"Five dollars."

"Too much. She was a good woman. Better woman than a lot of men I know," said Solomon.

"Now, see here. I won't be dallied with."

Cynthia came and stood by King Solomon's side. She looked defiantly into the preacher's eyes.

Solomon picked up the shovel at the bottom of the stairs. "Where is she?"

"Who?"

"My friend, goldarn it."

"She's in her bed, where she died."

"I'll meet you at the Main Street Burying Ground. By the time you get there, I'll probably have the grave dug."

"You expect me to *carry* her all the way to the grave?"

"I don't expect anything. I'm going to dig a grave. If you get there in time, you can put your wife in it. If you don't, we'll find somebody else to put in it. We don't have time to fart around."

"Bill Solomon, the Lord will settle up with you. Maybe one day you'll die of cholera, and Aunt Charlotte will want *me* to pray for *you*."

"Maybe so. I doubt it. Go get your wife, so you can stand at her grave and pray for *her*. Cynthia?"

"Yes, sir."

"Go be with Jem and Aunt Charlotte."

"No, sir. I'm going with you. You might need some help with the dirt." They walked together toward the cemetery, where the early morning sunlight filtered gently through the pin oaks. Up in the sky, a small bird was chasing a crow, probably because a nest of eggs had been disturbed.

King Solomon had the grave dug when the Reverend Josiah Abernathy appeared with his wife's blanket-wrapped body in his arms. "Let me help you," said Bill Solomon, his voice pitched unusually low at the sight of the woman for whom he'd once dug flower beds and planted a tulip poplar. He leaped into the hole and held up his arms to receive the form of Mrs. Abernathy. After he'd stretched her straight and smoothed out her gown, he covered her with the blanket and levered himself out of the grave. "Now you can pray," he said. Solomon took his shovel in one hand and Cynthia's hand in the other, stood nearby, and respectfully waited for Abernathy to finish.

"God of our fathers," proclaimed the Reverend Abernathy, "forgive this woman her mortal sins. Restore her to your loving grace. Assist this city and help this world to understand thy wrath. Reconcile us to thy everlasting mercy. Deliver us though we are undeserving, though we are sinners. Deliver us from this divine scourge. Amen."

After standing silent for a moment, he handed King Solomon a five-dollar gold piece, and said: "I'm sorry the way I spoke to you. Thank you for what you've done to help bury all these people, especially my wife."

"She was good to me. That's all I know. Maybe she wasn't such a sinner. But that's not for me to say."

Turning to go, Reverend Abernathy heaved a sigh and said, "Vengeance is mine; I will repay, saith the Lord."

As soon as he departed, Solomon filled in the dirt.

"Mr. Solomon," said Cynthia, "is God mad at us?"

"I don't know."

"What do you think?"

"I think I've never had a problem with God. But I've sure had my hands full with the preachers of God," said King Solomon.

"Does that mean you don't believe in God?"

"No. It means I don't believe in God's preachers."

"None of them?"

"None of them."

"Not even the Pope?"

"Especially not even the Pope."

"Where does that leave me?"

"What do you mean?"

"I'm Catholic. My mother and father were Catholic. Grandfather Charlie is a Catholic—probably not a very good one. My friend in Louisiana, Mr. Boudreaux, is a Catholic."

"Don't blame me."

"I'm not blaming you. You're all I have," said Cynthia. But then she remembered the words of Captain Lovingsworth: "Believe in yourself."

"We got mackerel-smacking Catholic priests in Lexington," said King Solomon. "Most of them mean well, but that don't mean they put their britches on any different than I do. Some of them like Ole Wildcat almost as much as I do. Some of them call it their spring tonic. Some call it their daily bracer. They hide it in secret places."

"I'm confused about priests. But not just priests."

"How so?"

"Since we left England, seems like most preachers I've met tell just about everybody they meet that they're sinners, tell them they're *born* in sin. I suppose they want me to believe my mother and father were sinners. Same thing with Grandpa Charlie."

"Brother Abernathy sure wants the world to believe his wife was a sinner," acknowledged King Solomon. "Like I told him, she was a goldarn good woman."

"I don't believe that cholera was God's punishment for her sins. Do you?"

Solomon leaned on the handle of his long shovel. From his hip pocket he took a new bottle of Ole Wildcat, which he'd added to his overdue account at Postlethwait's. He removed the cork and drank.

"Cindy, you make more sense than anybody I know."

"I'm twelve years old," she said, as if to remind him of something he should have known. "I'm about to be thirteen, and I know more than a lot of people give me credit for."

"Maybe we got a chance." He drank again and wiped his mouth with a long, leisurely swipe of his sleeve. Bill Solomon believed he needed alcohol the way he needed air. He was drunk much of the time. His capacity for whiskey seemed as deep as a bottomless pit. He didn't drink water for he instinctively believed whiskey increased his immunity to cholera.

"I'm afraid," said Cynthia.

"Of me?" Solomon belched.

"Least of all you."

"Then who?" He belched again.

"People like the preachers."

"They only talk. I don't pay any attention to them."

"I wonder if the cholera will kill us all."

"It might."

"But it won't be because of sin."

"And it won't be because of drinking Ole Wildcat."

"I think that's what may have killed the captain."

"He wasn't used to it."

"What's going to become of me?"

"You could go to the home for orphans."

"I will not!"

"Oh?"

"If you and Jem and Aunt Charlotte don't want me, just say so. I'll go away."

"Now, where would you go?"

"I won't tell you." She bit down on her lower lip until it hurt. She brushed back the auburn hair from her face. At times when the weather was hot, ends of her hair would stick to her face and irritate her eyes. Cynthia glared at King Solomon. He looked back with the sad eyes of a St. Bernard just given a long-distance command. A breeze stirred among the trees. An emaciated dog crossed the street and headed toward Town Branch. In the sky vultures circled, riding the currents. From time to time they descended toward the burying places. Rats ran in all directions in the deserted city.

Cynthia spoke: "Mr. Solomon, I'm leaving you. Please tell Aunt Charlotte that I thank her for giving me a chance to get a good night's sleep."

"Now, hold on—"

"Do you see those big birds up there in the sky? They're doing what they got to do. I'm doing what I got to do. I'm an orphan. I'm a long way from home. I don't know where my home is any more, but I think I want my home to be here *somewhere*. At least for now. I've got some money the captain gave me." Cynthia opened her purse and rummaged inside. "Take this, it's one of his gold coins. You and Aunt Charlotte and Jem use it any way you want to. Please don't buy more Ole Wildcat, but if you do I'll forgive you."

"Thank you," said King Solomon. "You do what you believe you have to do."

"On our way to the burying ground we passed a church. I am going there to pray, and I'm going to pray for you, for Aunt Charlotte, for Jem, and the woman we just buried, and I'm going to pray for her preacher husband because he called her a sinner."

Cynthia stopped to give her breath a chance to catch up with her racing mind, then she added softly, "I will pray for the nice lady too, the one the captain called a whore and Miss Abigail called *lagniappe*."

"What's *that?*"

"I'm not sure I know, but I'll pray for this world, Mr. Solomon," she whispered, tears welling in her eyes, "that people don't die such horrible deaths. I will pray that somewhere in the world somebody is working hard to find out why the cholera comes."

Turning away from Bill Solomon, she walked deliberately. At the door of St. Jude's Cathedral she glanced back to see King Solomon shuffling toward Town Branch, the long shovel balanced on his shoulder. He did not look back. The bottle of Ole Wildcat protruding from his hip pocket was more than likely just about empty. Storm clouds rolled in from what Cynthia guessed was the southwest. The air suddenly felt cooler, and thunder rumbled as heat lightning crackled.

Inside St. Jude's, Cynthia's forefinger was about to touch the Holy Water. She saw the particles of dirt settled in the bottom of the bowl. "Don't touch!" Her hand jerked back, and she made the sign of the cross without touching the water. She believed she had heard a voice. Perhaps it was St. Jude, or maybe only his presence. Perhaps it was the captain who caused her inner voice to speak so clearly. Maybe it was Sylva she heard.

"Don't touch what?" asked Cynthia, aloud.

"The water! Don't touch the water!" came the voice from within her.

Cynthia walked toward the altar. She double genuflected, her left knee following her right. She bent forward until her head almost touched the wooden floor. She closed her right fist and held it against her heart. Then she fingered the gold crosses, kissed them, and let them fall again to the end of their chains.

A voice startled her.

"Young lady," it said.

"Yes?"

"Do you wish to confess?"

Cynthia turned and saw an elderly priest standing nearby.

"No," she replied, "I have nothing to confess."

"Then you are not Catholic?"

"Yes, I was raised a Catholic."

"I see," said the priest with extreme weariness. "Then you have carefully examined your conscience in this hour of our vast calamity?"

"Sir?"

"You have examined your conscience and you have found no sin there," said the elderly priest, impatiently.

"I'm not sure what sin is," said Cynthia.

"Young lady," said the priest, "shouldn't you have your confession heard, so that you may do proper penance before it is too late for you? Please rise and enter the confessional. We do not have time to waste. There are too many souls to be saved! And may the Good Lord have mercy upon *all* our souls. May the Good Lord save us from the plague," said the priest, exceedingly fatigued, groping for the tops of the pews to guide his frail body toward the confessional.

"Father," called Cynthia to Monsignor Delaney, still making his way to the confessional in St. Jude's Cathedral.

"Yes?" replied the old priest, apprehensively, as if believing he was hearing a voice from the nether world. The refraction of light through the large window in the eastern transept often stirred the Monsignor's sacerdotal yearnings. He likened it to the Holy Spirit of the Blessed Trinity, which he loved and which he often included as sacred imagery in his homilies. The Monsignor had abandoned evangelicalism in favor of the primacy of papal authority. A Jesuit in a mixture of postpioneer crudeness and neoclassical pretentiousness, he lived and breathed a determined, uncompromising theology. Emanuel Kant's absolutism, his "categorical imperative," lived on in the pure and pious mind of Monsignor Joseph Delaney, while still there was a mystical part of him that refused to shut out any marvelous possibilities. The Monsignor turned, and for a moment the light through the stained-glass window struck him as possibly of divine origin.

"Yes?" he answered, expectantly. "Yes?"

"I wish to be alone with my thoughts," said Cynthia, evenly and assertively, like a slender strike of summer lightning. It was an unthinkable statement for one so young, especially with such poor timing. It stunned the Monsignor as surely as the nearly simultaneous crack of lightning and its accompanying clap of thunder that cut through theological theorems.

Monsignor Joseph Delaney stopped cold in his tracks, lowered his head, and made the sign of the cross. A Jesuit, he was obedient to the order's reestablishment by Pius VII, but Father Delaney had become bone-tired with the work of ministering to his stricken community. He and other clergy, Roman Catholic or Anglican Catholic, evangelical non-Catholic and Jewish had gone dutifully from house to house, from church to graveyard, risking their own lives, hearing confessions, administering last rites and final oblations in the hope of saving souls from the broken shells of human bodies. The last thing Monsignor Delaney wanted to hear was a sassy, healthy youth talking back to him. She'd be better off with a Good Shepherd Sister, some-one better equipped to deal with immature females, Monsignor Delaney thought.

"'I wish to be alone with my thoughts'? That is what I heard you say? 'I wish to be alone with my thoughts'? Well, well, well." Father Delaney was running low on charity. "Who are you, so young, to be *alone* with your thoughts? Should you ever reach the Kingdom of Heaven, you will tell the Lord that you wish to be *alone* with your thoughts? In the community of saints, you would want to be *alone* with your thoughts? Oh, what if *I* should want to be *alone* with *my* thoughts?" said the Monsignor. "You dare to want to be *alone* with your thoughts?"

"Yes, Father, that is what I want."

"Where are your mother and father?" persisted Monsignor Delaney.

"Dead."

"May their souls rest in peace," he said, making the sign of the cross. "Do you have any other family?"

"No. Not any more."

"Where did you come from?"

"England. Aboard a sailing ship, the *Cynthia Anne*. My parents died of cholera. They were buried at sea. We finally landed in New Orleans. A nice prostitute included me in a deal with the captain of the ship—"

"A deal with the captain of the ship. And a *nice* prostitute, is it? There are *no* nice prostitutes."

"This lady was as nice as anybody aboard ship. If it were not for her, I would probably not be alive today. I would not have met Captain Lovingsworth and his wife, Miss Abigail. They brought me to Kentucky. She died shortly after our ar-rival, and the captain died last night."

"Then, you are an immigrant *and* an orphan?"

"I suppose you could say I am. I have met King Solomon and Aunt Charlotte and Jem, but I would be one too many. Yes,

I suppose you could say that I am an orphan, as well as an immigrant."

"Then you should be in a home for orphans. You should be with the Good Shepherd Sisters. They know how to handle young ladies who've fallen into sin."

"No!"

"No, *what?*"

"No, I will not go to a home for orphans. No, I will go to no Good Shepherd Sisters. And no, I will not go to confession!" Cynthia snapped at the Monsignor as fiercely as a cornered animal.

"Then would you please remove yourself from this holy place. This is the house of God. It is not a house of prostitution. I am God's Monsignor, and I have asked you to obey my authority, and you have thumbed your nose. You have no respect for me, nor for St. Jude, who has correctly warned against ungodly persons who pervert the grace of our God. You are clearly lacking in grace. I have offered you the sacrament of confession, and you have rebelled. Therefore, penance is not possible."

Cynthia recoiled. Then she approached the Monsignor, who braced himself as well as he was able, like a tremulous lynx confronting an intruder on the boundary of its lair. Cynthia reached inside her blouse for the captain's envelope. She opened it and slowly unfolded the piece of paper. Another arc of lightning seen through the stained-glass window took Monsignor Delaney aback, the point of the shaft of light flashing for an instant across the piece of paper that Cynthia held protectively in her hand.

"I will read this to you," she said.

"I will read this to you?" he sputtered. "What right have you to *read* me *anything?*"

Beware of gold. Beware of silver. Believe in yourself. Don't let the sons of bitches get you down.

Cynthia smiled, refolded the paper, and confidently returned it to its resting place. The brief silence that ensued
seemed as loud as another clap of thunder. The woman-child
glowered into the eyes of the confused priest. He had never been
so confronted. It took his breath away.

"Who—wrote—that—garbage?" gasped the Monsignor.
"Where did you get that?" He asked.

"It doesn't matter who wrote it or where I got it. What
matters is that I believe it."

"Young woman," began the Monsignor, "you may read
what trash you please, and you may believe what filthy language
you choose, and you may consort with whom you please, including prostitutes in bawdy houses."

"Yes."

"You may not stand here in this holy place, you may not
remain on this sacred ground any longer speaking blasphemy!
This city is dying and you are a part of the cause of it. The
Lord's curse is upon us, and you are an example of the general
denial of the authority of Almighty God and Holy Mother
Church."

"No!" Cynthia wiped her nose and looked in unyielding
anger at the aging priest. "There is no divine curse!" she said,
calmly. "There is no heavenly affliction!" she added, marching
toward the front door. She turned and fired a final volley: "I
respect you for your age, but I judge you not a worthy representative of God!" As she looked toward the street, she proclaimed to herself, "I will gladly leave."

With dignity and without hurry, Cynthia turned and
marched out of the cathedral. As she walked through the rain
she held her head up, not caring that she was getting wet.

As soon as the door closed behind her, in exhaustion, Monsignor Delaney slumped to his knees. He prayed to St. Jude for
strength. He called upon all the icons of his faith, praying devoutly for forgiveness for himself and for all sinners throughout

the city of Lexington in the cataclysmic year of 1833. "Save that child," he pleaded.

Pale with grief, old hands trembling, the monsignor made his way to the sacristy. He went to a corner cabinet and took out a large medicine bottle. He removed the fragrant cork. He drank. He drank again and again and, through the window, he regarded the rain moving through the stricken city.

Owl Hollow, Kentucky

1833-1840

Soft zephyrs gently breathe on sweets, and the inhaled air gives a voluptuous glow of health and vigour, that seems to ravish the intoxicated senses. . . . Everything here gives delight, and, in that mild effulgence which beams around us, we feel a glow of gratitude for that elevation our all-bountiful Creator has bestowed upon us.

—Gilbert Imlay, 1792

CYNTHIA RETURNED TO Postlethwait's Tavern, ducked behind the counter, and opened the two bags left there by the captain. Hurriedly, she rummaged through his clothes, checking in each pocket for anything of value. Finding a small tinderbox, she put it in her own valise. She checked to see if Abigail's banknotes were there, counted to be sure there were twelve, rose quickly with the single bag, and walked out the front door. She headed north. Abigail's parasol was strapped to the outside of the awkwardly swinging bag, and Cynthia hoped she wouldn't have to use it. The rawhide thongs of the captain's leather money pouch were tied to her left wrist. She was fearless about the danger of robbery, resolving to find a permanent hiding place for the coins and notes. If anyone were to ask her what was in the pouch, she would say it carried her pet snake.

Turning her back on Lexington, Cynthia retraced the path she and the captain had taken as the cholera epidemic blew through Kentucky like heavy fog hugging the ground in hemp and tobacco fields. When a bib-overalled dirt farmer wearing a broad-brimmed straw hat with a sticky sweatband and sturdy, tied-to-the-top brogans stopped and offered her a ride, she climbed up beside him on his mule-drawn wagon and accepted the offer of a night's lodging with him and his wife at their farmhouse over on Owl Hollow Creek. One night became two, two became three, and before the winter of '33 had clamped its temporary lid on everything, including cholera, the orphan had found a home in Kentucky.

There were no other children in the family. Joshua and Louise Carpenter were in their fifties, and all their lives they'd wanted children of their own. Cynthia came as the answer to their prayers. By the time she was fifteen, she had grown accustomed to an unchurched life and accepted it without regret, although memories of the sounds of "mea culpa" and *"oremos"* and *"Dominus vobiscum"* remained in her consciousness like perennial flowers. Mr. and Mrs. Carpenter knew nothing of Catholicism or any other form of organized religion. To them the idea of a minister speaking in any foreign tongue was strange and fearful, the notions of Holy Water, signs of the cross, and penitence for sins as peculiar as witchcraft, the Virgin Birth as amusing as it was unnatural, and Original Sin a bad fit for their belief in the natural goodness of mankind. They bore with uncomfortable patience the regular rounds of Methodist circuit riders with their long faces and their grave pronouncements, gave them their supper and offered the hayloft for a place to sleep, but resisted stubbornly all attempts to be evangelized.

"But you will accept this important tract from the Missionary Society? You will allow me to leave it with you for your benefit in the event of emergency?"

"Friend, the only kind of emergency we have around here is when the chickens stop laying eggs and the cows stop giving milk. Don't imagine your preaching will start up eggs and milk, will it?"

"Man does not live by bread alone, Brother."

"Maybe not. But we're a dern sight better off with it than without it."

Joshua knew you'd not catch most ministers freezing their hind ends off outside when the cold made Owl Hollow Creek solid enough to walk on. You wouldn't find these tub-thumpers going out on Good Fridays to do something as simple as counting cows and calves or, after counting them, searching the fields for hidden newborns, like the one that had staggered into a wet weather runoff where the water was almost up to its nose. Just a little more water and a little more time and the calf would have been gone. It was the quiet, unchurched practitioner of pioneer animal husbandry who would pull the shivering calf from the water and place it on high ground, would look for the afterbirth and drape it over the calf's back, taking special care not to leave behind too much human scent. Joshua taught Cynthia to have the patience to watch the wary approach of the mama cow and the tenuous, maternal claiming, and it was he who—feeling the rain falling through the spare, early foliage of the wild cherry tree—would gather up the calf and carry it in his arms to the barn, trusting that the cow would follow and increasing the chances by making the sound of a newborn in distress. It was Louise Carpenter who would show Cynthia how to massage the calf's throat to stimulate swallowing. It was this simple Owl Hollow man and his plainspoken wife and their adopted daughter who would walk away to leave the calf alone with its young, inexperienced heifer-mother and, upon their return, silently rejoice that the calf was on her feet and had nursed and would probably live. There was a rhythm in it that could not be learned from Bibles or catechisms.

Cynthia came to love her new life and could not imagine departing from its simplicity and goodness. She came to know the seasons of the year and each of the intersessions when the weather was subtle and unpredictable. There was Indian summer when cool air replaced the cold snaps of late autumn, and light was diffused through multicolored foliage. Formations of geese dipped low from southbound passages, landing along Hinkston and Stoner creeks, then departing again with the blest, brief postponement of winter. Without consistency or reliable warning, the rains fed the pastures and the streams, and Joshua Carpenter told Cynthia about the old saying: "All the water that was here in the beginning is here now, and all the water that's here now is all the water there'll ever be." Cynthia felt as if she were an intrinsic part of the Kentucky soil, and it pleased her more than what she remembered about Oxfordshire and Southwark.

Cynthia turned the toe of her shoe in the summer dust, then looked directly into the eyes of the Methodist minister.

"And what about this fine young woman?" he implored.

"Cynthia Anne's her name. She's one of us. What about her?"

"She needs to have her soul saved."

"Why don't you ask *her?*"

"Daughter, it is not my way to ask permission to speak what I fully understand to be the truth. You will suffer eternally if your soul is not saved. 'Unto them that are contentious, and do not obey the truth, but obey unrighteousness, indignation and wrath, tribulation and anguish, upon every soul of man that doeth evil. Romans 2:8-9.'"

"Would that be a scourge of Heaven?" asked Cynthia.

"And what do you mean by your impudence?" retorted the circuit rider.

"I do not consider it impudent to tell you that my real mother and father died in the hellish cholera epidemic four summers ago. The man and woman who later took me under their wing also died—she of cholera, maybe, he of exhaustion while burying cholera victims. I have been exposed to much disease and death, but by some reason I do not entirely understand, I was spared. Why do you suppose *I* did not die?"

"By the grace of God, you have lived. Without the grace of God you have no chance whatsoever," said the dedicated missionary, cheerfully.

"I do not believe it," said Cynthia, picking up a rock, throwing it at the dinner bell, making it ping.

"How dare you blaspheme? The wrath of God will surely descend upon you and upon this house."

"I do not believe that God is wrathful. I believe that He is full of love," throwing another rock and causing the bell to ring again.

"You do not believe that God sends disease as punishment for man's sins?"

"I do not."

"Blasphemy! 'Bless the Lord, O my soul, and forget not all his benefits: Who forgiveth all thine iniquities; who healeth all thy diseases.' Psalm of David."

"Sir," said Cynthia, "you have judged me to be impudent and blasphemous. Perhaps you are correct, for I've not studied the Bible as you certainly have. I wish you no misfortune. I wish you good health and a long life. Surely, you will find your place in Heaven."

"Daughter—"

"Brother," interrupted Mr. Carpenter, "the child speaks past her years. She is a good young woman. She has had a hard life. Do you not have other stops on your travels?"

For a moment, the minister canted his bearded face and held his chin in the cup of his hand and looked at Cynthia as a father would at a daughter. "Good day," he said grimly, and turned to his horse. He mounted, and with the reins gathered in his left hand he reached into the leather saddlebag on his right. He removed a Tract Society pamphlet, looked at it for a moment, then called to Cynthia, "Daughter, please accept this as a personal gift from me. Read it as you grow in wisdom. My earnest prayer is that you will know, love, and serve the Lord. That is all, and all we need to know."

Cynthia stepped forward to accept the gift. She looked into the man's eyes, softening as fires cooling to ashes. She reached up and took the booklet.

"Thank you," she said.

The missionary smiled and turned the horse's head. As he rode away, the right hand of the man of God reached for his hat and brought it down in a flashing arc on the horse's flank. The three-gaited animal glided from its trot to a smooth, unbroken canter.

"He'll be back," said Joshua Carpenter. "He'll be back. He's one of those Methodist fellers what don't give up easy. He'll be back."

"If it's not him it'll be another one just like him," said Louise Carpenter, wiping her flour-caked hands on her Sunday apron.

Cynthia went to the corner of the room where she'd been given a bed with a feather mattress and a pillow stuffed with goose down. She removed her work shoes and stretched out on her back. Vivid in her mind was the strong image of the circuit rider's angular face, the breadth of his shoulders, his boots pushing outward the stirrups of his saddle. She opened the pamphlet and struggled to read the handwritten purpose of the American Tract Society: "To diffuse a knowledge of our Lord Jesus Christ as the redeemer of sinners and to promote the interests of vital godliness and sound morality, by the circulation of Religious Tracts, calculated to receive the approbation of all Evangelical Christians. . . . A missionary without a supply of Tracts is unprovided for his work."

The memory of Grandpa Charlie was beginning to fade, but Cynthia had inherited his intelligence, and it would flower on the Kentucky frontier, where children quickly and of necessity became young adults. From her father, Elton, had come simple goodness. With those two qualities alone, she'd stand a better chance to survive than most, wherever she happened to be, whatever the circumstances. From her mother, Sally, she had received physical beauty, both a blessing and a curse. Cynthia would want men to be attracted to her, but she would not want to be tied down by their selfish attitudes toward a woman who could actually think for herself.

Cynthia embodied a fountain of youthful imagination and creativity, combined with spontaneity and earthy intuition. Since the first day with the Carpenters, she had appreciated the miracle of seeds, the preparation and nurturing of soil, the acceptance of rain in whatever amount it came. "Charlsie" was at home and at peace with this new agrarian underpinning, reconnecting her with and, at the same time, separating her from her Oxfordshire birthplace.

Despite her resistance to his message, the strong maleness of the young circuit rider had created in Cynthia a gossamer of desire, stirring the sleeping passion. She fixed her eyes on the ceiling and loosed her mind to roam in the direction it chose.

She had been a perfect companion for Sylva on the voyage from London. They had huddled together in steerage, avoiding the temptations of self-pity, and bonding their womanhood to draw the strength necessary to survive. Yet there had been frequent moments of tenderness and surprising intimacy, beginning with the exhilaration of taking turns with the brushing of their hair. Sylva's reddish-golden tresses, when loosened, fell to her waist. When Cynthia slowly and carefully stroked the locks they crackled with static electricity, warm as the embers of a fire.

"Tell me," Cynthia had whispered, "what is it really like to be with a man?"

"You're too young to know."

"No, I am not too young to know. And you know I am not. Soon I'll be thirteen years old, and I am already beginning to have feelings deep inside me that I don't understand. I've told you of these feelings before. They won't go away. It's as if a bee has stung me."

"Be careful," warned Sylva.

"But be careful of *what?*" Cynthia retorted.

"Be careful of those feelings. And I am not talking about bee stings."

"Then what do they mean?"

"They mean—all right, they mean that the nature with which you were born, which came from your mother's womb, which came from *her* mother's womb, is ripening again in *you.*"

"Does it require a man to complete what I am feeling?"

"Yes and no. There are no easy or simple answers for such a complicated matter. Some women will fall in love with a man and they will marry and have children. Some women will simply fall in love with life, and they will not marry. Some women will *not* fall in love, but they will marry anyway."

"Why?"

"Because society expects it. Demands it. Reminds women of it almost every day. But then, some women will fall in love with God and commit entirely to that union."

"I don't understand."

"These are the nuns, who teach you in school. They have given their lives, a free and complete gift of themselves."

"Sylva, are you Catholic?"

"A long time ago. I used to think of the convent as a life so rich in possibilities that it defies the imagination. I loved the simplicity of a Sister's vestments, the sparkle in her eyes, the way she held the Cross to her lips."

"Then why—?"

"Yes, I know what you're thinking and what you're going

to ask me. I honestly don't know the answer. There are some women who will grow old in lonely bitterness, and there will be no completion of any kind, only a dying off. I have never wished to be one of those. Don't ask me why. It is simply the truth."

"What kind of a woman *are* you, Sylva?"

"Damn it. You are as blunt as anyone I've ever known when you want to be, Charlsie."

"I'm sorry."

"Don't be. I like your directness. Yes, I do. There is a sharp edge to it that I like very much. What kind of a woman am I? To be just as blunt, perhaps rough spoken—I am a whore. Some prefer to call me a 'prostitute,' others call me a 'bad woman.'"

"I think you're a nice lady."

"Oh, just hush. I mean—thank you very much. Thank you from the bottom of my heart." Tears were forming in Sylva's eyes. "Yes, I do have one. Thank you—Oh, I don't know what I mean."

"Why do you call yourself a whore?"

"Because that is what I am. My mother and father tried to make a living. They failed, and they tried again. Nothing seemed to work. I decided entirely on my own that I would work on the streets. I'm not ashamed. Over the centuries, there have been many thousands like me, no better and no worse. As Wellington has said, 'I never saw so many whores.'"

"What *is* a whore?"

"Too many men have been in the habit of defining it for us. I use the term out of a habit of turning the trick, so to speak, on them as well as on me. Necessity, perhaps. Stupidity, perhaps. Raw feelings, perhaps. Who is to say? To the Reverend Goodman I made a gift, which I calculated he would understand better than any other. He had something I wanted—my passage to America—the most important thing of all to me at that moment. He was human also. I would make the same gift to Captain Lovingsworth if I thought the benefits outweighed the disadvantages. Charlsie, I am not so much older than you are in years, but I am so much older in experience. One day, I will turn my experiences into a new life. I can feel it. You will see."

"But will that be right?"

"What do you mean?"

"Is it right to be so bad in order to be so good? And *can* you be good after being bad for so long?"

"There's the problem, Cynthia. There are those who spend most of their time determining for others the rightness and the wrongness of everything. How do they know?"

"They have the Bible."

"I know that. There are those who say they believe every word in the Scriptures. But the Bible is a guide. The Bible is word pictures. If you believe that everything in it is literally true, then you have a *real* problem. Take, for example, God's wrath. If God is punishing everyone because of sin, then the situation with cholera is very simple."

"Sin goes away, cholera goes away?"

"Exactly. And prostitution is a sin; therefore, if all prostitutes stop prostituting and if all men stop looking for prostitutes on street corners and in dark alleyways, then all of us will live better, moral lives. And there will be no prostitution—and no cholera. If everybody would just be *good,* then there would be no problems."

"That's not true, is it?" asked Cynthia, pausing for a moment in her brushing of Sylva's hair, and peering around her right shoulder.

"Of course, it's not true. Here is a better truth. When *more* men stop looking for prostitutes, when they stop talking out of both sides of their mouths about prostitution, *then* there will be no prostitution, no market for our bodies."

"So, I ask again. What is it like to be with a man?" asked Cynthia, brushing Sylva's hair again with long, deliberate strokes.

"It depends on the man. You can allow yourself to be abused. Or you can encourage tenderness. Many men, though, do not begin to understand what it is to be tender. Many are ruthless. They believe they must be 'manly.'"

"So, you won't tell me?"

"I cannot."

"Why not?"

"It is simply something that you must experience for yourself."

"What if I choose never to be with a man?"

"That is your choice."

"Do you advise it?"

"I cannot give that kind of advice. God has made you a woman. He has made you different from a man, in certain very real ways. You must accept the responsibility for making decisions based upon that physical reality."

"I think it would drive me crazy, never knowing what it would have been like to be with a man."

"Therefore, one day, you will be with a man."

"I am afraid."

"I understand. That is a part of it too. But think of it this way: men also are afraid the first time. They never wish to admit it, but it is true. They are probably more afraid than women."

Sylva turned around and looked at Cynthia, then took the brush from her hand. "Now it's my turn. You have glorious auburn hair that will glow if helped along. It is the color given you by our Creator. God brought into being all shades of color of hair, eyes, and skin. The Almighty loves differences, don't you think?"

"I think all my life I've been teased about my hair."

"Oh?"

"They said it was too short for a girl. They called me a boy, a redheaded boy."

"Heavens!"

"Now you're making fun too."

"Hush. Your hair is what your hair is. We shall comb it and wash it and comb it again and it will shine. You decide how long it should be. It's God's gift and it's *yours!*"

Cynthia smiled and turned her back. She crossed her legs and looked at the place where her mother and father had lain, their traveling bags the only physical evidence of their existence, except Charlsie herself. And where was she? Charlsie was gone, too, her place taken by this new creature, this Cynthia Anne Ferguson, who had gone through the bags and removed a small amount of money. Mr. and Mrs. Fischer were gone, and that kindly but terribly plagued preacher, the Reverend Goodman, was no longer moving among the passengers, urging them to give up their sins. Cynthia turned and looked into Sylva's deep green eyes.

"Sylva," said Cynthia, "I love you."

"I love you too," said Sylva.

Cynthia sank into a dark dream in which she was *Cynthia Anne* the figurehead, ocean spray dripping from her flowing hair as she plowed through the heavy sea surrounded by thunder and lightning. The moaning of the passengers in steerage rose in its own storm. The shouting of orders among the sailors in the rigging sounded from the main deck to the topmast like drovers controlling the movements of cattle on the trail to greener pastures. The animals were hungry. They easily stampeded, enveloped in a vision of clover and perpetually flowing springs. The sick, the old, and the very young were most vulnerable. They sat on their trunks and pieces of luggage, and they pressed their hands against their faces. The fallen were trampled. The bulging eyes of the living gaped, their nostrils distended, hot air shooting from them like steam jets. "Mind the jibs," the first mate squalled. "Sons of bitches," the captain screamed.

Cattle turned into lumbering rats, a community of starving rats scrambling, squeaking, running up the backs of brothers and sisters, aunts and uncles and cousins, mothers and fathers, grandfathers and grandmothers. There were frenzy and an orgy of feeding and breeding. Hungry emigrants trapped the fattest of the rats, cooked them, and ate them. The cattle drovers became embodied in one person. The Reverend Daniel Christian Goodman stood on the bow, feet firmly positioned above the figurehead of the *Cynthia Anne.* He held a whip in his right hand and he flailed the storm, his mouth as wide as a cave opening.

Cynthia was alone in a small boat, swirling down the Reverend Goodman's gullet and entering the twisting canal where creatures hung from the ceiling and walls of the upper bowel like bats with sharp, pointed horns. Their tails were long. They flicked like miniature whips. The bats became mice and the mice became fleas, and the tiny boat began to sink.

"Cynthia!" Mrs. Carpenter called as she tried to shake the child awake. "Cynthia!" The shaking seemed like the shifting of the cargo of emigrants during the first storm at sea in the summer of '33. Cynthia lurched bolt upright, eyes wide with fear, brow drenched with the dankness of deep despair, shoulders quaking like the beams of a sailing ship passing through the wall of a hurricane, entering the calm in the center, then hammered by the trailing edge. The nightmares were to persist through most of her life, plaguing her sleep, leaving her exhausted and frustrated.

On an early summer morning, three years after Cynthia came to live with the Carpenters, she was in the barn loft looking for the nests of contrary Plymouth Rock brood hens when she thought she heard a sound coming from one of the corners. She paused, then heard nothing. She took two steps and heard the sound again.

"Pssst."

"What in the world?"

"Shhhh!"

"Who in tarnation?"

"Miz Cindy. It's me. Jem."

"Good God," said Cynthia, dropping to all fours and advancing toward the corner where from the hay two big eyes peered back at her.

"Don't make no noise, Miz Cindy. I don't want to get cotched."

"How did you get here?" she whispered.

"I run off from Aunt Shawlette and the King. I'm afraid."

"Of what, Jem?"

"That somebody is going to cotch me and make me a slave again."

"I want to know how you found me," said Cynthia. "How did you?"

"The way you found me—by accident." He grinned. "I hides by day and moves by night. I saw you bringing in the milk cow early this morning. Sure is a stubborn old cow, thought to myself she'll never get her to the barn. Said to myself, Jem, that's Miz Cindy, I'll just be dipped if it ain't. I'm going to the loft of that barn and I'm going to look for a way to speak to her and nobody else. When I saw the hens nesting, I figured you'd probably be checking on 'em, so I just waited for you."

"What can I do to help you, Jem?"

"Bring me some food. I'm hungry."

"You stay put. I'll be back quicker'n you can say King Solomon!" said Cynthia, leaning forward and giving Jem a kiss on the forehead.

Outside the Carpenter house, Louise was starting a tub of wash. Joshua was down the hill, scything weeds around the tobacco patch. Cynthia went into the kitchen and loaded up her apron with a portion of cracklin' bread she'd made fresh that morning, a fried chicken leg left over from supper, a small, ripened tomato, and two apples from the trees Joshua had taught her to prune in the little orchard on the eastern slope of the home place. She carefully poured milk into a glass jar and stuffed a clean piece of cloth into the narrow neck.

"What are you doing, Cynthia?" asked Louise as she entered the kitchen.

"Oh, just heading out on a little walk. Thought I might like to have something to nibble on," she said, reaching for a piece of candle from the last batch she and Louise had made in February.

"Since when did you start eating candles?" asked Louise, picking up a square of lye soap and starting back outside.

"Never know when you might need a little light. Leastways, hope I won't."

Louise turned. "What's his name?"

"Whose name?"

"The feller you're going to see."

"What feller?"

"Ain't that Shelby fellow, is it?"

"Oh, *him*! Yes, well, to tell the truth, he's been looking my way, and I just thought I might meet him for a little picnic down on Boone Creek aways."

"Now, Cynthia Anne, you just be careful about John Shelby. He's big and he's rough, and around young ladies he bears watching."

"Yes ma'am," said Cynthia, "I understand."

"Joshua know about this?"

"No, ma'am."

"Well, I don't aim to tell him. You get back here afore you need that candle."

"Yes, ma'am."

Louise returned to her washtub and, as if she had all the time in the world, Cynthia nonchalantly headed in the direction of the barn. She climbed to the loft, using one hand to pull herself up the pegged stairs, the other to keep her apron from falling down and the bottle of milk from tipping over. She went straight to the spot where she'd left Jem, but he wasn't there.

"Pssst. Over here," said the voice.

"Lord God, you just enjoy scaring me."

"Most usually, I'm never in the same place twice. It's a little trick I figured out for myself. What did you bring me?"

"Enough to get by on for a day. There's a candle and a tinderbox in here too, if you happen to need them. Dadblame it, Jem, where you going from here? I don't want you to leave."

"I'm heading for the Ohio River. And when I gets there I'm going to figure out how to get across it. Swim it, if I have to. Get me a good piece a log and push it in front of me." With his teeth he tore off a mouthful of the chicken leg and followed it with a chunk of bread. "What's in this?" he said, pointing to the jar.

"Fresh milk from that contrary old piebald cow I brought in and milked this morning. She shook her horns and swished her nasty old tail and made it just for you! Said I might run into somebody today who'd appreciate it."

Jem smiled. "Let me sleep up here today, Miz Cindy. You won't tell on me, will you?"

"Why would I ever do that?"

He smiled again. "I'll be gone after dark. But now I know where you are, Miz Cindy, I'm liable to come back and see you again."

Cynthia kissed Jem, and she hugged him. "I'm going to be around the farm here most of the day, but I told Mrs. Carpenter I was going on a little picnic. I'll be down by the creek out of sight for a few hours, then I'll be back to check on you and maybe I'll bring you some more food to take with you. Drat it, Jem, I don't like you having to hide this way. It's not right."

"Don't you worry none about old Jem. He gonna be just fine."

"Please be careful, you hear? Get some sleep." Cynthia squeezed his hand, then descended the steps and headed from the back of the barn toward Boone Creek. She passed beneath the big buckeye tree where tradition held that Daniel Boone's brother was buried after the Indians killed him. She wished she *were* meeting John Shelby and that they would sit down together on the edge of the pasture where the cane grew tall and the wild turkeys hid. Cynthia took off her shoes and put her toes into cool water where schools of minnows played at recess. She stretched on her back, studying the puffs of clouds moving northeast. It troubled her that some nearby farms had grown so large the owners believed they needed slaves the way they needed sharp axes with strong handles. Cynthia declared that when she owned a farm it would never be so big that slaves were a necessity. She would pay attention to the smallest of needs—the ample garden, reasonably abundant orchard, crops of corn, hemp, and tobacco for reachable markets, well-conditioned animals for their various purposes. There was a nicely tuned rhythm on the farm, and she wafted herself through its cycles of seasons.

She was gone several hours but to her it seemed too long, much too long. There were so many things she wanted to ask Jem, and she didn't want him to leave, ever. When she returned to the house, Joshua was stacking locust firewood in neat cords so it would season and be ready when needed. Cynthia worried about copperhead snakes making homes in Joshua's cords of firewood. When Cynthia entered the kitchen Mrs. Carpenter was at her new iron stove, cooking supper. With a long-handled wooden spoon she stirred and found the movement relaxing.

"How was the picnic?"

"It was all right. It was just fine."

"Well you just 'member what I said about that John Shelby."

"Yes ma'am."

"You finished your chores?"

"No ma'am. I'm headed for the barn now," said Cynthia.

"Be thinking about catching me a young dominecker rooster first thing in the morning. I've got chicken and dumplings on my mind. By the time you have his scrawny neck wrung I'll have the water ready. We'll pluck him and put him to some good use."

"Yes ma'am."

As soon as Mrs. Carpenter stepped outside to fetch clothes dried by the sun, Cynthia grabbed another chicken leg, a wedge of cornpone, an apple with few enough specks to suggest a minimum of worms, and she bounded to the barn, her long, reddish hair flying. In the loft, she looked in all directions. Hearing nothing, she whispered: "Where are you?"

There was a fluttering of barn martins' wings and the keening of baby bats clinging to the juncture of beams in the loft above, but that was all. "Where are you?" Cynthia breathed. A barn cat meowed and darted away, leaving the complaints of a new litter of mixed yellow and gray kittens. The eyes of two Plymouth Rock hens blinked. "Well, I just be dadblamed, he's gone!" said Cynthia, feeling a stinging in her eyes. She slumped to her knees.

"Boo!" said Jem.

"We're even!" exclaimed Cynthia, "Lord, God, we're even. Now that's it. Never again. Absolutely no more of this scaring business. One of us is going to have the shivering fits."

"I'm sorry," said Jem.

"You'd better be, for goodness sake. Now sit down here. Brought you a little more fixings. Before you go, before you do another blessed thing, tell me, how's Aunt Charlotte and King Solomon? Tell me they're all right. Tell me they're taking care of each other. Tell me the King hasn't drunk himself into his grave. Tell me Aunt Charlotte isn't running up and down those stairs, gasping for air. Tell me—"

"They're doin' what they got to do. Same as me, Miz Cindy. I'm doin' what I got to do. It don't make no never mind what they think. I've heard too many talkin' 'bout rafflin' me off like a door prize. They say I got no business bein' free. They say all niggahs ought to be slaves, 'specially the young 'uns. So I just up and left, 'cause I know ain't nobody gonna fool with Aunt Shawlette or King Solomon, but I'm mighty fearful they gonna fool with me. One white man keep playin' with his knife whenever he see me. He talks about cuttin' out my privates."

"Oh, Jem!"

"Soon's it's good and dark I'll be gone. I wish old Jem could be like ever'body else, but he can't be—he's black."

"You're as good as anybody and don't you ever forget it!" Cynthia said, seizing him by the shoulders. "But I know you have to go. I've brought you another chicken leg and an apple that might hold up. Here, take it. Please get across that river and don't you come back until you're sure it's all right."

Cynthia and Jem embraced. She kissed him on the cheek. Slowly, she stood up and did what she knew she had to do. She climbed down the steps from the loft and walked back to the house.

"Chore's done?" asked Mr. Carpenter.

"Yes, sir," said Cynthia, taking her seat at the table, dabbling at her supper.

When Cynthia was seventeen years old she married John Shelby, the neighbor farmer who'd asked her to dance at the local agricultural exposition. It was 1838, the year of the first common schools in Kentucky. Cynthia had no time to attend them and neither did her husband. They were busy with their crops and the starting of a family. In the same year Oberlin College became the nation's first institution of higher learning to accept women as equals with men. That was irrelevant to anyone as unschooled as Cynthia Anne. Her marriage to John Shelby confirmed in her an obsession to learn whatever she could about agriculture and human nature, male and female. When word reached Kentucky in 1844 that a mob had murdered the Mormon leader Joseph Smith in Carthage, Illinois, and that the prophecies of the Adventist Reverend William Miller in 1843 and 1844 had proved untrue (there'd been *no* Second Coming of Christ), Cynthia scribbled some of her thoughts in a small, lined writing tablet: "Once again, man has shown his ignorance! Women are no better. They fall in love with men, they give birth to men."

Upon the passing of the Carpenters—bitten by a pair of copperhead snakes in the summer of 1840—Cynthia inherited their small farm and added its sixty-eight acres to the thirty-eight where she and John Shelby had built their cabin. The total 106 acres represented a hardscrabble homestead, but it was something she believed needed and deserved to be saved, something upon which she believed she might be able to build. The orphan girl from Southwark was determined to try it, alone if necessary. Cynthia had the strength and the will to split wood and plow fields, seeing no reason to surrender her entire essential being to any John Shelby, or to any arbitrary religious authority.

Owl Hollow

1844

Richard Oldham who lives in 3 miles of me fared
worse than any person I have heard of in this County,
his family were well at breakfast and before night he
had lost four of his family and the fifth one died a few
hours after night. He threw some of the last that died
in to a sinkhole and moved from his farm that night
and the ballance of his family remain in good health.
—Nelson Prewitt, to his brother, July 20, 1830
Montgomery County, Kentucky

THE DOGTROT CABIN built by John Shelby in 1838 was silent,
empty, and heavy with memories. Cynthia sat on the edge of
the bed where Little John was born the same month the last log
was chinked and the last plank of the puncheon floor was
pegged. Hadn't the birthing been more painful than she ever
imagined it would? Oh my God, yes! She was certain that she
would have died had it not been for Agnes Caudill, a traipsing
woman who, most of her long life, specialized in delivering ba-
bies. She knew exactly what to do and when to do it. She was
calm and methodical after the water broke, brooked no nonsense
on anybody's part, especially anybody the likes of a John Shelby.

Agnes rode an old mule named Leviathan, and she had a pretty good notion of where to point him without wasting time. When Cynthia looked into Agnes Caudill's eyes, felt the soothing hand with the dampened cloth on her heated forehead, there was gratitude for even that much. When the baby finally emerged, and Cynthia felt the incredible relief of delivery, she broke into a wide smile, seizing Agnes's hand, pulling it to her lips, kissing it while sobbing with joy.

"How shall we ever repay you?" asked Cynthia.

"Hush. I take no pay. Well, maybe an ear or two of corn for old Leviathan, maybe a slice of apple pie for me. Nothing more. Knowing you and this baby boy are well is good enough for me," said Agnes, cleaning the child, wrapping him in a piece of cotton cloth, nestling him next to Cynthia's breast.

"Now, Agnes Caudill," said John Shelby after he was permitted to return to the room, "what's this about you taking no pay for your trouble?"

"What I said."

"You need to take a piece of money," John insisted.

"Let me tell you something, friend, there's some things money can't buy. One woman helping another woman is one of those things. Now if you'll just do your part and look after your wife and son, I'll be upon old Leviathan and headed down the road."

Now, almost six years later, Cynthia stared fixedly at the puncheon floor and watched an ant cross near her feet. The creature scurried on and disappeared into a crack. Cynthia remembered well the day she gave up her Ferguson name to become a Shelby, remembered it as if it were yesterday, remembered that on her wedding day she felt as small as an ant and as hurried.

Cynthia Anne, to be twenty-three years old on her next birthday, growing old before her youth had scarcely begun, had been attracted by the strong masculinity of Big John Shelby.

The first time he put his arms around her and pulled her up tight to him, she felt weak in her knees as if they'd turned to water. Her nerves felt exposed with a forceful heat in her loins, her heart pounding. Yes! It was what Sylva must've meant by the "first time." John was a sturdy man, knew exactly what he was doing, and did it with intuition and, at the same time, as much kindheartedness as any bride had a right to expect. He was the lover of a young girl's sweetest dreams. But the ultimate act of creation, which Cynthia welcomed as the only way for children to be conceived, then nurtured, turned to demands, morning, noon, and night.

John had pestered her to be married. From the moment he had taken her in the barn loft, he had kept after her. She knew why. He wanted somebody to cook for him. He wanted some-body to haul his bathwater, somebody to plant and work his garden, somebody to carry in the firewood, slop the hogs, shoot the hogs, pinch the life out of the tobacco worms. He wanted her body in his bed. He wanted to roll over on her and take his pleasure whenever he felt the urge, which was regular.

There'd been laughter on that day in '38 after the simple wedding ceremony in front of the new fireplace made of Owl Hollow cliff rocks. Joshua and Louise Carpenter had never seemed happier. Their gift was a pair of yearling mules. There'd been cake and a wedding night in a featherbed with fluffy pil-lows. For a fleeting moment there'd been a thought, if not a feeling, of passion cresting inside her mind and body, the outer edge of her awareness as fragile as a leaf touching the defining edge of the distant horizon. Then, it was gone. It had been a single leaf dependent upon that unchangeably drawn line mark-ing her existence in a world she once thought she was beginning to understand.

After that she felt used. She felt damnably put upon. She cried but hid her tears in her goose down pillow. She would have liked to feel excitement. It was not that she was a cold woman. That was not it. It was more as if an essential part of her being was sleeping. Maybe it was hidden and she did not know how to discover it. Maybe a man could not discover it. She found it hard to admit pleasure. A woman who dared to admit that she really *wanted* a sexual experience was branded a whore.

Cynthia wanted love. And she wanted children. She was like other women she'd known, but she also possessed a quickness of thought and a desire to speak her mind. She fretted and rationalized that a barter would be necessary. She was willing to make a gift of her body, her work, and her daily presence, to do all God's chores, in exchange for the chance to be a mother. And when the time came, she rejoiced that she had received the gift of Little John. But then there had been three miscarriages. They always made Big John so short-tempered.

Only the day before, John had promised to take Little John to market. They'd gone in the wagon with the mules, You Know and I Know, pulling the load of tobacco, stripped and tied in hands, done up as neatly as skeins of bright spinning yarn. Little John had been eager to travel with his father. He'd been a good boy, had said his prayers, had not complained and not asked for anything. He'd earned a little favor, yes, he had. Until now, he'd never spent a night away from home. Father and son were traveling on the Cane Ridge Road, having one of their rare conversations. The November morning was crisp and clear.

"Little John, you're getting older. Gonna be six years old come your birthday. Now, you got to be real careful when we get to town. Just because the cholera has passed on, so to speak, there's always the outside chance that somebody might run up and give it to us. You know what I mean?"

"No, sir."

"Well, I'll tell you. You see, the year you was born, I was ready to look for my own pot of gold. Yes, I was."

"Why?"

"To make us rich. But your mama's forcing me to stay close to home."

"Naw, she ain't."

"Is so. Now, as it's turning out, she's probably right. Hate to admit it, but she probably is. See, if I'd go off, I might find the cholera instead of the gold."

"What's cholera?"

"Bad trouble. You might say it works a lot like gold."

"How's that?"

"Well, gold can make folks greedy. It can gobble them up. People will kill for gold. Cholera has its own way of gobbling up people."

"People like you and me?"

"Like you and me. Don't want it to happen. But it could."

"I don't want no gold nor no cholera neither," said Little John.

"Cholera's like being sat on by an elephant and swallered by a whale. Old Jonah knew all about the leviathan. Old Job, too. Now, Job, he'd had it up to here with the whole business of living and dying. I've heard my daddy say, just like old Job, he cursed the day he was born. So, maybe you and me will do just fine without the gold, or the cholera, or a whole herd of elephants or a whole ocean of leviathans!"

"What's a leviathan?"

"A big critter in the Bible. It's an elephant that lives in the ocean. He eats all the little fish he wants to. It's also the name of old lady Caudill's dadblamed mule."

"How we gonna be just fine?"

"Well, we'll raise our tobacco every year, and we'll bring it to town to sell. We'll raise a little corn. Make a little whiskey. We'll raise our hogs and butcher 'em for our table. We'll split our firewood, and go a-fishin'."

"Don't mama split most of the firewood?"

"You'll grow up and you'll find a sweet young thing just

like your mama and you'll bite the bullet and get yourself hitched."

"What's hitched?"

"Like You Know and I Know. They're hitched."

Little John stared at his father. Then he stared at the big rear ends of the mules. Where the leather rounded the rumps, a layer of sudsy lather foamed and dripped.

"You'll work your woman hard and have a passel of children just like their grandpa has tried to do. I wanted lots of sons, maybe ten of 'em, maybe more. But your mama has only dropped one and that is you. Natcherly, we'll take special good care of You Know and I Know. We couldn't hardly make it without *them*."

At the mention of their names, the giant ears of the sixteen-hand, half-ton mules flinched in anticipation of a "gee" or a "haw," but when the commands didn't come, the long ears returned to their forward, on-guard positions. You Know's and I Know's big, soft eyes blinked and studied each stone and each piece of limb in the road, avoiding them insofar as they believed it necessary to keep from bouncing out any tobacco. They knew a stick from a shadow, and whenever they saw a snake they didn't spook, they stomped. More intelligent, by far, than most horses, You Know and I Know felt as much members of the Shelby family as the coon dog, Rafe, or the barn cat, Starlight. Hauling tobacco to sell had a connection with corn in the crib and therefore with corn in their stall troughs, where they had the good mule sense not to eat too much. Wouldn't catch them foundering. They thought too much of their feet to be that stupid.

Conventional wisdom held that mules didn't stand a chance of anything called love because they couldn't *make* love to amount to anything in the first place. Even if they could, it was plainly doubtful that love played any part whatsoever in the activity, if there had been any activity, which there wasn't, so why worry about it? When Starlight came in heat she rolled over on her back, thrashed on the ground, turning this way and that, and screeched an open invitation for any tom anywhere to come put out the fire. When Rafe was in the middle of treeing a coon, if a bitch in heat presented herself, he'd breed first, tree later. John Shelby had plenty of company. So did Cynthia, come to think of it.

To say that Big John *loved* his wife was a good way down the Cane Ridge Road from the truth. He did not want a single life, forcing him to do many things he judged better suited for women. Was it not, then, a good trade that she did her work and he did his work? If anybody wanted to call that loving, they were free to do so. They could call it canoodling or being a man or claiming debt. John Shelby never once in his life told Cynthia that he loved her. It would be an unmanly thing to do. In short, his job was to do the thinking.

Big John looked off to the right at the Cane Ridge Meetinghouse, A Temple of Christian Unity, site of the great revival of 1800. His mother and father and grandmother and grandfather had been there on the day of the huge outpouring, the grand jumping up, and the glorious falling down. The Baptist, Methodist, Pentecostal, Presbyterian, and latter-day Lollard preachers who shouted at the praying, singing crowds countenanced no human reason but focused simple-mindedly on a sacred text. As many as twenty thousand people screamed, jerked, and fainted as if they had lost all good sense.

Big John himself had quickly and easily become *un*-churched. He had done his share of ridge running and howling at full moons. He could quote here and there from the Bible and drink several good men under the table, but he didn't know anything about praying, and he felt uneasy whenever a crowd formed to talk uproariously about Heaven and how to get there.

"Son," said Big John, "over there's where not so long ago all those religious folks had that whoop-de-do and organized the 'Christian Church.' Now, that's all right for those better suited for it, but as far as you and me and your mama is concerned, we're better off just staying out of it."

"Why?" asked Little John.

"Just told you. Some people's better suited for it. You and me, we got better things to do."

"Mama says there's a God and I ought to behave myself."

"Didn't say there *wasn't* a God."

"Mama says there's a place where all good people go. She says there's a Heaven. You don't believe in Heaven?"

"Putting words in my mouth. Didn't say it. Didn't say it at all. But I will say this: You give me half a chance at either looking for silver and gold here on God's green earth or walking around on streets of gold and drinking from silver goblets in God's stupendous and wonderful Heaven, and you know which one I'll take?"

"Which one?"

"The golden one. The silver one. Right here, right now. Ain't that right, You Know and I Know?" Big John guffawed loudly and snapped the reins against the backs of the mules.

The Shelbys crossed over Stoner Creek near the mouth of Houston Creek, where Stoner gathers speed and wiggles its way northwest to meet with Hinkston at Ruddles Mill to become the South Fork of the Licking River. Big John didn't have to remind You Know and I Know that they would be needing some extra pulling to get up to the courthouse on the hill in Paris, the county seat. The mules didn't strain, but he could see the dark, leathery muscles working from their necks, down along their sides and into their sable flanks, rhythmically moving with legs and hooves as steady and smooth and true as metronomes.

Big John Shelby pulled in the reins at the edge of the public auction site. He and Little John began unloading their tobacco under the watchful eye of company agents. Some of the leaf would be transferred to hogsheads and rolled by mule, horse, and oxen to river stations and loaded onto Kentucky boats for the long trip down the Ohio and Mississippi rivers to New Orleans for the overseas trade. Some would be processed locally for pouches of chewing, cigarette, and pipe tobaccos. Wherever it went, people were more than willing to pay a good price for it because it brought them pleasure. It was as simple as that.

Flush with their money, John Shelby and his son headed for Big Billy Scott's dry goods store, where they bought a bright blue ribbon for Cynthia, a pair of work shoes for Big John and two pieces of taffy for Little John. They slept in the wagon and the next morning they were on the way back home, the lightness of the load a noticeable and certain joy for You Know and I Know. It was the end of another season, autumn was blending into winter, when man and beast could sense the coming of the cold blowing down from Ohio. Like bears, they'd begun to think about curling-up places. It was the annual winding down, when older folk equated winter with the end of life.

Cynthia would never know what went wrong. Nobody would know. It may have been something as innocent as a drink of water from a common cup at the tobacco auction site. It may have been the use of the public outhouse; it may even have been the taffy pulled by some well-meaning churchwoman in town, or the licking of fingers to get every crumb. Hands most often went unwashed. Whatever it was, it hit as it usually did—suddenly and without warning.

The cholera pandemic, the global spread of the disease in 1832 to '33, had come and gone, and hundreds of people had died in Kentucky. In its wake there was a feeling of complacency. There were isolated cases; from time to time the dread disease would strike, and churchgoers would speak nervously of God's wrath. Others accepted cholera as stoically as the death of a calf or a suckling pig. It was all such a mystery, a fearsome conundrum that served to baffle a people who wanted hardly more than to live good and decent lives. Sometimes the disease seemed as capricious as a lone tornado, hitting a single family and then rising to drop down later miles away.

In that afternoon of November 1844, John Shelby and five-year-old Little John were sick, bad sick, before they got home. You Know and I Know, ears pinned back, were anxious for some better word from the driver or the boy. Big John and Little John slumped together, jostled apart, then collapsed together again. From time to time, John would call out "Whoa," and the mules would wait as the father and son spilled out of the wagon and squatted along the roadside. It seemed there could not be enough stops. Each time, it was more difficult for the two sufferers to climb back into the wagon. Each time, the reins were flicked on the mules' rumps more feebly than before. You Know and I Know knew it was growing darker and that they should not be stopping so often. They should head for home with no looking back. And they did. They broke into a pace so fast that the boy and his father began to vomit and defecate, profusely, as if their insides were coming out.

Cynthia was watching through the window, waiting apprehensively. The line of the horizon cutting across from Buzzard's Roost down to Owl Hollow Creek was, on the one hand reassuring but, on the other, an unwavering confirmation of her feeling of powerlessness to change reality. When Rafe set up a howl and bounded off the porch, and then Cynthia heard the unusually loud bouncing of the wagon, she ran outside. Big John and Little John struggled from the floor of the wagon to the ground, leaving You Know and I Know troubled about when they would be unhitched so they could amble on down to the frog pond for drafts of sweet glory water.

"I feel like I've been eaten alive," said John Shelby. "Feel like something real big done sat down on me," he gasped.

"Feel like shucks, Mama," said Little John, barely to be heard.

Big John, fumbling with his suspenders and the top button on his soiled pants, stumbled toward the outhouse he'd built with his own hands and presented to Cynthia with such all-fired pride in '38.

Cynthia scooped up Little John and carried him into the house and laid him on his bed. She fetched one of the bottles of calomel she kept handy as recommended in her *Family Medicine Chest Dispensatory*. She mixed a portion in grape jelly and eased a spoonful into Little John's mouth. He swallowed.

"Mama, am I gonna die?" he whimpered. "My legs hurt so bad. My stomach is on fire."

Cynthia had heard such words many times in her life, but hearing them from her own child was like the line of the horizon snapping. She touched her forehead with the thumb and index and middle fingers of her right hand and crossed herself. It was more than Catholic habit. It was an ultimate sign of surrender.

"In the name of the Father and of the Son and of the Holy Ghost."

Making the same sign on Little John and saying the same words, Cynthia peered deeply into the boy's sunken eyes. He no longer looked like a child. He seemed more like a small man, withered and rapidly fading. "We must all pass over, some day," she said, "but you must rest now and place your faith in God."

"Is God mad at me?" asked Little John, squeezing his hands together, tightly.

"Now, why should God be mad at you?"

"Maybe I've been bad."

"I don't remember you being bad," said Cynthia, looking again through the window to the distant ridge. The line of the horizon was still unbroken. She wiped her eyes with the back of her hand.

"I toyed with myself, Mama," said Little John.

"Hush. Just hush. How could God possibly care about such a small offense?"

"I've been chewing tobacco too, a little bitty chaw."

"God doesn't care if you chewed the whole dang crop."

"I hid it from you."

"If that's all you hid from your mama, she'd be mighty happy."

"Mama, I wish I wasn't such a bad person. Mama, where are my feet? I can't find them."

"Just stop it, now. You're *not* bad and your feet are right here where they've always been. You've not done anything wrong. God doesn't sit up there in Heaven, looking down here on his children, punishing them for little things like what you've told me about. God is not a monster. God is *good*. God loves you, Little John. He is a spirit and he loves you."

"Mama, I hurt. I hurt all over. I'm cold all over."

"Little John, I'm going to Flat Rock for Doctor Regan. Try to stay in bed. If you need to throw up use the slop jar, just do it. I'll be back as quick as I can."

"Mama, am I going to Heaven?" asked Little John in almost a whisper.

Cynthia heard the words, but they meant nothing to her as she hurriedly left the house. Outside, between the side of the porch and the outhouse, lay the body of John Shelby. His eyes were wide with dark circles around them and a distant stare. His mouth was slack. Saliva oozed from it. Cynthia knew death when she saw it, so she did not touch her husband's body, but she returned to the house and found a shirt to cover his face. When she climbed onto the wagon and took up the blackened, slathered reins, she wore her garden gloves, a special wedding present. Instinctively, she was being as careful as if she'd turned a large rock and discovered the biggest copperhead in the entire world.

By the time Cynthia and Doctor Walter Regan returned, Little John Shelby had crossed over. The doctor closed the boy's eyes, then turned to look at Cynthia, her head hanging down, her hands tightly twisted as she stood by the fireplace.

"I'm sorry," he said. He went to her and put his arms around her and held her while she sobbed.

Cynthia pushed back and looked squarely at the doctor. "It was cholera. It was cholera, wasn't it?"

"Perhaps," said the doctor. "It's not the season for it. Sometimes it comes when we least expect it. We seldom know for absolute certain."

"I know it was. They went to town healthy and they came back sick unto death."

"I advise you to see about burying them quickly. Tomorrow morning early would not be too soon. *Don't* touch the bodies. Let me wrap them in any bedclothes you may have. Is there somebody who could dig the graves?"

"I'm not sure anybody would want to. No, I have nobody to do it."

"Somebody's going to have to. Do you have coffins? Of course, you don't. I'm sorry I asked."

"A small one is all. The family that raised me left it up in the barn loft. They never had children, but they always said it wouldn't be right to bury a child unprotected. They bought it from the same drummer who sold them their Bible. I could drag it down and make it ready."

It was in full-moon brightness that Doctor Regan began to dig. He knew he wouldn't be able to dig very deep, but by dawn he'd done the best he could. While he dug, Cynthia was clumsily using the sharpened edge of her hatchet to score the name and dates below the coffin's small window.

Little John
1839-1844

The air was keen with hoarfrost on the morning of the burial of Cynthia's husband and son, the rising sun illuminating webs on the split-rail fences where spiders dozed and waited patiently.

Finished with the laborious digging of the graves and the covering of John Shelby's body, Doctor Regan sat beneath a tall, straight tree where the black walnuts were beginning to shake loose and fall to the ground. He watched as Cynthia reopened the iron coffin to look a final time at Little John. She adjusted the collar of his shirt and around his neck she considered placing the gold chain and cross his great-granddaddy had given to her. For a moment, she held the cross lightly in her hand, looked at it, pressed it against her lips then, shaking her head, spoke softly: "No, it is for the living."

She wished to leave *something* with the child. She looked at the farm around her—the calves bawling, hens scratching for grubs, You Know and I Know standing at the barn lot gate, ears forward. She saw a tall flowering goldenrod, pulled it up by its roots, and laid it gently on Little John's breast. Then she prayed: "Oh, my God, redeem my blameless child. Help us to understand why he died," Cynthia sobbed. "Deliver us from fear. Save us from ignorance."

She paused, then stiffened as she turned and looked toward Big John's grave. "I'll look after this place, John, I will. I'll work it with these hands—somehow."

Turning back, she closed the lid of Little John's coffin and lightly placed her hand upon its small window. "Amen."

Doctor Regan rose and helped Cynthia lower the casket into the shallow grave. Together, they covered it with dirt, dark and rich, brittle with November tackiness. Cynthia made the sign of the cross. "Doctor, I just don't understand it."

His head down, the toe of his boot nudging a piece of dirt toward the edge of John Shelby's grave, Doctor Regan waited for Cynthia to speak again.

"I haven't been able to figure out the connection between God and disease. I can't bring myself to believe that sickness and punishment are the same thing. It grieves me even more than death."

"Do you read the Bible?" asked Regan.

"A little bit. It confuses me."

"You're Catholic, are you not?"

"Yes, but that confuses me too. It is too damnably strict."

"I'm cursed by those who believe that God is the *only* healer," said Regan, turning his large bulk toward his old, gray, patiently waiting horse. "I'm damned again by those who believe scourges are sent from Heaven." He stirruped up, leaned forward, and looked down at Cynthia: "As long as there are authoritarian biblical mandates there's little hope for new medical discoveries."

"I'm totally alone," said Cynthia, "stripped bare and winter just beginning."

"A line in the Apocrypha sustains me, Cynthia," said Doctor Regan. "It's from Ecclesiasticus: Honour a physician with the honour due unto him for the uses which ye may have of him: for the Lord hath created him."

Cynthia smiled for the first and last time on this day she'd always remember. She said, "It's time for me to go to work."

"And I must go now," said the Doctor Regan. "Will you be all right?"

"I'll be just fine. It'll take some time."

"Call me when you need me," said the doctor as he loosened the reins, patted the side of the horse, and, touching the front edge of his hat, headed home to Flat Rock.

"God bless you," said Cynthia, waving. Finally, she turned back to look at her husband's grave.

When she heard someone approaching and Rafe barked a warning, Cynthia turned and saw a rider, tall and lean and wearing a peculiar smile. His hat was pulled low and his frock coat flared out, completing the appearance of urgency.

The Reverend Samuel J. Jones had seen Doctor Regan rushing from his house and climbing into Cynthia's wagon, and he was sure his services would be needed. Now he dismounted, removed his hat, stood on the edge of the Shelby graves, and began to preach hellfire like a man consumed. He wetted his lips with the flecks of spittle flying from his mouth. He dug at the ground with the heel of his boot, the Reverend Jones's ministry beginning at the tips of his toes and spreading through his body until it spewed from his tongue. "Hallalabamamababa-huh. Heyomamadeabba-huh. Holysabbamama-huh."

The Reverend Jones looked Cynthia dead in the eye, and wavered not one whit but that she and her son, Little John, and her husband, Big John, had each one sinned and, "Oh Gawd-huh," those two had paid with their *lives* for all their wrongdo-ing. The Reverend Samuel J. Jones quivered like the master of a hungry coonhound beneath a tall water maple on the creek bank in the dead of night. Cynthia was still too weak with grief to speak against the Reverend Jones, such a physical man of God, announcing the Word from God's Holy Bible the way he did. She just stared at him.

The heat of the Reverend Samuel J. Jones's exhortation had cooled down to a more indifferent but no less insufferable rumble. From the front gate a few neighbors had paid their hur-ried passing respects, all keeping their distance, for they feared exceedingly being even that close to anyone associated with cholera. When Cynthia unfolded her arms and placed her hands on her hips, only then did the Reverend Jones's demeanor di-minish from holy bombast to mealy-mouthed philandering.

"Honey," he said, "honey, this here's Gawd-huh's way. You know that, don't you?"

"No," said Cynthia, "I don't know that."

"See, your husband and your boy, they *sinned.*"

"No, they didn't. They didn't sin at all. Even if they had there'd be no way for you to know about it. And if you did know about it, it would be none of your business. So let's just leave it *right* there. They did *not* sin."

"They *must'a* sinned, else why would Gawd-huh have

slammed the door so tightly shut on them?" crooned the Reverend Jones.

Cynthia shook her head in disbelief. She tucked down her chin, while her eyes moved upward, where they became fixed like cats-eye agates.

"Mister Jones—"

"Yes, my dear?"

"I wish to God—"

"Yes?"

"That he would—"

"Yes, dear?"

"—slam the door tightly on *you!*"

"Now, you're overwrought, and I'd be obliged to explain everything to you in the days ahead," continued the Reverend Jones, ignoring Cynthia's remark, his arm searching and reaching and hanging across her shoulder, his breath not helped even a little bit by tobacco juice.

"You'd be better obliged to be on down the road," said Cynthia, removing the reverend's hand. It was as insufferable as it was inconceivable that such a thing should be happening to her with the dirt not settled in her husband's and son's graves. She was as vulnerable now as she'd ever been in steerage on the *Cynthia Anne*. She felt horribly alone but strong and vengeful.

"Now, I'll be coming back to check on you, you hear?"

"No!"

"I mean to be sure you're doing all right, is all."

"No!" said Cynthia, her back arching like a cat, bristling and about to spring.

"Don't you worry about nothing," soothed the Reverend Jones.

"Never you mind heading back this way. Now or ever."

"Aw, now's that any way for a little *lady* to talk?" he said, again putting his long arm around her shoulder and abruptly pulling her toward him, seemingly the protector, the consoler.

"You son of a bitch," Cynthia said, her voice low.

"What did you say?" the Reverend replied in astonishment, like a bull suddenly pole-axed.

Cynthia twisted loose from the heavy arm. In the same motion, from her apron pocket she brought forth Captain Lovingsworth's small pearl-handled pistol. She held it with both hands, and she aimed it directly at the frown between the Reverend's startled eyes.

She had learned to use the weapon with efficient authority, especially at hog-killing time in November. She would stride among the squealing, wild-eyed creatures and place the gun at the exact spot where it would be most deadly. She'd pull the trigger and walk on, while Big John followed and slit the throats of the fallen hogs. In their high-top leather boots, Cynthia and Big John walked in blood, and the steam rose from the hides of the animals in the vats, and it was good, knowing there'd be fresh sausage on the breakfast table and twenty-pound hams to be salted and hung from the meat house rafters.

Once, after the Carpenters' deaths, Cynthia had blown away the head of a three-foot copperhead staring from the Owl Hollow Creek water gap, the bullet entering the gaping mouth, sealing the sensory pits beneath the eyes. She'd peeled the hide and hung it to dry on the back porch.

"Nobody invited you to mind this burial of my boy and my man."

"Now, Miss Cynthia, don't get riled, now." The thought occurred to Jones to knock the gun from Cynthia's hand, but it was quickly replaced by another more sensible thought when he heard the slow, positive cocking of the weapon. Even the slightest of movements now would send the bullet into his brain, and he did not like that thought.

"You invited yourself. There was nothing for anybody to do," she said.

"Yes, ma'am. You're right about that. Yes, ma'am, you are definitely right about that."

"You would take advantage of anybody you could lay your hands on. Even me. Even now."

"No, ma'am. No, *ma'am*," the Reverend Jones pleaded.

"You're the Devil!"

"No, ma'am."

"You're humbug!"

"Yes, ma'am. Call me anything you want to. Humbug is right. Just, *please,* uncock that gun. You shouldn't be doing this," the Reverend moaned.

"You are—everything—that's bad."

"Yes, ma'am. I mean, no, ma'am."

"To my dying breath, I will do everything within my power to see that the truth is told on you."

"Yes, ma'am. Yes, ma'am, and Amen."

"You're like all the rest of the liars and the thieves."

"Yessum."

Cynthia slowly pushed the gun against his forehead.

"Oh, no. Please. Oh, no."

"Yes. You *are* the Devil. And I'm going to shoot you!"

"No!"

"You belong to him. You work for him. Now I'm going to send you *to* him. I'm going to blow your brains out, and then I'm going to skin you and hang your hide on the front gatepost for all God's men to see."

"Miss Cynthia, please put the gun down. I want to go. Honest to Gawd-huh, I want to go. I promise not to come back. I promise not to bother you *no* more."

"One day, and it will not come soon enough, God will take care of you. It will not be by me or anybody else killing you, but simply by Him *shunning* you, and you will go on living with the Devil and all his kind."

"Please, don't shoot me!"

"Turn around."

He gaped for an instant, then did as he was told.

"Head down the road. Don't *ever* come back."

She pushed the barrel of the gun against the back of his head and said, low down and coarse, "Git, you son of a bitch."

"Yes, *ma'am*," said the Reverend Jones. "Yes, ma'am. I'm gittin', I'm gittin'." He slowly began walking, each step quicker than the last, and then running. The farther he went, the faster he ran. When he reached the edge of a honey locust thicket, where huge thorns grew in impenetrable profusion from the bases of the trees to the highest top, the Reverend turned and cupped his hands.

"You'll burn in hell, daughter-r-r-r!" shouted the Reverend Samuel J. Jones as Cynthia walked with measured strides down the hill to her house.

"Lord, Gawd-huh, Almighty, you'll burn in hell-l-l-l!" hollered the Reverend Jones one more time.

She'd heard enough. She turned and fired three shots.

Out of range, the preacher heard the sounds, loud and clear. He vanished among the honey locusts and the pin oaks.

Cynthia muttered under her breath, "I wish I'd shot the son of a bitch."

From that day forward, Cynthia worked as hard as any man, harder than most. She knew what she could do, and she did it. She was a planter of seeds in the fertile ground of her adopted state. She gloried in the coming of each spring when she could set out the tomatoes she'd started from seed, plant her corn and her beans. She undertook only what she could handle herself, including a small patch of that bewitching vegetable, tobacco. She did not smoke and she did not chew, but she grew the weed for others to buy and to decide what they wished to do with.

Cynthia was the Jeffersonian and Jacksonian foundation of the future of Kentucky and the nation. She was five inches of topsoil upon which, with sufficient moisture, a civilization could grow. Her love of sowing and reaping, of conserving the soil and water, and her respect for the ways of nature were the basis of Cynthia's resolve to survive and to grow. Her independent, determined way of thinking was a direct link to her grandfather Charles, whose body now lay somewhere at the bottom of a Southwark mass grave, and her grandmother, Winifred, sleeping in an unmarked churchyard grave in Wantage, in the Vale of White Horse district of Oxfordshire.

Owl Hollow

1852

Gird on thy sword, O man, thy strength endue,
In fair desire thine earth-born joy renew,
Live thou thy life beneath the making sun
Till Beauty, Truth, and Love in thee are one.
—Robert Bridges, *Hymn of Nature*

THE CONFLICTING TALES about Cynthia Anne Shelby, her virtue and her wickedness, took root—stories spreading far and wide about the incident with the pistol and the threat on the life of such a well-meaning man of God as the Reverend Samuel J. Jones—and the many times she arrived just in time to save a neighbor's newborn, be it calf, lamb, or colt. She was variously described as a hellcat who drove hard bargains, an immigrant Catholic, somebody with a lot of money, and—by those who lived the nearest and knew her best—a good woman whose word was her bond.

From time to time, a gold sovereign would show up in town, and it would be designated a "Miss Cynthia." Those who shunned her because they feared her said it was a constant wonder that somebody didn't knock her in the head. It was a known fact that she could shoot the eyes out of a copperhead, and nobody wanted to take the chance of trying to sneak up on her. There weren't many who were willing to ask her for a job because she was particular about the help she hired, the long hours she worked, her disregard for threatening rain. Sometimes she did her own plowing. She swapped help with neighbors at tobacco housing time, but there were other days when the stubborn old fool pitched in and worked, she said, for the fun of it. She made no secret of the fact that she loved her land and said it would be a cold day in Hell afore she'd part with it. She seldom went to town, but when she did it was to take vegetables to sell at the courthouse square. Her melons were the juiciest, corn the sweetest, apples the firmest. She showed children how to cut scary faces in pumpkins, and she always told them to be careful about putting their dirty fingers into their mouths.

There was the one time when that known atheist Dr. Walter Regan showed up with Cynthia at Owl Hollow True Believers Evangelical Church. It was the last day of a revival, and a traveling evangelist was conducting a "healing" meeting. Several of the frothiest, wildest praying came down front, fell on their knees, and had their throat cancers relieved by a hard slap below their jawbones. Doctor Regan looked at Cynthia and she looked at him, and they walked out before the last Amens were finished. Not long after that, Doctor Regan died after treating a cholera victim, but it seemed that nothing could kill Miss Cynthia. When she attended his funeral in the Flat Rock cemetery, there were several strangers there, including a group of doctors from Transylvania University. One of them was seen whispering with Cynthia, and it was plain for anybody to see that they went off together in her wagon, toward the old Carpenter place.

"I had no idea I'd ever see you again," said Doctor Laurence Hanover.

"Lord God, nor I, you," said Cynthia, "but I sure am glad you're here. A talk with a sane thinking human being for a change will be the best thing that could happen to me."

"Why didn't you contact me?"

"Now, how could I find time to do that?" said Cynthia, the aging You Know and I Know pacing themselves, bringing the old wagon over the hills, across Boone Creek, and up the branch to Owl Hollow.

"My husband and son are buried over there," Cynthia pointed. "There's no marker. Cholera killed them. When are you doctors going to figure it out?"

Doctor Hanover looked where the bluegrass was lush, tiny seed heads bowing over in profusion, nothing to indicate a physical presence, yet the tips of the seeds were softly blue, alive with new growth. "We're working," he said.

"Will you sit on the porch for a spell?"

"Yes, of course."

Cynthia Anne Charlsie Ferguson Lovingsworth Shelby and Doctor Laurence Hanover sat in rough hickory-staved chairs she'd made with her own hands, and they talked about the last voyage of the *Cynthia Anne.* He listened with spellbound attention as she recalled the death and burial of Captain Lovingsworth, the little room containing Old Aunt Charlotte, King Solomon, and Jem, and the day they left Sylva at the entrance to the convent. Cynthia recalled the lives of Mr. and Mrs. Carpenter and her marriage to John Shelby.

"Enough of all that," she said. "What has happened to you?"

"I've traveled quite a bit. I've been to India. I suppose I've taken it upon myself to continue the study of cholera where it often begins and inevitably ends. But it's so frustrating. We're no nearer a solution, I mean a definitive answer. It has been fairly clear to me that despite the claims of the theologians, cholera, filth, and bad social conditions go hand in hand. After two major epidemics to hit here in Kentucky, even King Solomon realizes it. But people keep dying, and he keeps on digging graves."

"You live in Lexington?" asked Cynthia.

"Yes. I inherited my father's house."

"Will you retire there?"

"I hope it won't be much longer. I long for time in the library he left for me. There are so many books to be reread and some, I'm afraid, I've not opened the first time."

"There are those who think I'm strange," said Cynthia.

"Why?"

"Because I don't get much farther than the farmer's market in Paris, I carry a gun and just about everybody knows I can use it, I'm an immigrant Catholic with a foreign accent, and I have a deep-seated disgust for anything that smells like evangelical horse manure. On top of everything else, they call me an abolitionist—and they may be right."

"Cynthia Anne," said Doctor Hanover, "there'll always be the fanatics who feed on ignorance. With no justification for godless beliefs, witchcraft was punished by death not so long ago in this country. In fact, in colonial days, the Rev. Cotton Mather published more than three hundred and eighty books. I have two on my shelf, *Wonders of the Invisible World* and *Memorable Providences Relating to Witchcraft and Possessions*. I should not allow them to gather dust. I should go home today and read them once more to remind myself that these hideous doctrines have been promulgated and will be again if good people remain silent."

"Will you stay for supper?"

"No, thank you."

"Fresh asparagus, corn so juicy it'll run down your chin, leg of lamb cooked slow and tender—everything from right here on this farm!"

"Sounds wonderful, but I must catch up with my doctor friends who came to pay their respects to a good man of medicine. They're waiting for me at his widow's house in Flat Rock."

"Will you come another time and let me show you around my place?"

"I'd be honored."

"Then I'll take you back," said Cynthia.

Over the years, few visitors came to her door where the fragrant honeysuckle, the morning glory, and the gourd vines grew in such profusion, and the purple martins returned each April. But one bright day a man on horseback approached the front porch, dismounted, and haltingly called her name, his felt hat clutched tightly in his hands.

"Miz Cindy? You here?"

"Yes, what is it? What do you want?" she said, emerging from the shadows, guardedly, easing her right hand to the side, where her loaded pistol rested.

"Don't you *remember* me?" said the voice, low and soothing.

A moment's thought and then a huge smile broke across her face. She threw open her arms and into her embrace she pulled the tall, gangling, handsome man. His arms hung down, because he knew instinctively the recrimination such a situation could invite.

The young black man who appeared in Cynthia Shelby's doorway and who soon found himself in her embrace was a fugitive from freedom, trying to find unlikely acceptance. He had gone to Cincinnati and remained there, despite Aunt Charlotte's and King Solomon's pleading during his secret visits to Lexington. Although Kentucky was officially not a slave state, the weight of its true nature was more than any that abolitionists such as Cassius Clay could overcome. It had become a virtual slave marketplace for the South, where anyone with black skin and African features was stamped ineffaceably. Freed slaves were always on guard about the possibility of a contrived return to chains.

"Jem, Jem, Jem," said Cynthia. She held him tight and she would not let him go.

"Miz Cindy," said Jem, "I didn't know if I'd ever see you

again. I'd come to the top of the hill, but something always seemed to pop up. It's still not easy being a free black man in your neighborhood."

"Come into this house," said Cynthia. "Come into this house and sit yourself down and talk to me. Here, sit right here in this chair and prop up your feet and get me caught up. Aren't you just fine to look at? Yes, you are! All right, begin in the beginning, right at the very beginning. The last time I saw you was—how long ago?—more than fifteen years ago? You were hiding out there in the hayloft, and you were hungry, and I brought you food, and Mr. and Mrs. Carpenter never knew a thing about it. She thought I'd gone on a picnic!"

"I made it to the Ohio River and there was nothing to do but, in the middle of the night, slip into that muddy water with a log and paddle my way to the other side. I was lucky to wind up no more than a mile or so downstream from Cincinnati, and I walked back as soon as I was rested."

"What has become of Aunt Charlotte and King Solomon? Do you know? Have you seen them? You don't live there anymore. Where *do* you live?"

"Cincinnati—"

"How have you been? You're a man now, yes, you are. A grown man, and here I am an old widder woman talking her fool head off, not letting you get a word in edgeways. Do you know what some call me around here?"

"No."

"They say I'm a blamed old nanny goat."

"Why?"

"Because I'm different. I say what I think. I won't put up with foolishness."

"Miz Cindy—"

"And don't you call me any 'Miz Cindy,' you hear? You call me Cynthia Anne, because that's my name, and I give you permission to call me by my real name, for goodness sakes."

"I don't know if I can change *that* much," said Jem with a soft smile.

"Well, you just try," laughed Cynthia.

"All right. First of all, you're not an old nanny goat. You're a young woman who wanted me to be her brother. You fed me when I was hungry. You even gave me a candle and a tinderbox. I'm sorry to say they're at the bottom of the Ohio. And I'm sorry about the widow part. You don't have to tell me about that if you don't want to. But you're a fine *young* woman, Miz Cindy."

She looked down, warmly pleased, and then looked back into Jem's dark eyes. "Aunt Charlotte?" Cynthia asked, the words catching in her throat.

"She still lives in one of those rickety old places in Lexington, still sells gingerbread and other things on Water Street, still predicts another Town Branch flood. She's aging very fast. The King lives wherever he can find a place. He's still drinking Ole Wildcat and picking up cigars off the street and firing up those infernal things. Says his favorites were his hero's, Henry Clay, but now that the senator is dead, the King will just have to make the best of it. He's still digging anything anybody wants dug. The King is staying in shape for the next cholera epidemic, I suppose. But he's not getting any younger either!"

"Does he still *belong* to Aunt Charlotte?" asked Cynthia, beaming.

"Oh, no. The year of indentured servitude was long ago. I should ask you—do I still belong to you, Miz Cindy?"

"Oh, for goodness sake, stop that! What a memory you have, Jem! Why, of course, you still belong to me, and you always will, you hear? You just let somebody try to take you away from me!"

The two of them laughed, uproariously.

"Now, tell me about *you,* Jem."

"Well, I live in Cincinnati, but nobody calls me Jem."

"What do they call you?"

"They call me James!"

"Why, of course they do. James. Of course they do. Why didn't I think of that? But please, may I always call you Jem?"

"I wouldn't want it any other way. But on one condition."

"What's that?"

"I'll always call you 'Miz Cindy.'"

"It's a deal, Jem, it's a deal. Oh, let me hug you again," she said, and she threw her arms around him. "Now tell me, what are you *doing* in Cincinnati, that tremendous city across the river?"

"I'm studying at St. Xavier College—studying to be a doctor."

"Go on, now. You are not! How could you possibly be doing that? You are not!"

"Yes, I am," said Jem, smiling broadly. "Indeed, I am."

"But, how?"

"Well, I ran away from Lexington because I had to be more certain about freedom. I headed straight for Cincinnati. As long as I was going to be a 'free niggah,' I was going to be one in a free state. A Catholic priest picked me up off the river front and took me to a home for former slave children. I graduated from high school first in my class, and that got me a scholarship at St. Xavier. I'll be entering the University of Cincinnati's College of Medicine this fall."

"I can't believe it, Jem. Oh, yes, I can. Yes, I can. I *can* believe it!" cried Cynthia. "You'll be a fine doctor, and you'll be famous! You'll work with cholera patients, won't you? And you'll find out what causes this insane disease."

"Miz Cindy, if I could do that, I'd be one happy man!"

"I know. And I'd be one happy woman!"

"Do you remember telling me not to put my fingers in my mouth?"

"Yes, I do. And I remember it was only one of the things

a young doctor and a very nice woman told me on the ship coming to America. It is something I shall never forget as long as I live. That woman haunts me, Jem. Sometimes, after the sun goes down here on this lonesome piece of land, I go to thinking about her. The beauty of her makes me doubt myself."

"How do you mean?"

"Look at my hands, Jem. Hard as Owl Hollow rocks. Look at my hair. Coarse as summer straw. I'm a hag, a damned nanny goat as sure as you're born," said Cynthia, beginning to cry. "Whatever happened to my youth, Jem? That's what I'd like to know."

"Who was this woman you so much admire?"

"Well, she was a wayward woman, Jem, condemned for the way she was. But she had so much sense. And she had so much goodness. And she *knew* things, clearly, *really* knew them. The scourges of Heaven were so simple to her. 'Keep your fingers out of your mouth, and watch out for the water.' That's what she used to say. Oh, mercy, Jem, there was more to it than that. Sylva was as genuine as a day in May. And here I am, sometimes, feeling like I'm left out on the coldest night of winter. I suppose it's the price to be paid for loving the land."

"I have an idea," said Jem, shifting ground. "Maybe it's a pipe dream, but I have it all the same."

"What is it?" asked Cynthia, rising from her chair. "I'm going to fetch us some applejack, so you just go on talking." She turned suddenly and exclaimed: "It's a miracle! Your speech, I mean! It's the bloodiest miracle that ever there was." She turned back and reached above the oven for the earthen jar filled with the spirits she had distilled from her beloved orchard, apple trees descended from the seeds John Chapman had spread throughout the Ohio Valley. In 1845, the year he died, Johnny Appleseed told Cynthia of his belief that everything is filled with the spirit. She listened to his simple message and blessed the day he stopped at her farm.

"I'm not sure that all the good fathers at Xavier will always approve of my unconventional thinking," said Jem.

"What is it? Does it have anything to do with us old farmer women, for goodness sake?" said Cynthia, laughing. "Oh, mercy, it *is* so wonderful to hear your voice all grown up and *smart!*"

"It has to do with a scientific paper that was published last year in France."

"Concerning cholera or females or what?"

"It is certainly possible that it will provide answers to all diseases. As for females, I'm not sure what is the cure for that!" Jem laughed.

"Why not?" asked Cynthia, taking her seat beside him. "Don't we count for something?"

"I am certainly not a philosopher, nor am I a student of what the Frenchman Comte is calling 'sociology.'" Jem sipped the applejack. "This is really good."

"Then what *are* you, Jem?"

"Miz Cindy, you always did like to fool around with my mind. Do you remember how you put a stick between my toes?"

"Indeed. To check them for their ability to run," Cynthia laughed deep down inside herself.

"Yes, there was that. And you scared me, talking about ghosts. You haven't changed one bit. Now, why don't we stop trying to get Ole Jem to frittering away his time talking about what's right or wrong with *old* women. We could talk about slavery. We could talk about Mrs. Stowe's sensational new book, *Uncle Tom's Cabin,* that's just been published. If that doesn't start a war, nothing will. We could talk about that war that's certain to come one day soon."

"You're right, Jem," said Cynthia, sobering. "Talk about war scares me to death. I sometimes think I ought to get out of Kentucky too while the getting's still halfway good. I distrust slavery. I think it's evil, Jem. I know it is."

"And that's all there is to say about slavery. Let's talk about science. That's something I've come to love."

"You are amazing, Jem. And do you know, I've just now realized that I have never known your last name? What is it?"

"I hope you don't mind that I've named myself."

"You have? Why should I mind?"

"Since I never knew what my real name was, when the Fathers asked me, do you have any idea what I told them?"

"No."

"I told them it was Ferguson."

"James Ferguson. You'll be Dr. James Ferguson! Oh, Jem!"

"Then you don't mind? I had to think of something."

"Of course not. I'm honored. It takes my breath away, for a fact it does."

"I remember how nice 'Ferguson' sounded the first time I heard somebody call me that and understood it was my identity. I know I had a family name a long time ago in Africa, and if I knew what it was I'd take it back. But I don't have time to worry with it. You know, Miz Cindy, you did say something about me being your brother."

"Yes, I did. Thank God you didn't name yourself Lovingsworth! If you had come in here and told me that you were James Henry Lovingsworth, I think—well, I don't know what I would have thought. I would have thought you were a ghost for sure! Or a billy goat!"

"Oh, how the notion of ghosts used to frighten me. Now, they're replaced with *real* people. And I'm living in a world more real than I ever imagined. A young scientist whose name is Louis Pasteur, about my own age, could open many new doors and solve many awful ghost stories and mysteries of pestilence, and the ancient 'scourges of Heaven' may at last be laid to rest."

"Jem!"

"You see, Miz Cindy, we've begun to postulate that disease, including cholera, is the result of tiny *organisms.*"

"What in the world are they?"

"In nature, there's a complex web of life. There's nothing simple about it, certainly nothing as simple as a ruling God and a squirming, subservient mankind. You and I, for example, are complex entities."

"How *have* the Fathers put up with you at Xavier, Jem?"

"Not too well, I'm afraid. But some are my friends, and I can talk with them. Some are far ahead of their time. It would be a mistake, Miz Cindy, to dismiss all churched people as a bunch of know-nothings. We have enough of those in politics."

"They're all around us, Jem. The Know-Nothing Party hates immigrants and Catholics. Too many around here hate abolitionists. I think the supporters of slavery would love to have us in chains too. I have feared for my life. Oh yes, I have, Jem."

"There is fear on both sides of the river. In Ohio, I've found hatred and distrust, but at least slavery isn't institutionalized there. But crossing over does not ensure safety or salvation. And after my visit with you today, I've got to figure out how to return to Cincinnati without some maniac kidnapping me and accusing me of something, some authority denying my papers of manumission, some slaver buying, selling, and shipping me down to Mississippi."

"Oh, Jem, Jem. I've no right to complain about anything, have I?"

"You've a right to complain about anything you want to. You say you're a widow. Then how are you able to manage here on the farm?"

"I do the best I can. I love it. I give the crops and the animals all I've got. And I haven't stopped respecting people as long as they act halfway decent. There are those all around me buying and selling the God-given land as if it were nothing more than plunder. Sometimes I say if I do no more than live here and be, as long as I draw a breath and care for my land, I'll be fulfilling my mission. Other times I'm not at all sure. I have an unexplained longing for spiritual fulfillment. I hunger for God's benediction."

"'The flowers appear on the earth; the time of the singing of birds is come,' *Dominus vobiscum.*"

"Have the fathers at St. Xavier converted you to Catholicism, Jem, for Heaven's sake?"

"Not quite. They're working on it. I think they believe if they can bring me into the fold, they can afford to indulge me in my scientific experiments," said Jem, laughing.

"Don't you let them hog-tie you, Jem, don't you dare!"

"So, that's where we are, Miz Cindy. You and I and the rest of the world are right on the edge of all this new understanding, and at the same time we're on the terrible verge of civil war. Wouldn't it be wonderful if religion and science could be integrated, could be united with one people and end the division and the distrust?"

"A black man in a white widow's home. An immigrant Catholic and a freed slave, in a tub of Know-Nothings. Jem, we are truly in mortal danger."

"I know. And that's why I'm going back as fast as I can to the other side of the Ohio River. Will you join me there? But that's another crazy idea, isn't it?"

"Oh, Jem. How could I? If I could raise a magic wand and if I could ride a magic carpet, I would sail it with you. But I am what I am, and you are what you are. We have our missions. I'm sitting here thinking and wondering how it is that one little black boy has grown up so fine and has such an incredible mind, and how one little white English girl has grown up and is sitting here in his shadow."

Jem smiled and said:

When I from black and he from white cloud free,
And round the tent of God like lamb we joy,
I'll shade him from the heat till he can bear
To lean in joy upon our father's knee.

"Whose words are those, Jem?"

"William Blake's. One of the Fathers at St. Xavier challenges me to read the literature of your country, Miz Cindy. Not always easy, often condescending. Nonetheless I find enrichment in it."

"I can hear Grandfather Charlie now in Southwark at the Billy Goat Strut. Why, he'll never die, Jem. In my mind he lives and his voice is strong and he makes as much sense as he ever did."

"Well, there were many minds at work before ours, weren't there, Miz Cindy? I went back before Pasteur to discover them and connect them for my thesis: Bassi and Redi, the Italians, and the Roman scholar Varro, who wrote hundreds of volumes on many subjects a century before the birth of Christ. And, of course, hundreds of years before Varro there was Hippocrates. He understood the distinction to be made between religion and medicine, between pseudo-theological medicine men and the kind of educated doctor I want to be."

Cynthia looked intently at Jem. The image returned of the frightened black child with bulging eyes peering around the corner of the bar at Postlethwait's. She reached out to touch his hand and his arm and the side of his face, to reaffirm that he was real. His skin felt as she remembered it—like satin. She withdrew for a moment and sat in awe of what she was sure was a transfiguration. A feeling swept over her, a sensation of revelation. "Please don't stop talking," she said, with a catch in her throat.

"Well, it was Francesco Redi, in the seventeenth century, who wrote 'Observations on Living Animals Which Are to Be Found within Other Living Animals,' and this theory brought the Frenchman Pasteur to the concept of microorganisms that I want to continue studying. Perhaps after we've identified the creature that lives inside the victims of cholera, we'll be able to build on that knowledge and solve other mysteries. Bloodletting, Miz Cindy, is not the answer. Neither is the business of the 'scourges of Heaven.' It's time for people to stop praying at least long enough to start digging sewers! Miz Cindy, the cholera pandemics should not have happened. Your mother and father should not have died of it. None of your family or anybody's family should have died of it. These are not the scourges of Heaven; these are diseases perpetuated by ignorance."

"Oh, Jem!"

Jem looked about him, his dark eyes drawing in the light of the fireplace that brightened the hearth broom hanging from a leather thong. He imagined how the candles on either end of the mantelpiece would look when lighted later as darkness fell.

"Jem, you must spend the rest of the day with me. And you must take supper, and you must spend the night!" said Cynthia.

But Jem did not want to be surprised in a widow woman's house in Kentucky, especially a white widow woman's house. He wanted to cross the Ohio River before the next day's night-fall, and he knew his trip could be dangerous. Jem was not lacking in courage, but he was virtually devoid of vainglory. He had heard too many accounts of lynching.

"No," said Jem, "No, Miz Cindy. Maybe if we were to live one hundred years more, maybe then. But, no, not now. Jim Crow lives in Kentucky, and there's too much of him in Ohio. People have neither forgotten nor forgiven Nat Turner. They hanged him, and they'd hang me if they found me spending the night with you. There's so much racial hatred, so much *nonsense*. The churches in the South are preaching a segregated Heaven. Can you imagine anything more absurd? It will have to change, Miz Cindy, but I'm certain it will not be put to rights until there's been a godawful war. Signs of it are everywhere. Many in the North are coming out to hear Sojourner Truth, who would be tarred and feathered in the South. Oh, Miz Cindy, I wish you could come just once with me to hear Sojourner Truth speak the words 'Ain't I a woman?' She has the passion of Frederick Douglass, indeed she does. And you may not have heard of Martin Delany. He's one of the first blacks to be admitted to the Harvard Medical School. One day there'll be a lot more of us doing important things than most whites think or want to believe. We're not devoid of intelligence. We're not beasts. But you, of all people, know that. We have brains as well as hearts. And whites should understand that the same organisms growing inside them live inside all of us."

"Jem, I want you to know something. As long as I live, you have a home here or wherever I am. You are always welcome. As I look back on our lives, it was a blessing that we became separated. I mean, if you had tagged along with me, you would always have been subjected to an unfair, unpromising comparison with those of us who are *somebodies* only because of the color of our skin. You were *blessed* with being freed. Think how many have not been! Think how many are still being bought and sold up and down the Ohio River. Think how many are in chains even as we speak, how many families are broken apart like bundles of lumber."

"My heart bleeds for them, and yet I am willing for the Sojourner Truths and the Frederick Douglasses to do that important work for me, while I try to become a medical doctor and scientist worthy of the name. I am selfish. I admit it. But I know that this is what I must do. It is my passion."

"Will you come back and visit me, Jem?" asked Cynthia, tears forming in her eyes.

"Yes. And will you come up North to visit me?"

"I would like to say I will, but there's not a lot of traveling left in me. You are stronger than I am, Jem. My husband, John Shelby, never understood me. In fairness, maybe I never understood him. I thought he valued me the same way he prized a plow or a wagon or a fresh team of mules. I've lost my only child to the cholera. I fear another epidemic, and I want you to be so careful wherever you go. There's something else I want to share with you, Jem. And that is my feeling about this place, this spot of earth, where a man and a woman who had no children of their own took me in. They gave me a farm to watch over. And I know that this is what I must try to do. The only trouble is, I don't know how much longer I can do it."

"Have you thought of selling the farm?" asked Jem.

"Yes, I hate to admit it, but I have. The truth is, I am a woman with limited physical strength. There's no getting around that point. But even if I had a man, there would only be so much he could do or *would* do. Farm work is for generations of families as much as it is for seasons. It covers decades. It covers centuries. There's nothing easy here. When it rains, it rains. When it snows, it snows. When a heifer comes in heat, she breeds. There's no turning anything off, is there, Jem? Maybe you can turn things on and off in the places where you perform your experiments, but that is not the way it is here on the farm. The same is true of religion. It's all bound up together. I am one silly old woman with two ancient mules named You Know and I Know. In my heart, Jem, there is love for you, a woman's love, because you are a special man. You've grown from a little black boy to a sensitive and educated *man.*"

Jem rose to go. He and Cynthia met in the middle of the room and their arms went around each other, holding on tightly for a moment. She kissed him on the cheek. Taking her face in his hands, he pressed his lips to her forehead. Suddenly, her lips met his.

"I love you, Jem."

"I love you, Miz Cindy."

Then, they pulled back.

"I want you to have something," she said, unbuttoning her close-fitting collar. She removed one of the two small crosses, and refastened its chain around his neck.

"I have worn two of these for a long time. My grandfather

gave me one. Captain Lovingsworth gave me the other. I should like for you to have the one Grandfather Charlie gave me. I think it would have meant so much to him. And wearing the captain's gift will remind me of the importance of closing the gaps that separate us all."

She stood in the doorway and watched as the tall, handsome man stirruped up into the saddle of his horse. Old Rafe's son, as flea-bitten a hound as his father, raised his head up, then put it down. Jem waved good-bye, and he was gone. Cynthia knew she'd probably never see him again. She worried for his safety. No strange black man riding in broad daylight unannounced through most towns in Kentucky was secure. The hot winds of war were gathering as ominously as storms over the Isles of Scilly. She believed, somehow, that she'd be involved in it.

Cynthia thought of following Jem. Her heart said she should. But her reasoning told her something else. Her ambivalence was burdened by the demands of the farm and an incompleteness that festered when she prayed. She believed there could be an incorruptible calling in her life. She knew not what that might be. For now, she convinced herself that she was rooted to her place on Kentucky soil, where the issue of black and white was as paramount as it was divided and unresolved.

New Orleans

1855

I have urged on woman independence of man, not that I do not think the sexes mutually needed by one another, but because in woman this fact has led to excessive devotion, which has cooled love, degraded marriage and prevented either sex from being what it should be to itself or the other.

—Margaret Fuller

CYNTHIA ANNE FERGUSON LOVINGSWORTH SHELBY raised the shining brass knocker on the mammoth oak door and let the hammer fall. The sound startled her. She had not expected it to be so loud. Within a few moments a small peephole slid open and an eye appeared. From Dauphine Street the eye looked like any other, but the voice was softer than the outside discordance of drivers urging on old dray horses and the shouts of the vendors hawking their wares.

"Yes? With whom do you wish to speak?" asked the nun.

"I'm inquiring whether there is someone, someone by the name of Sylva, living here at the convent," said Cynthia Anne.

"And who might you be?" asked the youthful nun, the wary, cloistered eye growing larger in the peephole.

"I would like to believe that I am an old friend."

"I see." The eye blinked doubtfully.

"We came over from London together on a sailing ship when I was a little girl. My parents died aboard ship, and had it not been for Sylva I doubt whether I'd be alive today."

"I see," said the nun again. "One moment, please."

Cynthia waited. She turned when she felt a distinct presence. A black child approached her on the dusty banquette and began to dance. He was a professional street performer, and the snapping sounds and flashing movements mesmerized Cynthia. She thought of Jem, the memory of the first time he'd rolled his eyes at her in Postlethwait's Tavern still vivid, his steely look in the Carpenters' barn loft, the deep loveliness of his newfound bearing when, upon his last visit, they had kissed as lovers do.

Before the youth had finished dancing, the front door of the convent swung open. Another nun was standing there in the opening. The sunlight streaming in brightened the whiteness of her coif and guimpe. At first she did not speak, but her smile was as radiant as it was unmistakable.

"Sylva!"

"Cynthia!"

The two women held each other until it seemed they had squeezed out all the air in their lungs. Sylva pushed back, but she held to Cynthia's upper arms, like a proud parent.

"Let me look at you. Let me just look at you. My, you've grown up and become a beautiful woman. Come in. Do come in and let's talk. Right over here in the parlor!"

The dancing child picked up his cap from the banquette, slung it stoically upon his head, and began to skip away, rueful but unregretful, like a philosopher who has cast for an idea but come up with an empty hook.

"Come back here, you!" called Cynthia. "I did not *give* you anything," she said reprovingly, pressing a coin into the palm of the child's eager hand. "There's no telling what you might become should you put your mind to it."

The street dancer removed his cap and with a grand, sweeping motion made a graceful bow that brought his face close to the ground. He smiled and turned to go.

"Come back here, you!" Cynthia ordered with more mock authority. "A little *lagniappe,* Sir. Everybody deserves a little *lagniappe,*" Cynthia said, flipping a coin high into the air. The boy again whisked off the cap and caught the coin in midair, as deftly as a collector of butterflies.

"We must not forget our little *lagniappes,*" she said, smiling as she squeezed Sylva's arm.

"Now, now, young lady," said the Sister, "let's not recall *too* much about our dim, dark past. Let's not remember too much!" she laughed, drawing Cynthia into the parlor. Spare, clean chairs with straight backs were the only furniture in the small room. On one wall hung a likeness of Jesus, pointing to his sacred heart; on the opposite wall, a likeness of the Virgin.

"Sit here and tell me everything. You were with that awful, awful captain the last time I saw you, although I suppose I should have learned by now how useless it is for us humans to be judgmental."

"Let's just say, the captain was the captain, and he was like most captains," said Cynthia, smiling.

"He imagined himself to be a replica of God," said Sylva. "That doesn't sound right, does it? For I had considered myself some kind of goddess. Where is he? Where is the captain?"

"He's gone to his reward, if that's what we should call it."

"Oh, I'm sorry. Somebody killed him?"

"No. Some *thing* killed him, I'm not sure what. It could have been cholera but more likely his heart. He really just dropped in his tracks."

"All right, then, from the beginning," beamed Sylva. "I want to know about *you.*"

"Well, the captain took me into his home here in New Orleans. At the corner of Dauphine and St. Peter. His wife was a sweet lady, but she was not well."

"*Was* not well? She has gone, too?" asked Sylva.

"Yes. We weren't sure if it was cholera or just a case of crumbling apart. Do you know what I mean?"

"Perhaps."

"The captain took us back to Kentucky, which was their original home, trying to outrun the cholera. Miss Abigail died shortly after we got there."

"How did you make the trip?"

"Steamboat. The same way I got back here to find you. Sternwheelers are the most fun I think I've ever had—the huge, red paddlewheel turning through the sunrises and sunsets. But it was hard on Miss Abigail, the straw that broke her will to live. She was buried at Washington, Kentucky, not far from the Ohio River, which *she* thought was the ugliest body of water she'd ever seen. Maybe when she was a young girl she saw it differently, but by 1833 her life was falling into little pieces. Even the state banknotes she prized and hid from the captain turned out to be, as she feared, worthless."

"I see," said Sylva, soberly, in a hushed tone.

"I know you must remember Laurence Hanover, the ship's doctor on the *Cynthia Anne*."

"Yes, he was a beautiful man and I remember telling him so."

"Well, he still is beautiful, and he's a doctor in Lexington. He visited with me and later I went to see him in his home. One year when things weren't going well on my farm, I asked him to check on Miss Abigail's banknotes. I think that in their own valueless way they sustained her through those years of misery."

"And?"

"Well, there was a worth in their worthlessness. They taught me a lesson, taught me that pieces of paper many times are just that—pieces of paper. They're no substitute for sunrises on the farm. Documents don't mean anything when a ewe won't claim her lamb. All the written notices in the world will not produce a single drop of water."

"It is true," Sylva beamed with pride for Cynthia.

"There was another piece of paper, though, which the captain left in his belongings. I brought it with me to share with you." Removing the wrinkled and faded note from inside her dress, Cynthia handed it to Sylva.

She read it, and the smile broadened on her face. She laughed and replied: "Oh yes, oh yes. He too saw the light about riches, but at the same time not forgetting," said Sylva, leaning forward and whispering to Cynthia, "there'll always be sons of bitches." Sylva clasped her hands and looked heavenward. "Oh, Lord, forgive me one more time," she said, cupping her hand against her mouth. "Tell me, child, what was it like during that time?"

"Well, I was lost and everything was strange. I mean, there was Abigail losing her mind, and then the captain began to lose *his*. When he took me on to Lexington he was acting strangely, irrationally. It didn't come all at once. Little by little, I realized that everything for him at that time was becoming a nightmare. The coming of madness, do you think? Is that possible?"

"Oh, my dear," said Sylva touching her lips lightly with her forefinger. She took a short breath and waited for Cynthia to continue.

"Lexington was almost deserted. Just days before, word had come that cholera was on its way. It was there when we arrived. It was like riding into the gates of Hell—I mean—"

"You mean *HELL*," said Sylva, softly, looking again toward Heaven.

"Yes, I do. Well, we stumbled upon a little black boy, Jem, a story unto himself, and Aunt Charlotte, a sweet, well-meaning, and wonderfully uppity freed black woman, a story unto *her*self—oh, I forgot, there was Lou Belle, who belonged to Abigail here in New Orleans."

"A story unto herself!" said Sylva.

"Yes, and I've not yet tried to find her. She's probably gone to *her* reward—yellow fever, or cholera or the Lord knows what else. Abigail's and the captain's place is more than likely gone too, or been condemned. I promised myself I would come to see *you* first. You're the main reason I've returned on this visit to New Orleans."

"Thank you," said Sylva, looking down at her hands, clasped now in modesty.

"I have so many questions, but most of all, I'm lonely. I've missed you terribly, Sylva."

"And I've missed you. I've wondered whatever happened to you. And now here you are again—Charlsie!"

"Lord, I've not been called that for so long," said Cynthia, a catch in her throat. "You know, there comes a time of reckoning, of adding everything up?"

"Yes, of course," said Sylva, "each day we ought to count our blessings and put our curses behind us, along with all those self-worshiping captains and those creatures of God who act as if they *are* God."

"Well, but let me tell you—of all the people I've met so far in my life, there's been none the likes of King Solomon."

"*King* Solomon?" Sylva laughed. "Do tell me more. A *black* King Solomon in a Louisiana bayou?"

"No, a white King Solomon in Kentucky, as strong as the capstan on the *Cynthia Anne.* From the time I arrived until the time I left in that summer of '33, the King was in the graveyard burying cholera victims as fast as they could be carried in or dumped at the gate. The captain went to his grave along with all the others. Doctor Hanover told me King Solomon was still burying victims in the second epidemic of '49. He died of cholera himself last year in the Lexington poorhouse."

"And you?" inquired Sylva, leaning forward. She lightly touched Cynthia's hand. "I want to know about *you*."

"Well, after the captain died, I hitched a ride with a kind and generous farmer, who took me to his home in Bourbon County, as beautiful a place to farm as any in England, or any-place in the world for that matter."

"Nothing like our Bourbon *Street?*" Sylva asked, straight-ening her shoulders.

"Not unless your Bourbon Street has grown bluegrass."

"Not quite, I'm afraid," Sylva chuckled.

"Well, those two good keepers of the earth, Mr. and Mrs. Carpenter, took care of me until I was old enough to make a huge mistake."

"And what might that have been? Could it possibly have had something to do with a man?"

"At the ripe old age of seventeen I got married."

"Huge mistake," said Sylva, shaking her head with mock seriousness. "Huge mistake. Go on."

"Well, I'd seen all this birthing—lambs, calves, even barn swallows—and I wanted children."

"I understand. I wanted them, too."

"I married John Shelby. In nine months, there was Little John, and I had the child I'd always wanted. Then there were miscarriages."

"Are you *alone* now?" asked Sylva with bleak seriousness.

"Yes, I am."

"Do you want to tell me what happened?"

"Cholera did it. Cholera—"

The two women were silent.

"I'm sorry," said Sylva. "I'm very sorry."

"My husband and my son went to market early one morn-ing and returned home the following day. They died before sun-down. That was more than ten years ago. Since that time I've been rebuilding my life. I'm pleased with the goodness of it. I love the soil, Sylva, and I wish you could visit Kentucky sometime. You'd see what I mean. Yet I fear the coming of more cholera almost as much as I do the war that seems inevitable."

"Dear child, my dear, beautiful child. The victims of war and pestilence have been victims of unsolved mysteries, haven't they?"

"People still call them the scourges of Heaven."

"I know they do, and I hate it each time I hear the expression," said Sylva. "You don't believe that nonsense, do you?"

"No, I don't. At least I don't think I do. When I become discouraged and worn out with just the idea of living, I begin to think, well, maybe the preachers are right after all. God is wrathful. God *does* lose his patience with us. He's actually *offended.*"

"Stop that nonsense! You know better. You have much too fine a mind. What's the *real* reason for returning to New Orleans? You didn't come all the way back down here just to check on old Sylva, *did* you, for Heaven's sake?"

"Yes, I did, actually. I decided I had to find Sylva again to see if she was still in that convent or back out on the street. I prayed I wouldn't have to go house-to-house looking for you!"

"Your prayers have been answered," said Sylva, "and so have mine. I prayed that one day you'd knock on the right door, and I would not disappoint you. Tell me, how may I help you?"

"After more than fifteen years, Jem has reappeared in my life."

"The black boy? How did that happen?"

"That black boy I'd first met in Lexington was a freed slave. About three years after the Carpenters took me in, I went out to the barn one morning and found Jem hiding in the hayloft. I gave him food, for he was hungry. I gave him a candle and a tinderbox. That night he was gone again on his way north. He swam across the Ohio River, and a Catholic priest in Cincinnati found him and took him in. Gave him clothes and something to eat. Put him in school. That little black boy, Sylva, has grown up to become an educated man, the head of his class, a genius, a beautiful human being, truly. He has come back again and this time he has asked me to join him in Ohio."

"And you are in love with him?" sighed Sylva.

"I suppose I'm more in love with him than with any other man I've met. I think he loves me. How fine it would have been for us to be together. But it is impossible, we both know. There is no way. First of all, a white woman does not marry a black man, certainly not in Kentucky in 1855. It would be suicide. Besides, Jem has such an important future. He's going to become a renowned doctor, a brilliant medical scientist, and I wouldn't want to do anything to stop that. Our earthly *bodies* should not be obstacles to so much good."

"'Our bodies are our gardens, to the which our wills are gardeners,'" said Sylva. During her initial, lengthy penitence, a kind priest had quoted that line from *Othello,* and she had remembered it as one of her treasured proverbs.

"So you forsook prostitution?" asked Cynthia.

"So I stopped being a whore," said Sylva.

"And now you are free to love, really love?" asked Cynthia.

"'My boat sails freely, both with wind and stream,'" said Sylva, quoting Desdemona.

An elderly nun appeared in the doorway of the parlor. "Sister Mary Magdalene," she said, "may I have a word with you in my office? At your convenience, of course."

"Yes, Mother," said Sylva, "I am coming now. May I introduce to you an old and dear friend? Her name is Cynthia, and she's here from Kentucky. But before that she was from England and for a brief time she was from New Orleans. She has come to ask questions, perhaps about how we live and how she might become a part of our order. I believe she may have a spiritual calling."

"Bless you, my child," said the aging Mother Superior. "A

friend of Sister Mary Magdalene is a friend of mine. I admire the honesty of your plain dress. Do you live on a farm?"

"Yes, I do. I suppose you could say I work very hard with these two hands to hold onto the land that was passed along to me."

"Then I admire you all the more. I can think of nothing as important as the preservation of soil. After all, it feeds us. Makes our bodies strong so that we might then be able to pray for those who are hungry, and look for opportunities to feed them. We'll be having our midday meal in a short while. I'm told Sister Mary Paul has a little surprise for us today, and she's quite a cook. Will you join us?"

"Yes," said Cynthia. "Thank you, I will."

"Continue your conversation, but don't make any rash, unsupported decisions. There'll be plenty of time later to meet with me, Sister Mary Magdalene," said Mother Superior, as she turned and walked slowly down the hallway.

"At this time in her life, Sister Jerome is very conscious of the possibility of falling, and she does not wish that to happen. She steadies herself with that simple mahogany cane given to her years ago by a poor Haitian farmer," Sylva explained to Cynthia. "She told me she accepted it with reluctance because she knew it meant another small tree wrenched from a hillside, the beginning of another deep path for the water of a sudden storm. Her years as a missionary in Haiti brought her face to face with the disastrous consequences of bungled agriculture. On the other hand, not to have accepted the gift might have constituted an even deeper hurt."

Cynthia nodded, remembering the ruination of hillsides in Kentucky, often when corn was grown where there was no good reason for it to be, or when forest was destroyed, or prime agricultural land raped. To an extent, such practices were as prejudicial as sowing seeds of conflict, as perverse as they were careless.

"As Mother Superior, Sister Jerome has much important work left to be done. She has always had a most special place in her heart for all young women, even those with a past like mine. It is Sister Jerome's vocation to be helpful to all women, no matter the sacrifice, no matter their previous condition. She has instilled in me a passion for reaching out to the prostitutes here in the Vieux Carré to show them a different kind of life. They are the best reason for there being a chapel of Our Lady of Prompt Succor," explained Sylva. "Since the founding of the order by St. Angela Merici in Italy in the sixteenth century, the mission of the Ursulines has been to educate and nurture girls. That's the way it has always been, and that's the way it will be in perpetuity." Sylva smiled. "You'll find that Mother Superior accepts you for the person you are at this moment and no other—as a steward of the God-given Lord."

"I feel honored to have met her."

"Cynthia, since we'll be having lunch very soon, if you'd like to use the chamber set, it's right over there behind that little door. Don't forget to wash your hands!" said Sylva, joyously. "I'll be back as quickly as I can. Don't you dare leave this convent until I return. Do you understand? If you were to walk out that door, and if I should never hear from you again, my goodness, I could not bear it. Do you understand? Do you?"

"Yes, I do," said Cynthia. "And I couldn't live with myself."

She stood at the doorway leading to the garden in the inner court. Her thoughts returned to her home in Kentucky. She had often wondered about the future of the Bluegrass, where the pastures were so lush, the woodlands so virgin. She remembered the wild columbine with its lavish yellow and lavender blossoms growing outside her kitchen window. Each April she awaited the return of the purple martins to the gourds she'd carved and hung up high for nests. She fed the cardinal pairs in winter and rejoiced with the first appearance of the robin scouts.

Who would be taking care of all this beauty in the next century and the century after that? Would it be buried by the machines of war, bloodied by falling soldiers, replaced by great cities with no semblance of agrarian foundation?

Had she not considered running away from Kentucky? To Ohio to be with Jem? To Louisiana to be with Sylva? Or was this to have been only a brief visit to New Orleans? A time to look for Sylva before it was too late? A time to discover another piece of the paradox of Captain James Henry Lovingsworth? More than once it had occurred to her that she might abandon her home in the Bluegrass, as Grandfather Charlie had fled Oxfordshire. Now Cynthia sensed that she was hurrying *toward* something. But what? It might be a spiritual goal, principle rising above materiality, above the carnal. Each inner component of the grand design was as important as each rock in Owl Hollow Creek.

She had always been drawn to the remembrance of Sylva. An idea was evolving that awakened Cynthia to the possibility that prostitution has many forms. It did not have to be sexual. In such a narrow sense, it was another convenient way to abuse women and at the same time to be nicely blinkered to non-sexual debasements. Cynthia was drawn to the idea of womanhood in a less mean, less petty form. Why could *she* not be on the long, painful road to the community of saints? On the other hand, why should she not resolve to be the best steward of the land? The answer at times seemed clear, but she believed she needed to face Sylva one more time and talk it through.

Before leaving on the stagecoach for Maysville, Cynthia had closed the doors of the Carpenter home place and stood at the spot where Little John and his father were buried near the old log cabin just off Owl Hollow Road, only a trace for farm wagons and people walking. She had decided not to mark the location with a stone of any kind because she wished her husband and son to be subsumed, incorporated back into the land. She had no desire to raise monuments. "Let them rest in peace," she thought.

"Let them rest in peace." She had knelt and crossed herself. "In the name of the Father and the Son and the Holy Ghost. Amen."

The reunion with Sylva was a part of Cynthia's maturing spiritually. Was it not a physical maturing as well? Cynthia guessed that her designated time on earth would be sorely limited, and she was determined to make the most of it. Some women would live long and richly fulfilled lives as mothers and grandmothers, enjoying each level of procreation. Others would experience withering virginity, never knowing the nectar of lovemaking. Sylva had explained that long ago.

"Cynthia," said Sylva, interrupting her revery, "it's time for our meal. Mother Superior says she's delighted you are going to be with us. I hope you'll enjoy our modest fare."

Cynthia turned from the courtyard door. She smiled and walked directly to Sylva and threw her arms around her. Both began to cry, softly. "Now then," said Sister Mary Magdalene, "we should go in—they don't like tardiness."

The meal was taken in silence. It gave Cynthia an opportunity to be at peace with herself and to work out thoughts of selling the two small farms in Kentucky, of sending You Know and I Know to the highest bidder, of putting up for absolute auction all the tools and furnishings accumulated by the Carpenters and the Shelbys, of being rid of everything that would not fit into a small traveling bag, cashing it all in and seeking safe haven with Sylva. She'd been certain in her conviction about not returning to England. That had been settled years ago. But she was pulled to this place of worship and service on Dauphine Street in the Vieux Carré for one more affirmation, the way a swallow unerringly migrates to a seasonal home.

Two questions troubled her. Would the Sisters accept her? And could she accept the subservience required of all novitiates? Cynthia doubted whether she could always and in every way be obedient to any Mother Superior. What if she encountered or confronted a wayward Bishop of New Orleans? She was certain what she would do about burned-out monsignors, and most male parish priests would require more time than she was willing to invest. Cynthia treasured her individuality. She was determined not to lose her right to speak out when she perceived a different truth. For her, the possibility of entering a convent was an ambivalent one. For any woman, life in New Orleans or life in Kentucky—or life anywhere—was a challenge, many times a harsh reality. It was especially true on the farm, where she'd learned the lessons of natural order, evolutionary selection, the power and beauty in the bursting of one seed, the fact of gravity as Owl Hollow spun through the universe, each of its rocks hugging the creek bottom, each of its trees reaching deep for nourishment.

Following Sister Mary Paul's simple lunch—fresh-baked bread, gumbo, the surprise crab cakes, and tea—Cynthia confronted Sylva with these and many other uncertainties as they sat again in the small parlor.

"Are you by any chance considering becoming a nun?" asked Sylva.

Cynthia looked quickly into Sylva's sparkling green eyes, then lowered her head and studied her fingers, sunburned, cracked, and hardened. "That would be a very big decision, wouldn't it? On the other hand," said Cynthia, "it could be a very small decision." She raised her head again and looked deeply into the lively eyes, confident smile, and firm eyebrows touching the edge of the coif.

"It *can* be very tiny if your mind and your heart tell you it's right. Hardly anything has to be big to be good," said Sister Mary Magdalene. "But it would be wrong to seek admittance to a convent out of a sense of loneliness or desperation. A religious community is not a place to fall back into."

"If there ever is such a decision, I should like for it to come from a desire for purity, I think," said Cynthia. "Doesn't sound like a farmer talking, does it?"

"Ah! 'Decision' and 'desire' are objective matters. 'Purity' is quite another complication. And I should be better qualified than most to know the 'truth' of that, don't you think?"

"I should like to know—" Cynthia began.

"You would like to know how such an 'evil' woman as I came to be accepted here in this order?"

"Yes. Will you tell me?"

"Well, I'll tell you, and I'm assuming that you are here neither on a lark nor out of a sense of morbid curiosity."

"That is true. Whatever truth is," Cynthia added. "Maybe truth is no more than a chick pecking to escape from its shell."

Sylva smiled. "When I knocked on this door after you and the captain left me here, I entered and found other women with stories of survival. They were trying to make sense of their human condition and their spiritual future. How many of us were virgins, you may ask? I don't know. All I know is that I certainly was not. I shared my secrets with Mother Superior, and I confessed them all to the priests in the proper way. I suspect I shocked them as they'd not been shocked before, although it is generally believed that priests, like prostitutes, have heard it all and more besides. Being a representative of God is not an easy responsibility. Some are definitely not suited for it, but they are easy to spot. Now then, how can a prostitute be saved? Cured? Cleansed? Do you remember what Jesus said about the adulterous woman?"

"He who is without sin—?"

"Yes, in the Book of St. John: 'He that is without sin among you, let him first cast a stone at her. When Jesus had lifted up himself, and saw none but the woman, he said unto her, Woman, where are those thine accusers? Hath no man condemned thee? She said, No man, Lord. And Jesus said unto her, Neither do I condemn thee: go, and sin no more.'"

"You have found forgiveness?" challenged Cynthia.

"I have found it. Actually, it found me. As it found Mary

Magdalene. She found me. Here I am no longer Sylva. I *am* Mary Magdalene. She had been possessed of seven devils, but Jesus healed her and she became his friend. I was an outrageous prostitute at a time when good people were either starving or dying of plague. Mary Magdalene and I were at our wit's end, but we both had the good sense to accept the gift of the fullness of God's love within a discipline. You, on the other hand, Cynthia, are more Cynthia than anybody else. I mistrust as to whether you are a Mary Magdalene, even a Mary Paul."

"Sylva," said Cynthia, "don't be too hard on me. I feel pulled apart. A voice inside me says I must not sell anything in Kentucky. It's all I have, it's like saying the land *is* Cynthia and Cynthia *is* the land, and that's all there is to this Cynthia. Another voice says I have a spiritual responsibility, perhaps with you and the Sisters and Mother Superior. I feel pulled out of the ground. Then there's the captain's property here in New Orleans. It did not pass to me. I was never formally adopted. But if I had been, if the inheritance had been mine, would I have lived in it with another Lou Belle or would I have given it to you and the Sisters?"

"You have the *spirit* of generosity, and that's *all* that matters," whispered Sylva.

"I want to spend some days here in New Orleans. I want to look for Lou Belle, see the old house, maybe take a buggy ride out to the Rigolets. It would be a miracle if I could find that old driver Mister Chawles, but by now I'm sure he has crossed over in his chariot. Boudreaux has probably been swallowed by the swamp, and he's surely as happy as he's ever been. It doesn't matter anymore that I've never known and most likely never will know where Captain Lovingsworth's fortune is hidden, if it ever existed in the first place. It might as well be at the bottom of the ocean with my mother and father."

"Would you like to stay in the convent while you're tying up the loose ends of your quandary?" asked Sylva. "You could stay as long as you like. I know Mother Superior would approve of it, and Sister Mary Paul would love to have one more stomach to feed. Did you see the look in her eyes when she served you? It said 'love' and 'trust.' Staying here would give you an idea of how it is to live the way we do—no cows to milk, no eggs to gather! By the way, who's doing the chores for you while you're here?"

"There's a neighbor lad and his wife. They're looking out for me until I return. I never told them of the possibility that I might become a nun."

Cynthia considered for a moment. "I have a dwindling pouch of gold, only that much of the secret the captain shared with me. I am willing to make a contribution to you and the Sisters for the benefit of young women, especially the prostitutes here in the Vieux Carré. But I somehow fear that would not be enough, only a token actually. I want Charlsie to amount to something, Sylva, really amount to something beneath God's Heaven."

"What about something as simple as helping your neighbors in Kentucky?"

"I had not thought of them."

"They'll always need your best. You must understand, Cynthia Anne, that nobody buys her way into this convent. I don't know how else to say it. I don't wish to be harsh."

"You don't want me?"

"Hush. Of course I want you. This order of nuns will always want you. And yes, we need you, too. But as your friend, as your confidante, I know you must have a place and there must be people in Kentucky who need you more than we do. Isn't that right?"

"The truth is I've failed to ask. Too often I've lacked patience. I've been unforgiving."

"Well then, the way is clear, isn't it? Here in New Orleans I will continue to touch and tie together the torn shreds of humanity in men and women of every condition. You, in Kentucky, in a different way—plowing and planting with your neighbors—will be doing the same thing. It is our work!"

"Sylva, I so needed to come here and find you. Needed to talk to you again. Needed to see your smiling face and hear your wonderful voice. Needed this confession. And your blessing. You're right—the convent is not the place for me. But the thought of becoming a nun will always be a provocative one as long as I live. I'll have to walk a fine line between opposing feelings."

"Yes, you will," said Sylva, "and it will make you a finer human being."

"Then the gift is given. I'm returning to Kentucky," said Cynthia, smiling with resolution born of better understanding. "New Orleans is at one end of a pair of compasses, the other, what Grandpa Charlie called the fix't foot, is in Owl Hollow, Kentucky."

She hesitated a moment before continuing. "I must tell you everything, mustn't I? This must be as perfect a confession as I can make. I had considered the possibility of running away with Jem. Or of finding some place where I could just block out the sounds of war. Finally I discovered what I see now was the biggest deception of all—rushing to what I thought represented safety, back to you, Sylva, to hide in a convent's womb. Could those be things I actually contemplated? Yes," said Cynthia, decisively answering her own question.

"Perhaps I do not entirely understand," said Sylva, turning her head to one side, as if to catch a new light from the world outside. "Are you disappointed in me? Have I let you down? I pray to God I haven't."

"I'm disappointed in myself, disappointed that too often I've retreated from those who've misunderstood me. They don't know the real Cynthia Anne. And they sure don't know Charlsie the way I believe you always have. I'll give them the room and the forgiveness they need to come around. I won't be sitting on my hind end, holed up in a house full of bad memories. If I thought for a single moment that Jem and I needed each other now as much as we did when we huddled together beneath that big tree where King Solomon dug graves—needed each other as much as we did when he was running toward freedom—then I would go to him and become his mate and his helper. But probably he doesn't need me now nearly so much as I think. And if I thought the sisters of this convent, especially Mary Magdalene, really needed me here—scrubbing floors, teaching children, visiting prostitutes—I'd stay here right now. But I see now that I'm not needed in this way at this time. Since I have no husband and no children, I suppose I might become a midwife, like Agnes Caudill, who delivered my child. Doctor Hanover says midwives are needed as much as farmers, and there aren't enough good ones. I've always been fascinated by birthing. So I can offer my help to my neighbors. And when the terrible war comes, as I'm sure it will, perhaps I'll be a nurse, if they'll have me, wherever I'm needed. It won't matter which side the wounded are on."

"Cynthia, Cynthia," began Sylva.

"Listen," said Cynthia, "in these few hours together you've heard me and given me a blessing of truth. After a week or so in New Orleans, I'm going back to Kentucky where I belong. I'll beg, borrow, juggle, cajole, wrestle, persuade—and I'll hold onto the farm. We can't all be joining convents, now can we?"

"You are a wonder of wonders, Sister Cynthia! And you *do* have my blessing. You'll be in my prayers, constantly."

"I will build upon the land as well as I am able, Sylva, as long as I am able. And my last will and testament will make proper provision for those who deserve another chance, whoever they happen to be."

The two women embraced, tears falling without restraint. They pulled back for a moment and smiled and embraced again.

Suddenly, Sylva pushed Cynthia from her and declared: "Did you know that the captain's ship is on display at the Louisiana Dry Dock Museum?"

"No!"

"Yes! Would you like to go and visit the *Cynthia Anne* while you're here?"

"Yes, oh yes! Such a visit will be painful, but I want to see it."

"Mother Superior might approve. I will ask her right now. Perhaps we can chaperon a class of our young girls. They will be fascinated that there is a *person* Cynthia Anne and an ocean-going ship *Cynthia Anne!*"

"And the scourges of Heaven—what will we tell the young girls about that?" asked Cynthia, with one hand on her hip and the other hand pointed toward Heaven.

"We will tell them that God is love," said Sylva.

Mt. Sterling, Kentucky

October 1998

Whatever befalls the earth befalls the sons of earth
Man did not weave the web of life
He is merely a strand in it
Whatever he does to the web
He does to himself

—Chief Seattle

MABEL STONE, THE CLEANING LADY, was sweeping the floor of Mother of Good Counsel Church in Mt. Sterling early on the Saturday morning of October Court Day. It was her self-imposed weekly ritual to work from the altar up the main aisle to the front door, using a small broom with stubborn little tufted straws to move a handful of dirt and bits of torn paper. The church was otherwise immaculate. Mabel had carefully dusted the Stations of the Cross, making sure that no particles of dirt clung to the corners. Daily devotions before each of the stations had become a rarity, though. In the minds of the young, the Fourteen Stations were hardly more than pictures to adorn the walls and alleviate the bareness.

Joseph O'Malley opened the front door and stepped inside the small vaulted vestibule. The only sound was Mabel Stone's broom scratching against the floor. Her narrowing eyes examined Joseph. The shuffling old man's dishevelment did not betoken trespassing or any other likely trouble. Mabel Stone only knew that somebody ought to strip off his clothes and throw him into a tub and go over him inch by inch with a stiff brush and a cake of lye soap. The earnest, scrupulous woman would have made brief, circumspect eye contact if Joseph had been able or willing to look directly at anybody, even for a second. He was much too shy to do that.

He went first to the smooth marble bowl containing a small amount of Holy Water, freshly blessed that morning by Father Clarence Harper, a personable, outreaching young diocesan priest who thought of himself as one who walked in the footsteps of Francis of Assisi. Father Harper was a gentle man, loving both God and God's people. He revered the words of St. Augustine: "Our hearts are restless and are made for God and will not rest until they rest in Him." Yet Father Harper recognized within himself conflicts related to the imperfections of humanity as expressed by the Apostle Paul: "We carry this treasure in earthen vessels."

Since his ordination, Father Harper had become less sure of perfection. "Beware of absolutes," a priest in seminary had often written in the margins of Clarence's written assignments. Keen intellect rejected oversimplifications. For the most part, Father Clarence could rationalize the special needs and degrees of poverty and obedience, but he could not deny hormonal feelings. He struggled daily with the practical effect of the Church's law that if a man could not keep a vow of celibacy, the moral alternative was to leave his ordination and marry a woman until death did them part. He wrestled with the Church's rigid stand on fornication, heterosexual or homosexual. He truly disliked the word "fornication" because it sounded and looked so much like a mark of depravity, another scarlet letter.

The original Latin from which "fornication" derived depicted whoredom, and Father Clarence despised the conventional implications of that word even more. The young priest knew, as one who respected language, that the same linguistic stem responsible for "whore" also produced "caress," "cherish," and "charity." He delighted in the work of a college friend, a woman scholar, whose research focused on the essential differences separating "prostitute," the person, and "prostitution," the inevitable result of a social condition within a political system.

Unaware of the young priest watching through the doorway of the sacristy, Joseph O'Malley shuffled directly to the northwest corner of the church, past the fourteenth Station of the Cross depicting the lifeless form of the Savior. He began to feel much better in the presence of the statue of Mary, so much finer than his own. Both hands were in place. Her outer raiment was soothing pale blue over a white robe signifying innocence. A crown rested on Mary's head. Cradled in her left arm was the infant Child, the baby Jesus, a globe of the earth upon the palm of his extended left hand. A statue of Saint Joseph stood beside Mary, his plain brown garment reminding his namesake of the soil and its fertility.

Joseph had come to Mother of Good Counsel to make his confession. First, he would light a candle, then he would look for Father Devereux, who was also elderly and who could be counted on for a worthy, uncomplicated number of Hail Marys and Our Fathers. Joseph took one of the long, used match stems and held the end of it over the flame of a burning taper. Then he lit a new wick. He made the sign of the cross. From his pocket, he extracted several coins, three quarters, and dropped one of them into the coin slot. It made a sharp sound as it hit the bottom.

Mabel Stone looked in the direction of the noise and then returned to her sweeping. Father Harper stepped from the sacristy into the sanctuary. He bowed before the altar, then came to the opening in the center of the railing. He wore a tartan sweater over an open-collared shirt. His blue jeans were worn and faded. Father waited until Joseph turned.

"May I help you?"

"I'm looking for the priest."

"I am the priest," said Father Harper with a gentle, inviting smile.

Joseph looked directly into Father Harper's eyes.

"Don't look like no priest," he said.

"Yes, I know. Excuse me for being out of uniform. It's Saturday, and I thought I'd check out Court Day."

"Where's Father Devereux?" asked Joseph, looking toward the sacristy.

"Father Devereux is not feeling well. Perhaps you did not know that I am taking his place here."

Joseph felt uncomfortable and betrayed. Mabel Stone made a small but unmistakable clucking sound of disapproval. Joseph looked back to the sacristy door, twisted his mouth, and bit down on his lower lip. He turned to go.

"Please stay," said Father Harper. "I'd like to help you. I'll put on my collar and coat, just for you. By any chance, did you come for confession?"

Joseph O'Malley stopped and turned back to Father Harper.

"Yes, I come for confession. Will you hear it?"

"Of course, I will."

"Don't have to put no collar on."

"You're very kind," said the young priest. "Come, let's walk together to the confessional."

Unlike some of his arbitrary and tormented predecessors, Father Harper believed his role in the sacrament of confession was quite simple: to embody compassion and forgiveness— Christ enfleshed today.

Mabel Stone mumbled under her breath, so that no one

could hear. "I'd make him wear his dern collar. Hummmph. 'Thought I'd check out Court Day.' Still wet behind the ears."

"Mrs. Stone, you've got the church looking just fine. Would you mind going back to the sacristy to see about my robes for tomorrow? My surplice and cassock might need a little touching up. I hope you don't mind my being so fussy!" said Father Harper, kindly yet as resolutely as one might send away a pigeon pecking on the church's front steps. He felt more comfortable when Mabel Stone did not hover near the confessional door.

"No, Father," said Mabel, unsmiling and pained, "I don't mind you being so fussy." Halfway to the altar railing, she again spoke under her breath. "'Would you see about my robes for tomorrow?' I *bet* they need a little touching up. What *we* need is a real *man* for a priest. We don't need no fussy butt."

"Now then, my friend," said Father Harper to the old man standing patiently by his side, "I'm Clarence Harper. What's your name?"

"Name's Joseph O'Malley," the old man said with obvious embarrassment as he studied his feet.

"Splendid Irish name. I'm most pleased to meet you. I'm sure you know that the Irish had quite a lot to do with the founding of this church."

"No. Didn't know that."

"Yes, and there have been anonymous benefactions, large and small."

"What's that?"

"A benefaction? It's a gift truly given. Anonymous means having an unknown origin."

The words were a mystery to Joseph, but he accepted them as good enough for the moment. He remained silent as Father Harper continued: "Who knows? Maybe one of your ancestors came over on an immigrant ship and was among the first to worship here. Are you interested in genealogy?"

"Don't know what that means either."

"Family connections."

"Like to make my confession."

"Of course. Here, let me help you into your side," said the young priest, who intended to make one of his first building improvements the modernization of the confessional at Mother of Good Counsel. He had inherited the forbidding and constrictive architecture of the 1950s confessional that resembled a dark, tight little torture chamber more than a haven for one human to listen to another's sorrow and regret. Why not the comfort of extra space and the option of speaking directly with eye-to-eye informality? In the case of Joseph O'Malley, though, the old, more secretive, and private approach would probably serve best.

When Father Harper was seated on his side, he picked up the linen stole emblematic of his authority to forgive sins. He sighed. Is it really true that I have so much power? the young priest asked himself, a question that would weigh heavily upon him throughout his priesthood. Oh, God, give me patience, wisdom, and compassion, he silently prayed. He kissed the stole, freshly pressed by Mabel Stone, and placed it over his shoulders. Then he raised the small panel covering the screen that separated him from the side where Joseph was kneeling. The old man made the sign of the cross.

"Bless me, Father." Joseph cleared his throat and continued. "I confess to Almighty God and to you, Father, that I have sinned."

Father Harper listened with his right ear against the gauzed fabric through which Joseph was trying very hard to say precisely the right things. His mother had drilled the traditional prescriptions of the Baltimore Catechism into Joseph's brain with such repetition that there was little chance of his ever forgetting them.

"The last time I went to confession was last Easter. I said

the penance given to me by Father Devereux, and I took Holy Communion."

"Very good," said the priest, who had not believed he would hear opening words of confession spoken so perfectly. Hearing them from the mouth of a man as simple as Joseph O'Malley made it sound as grand as the Mass said in Latin at seminary.

"I have committed a mortal sin. I have also committed many little sins."

"Yes," said Father Harper, "what was the mortal sin?"

"I dug up a body."

"Excuse me?"

"Luther and me dug up a body."

"A body of what? Whose body? Luther who?"

"Little John's body."

"Who?"

"All I know's his name was 'Little John,'" said Joseph, beginning to frown, because he was not expecting so many questions so fast. If he had said the same words to Father Devereux, the priest would have taken longer and then said nothing more than, "Yes, my son." Or he might have said, "You were wrong to do that, my son. That will be five Hail Marys and five Our Fathers. Go and sin no more." Or he might have fallen asleep, and Joseph would have politely awakened him.

"O.K.," said the startled Clarence Harper, "let's see if we can understand this. Now, who is this *Luther* person?" He smiled at the mention of the name that had lived too long in Catholic infamy. Another decade of maturing ecumenism was pointing toward a new century of reconciliation with many Protestant denominations.

"Luther Duncan."

"I see. And he is—?"

"He hired me to help him dig a water line to his house."

"Go on."

"He rented a backhoe, which I never would do."

"Why not?"

"I'd rather use a shovel."

"To dig a water line? You'd rather use a shovel?"

"Yes."

"Why?"

"Don't think too much of engines."

"Interesting."

"They can get you in a lot of trouble. Which is what it has done to me. It has caused me to commit a mortal sin."

"I don't quite understand. Could you tell me more?"

"Tell anything you want to know."

"What happened next?"

"Well, after we uncovered the old coffin, we looked through the little window at the front end of it."

"And?"

"Isn't that a mortal sin?"

"Is what a mortal sin?"

"I mean, because—well, I don't know. I thought Father Devereux would know. I thought he would be here to give me my penance. I never thought I'd be making my confession to somebody who doesn't look like a priest, or doesn't act or sound like one either."

"After you discovered the coffin, did you report it to the authorities?"

"No."

"Why not?"

"I'm reporting it now to you."

"Where is the coffin at the present time?"

"We left it where it was. We covered it. We dug the water line around it."

"All right. You have committed a mortal sin." Father Harper sought to be as helpful as possible to someone so earnest. Unlike the typical priests of the old school, he was sensitive to the reality that how he conducted himself in the confessional had as much potential for hindrance as for help. Each individual caught in a unique set of circumstances deserved to be treated with special care. "So, I must set your punishment. Isn't that true?"

"Yes, Father."

"Is that what you really want me to do?"

"What?"

"Give you your penalty."

"I'm ready."

"Your penance is five Hail Marys and five Our Fathers. We'll add an extra Hail Mary and Our Father for your venial sins, which I don't think we need to hear."

"Father?" said Joseph.

"Yes?"

"You don't want to know anything about—about—thoughts about—*other* things?"

"What do you mean?"

"I don't have no woman."

Father Harper knew what was probably coming next. He wanted to avoid it if possible. It was a throwback to the days of confessions beginning and ending with admissions of everything from masturbation to bestiality. The crudeness of the exchanges in the confessional was legendary. There were priests who believed and wanted their congregations to believe that masturbation caused mental institutions to fill up quickly. Bestiality resulted in sick jokes, which only served to increase insensitivity toward other people, especially women. Confessions of loss of virginity were popular with some priests, whose fantasies competed with their celibate lives.

Father Clarence Harper, who supported the cause of optional celibacy, had no intention of using the confessional as a clearinghouse for the joys and pitfalls of sex. Recognizing that any kind of committed life is difficult, he believed that the Holy

Spirit was leading mankind in new directions. Many were not coming into the priesthood because of the rule of sexual abstinence. Optional celibacy, therefore, should include everybody, male and female, married and single. It should embrace individual sexual preferences. God loves variety, Father Harper believed, because everyone is a child of God; therefore, it makes sense for God to call for variety and for all to serve in his vineyard. But although more than half of the laity supported a relaxation of the celibacy rule, less than half of the clergy did. Among bishops it was only twenty-five to thirty percent. Reform was an uncompleted task.

"Joseph," said Father Harper, "what about 'Little John'?"

"What do you mean?"

"What have you learned from what happened?"

"Well, Luther's Old Lady says we stumbled onto a cholera victim."

"That's very possible. Indeed so."

"She told Luther that all the people who died of cholera a long time ago died because God was mad at them."

"Do you believe that? That God was mad at everybody back then?"

"I suppose He's *still* mad at just about everybody. Luther said Old Lady called it one of the scourges of Heaven."

"Joseph," said Father Harper, "what do *you* think the scourges of Heaven are?"

"Like I said, God was put out and fit to be tied. I guess that was it. So, he was punishing people for doing wrong."

"Is that what you believe?"

"I don't know what I believe. I'd rather you tell *me*."

"All right. For now let's close this confession. You have left the child's coffin in the grave. You have covered it over. You were worried that maybe you offended God by looking through the window of the coffin. Is that right?"

"Yes."

"If you believe that was a mortal sin, then perhaps it was. If you believe I can forgive you for committing the sin, then I do. In the name of Jesus, I absolve you of all your sins. You are forgiven. You know the penance, five Hail Marys and five Our Fathers with an extra one of each for all your venial sins. Joseph, God loves you as much as He continues to love Little John. And God does this because He *is* love. God does not send scourges as a form of punishment. You tell Luther to tell Old Lady that there's a priest at Mother of Good Counsel who does not believe in *any* scourges of Heaven. Joseph, I absolve you of all your sins. Make a good Act of Contrition and go and sin no more."

Father Harper listened respectfully as Joseph made his Act of Contrition.

"O my God! I am heartily sorry for having offended Thee, and I detest all my sins, because I dread the loss of Heaven and the pains of hell, but most of all because I have offended thee, my God, who art all good and deserving of all my love. I firmly resolve, with the help of Thy grace, to confess my sins, to do penance, and to amend my life. Amen."

When he heard Joseph opening the door on his side, the young priest hurried to assist the older man. "Let me help you to a pew." In Father Harper's eyes Joseph saw compassion, but he still missed Father Devereux.

The two men knelt together as Joseph began his penance. When the final Hail Mary and Our Father had been said, the priest took Joseph's hand, held it aloft, and prayed aloud. "God in Heaven, Joseph and I thank you for your love. We thank you for our creation. We thank you for our minds. Give us, O God, the courage to return our love to you and to share our love with our brothers and sisters. Amen."

Father Clarence Harper turned and looked at Joseph. "Well, how's about us going out there and seeing what's happening at Court Day?"

Joseph said, "No, Father, you go. I'm heading home. It's

a long walk. If you don't mind me saying so, a priest ought to wear his collar *all* the time. That way, people will know who you are."

"Yessir, you are right," said Father Harper at the front door of the church. As he watched Joseph walk east on Main Street, the young priest made the sign of the cross. He remembered Psalm 104:

> O Lord, how manifold are your works!
> in wisdom you have made them all;
> the earth is full of your creatures.
> Yonder is the great and wide sea
> with its living things too many to number,
> creatures both small and great.
> There move the ships,
> and there is that Leviathan,
> which you have made for the sport of it.

Joseph walked north on Maysville Street, like a lost trout heading back out to sea when all the other fish were coming in to spawn. He passed the Indian mound of the Adena people that folks said dated back to five hundred years before the birth of Christ. Joseph was befuddled by the thought that such a burial place could survive in the midst of McDonalds, Wendy's, and Kentucky Fried Chicken.

Joseph crossed the bridge over Interstate 64, past the newly constructed stone entrance to a complex of other restaurants and overnight lodgings, where only a short time ago there had been a lane leading to a farm. He passed places where other stewards of the land had come and gone, had lived and loved, had played the game of survival as best they knew how. Some had done it well; others had been shadowed and overtaken by trouble.

Joseph headed home to his beloved plaster of Paris Virgin

Mary in the shack in the woods. In one way, he felt quite old, but there was a piece of newfound happiness in him since his visit with the young priest, who really ought to have enough sense to put his collar on every day.

~ FINIS ~

Afterword

The original stories of Asiatic cholera in nineteenth-century Kentucky exist today only in scattered bits and pieces. There is no published volume that attempts to bring the subject together in a form that communicates the despair and destruction caused by the disease, which was endemic to India by 1817 and swept to England in 1832, to the United States in 1832-35. Asiatic cholera returned to Kentucky in 1848-54, 1866, and 1872, and in this state alone untold thousands of lives were lost.

All of the characters in *The Scourges of Heaven* are fictional or fictionalized. I have sketched them across a historical background that is real so that readers may gain a sense of a worldwide tragedy unfolding with uncompromising dimension. The names of churches in America are invented.

An account of the real William "King" Solomon appears in James Lane Allen's first book of nineteenth-century fiction, *Flute and Violin*. This single heroic tale has kept alive another generation's memory and respect for a giant who stood his ground and refused to run away from "the destroyer." *The Scourges of Heaven* picks up King Solomon's story from the point where Allen leaves it.

The year 1833, when the fictional Cynthia Anne reached America, saw the abolition of slavery in the British Empire, but it was another year in the institutional growth of human bondage in the United States, whatever the efforts to escape it. In that year, more than one hundred blacks assembled in Louisville and joyfully scrambled aboard the steamer *Mediterranean* for a trip down to New Orleans and on to Africa. Salvation! The answer to prayers! They expected to regain the Promised Land, but many died even before reaching the Crescent City, overtaken by cholera. A similar disaster occurred on April 20 of the same year, when nearly one hundred former slaves from Kentucky and more than fifty from Tennessee boarded the *Ajax* in New Orleans. They were freed blacks headed for Liberia, but cholera caught up with them, too. Before they reached Key West, nearly thirty were dead.

The fictional Cynthia Anne would live to see the slaves freed in the United States in 1862 and the discovery by the factual German bacteriologist Doctor Robert Koch, in 1883, of the specific cause of cholera, one of God's tiniest creatures— *Vibrio cholerae*—which fifty years before had killed the fictional Sally and Elton Ferguson, Harmony and Jasper Fischer, the Reverend Daniel Christian Goodman, First Mate Thomas Moreland, and the Southwark family, and later took the lives of John Shelby and Little John.

Ironically, 1833 was also the year of the birth of Alfred Bernhard Nobel, whose invention of dynamite would amass the wealth to make possible the Nobel Prize, which Doctor Koch in turn would receive for his work in solving the riddle of infectious diseases. Cholera was but one. There were also smallpox (which had spread from China and Asia Minor to Europe by 600 B.C.), yellow fever, scarlet fever, measles, mumps, and tuberculosis.

Cynthia Anne was born before antiseptic surgery, before the discovery of the leprosy bacillus, before Koch's discovery of anthrax bacillus, before Laveran's discovery of the malarial parasite, before Pasteur's discoveries of a chicken cholera vaccine and a rabies vaccine.

Cynthia would not live to see women, black or white, gain

the right to vote. Her quiddity would follow by three hundred years the life of Saint Theresa of Avila, founder of the reformed order of Carmelites, whose legacy was *The Way of Perfection*. When Cynthia was fifty-two years old, Saint Thérèse de Lisieux, "the Little Flower," was born in France. *The Story of a Soul* would become her bequest. Cynthia, although not a saint, shared in this community of universal goodness.

Cynthia and these women preceded the telephone, radio and television, the automobile and airplane, the computer, the internet. Yet they lived only about a hundred and fifty to four hundred years ago—nanoseconds of time. If history were to repeat itself, if it were necessary to start over again from the beginning, would the same mistakes be made? Where would be the individuals who could still see clearly without supernumeraries to guide them? Would there be even one Sojourner Truth? one Harriet Tubman? one Harriet Beecher Stowe? one Mother Teresa?

Cynthia would not live into the twentieth century, when there would be successors to Cotton Mather and the fictional Daniel Christian Goodman, Monsignor Delaney, Josiah Carter Abernathy, and Samuel J. Jones—Jim Jones, David Koresh, and Do Applewhite. She would not live in the time of Peoples' Temples, Waco Compounds, and Heaven's Gates.

It is understandable, perhaps, that so many clergymen saw in the calamity of nineteenth-century cholera pandemics a responsibility if not an opportunity to rally their congregations. The first Episcopal bishop of Kentucky, Benjamin Bosworth Smith, who lost his wife and one child to cholera in Lexington on July 2, 1833, composed and distributed to his parishioners a proclamation notable for its omission of anything unrelated to God's wrath.

My Dear Friends:
If the calamity which we have suffered does not turn

all hearts to the duties of a pious life, what can? Shall these corrections be lost upon us? Dare we provoke worse punishment, by refusing to humble ourselves under what has already been laid upon us?

It is not affliction which makes people better, but God's blessing upon affliction! Public calamities are unmitigated curses, save only where the Bible and the Lord's Day combine their influence to convert them into blessings.

My first most urgent plea with you then, is, fly to your Bibles, and to the house of God!

Yield your hearts, wholly, to learn those lessons of wisdom which God would fain teach you by affliction. Be humble! Be patient. Let your chastisements heighten your sense of sin and deepen your sorrow and abhorrence for it.

Henceforth live to God. Amen.

B.B. Smith

In Bishop Smith's pastoral letter there was nothing to suggest a possible cause of cholera other than God's punishment for sin, or any cure other than fervent prayer and regular church attendance and Bible reading. There was no mention of sanitation or the improvement of general living conditions.

Historically, there had been keen competition between scientists and doctors as healers, and clergy as intercessors. In the fifth century the kings of France believed they had worked closely with God to effect the healing of mere mortals, and, not to be outdone, Edward the Confessor in England claimed a cure for "The King's Evil," more correctly identified as scrofula, a swelling of lymph nodes in the neck. To some, it was another "scourge of Heaven," but the cause was unpasteurized milk from sick cows.

In 664 A.D. there was an outbreak of plague in Saxon

England. In 750 there were epidemics of St. Vitus's dance, Sydenham's chorea, in Germany. ("Chorea," unlike cholera, is a disorder of the nervous system.) Thomas Sydenham (1624-89), "the English Hippocrates," was one of the principal founders of clinical medicine and epidemiology. Another hundred and fifty years would pass before Rhazes, a Persian physician, would describe "plague" as an infectious disease, and before the noted medical school of Salerno would be founded. From this lonely outpost of the Middle Ages would come the "Practica" of Petrocellus and the *Regimen Sanitatis Salernitanum* of multiple authorship, the source of Jonathan Swift's "The best doctors in the world are Doctor Diet, Doctor Quiet, and Doctor Merryman."

As the end of the "first thousand years" approached, there was widespread fear that the apocalypse was at hand. But two more decades passed and there were more St. Vitus's dance epidemics in Europe. Not until 1071 did Constantine the African bring Greek medicine to the Western world. It was another half-century before St. Bartholomew's Hospital was established in London. The year 1230 is now remembered as the year when the Crusaders brought leprosy to Europe. In the next century bubonic plague began in India, and by 1359 the "Black Death" had killed a third of the population of England. Another three hundred years passed, and in the execrable plague years of 1664-65 there were an estimated 108,000 deaths in London.

Prophetically, 1833, the year cholera reached America, was the year of the birth in London of Charles Bradlaugh, who as a youth would be equally acclaimed and reviled as "Iconoclast," a breaker of traditional thought as well as religious symbols. Bradlaugh's writings went beyond theology to attack conventional wisdom, that attack constituting their greater significance, for his efforts were instrumental in helping to open doors for scientific medical principles. To say that organized religion was impeding the progress of medical science quite possibly represents the depths of understatement. It is true, however, that as early as the Middle Ages there were instances of religious groups establishing hospitals in an effort to combine spiritual and physical healing.

Another decade would pass before Dr. John Browning presented to England's House of Commons his "Resolution Relating to Quarantine Laws and Regulations":

> There is little difficulty in discovering the sources of plague. Where no attention is paid to the accumulation of filthy matter—where there is no drainage to remove nauseous accumulations—where foul air and stenches remain unventilated, and are allowed to create an active pestiferous influence—where streets are foul and narrow—where stagnant waters abound, and the remains of dead animals and putrid vegetables are brought together, there you will find the elements out of which plague has its birth. . . . When the plague breaks out, the ravages are always greatest among the poorest and least civilized of the population. . . . The ravages of plague are not to be checked by superstitious fears and dreams, but must be controlled by the general attention to public health which is now applied to stop the progress of other disease . . . the amount of disease depends on the condition of the people.

Another nontheological explanation for the rapid spread of cholera was advanced by Lunsford P. Yandell in the *Transylvania Journal of Medicine* for 1833. Cholera, he said,

> found our municipal authorities without the means either of ministering to the wants of the indigent sick, or of taking account of the progress of the disease.

No Board of Health was organized, no reports made, and hence we are now left to guess at the mortality. No available hospital was prepared. When the disease had been a week in progress, an attempt was made to open one, but it was then found impossible to procure the necessary attendants, and the project was abandoned. The result of this was, that as the sick were scattered over the whole city, much unnecessary labor was performed by the physicians, and as a necessary consequence, they were soon exhausted. During the first ten days of its prevalence Drs. Boswell, Challen, and Steele died, and nearly every other practitioner in the city experienced an attack of the disease. . . .

At one period, when the disease was most violent, and time, consequently, most precious, it was almost impossible to find a physician after night. Many were therefore obliged to wait until morning, when too often they had reached a hopeless condition. If to those who suffered in this way, we add the ignorant who were little acquainted with the early symptoms or the danger of the disease, and the indigent who could command neither nurses, nor messengers to send for a physician in time, we have a very large class for whom it may be said the resources of the profession were as nothing.

The extent of suffering and death would remarkably increase with the second cholera pandemic in 1849, for many people remained remarkably blind to their own filth. Had the popular culture been less encumbered by theological fantasies and had there been a more widespread yearning for new scientific discoveries, something as sensible as the modern sewer system might have come sooner.

William "King" Solomon died in 1854. Death came to him in the Lexington poorhouse, one more victim of cholera. He was buried in the new Lexington Cemetery, where in 1908 his monument would be dedicated with the words: "For Had He Not a Royal Heart?"

Solomon was not the only man to bury victims of the cholera epidemic voluntarily. "Cupid" Walker, the sexton of the Presbyterian Church in Nicholasville, Kentucky, buried many cholera victims. In 1850, at age seventy, he himself succumbed to the disease and became the first black to be buried in the Maple Grove Caucasian cemetery.

At Springfield, in Washington County, a slave named Louis Sansberry remained in town when his owner, George Sansberry, and his family fled from the approaching epidemic. Granted freedom shortly after the death of his master, Louis Sansberry, like King Solomon and Cupid Walker, had a curious obsession to stand his ground and bury cholera victims. He died April 12, 1861, at age fifty-four, and was buried at St. Rose. No stone marked his grave. With the passing of time the exact site of the cholera burials was forgotten. These unmarked graves were found during the installation of a water line.

In Glasgow, Kentucky, a slave named "Old Bob" every day drove a wagon loaded with meal and grain and brought it into the town during a cholera epidemic spread by the visit of a circus.

The year 1854 saw various manifestations of the prejudices of the time and hope for a better world. In Louisville, supporters of the Know-Nothing party rioted. They attacked Catholics and Irish and German immigrants, killing twenty people. In Salt Lake City, Brigham Young ruled that a single drop of black blood makes a man unfit to enter the Mormon priesthood. In New York City, Frederick Douglass published *My Bondage, My Freedom.* In London, England, sewers were modernized after another outbreak of cholera.

More than a century and a half after the first cholera pandemics, despite the medical and social progress of the human species, the July 1996 issue of the *Journal of the American Medical Association (JAMA)* concluded that "cholera has increased in the United States since 1991, reflecting global changes in cholera epidemiology, and is now primarily travel associated and antimicrobial resistant. . . . In 1994, cholera cases were reported by 94 countries, the largest number ever in a single year."

Dr. George Alleyne, director of the Pan American Health Organization, was quoted in 1985 by *USA Today:* "The scourge of cholera that came to us (in Latin America) a couple of years ago was almost an affront to those of us who thought the days of large-scale plagues were over. . . . In spite of our many triumphs, the microbes are with us and will always be with us."

David Dick

Acknowledgments

My grateful appreciation for the use of facilities and resources
goes to the following institutions, each location enlivened by
caring, enthusiastic, talented librarians: Asbury Theological
Seminary Library, Wilmore, Kentucky; British Museum Library,
London, England; Lexington Theological Seminary Library,
Lexington, Kentucky; Louisiana State University Library, Baton Rouge, Louisiana; Monroe County Public Library, Key
West, Florida; National Library of Scotland, Edinburgh, Scot-
land; National Maritime Museum, Greenwich, England; Ox-
ford University Bodleian Library, Oxford, England; Paris and
Bourbon County Public Library, and the Historical Museum,
Paris, Kentucky; Public Record Office, London, England;
Southwark Community Library, London, England; Transyl-
vania University Library, Lexington, Kentucky; Tulane Univer-
sity Library, New Orleans, Louisiana; University of Edinburgh
Library, Edinburgh, Scotland; University of Kentucky Library,
Lexington, Kentucky; Wellcome Medical Library, London,
England; and Wilkinson County Public Library, Woodville,
Mississippi.

I also thank the staff of the University Press of Kentucky
for their support and their belief that such a work of fiction is
timely and constructive.

Others who have been singularly helpful include Douglas
A. Boyd, former Dean, College of Communications and Infor-

mation Studies, University of Kentucky, and David S. Watt, Vice-Chancellor, Research and Graduate Studies, University of Kentucky, for the grant that enabled me to walk the streets of Southwark and the wynds of Edinburgh; to visit the National Maritime Museum in Greenwich, where I first read the accounts of the emigrant ships to America; and to view the rare illustrations of cholera scenes in the archives of the Wellcome Medical Library. Thomas D. Clark, historian laureate of the Commonwealth of Kentucky, was a guiding light. Paul A. Willis, director of the William T. Young Library, University of Kentucky, and William J. Marshall and James Birchfield, Special Collections, University of Kentucky, were unselfish with their time and professional expertise.

Carole Boyd read the early versions of the book as they evolved. Dr. J. William McRoberts at the Kentucky Clinic read the manuscript from the vantage point of medical science; the Reverend Sharon Fields of the Protestant Second Christian Church of Midway, Kentucky, from the perspective of the female African American; Father Thomas Farrell of the Newman Center at the University of Kentucky from the Roman Catholic point of view; and Father William Faupel of Asbury College from the vantage point of the Church of England. Virginia Buckner offered her perspective as a retired teacher. At Mayflower Farm, English expatriate Miranda Hendrix enlivened a rainy Kentucky afternoon with memories of her mother country.

I thank my wife, Eulalie ("Lalie") Cumbo Dick, and our daughter, Ravy Bradford Dick, for tolerating three years of neglect and, too often, ill temper. Lalie was with me every mile and every word of the way. She conceived the cover design and created the endleaf maps. It is *our* book, not mine. I also thank Lalie's gracious mother, Eulalie Harvey Cumbo, and her extended New Orleans family for making me a gift of one of America's outstanding immigrant cities. Percival Beacroft and

Ernesto Caldeira opened many doors of the Vieux Carré, including the one to Clarke "Doc" Hawley, one of the last of the Mississippi riverboat captains.

I am especially indebted to Sister Ruth Gehres, former president of Brescia College, a member of the Ursuline Sisters and Associate in Communications for Marian Heights Academy in Ferdinand, Indiana, for her compassionate and judicious reading of the manuscript. Her insight and sensitivity were essential to my understanding of modern Catholic thought. The creation of the fictional characters, especially Sylva—Mary Magdalene—are entirely mine, however, not Sister Ruth's.

The relationship of disease and theology has always been an individual consideration. Everyone must decide for herself or himself to what extent, if any, there is a connection.

If this novel promotes lively discussion and responsible actions, its purpose will be achieved.

The Scourges of Heaven honors my real great-grandmother, Cynthia Anne Hedges Kennedy Crouch (1830-1865). As a teenager she probably lost her first husband and young son to cholera. She later married my great-grandfather and bore him seven children, five of whom survived. Cynthia Anne's real story remains shrouded in mystery.